PART 1

NOTHING REMAINS THE SAME

CHAPTER 1

Walking down this street at this time of night revealed how desperate and stupid Jet really was. Searching for a missing student made the entire risk close to being worth it. However, if Jayco was right, this might turn out to be nothing more than a trap. An alley ahead on his left seemed like it could be the right spot. Glancing up and down the sidewalk, he found himself alone. Long shadows hung on to the ground as if afraid for the night to completely take over from the day.

His footsteps came to a halt on the brink of the narrow passage. The passageway was far darker and more unsettling than he wanted. He wished he had brought Iris with him, but she was off protecting Mckenzey. The golden panther was sensational at keeping out of sight.

A movement caught his attention from the doorway, across the alley, about ten feet away. This was the type of movement that made you question if it really happened. Jet pushed his vision to magnify, but only slightly, and his eyes found a figure sitting on the ground, with a hood over her head. She was likely homeless. The girl's face was partially hidden, but she was pale, with dark smudges of dirt around her eyes. She couldn't have been much older than he was. After everything he and his friends had been through, he wasn't convinced that she was just sleeping.

Instinct told him that this was a distraction, intentional or not. He had to find Kevin tonight, no matter who or what got in his way. The homeless girl's eyes flew open, and a small shriek escaped Jet's lips. Her eyes glowed a scarlet red, which somehow enhanced her beauty. A sound from down the alley pulled Jet's concentration from the girl. He prepared for an attack. Nothing came. He allowed a slight glance to the doorway, only to find the space empty. He was confident that there had not been any movement from the homeless girl. Scanning the street, he discovered that he was still alone. Taking a deep breath, he strolled into the darkened alley.

Jet choked back bile as he was assailed with the smell of rotten food, urine, and wet dog. The darkness swallowed him, and suddenly it felt like he stood on the streets of London. Nothing about this alley spoke of anything inviting, but it had to be searched. This was the fourth street along North Broadway in Chinatown he had investigated. The night air appeared to mock him in his futility. The first part of the alley was narrow, with brick buildings on both sides. After a dozen feet or so, he thought that it might open up to a small parking lot.

He listened intently as he cautiously moved forward. He had less than a quarter of an hour to rendezvous with Mckenzey, the only other member of the Echoes willing to drive to Los Angeles from Chadwicks on this pursuit. To his right, instead of the alley opening up like he thought, it was a parking lot with a few covered stalls. Cars were already parked in two of the three stalls; the third was full of furniture and other trash. Locals used this area to sleep at night. As he continued forward, the darkness seemingly was getting darker.

Like a metal hook cutting into a plastic bottle, a grating sound resonated from behind him, and Jet flew into a shadow, remaining hidden for a full two minutes. When he thought it was clear, he poked his head from the archway of a back door. A stray cat scurried from under the back fender of one of the cars and darted under a metal door.

Further down the alley, the foul smell of food decay was replaced by a more pungent odor. The width of the passage doubled, and as the back wall came into view, the smell intensified. He was cautious with each step, understanding that this was likely a trap. Pulling three golden orbs from his pocket, his anxiety dismissed significantly. These beauties were the size of small rocks, and lethal. Rotating them around his hand felt natural. They'd saved his life a few times before now. He kicked out at a half-broken cardboard box, expecting to see rotten food staring up at him from underneath. Instead, a smeared red substance covered the ground, heading in the direction of the farthest trash bin in the corner.

Peering over his shoulder, a cat watched him from under a dumpster, unconcerned. Pushing forward, he strolled to the edge of the bin next to the wall. This bin had been shoved into a tiny area adjacent to a second, larger black trash bin.

"Do I even want to take a look?" Jet asked himself, his voice strained.

Gripping one side, he tugged the smaller green bin, and it moved several inches. He shuddered as the grinding sound. Jet swore silently as he recognized a blue sheet hanging partially out. It was a match for one of the sheets used by Chadwicks boarding school.

As he stared at the blue sheet, he feared what he was about to find. After placing the orbs into his pocket, he shoved open the lid. The sheet was wrapped around an object, but he couldn't tell what it was. There was dried blood spattered everywhere. Reaching inside, he pulled hard at the sheet, but it was stuck. Stepping onto a wooden crate, he placed one hand on the fabric, intending to pull. He recoiled as he felt a leg below the sheet.

His next yank was like swiftly removing a Band-Aid from a cut. The sheet peeled back, and another wave of stench stunned him. He glimpsed hair, pale skin, and a sunken face. He vomited into an empty cardboard box against the back wall.

Is this really happening? Jet peered closer at the dead body and easily recognized the face staring up at him, unblinking, but it wasn't Kevin McCormick.

"You're the last person I expected to see here." A voice echoed from behind him.

Bounding off the cardboard box, Jet reacted as if he was going to be attacked. As a dark figure stepped into view, Jet asked, "What are you talking about?"

"We checked you out months ago, and nothing. Since Silverton, we've been watching you more closely. Zip. I told Shane that you were a waste of time. We tested you with red powder, and you didn't change colors like the others. I guess you proved me wrong."

"No clue what you're talking about." A slight smile spread across Jet's face. "My car broke down, and I'm lost."

"I watched you pull back that trash bin, find the body, and puke. I thought you were stronger than that. Wrong again."

"Good to see you Vinny Estes, but you've got me confused with someone else. I was walking by, looking for a gas station, when I smelled something foul down here."

Jet cringed at the stupidity of his own excuse. He continued, "I'm traumatized at what I found." For the first time, Jet noticed the sword blade in Vinny's right hand.

He willed for his vision to change and was relieved when his eyesight magnified. This had happened before. His peripheral ability to see expanded to include almost everything in front of him, on both sides and most of the area directly behind him. The sword was an exact match to one he'd seen inside a cave near Silverton a month ago.

Using the sword Vinny pointed at the trash bin. He asked angrily, "Do you know who that is?"

"Why would I?"

"Because I'm certain that you or one of your friends was there when he died."

Jet took a step to the side and challenged him. "Vinny. What on earth are you talking about?"

"Shane said that if we put out the word that Kevin had been spotted in Los Angeles that the right people would come running." Vinny sneered and spat on the ground. "And boy, was he right."

Jet stared closely at Vinny; something was off, and he was about to lose it. His eyes had a yellowish glow, and dried froth was caked to the corners of his mouth. "What's going on here, Vinny? You're talking crazy." Jet took another step away from the trash bin.

Vinny stopped him with a shout. "I don't know if you're the Mikado or an Occultist, but my Runic magic and my protection are stronger than anything that you can throw at me. Shane also announced that he fought one of you and you cheated to escape. Not sure if that was you. The weapon of choice for that coward was three small orbs. Is that you, Black?"

"Have you lost your freaking mind? What's this about fighting Shane? Now you have a sword and are screaming at me."

"Thy mouth doth protest, and I conclude that you are guilty. Tell me where the fragment is, and we won't kill the others. You guys killed my roommate and best friend."

"Who's the dead guy, Vinny?"

"Didn't you recognize him?" His voice rose to a tortured scream.

Jet said nothing but shook his head.

"That's Jake Hurley." Vinny shook, tears running down his face. "You do remember him, don't you?"

Jet knew that Jake and Vinny were more than just friends. They were goons of Shane Fallon, who had been searching for an ancient artifact. It had been a race to find the first missing piece, and Jet and his friends had reached it first. Jake, Vinny, Shane, and several others had chased them, trying to recapture the artifact. Jake and Vinny had caught up, and Jake had pinned Mckenzey to the ground, a few seconds away from killing her. Jet had been fortunate and unlucky enough to stop him. He had killed Jake, dreaming about it every night for the last three and a half weeks.

Jet reacted, his voice far calmer than he felt. "I remember Jake. I mean, we weren't friends, but who could forget all the bullying and name-calling you guys did. Sorry to hear that he died."

Vinny seethed, shaking his sword at Jet. Spittle flew everywhere. "I'll kill you, Black. I don't really care about this war, releasing Arisol, or finding all the hidden pieces. You took my best friend, and I'm going to end you."

Jet's shoulders sagged. "Okay. Fine. I'll tell you the truth. I heard about what happened, but I wasn't there. You guys have this all wrong. The Mikado doesn't even go to Chadwicks, I think he or she attends San Mateo. I was brought in to help look for Kevin. I've no idea how Vinny died."

"What? San Mateo? That doesn't make any sense. Shane is convinced that it's someone from Silverton who is going to school at Chadwicks, right now."

"Sorry to disappoint. I have known Kevin since elementary. That's the only reason why I'm here."

Vinny didn't appear to be buying what Jet was selling, and he didn't know how he was going to escape. Jayco had warned him not to go looking for Kevin, but Jet couldn't allow someone else to suffer.

"That means that you know what the Mikado is. You are involved." Vinny swung the black blade expertly. "There are ways I can get the truth from you."

This time Jet was curious. "What are you talking about?"

"We can control your thoughts and emotions. We can't force you to do anything against your will, but we can cause a nuisance. I'm proficient enough to get you to tell me the truth."

"Why do you have a sword?"

"Stop playing stupid." Vinny rolled his neck as if fixing to attack. "We also found some weapons that night in the cave. You think you were the only one. I can smell the fear from here."

Jet scoffed. "The smell isn't coming from me; it's coming from that stray cat. But what you smell is pheromones. She's in heat, and she has her eyes set on you."

"You're a dead man walking."

"We'll see." Jet reached up and pulled the hood of his cloak onto his head and disappeared. A gust of air swirled around the alley.

Vinny had been prepared for this action, and using the pointer fingers on both hands, he touched an invisible spot near each temple. Jet watched as a purple film slid over Vinny's entire eyes. Once it was in place, it was unnoticeable. "That's interesting. You disappeared, but I can see your vague shape. I can't tell who you are. Shane will be very interested in this little fact."

With both hands, Jet arched his wrist, and a small jet of air propelled him into the air, a few feet off the ground.

"So your cloak helps you control your primary element, which is air. You can't be the Mikado, but you'll have enough answers to make this ruse worth it." Vinny held the dagger in his right hand. From behind his back, he pulled out a device that Jet knew all too well. It was a Y-shaped item, similar to a slingshot. It shot a powerful blue rope that could bind him.

Jet pulled out his own sword, but it wasn't magical or impressive, and he held it for only one purpose. When Jet and his friends had escaped Silverton, they had managed to capture a rope from this Y-shaped device. Only two things worked, cutting the rope with a magical item or an immense amount of heat. Silently Jet whispered a spell that poured energy into the sword. He hoped that Vinny wouldn't notice.

"That sword isn't going to protect you."

"As I told you, I'm not in the inner circle. This is all that I have."

"How did you get involved?"

"After Shane attacked several students on campus at the memorial, San Mateo sent recruiters to Chadwicks. They started with Jayco and Grantham, who ended up not having a lick of magical talent. I had very little, with air. I was supposed to keep tabs on Shane, but none of the heavy lifting."

"Why would you freely give me this information?"

"I've heard about that sword and those things you have. You must be someone important. I can't beat you. But I can give you enough information for you to leave me alone. It's the Mikado and his followers that you need to worry about."

"Who is it?"

"Don't be an idiot. You think they would give me that information. I'm nothing more than an errand boy."

"You've kept up that air spell for a long time."

"I can do one thing; that's it. That's how it works for our Elemental magic."

"Let's let Shane decide what to do." Vinny aimed the Y-shaped device, and Jet recoiled.

As the rope was launched, time slowed, and instead of allowing the rope to snare him, Jet flew at the rope, lifting his sword, and cutting cleanly through the cable. It sailed past him harmlessly.

Vinny raised his black sword and prepared for an attack.

Jet yelled, "Aquaenaeth," and a green aura appeared, and he knew that he'd chosen the correct spell. A water deluge sprang upward and smashed into Vinny's body. However, a protective shield, like an unseen helmet, prevented the water from hitting his face. He was still knocked off balance.

Somehow Vinny swung his black sword, and it connected with Jet's simple sword. Despite the heat the sword shattered into a dozen pieces. Jet released the handle as it disintegrated. He plucked a golden staff from his back and swung it forcefully at Vinny's head. Jet knew that Vinny couldn't react in time. Then the unexpected happened, and Jet learned of Vinny's talent. The boy side-shifted three feet to his left and reappeared. Jet's staff only connected with foul-smelling air. A cruel smile crept across Vinny's lips.

Jet yelled, "Aer," and a green tornado of air with a green aura sped toward Vinny's face and connected hard. Vinny's head snapped back, and he hit the wall. The purple contacts vanished, and Vinny slumped to the ground, dazed. He was no longer visible and could escape easily.

There had been a slow and steady decrease in his energy, and Jet knew that he couldn't remain hovering forever. He planned to go two blocks and drop onto the ground and meet up with Mckenzey.

As he soared out of the alley, the movement behind him was so fast that even Jet's enhanced vision barely caught it. Turning, he watched as something sprinted into the alley and went directly at Vinny. Jet could have never reacted in time. What he beheld was unimaginable. The creature was over eight feet tall, with long legs and dangling arms. It was covered from head to toe in black fur and ran on four legs, but as it approached Vinny, it stood on its hind two legs. There were three antlers in total. The first two were large and typical, but the third was smaller and on the top of its head. The creature had fanged teeth and a deer's head and body. The animal's arms reached for Vinny, who was still dazed as its jaws opened. The boy was pulled close, and the creature clamped down on the back of the boy's neck. Vinny was suddenly lifted into the air as if he weighed nothing, and an unnatural sound reverberated through the air as the creature's head shook back and forth. Vinny's neck was broken, and his body was severely beaten. An orange glow transferred from Vinny's neck to the creature's mouth, and the animal gained bulk before his eyes.

Jet reversed direction and advanced closer to the creature, removing the orbs from his pocket, intending to attack. He hovered twenty feet in the air, remaining silent and invisible.

The antlered deer tossed Vinny's body aside like it was a dead dog, and his milky white eyes stared up directly at the spot where Jet was hidden. Almost as fast as it could run, the creature removed a bow from its back and unleashed an arrow at Jet. There was barely enough time to react. He twisted, and the arrow slammed into his back. The golden shield linked to his back took the brunt of the blow. Just like his simple sword, the shield shattered, and Jet was propelled through the air at an alarming speed. Most of his energy vanished, and he had no control of where he was going.

When Jet finally hit the ground, he was a mile from the alley. He landed hard on his left side. Pain shot through his entire body, including his back; his face was gashed, and he had failed at almost everything tonight. None of that mattered right now. He needed to find Mckenzey so they could escape. Pulling himself off the ground, he ran as fast as he could in the direction of Union Station.

With every turn he was convinced that the antlered deer was closing the distance. He hated the idea of being chased by animals. He was about to set up a red flare when intuition told him to avoid any magic. He was already low on energy, and if he overexerted himself, the consequences could be severe. Without slowing, Jet crossed a busy intersection. Cars swerved and honked, but he kept running. A grouping trees came into view off to his left, and he changed course. As he ran he fished out his cell phone to call Mckenzey, only to find that it had shattered. He entered the far side of a parking lot and found Jayco's jeep at the far end. It appeared empty.

He ducked behind the far side of the jeep and searched the area. Every movement caught his attention, but there were no signs of an attacking deer, Iris, or Mckenzey. Unlocking the jeep, he reached inside and pulled his backpack closer. They'd prepared some homemade energy drinks. Magic drained Jet's energy, but he had realized early on mud and water could give back some of it. After returning from Silverton, Grantham began experimenting with the best possible mixtures. Turned out that lemongrass herbal tea and gray clay offered the best bang. Jet guzzled two full bottles and felt a measured return of his stamina.

From back across the parking lot, Mckenzey appeared, and she was sprinting fast. Off to the side, closer to the buildings, Iris, the golden panther, was mimicking her. Jet jumped to the front seat and started the engine. Thirty seconds later Mckenzey fumbled at the door, finally opened it, and let Iris leap inside first. She followed closely behind. Jet hit the accelerator, and they shot off.

"Well, that sucked worse than cafeteria food." Mckenzey rested back in the seat, sweat dripping off her forehead.

"Ain't that the truth," said Jet.

"Remember a few months ago when Shane cornered us, and you tried to punch him.

"How could I forget?"

"There was this stocky guy with Shane; I think his name is Clyde. And the girl I knocked over, Jessiva."

"Great memories."

"They're here."

"Did they see you?"

"Maybe. Hard to say. They might've been following me. If so, I'm not even sure that they recognized me. They got a phone call and headed in another direction. That was when I sprinted back to the jeep."

"Kevin was never here." Jet's voice was distraught. "This entire thing was a trap. I found Jake's body in a bin of trash. Vinny Estes, Jake's friend, cornered me in the alley.

He recognized me, but I found a way to escape. Something came into the alley and killed Vinny."

"What are you talking about?"

"Sorry. I'm all over the place. There was this antlered deer, moving faster than anything I'd ever seen. It shot into the alley and attacked Vinny. I was up in the air, and the thing tried to shoot me with an arrow. I'm not sure what to even think. How many creatures do we have to fight?"

"It attacked both of you?"

"Him first, then me."

They lapsed into silence as they both caught their breath. Twenty minutes later, on the freeway heading north, Mckenzey asked, "Are we heading back to campus?"

"I think that's the best idea. We need to tell the others what happened."

"Are you sure this is the best plan?"

Jet watched Mckenzey closely. He thought she was struggling with something, even before tonight. He didn't want to pry, but she hadn't been herself the last few weeks. She had been distant and secluded. They hadn't kissed or snuggled once since Silverton. It felt like she didn't want to be alone with him. He was surprised when she volunteered to come along with him. He said, softening his voice, "We only have four days before Christmas vacation."

Mckenzey glanced over and asked, "Are you still considering traveling to Argentina the day after Christmas?"

"I don't know that we have a choice."

"We're not ready," Mckenzey said, slightly frustrated. "Besides you, none of us can do any magic to speak of. We need more time."

"Maybe you need to be pushed into it." Jet wiped his forehead.

Mckenzey answered quickly, "Jayco's right. This has turned into a vendetta with you."

"No way," Jet said. "That's not the case. I'm just trying to do what's right. If we wait too long, Shane will get the next piece of the Phoenix first. Is that what you want?"

Mckenzey practically screamed, "Of course I don't. But we've been watching him, and he hasn't made a single move."

"Not until tonight."

"Fine." Mckenzey relented. "You refuse to listen to anyone else's ideas. I guess we have to do it *your* way."

CHAPTER 2

Two hours later they exited the freeway and drove north toward campus. It was dark, and the road wound back and forth. Mckenzey hadn't said a thing the entire drive back to Chadwicks. Now, as they drove the winding road, Jet considered the size of Chadwicks. Students rarely ventured this far south, except when leaving school. It was far easier to get to Santa Barbara if you took College Avenue north out of the school, so this direction was seldom used.

To their left was the ocean, and soon the bay adjacent to the school buildings would come into view. Trees, hills, and a few mountains were to their right. Out here, you could get lost in all the acreage that the school owned. Jet thought about a campus-wide event at the beginning of school when they had gone rock climbing. He'd almost fallen to his death, not one of the highlights of his time here. Mckenzey rolled down her window to let in the fresh air, but she remained stubbornly aloof. Jet wanted to reach over and hold her hand but thought better of it.

As they drove over the next small hill, the lights of the school came into view. Iris loved the back seat, and she mostly cuddled up or stared out the window as they drove. Only a few times during the drive would she step onto one of their laps. Usually, this caused a smile or two from everyone in the car. Tonight, however, Mckenzey's hand pushed Iris away. When the school came into view, Iris jumped up to share the driver's seat with Jet.

"Good girl," Jet said and stroked her golden fur. She bit his fingers playfully and nuzzled his hand to continue giving her attention.

Coming to Chadwicks had never been on his radar. That was until he received a letter telling him that he'd been given a scholarship. Nana wasn't surprised, but he had never filled out an application. Calling his friends, he learned that they also have been given scholarships. It was one of the ten most prestigious boarding schools in the country and probably the top school out west.

As they passed the buildings, Jet stared at the cobblestone walkways and the gigantic trees. On the left side were the dorms, dining rooms, and the classrooms. On the right side were the sports fields, the CeU building, the administrative offices, and some of the teacher's apartments, if they lived on campus. Most of the twenty-two hundred students lived on campus. The school was formatted as a coed school from ninth to twelfth grade. After he started, he learned that over two hundred students who survived Silverton had also received a scholarship.

For a Sunday night, the campus felt deserted. He parked Jayco's yellow jeep in one of the most northern lots, next to the bookstore. Before getting out, Jet spoke, "Pyramis of Aurum." A small light flashed, and Iris changed back into a golden pyramid. He grabbed his backpack with his most important possessions and added the pyramid.

Jet and Mckenzey were alert as they headed towards the beach. Their closest friends were waiting for them to hear how things had gone in Los Angeles. Their steps changed from the asphalt to the wooden boardwalk that continued south along the entire length of campus. From here Jet could see a half dozen campfires. Once they reached the sand, they curved right and made their way up to their usual spot.

As they stomped through the sand, Jet's mind shifted back to Mckenzey. He thought he knew what had come between them, but he couldn't change what had happened. He wondered if she regretted turning down the opportunity to transfer to Dillon Lake.

Before he could ask her, Seyanna's voice cut through the night air. "I think they're about here."

Latisha swore. "I can't believe you heard them before my night vision allowed me to see them."

"Why is it always a competition with you two?" Grantham asked. "Are you guys ever going to be normal?"

Jayco hissed, "This coming from the guy that can climb like Spider-Man."

"It's just annoying, that's all," retorted Grantham.

Jet shook his head as the shadows of his friends flickered in the campfire. They were still twenty feet away.

Mckenzey whispered, "Sorry."

"For what?"

"You'll see." Mckenzey hurried ahead for the last several steps.

As Jet made his way toward an empty chair, Jayco asked, "Was it pointless or a trap?"

"A trap."

"Grantham loses again." Jayco lifted his hand, motioning for Grantham to pay up. A dozen gold coins were tossed at Jayco, who caught most of them before they hit the sand.

"Haven't seen those before," Mckenzey said coldly, and she sat in her chair, opposite Jet. "When did you find those?"

"Yesterday or the day before. I can't remember."

Seyanna, sensing the tension, changed the subject. "What do you mean it was a trap?"

Mckenzey adamantly stared at the ground. Jet began, "We found a body, but it was Jake Hurley and not Kevin McCormick. Vinny Estes cornered me in an alley, and we fought. He recognized me."

"We're screwed," Latisha shouted.

"Did you kill him?" Jayco asked.

"No," Jet said over the commotion. "I tried convincing him that someone from San Mateo was leading things."

"That shows you know what's going on," Grantham said. "By tonight the word is going to get back to Shane, and he's going to come after all of us."

"Isn't that what you said to Shane after you fought him in that bubble outside of Silverton?" asked Seyanna.

"Well, not exactly," he said quickly. "But it doesn't matter. Vinny isn't going to be telling Shane anything."

Latisha questioned, "What's that supposed to mean?"

"Vinny and I fought, and I escaped. But as I was leaving, something with horns rushed into the alley and killed Vinny. It was not a pretty sight." Jet explained finding Jake, the confrontation with Vinny, and watching him die. He also described what Mckenzey had seen and about being followed by Clyde and Jessiva.

"Could this be a pissed off cousin of the creature you fought in Silverton?" asked Latisha.

"I'm not sure."

"Did your book tell you anything?" Seyanna asked.

"It still hasn't opened since we drove away from Silverton."

Grantham added, "Can I tell you how frustrating it is to be left in the dark like this. Why isn't your special book opening?"

"I have no idea."

"Take it out and let's look at it again," suggested Seyanna.

Reaching inside his backpack, he removed an ancient book entitled *The Sorcerer's Guide*. This book changed Jet's life but it also allowed him to accomplish things he would've never dreamed of. Without a word, he gave it to Latisha who examined it closely.

"Tell me this," Seyanna said. "Why do you think the book that has given us the fable, explained about the Rivalry, helped us down The Path of the Phoenix, splashed a tattoo on your back and arms, and has given you spells of Elemental magic has suddenly closed up tighter than a clamshell?"

Jayco asked, "Did you do something to piss off Wier?"

"All those things are true," replied Jet. "I'm telling you, something weird happened after Silverton. A page became charred that had a curse or something on it. Wier isn't willing to talk to me right now."

"You've told us this. But there has to be something more."

Mckenzey remained quiet during this conversation.

Latisha said, "You talk about Wier like he's a living being."

"He was at one time. But a spell put him into the book as my mentor."

Seyanna said, "There are written letters inside the book. How do you think that those got inside?"

Jet replied, "I think the Brotherhood has a word they can use to open the book. It gives them very minimal access."

"Like a spell?" Grantham asked.

"More like a key phrase."

Grantham whispered, "Seems like the same thing, just semantics."

"If you say so."

"Did you ever wonder why your parents put the book–?" asked Grantham.

"Tome," Jet interrupted.

"The tome…" Grantham said quickly, "inside your shadowbox? Why did they hide it from you in the first place?"

"No clue," Jet replied. "I've often wondered, were they hiding it for me or *from* me."

Jayco said, "I remember your mom and dad. They always seemed supercool. It's amazing that we all met during elementary school, and here we are, years later, in high school together."

"I, for one," Seyanna said, "would've never imagined it."

"Even crazier," Grantham pointed out, "since we all came back alive from Silverton, we can each do a little magic."

"That was a trip," Latisha said. "Going back to Silverton almost four years from when it was destroyed was beyond stupid. I still can't believe we escaped with the golden items and the piece of the Phoenix. Shane has been pissed for the last four weeks. I'm never going back to Silverton."

"I might," Jet said.

Seyanna asked, "Why?"

"I promised myself that I'd take a peek at my house." He glanced over at Mckenzey, but she glowered at the ground. He continued, "I want to see what happened after the earthquake and volcano destroyed the town."

"Are you crazy?" asked Jayco. "We saw the town. Your house has to be much worse. There might not be anything left."

"I know. One day I'll go back."

The fire crackled and burned. Grantham tossed on another log. Staring into the fire, Jet thought about the first time the tome opened. It was near his sixteenth birthday, just a few months ago. It only opened a page at a time and only he could read the words. Soon the tome was teaching him how to do Elemental magic and the importance of finding an ancient tablet called the Phoenix. It took days and weeks to learn that the first tablet piece was hidden in Silverton and that was why the town had been destroyed. Argentina, their next adventure, was where they thought the second piece might be.

Jayco interrupted Jet's thoughts. "Is it possible that Shane sent that creature after you tonight? And maybe Vinny just got in its way? We need to be on guard for something like that here on campus. Didn't I tell you it was a trap?"

Mckenzey stood abruptly and said, "Hey, guys, there's something I need to talk to you guys about."

"Not now," Latisha whispered.

"It has to be now," Mckenzey countered loudly. She and Latisha were close friends and roommates, but Mckenzey's voice was demanding and harsh. She paced back and forth. Her brown hair was pulled back in a ponytail, and her golden eyes were ablaze with hysteria. "I don't think any of us realized how difficult it would be to have talents and these abilities with magic. Jet told me how weird he felt, and I just didn't understand. We have so many responsibilities that sometimes it's just too much."

Jayco asked, "What are you talking about?"

"You and Grantham have been screwing around for the last three weeks. You've been cliff jumping, diving, finding treasure, and building a new hideout. I know I've been helping, but it has been pointless. Seyanna is starting school in January, but she hasn't been helping as much as we need her to. I know that she's been looking at some of the data from the disaster in Washington, DC."

"That's not fair," Seyanna protested.

"We've all had a purpose," Grantham countered. "I thought you were on the same page with us."

"Well, I wasn't," screamed Mckenzey.

Jet, slightly confused, replied, "I'm sure that we can figure all of this out. What do you need?"

"I can't anymore," Mckenzey said.

Jet felt his stomach tighten. "What do you mean?"

"I'm going home. I want to see my parents and have some normalcy for a few weeks. Can we push the trip to Argentina back a few weeks? After Silverton, we could all use a break."

"We already have the tickets," Jet said.

Mckenzey stopped pacing and stared at Jet defiantly. She hissed, "I'm not going."

Jet tried hard not to smile, but he couldn't.

"Are you laughing at me?" she demanded.

Jet lifted both hands as if warding off evil. "Ice crystals are shooting out of your cloak."

"I hate this thing." She tore off her black cloak and tossed it onto her chair. When she glanced at Jet, there was despair and uncertainty. "I'm flying home after classes on Wednesday. I won't be back until after the holiday. I'm tired of seeing and hearing about people dying. I'm tired of this war, and I am tired of all of you guys." Without another word Mckenzey stomped back toward her dorm.

"Follow her," Grantham hissed.

Latisha shouted, "That would be a terrible idea. You can't change her mind."

Jet asked, "How long has she been talking like this?"

"Two weeks," Latisha said, watching her roommate and best friend leave. "She's not sleeping well. She needs a break."

Grantham asked, "Are we still going to Argentina?"

Jet said, "I'm going. Each of you must make your own decision. Let me know what you decide by Tuesday night. Catch you later." He picked up his book and Mckenzey's cloak and marched back toward Jayco's jeep. Inside the vehicle, he grabbed the broken pieces of his shield and the staff.

He mumbled, "Why am I not surprised." Hidden under the passenger seat were Mckenzey's throwing knives.

He couldn't keep these items inside his dorm, so he decided to cross the length of campus to the science building, where he'd been hiding the rest of the weapons following a break-in at his dorm. As he walked he considered Mckenzey and what she meant to him. They had been friends since fifth or sixth grade, when Mckenzey first moved to Silverton. Jet developed a crush on almost immediately. A month before the battle at Silverton, the group had gone to Switzerland to find a casket that had previously held the Phoenix. While in Switzerland they kissed for the first time. It was one of the best days of his life.

As happens, they hit a speed bump when Jet found out that Eric, a boy from Colorado whom Mckenzey had been seeing, was visiting Mckenzey's parents and sisters for Thanksgiving while they were on their adventure in Silverton. To make matters worse, Jet had been forced to kill Jake Hurley, right in front of Mckenzey. He'd saved her life, but she'd taken the fellow student's death hard.

Jet took an unusual direction to the science building, in case he was being watched. He crossed College Avenue immediately after leaving Jayco's jeep. On this side of campus, he saw no one. He stayed in the shadows and passed on the backside of the CeU building. He crossed the baseball field without any concerns because it was completely dark and empty.

The science building was the building that Jet visited the most. He had a class, his favorite, a geology lab, there. He was also a TA for this class and needed to set up the lab. He found a hidden room in the basement that had been a perfect hiding space.

As he went past the tennis courts, he thought he heard something just south from there, in a field. It was an unusual clicking sound and a rush of movement. There were no other buildings in this area. Jet crouched down behind a large bush and listened. The dimness prevented him from understanding what was happening, and sounds were still some distance away, but they seemed to be far more than a single animal or someone trying to follow him. Ahead he noticed a large tree that would give him enough protection. It was situated on a small hill.

Jet sprinted to the trunk of the tree, lay on his belly, and crawled forward, up the slight incline of the hill, completely shielded by the tree. His backpack became caught initially on one of the lower branches. He was forced to remove it and place it next to the trunk. Between branches he could see out, but doubted that anyone could see him.

Flashlights illuminated the ground and figures bent low as if they were doing something with the ground. After five minutes he guessed that they must be digging a trench or creating an area to put fence poles in. But he couldn't see any additional tools or large pieces of equipment or fence poles. They were spread out, creating holes in the ground. Something as small as a football was dropped into the hole and quickly covered up.

"Hurry up," a voice bellowed from fifty feet away, to Jet's left, back from whence he'd come. "We need to find out if this is the right area."

Jet recognized the voice of Shane Fallon, and hot anger boiled within him.

A few minutes later, a voice that Jet also recognized echoed from the dark. "Several of the Claustra have been buried." This voice belonged to Raul Flores, Jet's old roommate.

Anger boiled in Jet's stomach. What was Raul doing out here, and why was he working with Shane? Shane must've recruited him to be part of his secret groups. Jet wondered if this meant that Raul could do Runic magic.

Shane yelled, "Move out. We need to clear the area to see if this works."

"What if it doesn't?" another voice asked.

"Then we get to start over tomorrow," Shane shouted. "If this doesn't work, you're not going home for Christmas break."

There was no other person that Jet loathed more than Shane. It wasn't enough that Shane knew Runic magic and Jet knew Elemental magic or that they were on opposite sides of the Rivalry. But rather the fact that Shane had spent every moment over the last year and a half bullying and harassing Jet at every turn.

Shane was the Czaric, the leader of the Runic magic, just like Jet was the Mikado. He had a book that taught him called *The Mage's Letters*. They were competing against each other to find the five remaining tablet pieces of the Phoenix and prevent Arisol from escaping. After Silverton, he and Shane fought in a magical dome. Shane was stronger, and Jet had been lucky to escape. The most curious part of the contest was that Shane couldn't discern who he was. The identity of the Mikado was still unknown.

"Clear," a voice bellowed.

"Continue with the countdown," Shane shouted, his voice farther away. Jet thought they must be on the softball field. "I will mix the two types of powder together and try the rune. I need you to throw the balls at the wall that is produced. Can you do that?"

"Yes," Raul shouted. "Will we see the wall?"

"I don't know."

Pushing aside some branches, he crawled forward another foot. A figure, likely Shane, stood near a fence and began drawing something that involved several shapes into the air. His hand flew in a blur, and a bright light engulfed the night. It was like Shane was trying to create a gigantic protective bubble. The glowing light covered two hundred feet and held steady.

"Throw the balls now!" Shane shouted.

Jet watched as four or five figures held white glowing spheres on the opposite side of the glowing wall. They threw them one after another. The spheres bounced off as if they were being repelled by the barrier.

Raul threw the seventh or eighth globe. This time, the wall vanished, as did the bright light and the ball hit another figure standing next to Shane.

Shane screamed, "What did you guys do? It was holding."

Jet dragged himself from under the tree, retrieving his backpack. He did not want to be seen and began running all the way to the science building. Using a key he'd been given by Professor Blum, his teacher, he unlocked a door in the alley.

After closing the door, Jet padded down the hall and into the basement. He didn't like what he had just seen. He wondered what Shane was trying to do. A protective barrier was meant to keep something out or something within. He'd have to tell his friends and make sure that someone kept a far closer eye on Shane and his cronies.

CHAPTER 3

The hidden room in the basement could only be accessed through a door at the back of another room. Before finding this space, Jet was sure that no one had been inside in fifteen years. The mothball was reasonably convincing. Now, the area acted as a treasure trove of magical items. In total, there were four golden pyramids. Jet hung up Mckenzey's cloak and placed her throwing knives into a bin Grantham had built into the back wall.

He placed the remaining pieces of the broken shield next to the other five shields. The golden staff was added to the other five staffs. Additionally, there were jars filled with black powder, multicolored stones, dried corn, feathers, red dirt, eagle talons, sharks' teeth, and arrowheads. Back in Silverton, he'd used the dried corn in a desperate time of need, and it had helped him escape. When swallowing the corn, it created exact duplicates of yourself doing what you were doing. Very useful.

There were a few necklaces and rings that, if used correctly, could give power, energy, or something more. Inside Silverton, they found gold and black weapons. Only Jet and his friends could touch the golden items. Jet was given his three orbs, and Mckenzey her throwing knives. Jayco had bracelets that, when moved into place, increased his strength tenfold. Grantham was given a long shaft with a half-circle of golden metal. His staff was flexible and strong and could be elongated for specific needs. Latisha had a golden chalice with black powder, which caused an area to become dark and impassible. Lastly, Seyanna was given a golden set of bows and arrows.

The crown jewels, though, were a black casket with symbols and Egyptian markings on the outside. The Echoes had tracked down this item to Switzerland. It was an adventure sneaking it out of a museum in Bern. The casket now held the fragment of the Phoenix. It had six sides, a front and back, and four other sides. Of the four sides, two were smooth, and two were jagged, like a puzzle piece. It was as clear as a diamond, but there were words in a language he had never seen.

Returning the fragment to the crate, he needed to get back to his dorm before he was later than his curfew allowed. He locked up the room and left, keeping alert to anyone around him. The walk back to his dorm was calm, and he didn't see another person along the way.

Without Mckenzey in Argentina, they were taking on a much bigger risk. There were too many unknowns. Was the second fragment piece even there? Was Argentina connected to the other natural disasters? If they didn't go, these questions would be impossible to answer. Seyanna and her parents were experts in all things scientific and had been chosen a few months ago to go to Argentina to study a disaster that had been like the tragedy in Washington, DC.

After returning, Seyanna confirmed that the catastrophe was more likely supernatural than natural. She had hinted at a blue fog. Through happenstance, Jet learned that a man named E.T. Forester had found meteorites in Silverton, just like the one that affected Jet. He had later died in a climbing accident in Argentina. Coincidence? Maybe. All in all, it was risky to proceed without Mckenzey, but they couldn't let Shane beat them to the spot.

In Jet's mind Silverton had been the first natural disaster. Later in the same year, Argentina had happened, and a few years later, just two months ago, two storms had collided over Washington, DC, that had killed more than a hundred thousand people. In his bones, he felt that these storms were connected. Jayco and Grantham were wholeheartedly on board with another trip. The girls were far more skeptical.

Ducking into his dorm at Kelci Halls, Jet searched the open space for anyone paying him too much attention. Since returning from Silverton, he'd adopted a spy mindset. It sounded so stupid when he really thought about it. It was also narcissistic to believe that all his classmates were watching him. But he'd seen enough this year to know that there was a bigger picture. He'd been attacked by Shane a few different times, someone had smashed his dorm, and someone else had tried to do the same with Mckenzey's dorm. Having the tome, a piece of the Phoenix, and the other items, he felt anxious all the time.

Napoleon Bean, the hall monitor, strolled down the stairs and caught sight of him immediately. Napoleon wasn't his real name, but no one ever called him anything else. The tall, awkward boy scurried over and whispered, "Black. So glad to see you. Let's not burden ourselves over the fact that you're five minutes late. I truly need your help."

Jet was taken by surprise. Normally, the only time Napoleon talked with him was to schedule a time to check on his dorm, or when he was in trouble. He muttered quickly, "What's up?"

Napoleon's face contorted. "I need a favor."

"It depends."

"Darla and I need to borrow a car for tomorrow night. We're going to take a drive to Disadol Peak."

"The make-out center of Central California?" Jet blurted.

Napoleon's face appeared devastated. "It's the perfect spot to use our telescope."

"I knew that," Jet said quickly. "If you follow me up to my room, I'll get my keys. It isn't perfect, but it works."

"Oh," Napoleon said quickly.

"Is there a problem?"

Napoleon recovered quickly. "No. I was just asking if I could borrow that jeep that your friend Jayco drives."

"Uh." Jet took a step back. "I'll check. He doesn't allow a ton of people to use it."

"Didn't I see you driving with Mckenzey earlier tonight?"

"Only because it was an emergency." Jet swore under his breath. It shouldn't have been surprising that someone had caught sight of them.

"Can your car hold my telescope?"

Jet stifled a laugh. "I'm sure it can."

"Okay. I'll follow you."

Together they headed up the stairs. Jet's dorm was on the eighth and top story of the building. During the day, using the stairs was far more effective than the single elevator. Sometimes, you had to wait twenty minutes before it reached you.

Near the seventh floor, Napoleon said, in between deep breaths, "Autumn Bells stopped by an hour ago looking for you. She wasn't sure if you'd made it back from Los Angeles yet. I hadn't seen you, so I told her I wasn't sure."

"Los Angeles?" Jet questioned.

"That's what she said." Napoleon opened the door and held it for Jet. He added, "What was the emergency that you ran into tonight?"

"My grandmother came to see me. I was dropping her off at the airport."

"A few days before Christmas break?" he asked.

"I didn't get to see her at Thanksgiving," Jet said quickly. "And she isn't going back to Portland. She and some of her friends are going to Hawaii for Christmas?"

"How fun," Napoleon said as he followed Jet toward his door. "Are you meeting up with her later this week?"

"I wish," Jet said. He then relied on the cover story he and his friends had made up. He added, "I'm going on a service trip to South America. I guess we are going to be helping with housing, or electricity, or even some running water."

"That sounds—"

Jet said quickly, "Boring."

"No way. I was going to say exciting."

Opening the door to his dorm, Jet found that his roommates were busy and that there were a few other students with them. He located his keys and passed them to Napoleon.

"Is it cool if I return these tomorrow night?"

"Definitely. You know where it's parked?"

Napoleon nodded.

"Have a good time."

"We will," the boy said excitedly.

Closing the door, a massive eruption of laughter came from the entertainment room. Jet found his roommates Rick Fish and Jackson Crawley playing a board game with two attractive girls. One Jet recognized as Keesha Davis, a girl who was often seen around the boys' dorms. He'd first talked to her after Shane and his friends had first attacked Jet.

Glancing up, she recognized him, and gave a small wave. Keesha added, "Glad to see that your face healed up nicely."

"It was touch and go for a few days."

Rick added, "Wasn't that when you crashed riding your bike?"

The other girl, a lanky brown-haired girl who Jet had never seen before, added, "Didn't you also fall and break your arm?"

"It was my collarbone," Jet said quickly. His first impression of the second girl caused him to cringe. It wasn't that she wasn't pretty, but she seemed almost gleeful at his injury. Her smile was disturbing.

"You've had a rough start to the year," Jackson agreed.

"Tell me about it," Jet said. "What are you guys playing?"

"Risk," the brown-haired girl said. "You're not invited."

Jet laughed. "Fine by me."

Jackson kneed the girl under the table. He said, "This is Paisley Samuelson."

"Nice to meet you."

"Without a doubt."

The girl was either self-confident or a total jerk.

"It appears you already know Keesha," Rick said. "We're starting to do a game night on Sundays, and these two were the first to volunteer."

Paisley added, "My mom was just telling me the importance of making new friends."

"No better time than game night." Jet agreed.

Jackson stood. "Who wants a drink?"

"Do you have premier bottled water?" asked Paisley. "That's the only water that doesn't cause me stomach problems."

"Ugh. Sorry, we don't."

Keesha smothered a smile. "I'll take whatever."

"Coming right up." Jackson hurried from the room.

Jet said, "Night all. I'm heading to my room."

Rick asked, "Why did Napoleon stop by?"

"To borrow my car. He wants to take Darla to Disadol Peak."

"To make out?" Rick questioned.

"To stargaze. It's totally innocent."

Rick teased. "If we were talking about anyone else, I would've called you a liar. But Napoleon wouldn't dream of kissing a girl this early in their relationship."

"He has good sense," Paisley pointed out.

This time, a laugh escaped Keesha, and Jet quickly covered by saying, "I'm hoping we might get some brownie points, and I don't want to clean before I leave for Christmas vacation."

Jackson returned with his hands full of drinks. "Are you heading home for Christmas?"

Jet knew this question was going to be asked a lot over the next few days. "No. Nana is going to Hawaii with some friends. I'm headed to a service opportunity in South America."

"Sounds fun. I've never been to Hawaii or South America," said Jackson.

"Me neither. I guess we'll see how it goes." The truth was that Nana wasn't in Hawaii, and in fact, she was in Canada, near Calgary, the last time he'd heard. Men had come to Jet's home in Portland the same day he'd gone to Silverton. They had come asking about Jet and his friends. Nana had escaped, and Jet had only talked with her a few times over the last few weeks. He was pretty sure she didn't know they were planning on going to Argentina.

Keesha asked, "Where are you from?"

"Silverton originally, but now I live in Portland."

"That's where all those people died," Paisley said. "From an earthquake."

"Yes, it is."

"Why didn't you die?" the girl asked in a cruel voice.

"What are you talking about?" Jet asked, now tired of her behavior. There was something off with this girl.

Rick and Jackson glanced at each other with bewilderment on their faces.

Paisley stood, her face shimmering slightly. Shaking her head as if she wore a mask and was trying to keep up the illusion. In the next instant, the disguise fell away. Standing in his dorm was Jessiva, a close friend to Shane Fallon. She wore a breastplate very similar to the one Shane had worn when they had last fought.

Jessiva hissed, "I saw you running around Los Angeles. What a fool you are, but Mckenzey was even more lost than you were."

"What's going on here?" Jackson demanded.

Jessiva opened her hand, and Jet thought he saw a small amount of yellow powder. She blew on her hand, the powder dispersed, and instantly Rick, Jackson, and Keesha were frozen where they stood. She added, "If they were part of this, the powder wouldn't have caused them to stop. They have no idea what you are."

"Not sure what you mean."

Jessiva took a slight step forward.

Jet could see Rick's eyes following her movement. "Can they see and hear what's going on?"

"Precisely. You've seen so much; you aren't even surprised." Jessiva pulled out a black whip with a black handle and unwound the far end.

"What are you doing?"

"Give me information or the tablet piece, and no one has to suffer."

"You need to leave."

"Is Jayco in charge? Is that why you had his jeep?"

"I was in Los Angeles looking for my friend Kevin McCormick, who has been missing for several weeks."

"Blah blah." Jessiva swirled the black whip close to her body, creating a small tornado of wind with its movements. "There's so much more going on than you could ever possibly understand. It isn't Shane's followers against Grantham's followers. You don't have to protect him any longer. Each of the five boarding schools is involved in searching for the special items. Silverton has two groups. Shane recognized Jayco during your last encounter, and he thinks Grantham, or you, fought him. My bet is Grantham. But after you escaped, two more groups arrived at Silverton and tried to rid the entire hill of any trace of magic. They had power you've never even dreamed of. Shane needs the tablet piece more than you do to stop them and control Arisol. He's trying to protect Chadwicks. I doubt you can say the same thing. Kevin is alive, and Shane will switch him for the tablet piece by Wednesday. We know you're headed to Quebec City, where the largest rockslide in the world happened a year before Silverton. Trying to divert us to Vancouver was childish."

Jet tried processing what she was saying. As a diversion he added, "If Shane thinks we have the tablet piece, why doesn't he just come and take it?"

"You're so laughable," Jessiva said. The cruelty in her voice was clear. "I'm almost embarrassed for you. Grantham has shared nothing with you, has he? You really have no relevance in this war, after all. Shane was right to have dismissed you so quickly."

"Enough," Jet said.

Dismissively she added, "There are magic ley lines throughout the world. Can we agree on this?"

"Go on," Jet said, trying to not sound as lost as he felt.

"Each of the five boarding schools was built on the only five locations in the United States where three ley lines connect together. The schools were built to protect students wishing to learn magic. But magic was lost for so many years, until just recently."

"What are you saying?" Jet asked.

"The schools are mostly protected against a magical attack from the outside. Additionally, neither Shane nor Grantham can actively attack someone else on campus with much success."

"Are you sure?" He'd seen Shane use a rune to attack one of his friends.

She seemed to guess his disbelief. "Look. He can throw a punch and break into a dorm, but he can't cause any serious damage. Trust me. He would've attacked every one of you from Silverton the moment you stepped on campus."

"What about Trina?"

"If she had not been protected by this school, she would've died."

Jet felt he had no other choice but to ask, "What were Shane and his goons doing out near the baseball fields, digging up the ground?"

"No idea. Since I got back from Los Angeles, I've been waiting here for you to come home."

"Was that magic you used to hide your identity?"

"Yes, but again, magic works differently where the ley lines connect, and I wasn't using it to attack you. Before magic was reawakened, it could be used, ever so slightly, at each of the schools. But now it's much more powerful. That's why Grantham was able to trick Shane; he didn't know his own power. Now Shane does, and you can bet he won't make that mistake twice."

"I think you should be going," Jet demanded.

Still swirling the whip, Jessiva added, "We're not finished here. I've given you information, and now it's your turn." Jessiva cracked the whip, and it smacked Keesha in the leg. Despite being frozen, her face contorted with the pain. More demandingly Jessiva asked, "What can you do?"

Considering his options, Jet didn't want to give away anything, but he felt that he had to give something back or Jessiva would cause more damage. If she challenged him, she would learn far too much. Jet nodded. "I can only do one thing." He avoided looking at Rick or Jackson. He loathed the idea of how they would treat him in the future. He whispered, "Aer," and a gust of wind shot outward from him. It wasn't much, but a few things rattled, and some papers shot into the air.

"A wind Occultist. Not bad, just not that powerful. You'll have your uses to Grantham. But I see why he didn't invite you to the inner circle. I bet you didn't even go to Silverton."

Jet's face reddened as he tried to appear embarrassed.

Jessiva smiled nastily. "I wonder why he sent you to Los Angeles?" A moment later her face lit up with such pleasure that Jet was shocked. "He knew it was a trap and sent someone expendable."

"It's not that…"

The next words were shouted with anger. *"Where is Vinny?"*

Jet thought she was about to explode or attack. He calmly asked, "What about Vinny? I didn't see anyone there."

"You were running away from where he was assigned. Did you see him?"

"No." He lied. "I saw no one. Mckenzey recognized you and Nash following her and wanted to leave. She called me, and we left."

"We couldn't find him or Jake."

"Jake?" Jet asked, feigning being shocked. "How could he have been there?"

"So you heard? One of *your* friends killed him."

"I'm totally confused."

"It wasn't Kevin that you were going to find in Los Angeles but Jake. That was the trap. We should've known Grantham would send a nobody." She muttered something under her breath. "Vinny never came out of the alley where they had put Jake. When the others arrived, Vinny and Jake were gone."

"Maybe Vinny left."

A hint of anger crossed Jessiva's face, and she flicked her black whip, and it expertly wrapped it around Rick's neck. Foam emerged at the corners of his mouth. She seemed barely in control of her emotions. "No one skips out on their passion."

"I wasn't saying that. It's just that there were some weird things going on in Los Angeles. I thought I saw a shadow following me."

"I doubt that." She released the rope, and it uncoiled from around Rick.

Taking a deep breath, Jet asked, "If magic doesn't work as well at Chadwicks, how is that powder keeping my roommates so still?"

"I'll be going. You have the ultimatum—the tablet piece for Kevin by Wednesday. Pass along the information to Grantham. You're pathetic. He would've never disclosed so much knowledge. But really, that's his fault for not giving you more information. What I told you is known to every one of the Czarics. It's clear that you aren't trusted and are on the wrong side. Choose better next time."

Jessiva swept away from the dorm, leaving Jet to pick up the broken pieces.

CHAPTER 4

"Who was that tramp, and what in the inferno was she talking about?" demanded Rick as his hands groped at the marks on his neck.

"Are you part of this?" Jackson asked. "Do you know who that was?"

Jet rubbed at Rick's neck. The marks were going to last a day or so, but they weren't permanent. Glancing at Keesha, he found that she was glowering back at him as if he'd just snuck into her dorm.

"Don't look at me like that," Keesha said. "I'm not going anywhere until someone explains what I just saw."

Jet growled and kicked the coffee table.

"She got the better part of you. She was name-calling and roasting you over and over again. I would've slapped her something fierce."

"Who invited that little troll in the first place?" asked Jet as he sat on the couch.

Rick and Jackson slumped across from him. Jackson said, "She just showed up."

Keesha disappeared for a moment, and he heard the faucet running in the bathroom. When she returned her face was damp.

Jet asked, slightly hopeful, "Did you guys see and hear everything?"

"Don't be an idiot," Jackson said. "She said some crazy things, but you didn't stop her."

Keesha added, "I don't think that girl likes you very much."

"You think!" Jet said sarcastically. "She's going straight to Shane. This is a total disaster."

"Are you talking about Shane Fallon?" Rick asked.

"The same."

Jackson added, "I think he's in a band or a group. All his friends wear the same clothes."

Keesha lifted a finger and pointed it directly at Jet. "Who are Vinny and Jake? Do they go to school here? And what is a Czaric?"

Jet groaned again. "I don't think it's a good idea to tell you anything."

"Why not?" Jackson asked. "It's not like you can take back what we saw. Might as well help us understand."

"If I tell you anything, it's either going to get you in trouble, or you won't believe me and go to the admin and try to get me kicked out of school."

"You know us better than that," Rick replied. "You've been acting weird since you came to school this year."

"What are you talking about?" Jet asked.

Jackson laughed. "Someone broke into our dorm a few months ago. They only searched *your* room. One time we had to throw you in the shower because you wouldn't wake up. Don't mention all the times your friends Ariana, Autumn, and even your old roommate Raul stopped by looking for you."

Keesha added, "Then there was that time I saw you with your face looking like you had been in a fight with a troop of monkeys. I barely know you and am already freaking out."

"I get the picture," Jet said, his voice resigned. "But if I tell you, you won't believe me."

Rick smiled. "After what we just saw, bro, I think we'll believe anything."

Wishing he had a spell that erased memories, he reluctantly held up his hand and spoke. "Chango." There was an immense increase in the temperature of the room, so much so that the other three recoiled slightly. Jet released the spell, and the temperature normalized.

"Did you do that?" wheezed Jackson.

"Shane Fallon knows magic, but of a different kind. He uses his to attack and hurt others. He and his friends are searching for something. So are we."

Keesha stood quickly, and for an instant, Jet was wary of who she really was. She said, "That girl said that Grantham is leading the group. He's in my English class. I've never seen him do anything magical."

"Grantham is part of our group. I don't think we have a choice, but have you meet the others."

Rick leaned forward. "Why are you telling us?"

"Knowing only a little will get you in trouble. What we're fighting for is big. Shane seems like the top dog, but there's something bigger going on."

Keesha asked, "Did you guys kill Kevin?"

For a moment Jet was confused. It took a few seconds for the pieces to fall into place. He said, "No. No. Kevin is missing. He's from the same town that I am—Silverton. Shane attacked him, and now he's disappeared. I was in Los Angeles looking for him. Vinny was the one that was killed. He tried very hard to kill my friends and me. Instead, he was the one that died."

"Are you serious?" Rick said. "A student from here has died?"

Jackson asked, "Why haven't we heard about this before?"

Jet answered, "The rumor is that Vinny dropped out after the Thanksgiving break. I'm not sure the school even knows what really happened."

"Was that magic you did there?" asked Keesha.

"A little," Jet said quickly. "I think it's best if you guys meet the others first. Probably tomorrow. I've no idea where this is going from here. The entire group will have to give the approval to say anything more."

"I'm interested," Keesha said. "I've seen Shane around a lot, and he's definitely a suspicious guy. Wasn't Silverton mostly destroyed? What's the big deal?"

"It's where everything started. Plan for tomorrow, and I'll let you know. My cell phone is dead, but don't worry, I'll contact you as soon as I know."

Rick said, "Can't wait."

As Keesha was heading out, Jet said, "I'm sure this doesn't need to be said, but please keep this between us."

"Who would believe me?" she asked.

"Still," Jet answered, "we can't take the risk. There's a lot at stake."

"I won't," she promised as she closed the door.

Rick and Jackson smiled widely as they said in unison, "Dude!"

# # #

Jayco chose the location of the meeting, under the bleachers of the football stadium. The Chadwick Dolphins had won a regional championship about four weeks ago and he wanted to brag. The season had been far from smooth because of the unprecedented heat that had lingered around the lower forty-eight states through October, when one of the largest natural disasters on record unleashed a storm of massive proportions. California received rain, but it had caused significant delays and changes to the sports seasons all along the West Coast. The East Coast was far more severely damaged. Jayco was a top player on the football team. In his eyes, under the bleachers was the perfect spot.

After an uneventful day in classes, Jet found Rick and Jackson in their dorm, and the three of them waited an extra fifteen minutes before Keesha arrived. She was unapologetic and tried saying how tricky it was getting away from her roommates. The walk to the stadium had taken five or six times longer than it should. Rick and Jackson were excited, while Keesha was far more reserved.

Last night, after talking with Rick and Jackson, trying not to give away any more than he should, he had called his friends and set up this meeting today. His classes for today were English, math, and PE. Tomorrow he had French class and geology lab. For the first time all year, he no longer wanted to be a TA for his Geology lab. He didn't want to see Autumn or anyone else, for that matter. He'd seen Shane twice during school today, and the smile on his face had been condescending and knowing.

First Jet led the group to the southern end of campus, near the science building. He continued to where College Avenue exited the campus, crossed the street, and headed back in the direction of the football field. Jet purposely passed this area and wanted to get a glimpse at what Shane had been doing last night. As he walked by the field, it was hard to see anything out of place except for some random holes in the ground that had been covered back up.

"Why are we going here?" Keesha asked, and they stepped through the main gate of the field.

"This is as good a place as any," replied Jet. "Secluded but still open enough."

As they approached the easternmost bleachers, Keesha added, "Still seems weird."

"No one's going to see us," Jet said.

Rick said, "I hate football."

"Stop worrying," Jet said, and they found a medium building behind the bleachers with bathrooms and locker rooms.

"This is sweet," Jackson said. "I didn't know there was this much room back here."

"I only found out about it because I've spent two years making this my home," Jayco Carter said as he stepped out from behind a door of the building. He was the tallest of the group, with massive shoulders and beach blond hair. He always had a tan and almost always wore shorts. He personified the typical Californian.

Grantham Mitchell trailed closely behind. He was just over six feet tall and was slender, with long legs, and a very athletic build. He was a long-distance runner and on the high school team. His skin was black but not as dark as the third member of their group, Latisha, who followed closely behind Grantham.

Latisha was well-dressed, with the latest and most expensive of the fall collections. She was beautiful and intelligent. She hated sports and would've preferred another location on campus. In the beginning, she was by far the most skeptical of the group about magic and was hard to convince otherwise.

Jet searched for the rest of the Echoes. But no one else came out. "Where are Mckenzey and Seyanna?"

Latisha said coolly, "Not coming. They're busy."

Jet had hoped that Mckenzey's mood from last night had improved, especially after hearing that Jessiva had been in Jet's dorm, threatening him.

Grantham added, "Keesha is in my English class, so I'll make the introductions." Pointing to Latisha, he said, "This is Latisha Rivera and Jayco Carter."

Keesha said, "Nice to meet all of you."

Jayco said, "We all know Rick and Jackson. Good to see you guys again."

"Same," Jackson said.

Latisha added, "Welcome. I'm not a big fan of sharing our secrets, but it looks like we didn't really have a choice."

"Jet showed us magic," Rick said.

"What?" Latisha asked. "Tell me you weren't that stupid."

"Jessiva disguised herself as another student, and she tricked her way into my dorm. She used a weapon, a black whip, around Rick's neck. She used Runic magic to keep them in place. It's not like they could unsee what she did."

Rick pointed to his neck, which was starting to bruise. "I appreciate the help. That was a tight spot."

Jayco demanded, "Does that mean Shane knows that we can do magic?"

"Jessiva thinks that Grantham's in charge and that he fought Shane."

"Sweet," Grantham said. "I guess he can see real talent when it's there."

"What about me?" asked Jayco.

"He knows that you're involved."

"Why Grantham?" Latisha asked.

"I'm better looking," Grantham said quickly. Keesha laughed then covered her mouth with her hand.

Jet said, "They knew it wasn't Jayco. They recognized you in the forest before the fight." He noticed that Latisha was glaring at Keesha, slightly jealous.

"Who's going to tell us what exactly is going on?" asked Rick. "Whatever is going on, we want in."

"We haven't decided to bring you in," Jet answered. "I was hoping we would have a full vote."

"Can't be helped," Jayco said flatly. "Mckenzey flew out to Colorado today. She arranged things with all of her teachers."

"What?" Jet asked. "She left without telling me?"

Latisha said calmly, "She wanted me to tell you. She's a mess and needs to see her parents. She just wants a break for a few days."

"Do we vote without her?" asked Jet.

Jayco said, "Keeping them in the dark isn't our best option. But we need to know that we can trust you."

"What does that mean?" Keesha asked. "Maybe it's you that needs to earn our trust. I know Jet a little and Grantham, but that doesn't mean I trust any of you, especially after what we saw last night."

"Trust means that we aren't going to let you play with all the toys. But we might be able to help protect you."

"Why would we need protection?"

Latisha answered, "The same reason that we do. There's something big going on here, and you three have found yourselves smack dab in the middle of it. But now Shane will know that you've seen magic. He might want to get to you, to get to Jet."

"This is all Jet's fault," Rick said.

"It usually is," Grantham answered.

All eyes focused on Jet, who said, "I guess that means that I get to explain. Okay. There are two types of magic.

Runic and Elemental. Until a few months ago, maybe longer, magic was lost. I'm not sure which. But now magic has been reawakened, and we have some level of talent with Elemental. Shane, that girl from last night, and several others, are using Runic magic. Does it make sense?"

"No, not really," Keesha said. "You warmed up the room last night; I guess that's Elemental magic. What is Runic magic?"

Grantham answered, "Runic magic is the use of drawing a picture. From that picture comes an event or a reaction. Almost like chemistry—there's a movement and an action."

"Where did you learn all of this?" Jackson asked.

"Mostly from Jet."

"Why him?" Keesha asked.

Jayco added, "It would be easy to say he was chosen, but rather he lived through a natural disaster that almost killed him. 'Chosen' is too easy of a word. He survived."

"How do we know this is all real?" Keesha said.

It was obvious that Rick and Jackson were already on board with what they heard. Jet wasn't surprised. He asked, "Where are you from?"

She shrugged. "I'm from Sacramento. What does that matter?"

"What do you think of Shane?"

"The guy's a jerk."

Jet settled himself between Grantham and Jayco and stared directly at Keesha. "What do you think about the possibility of magic?"

"Never really thought about it." Keesha almost imperceptibly glanced away.

"I don't think you're being totally honest with us, Keesha. What are you hiding something?"

"Nothing," she said quickly, but she refused to make eye contact with anyone.

Latisha said, "It's better if you come clean with things now."

In a hollow voice, she asked, "Do you guys remember Chin Nguyen?"

Jet exchanged glances with his friends. He said, "I've no clue who he is."

"Me neither," replied Jayco. "Does he go to school here?"

"Not anymore."

Rick interjected, "Maybe. I think he was in my freshman biology class. He would've been a sophomore like the rest of us, but he moved to a different school."

"He transferred to a school in Florida called Valley Sun Academy." She paused for a moment, then continued, "Chin was befriended by Shane about halfway through our freshman year. He and I were dating at the time. After Christmas Chin stopped talking with me. I had no clue what was going on. One night, sometime in January, I cornered Chin and tried to find out what was going on. He told me very little but that he was getting recruited for a secret group. He wouldn't tell me anything except that he wasn't allowed to talk with anyone outside of the group. I figured we were breaking up."

Jayco said, "I think we can answer some questions."

Keesha appeared relieved. She continued, "Late January I was out with some friends, and I happened to see him running across the courtyard between the beach and the boys' dorm buildings. I followed but couldn't really keep up with them. I'm pretty sure they went inside Kelci Halls."

"My dorm building?" Jet asked.

"A few hours later, there was an ambulance and several of the administrators around, including Principal Jan Fletcher."

"When was this?" asked Latisha.

"About a year ago, in January."

Jet paused for a minute, then said, "That was right around when my roommate tried to hurt himself. I can't see that they would be connected."

"The day Raul, your roommate, went to the hospital, was the last day I ever saw Chin. He transferred to Valley Sun and won't return an email or phone call."

"Maybe a coincidence," Jet said.

"Seems like far more than a coincidence," Grantham said.

Jayco asked, "So you're here to learn more about Shane and what he's been doing?"

"For the last year, I've tried to find a way to become friends with Jet and the rest of you. I hoped that you could give me answers. Jet was always so preoccupied, so I tried becoming friends with Rick and Jackson."

Rick said, without a trace of displeasure, "You used us. I feel so gross inside."

Keesha smiled playfully.

Jackson added, "You loved it."

"Shane," Jayco explained, "is the leader of several secret groups on campus. Each leader is what they call a Paramount. Each leader reports to Shane. I was also recruited about the same time as your friend Chin. I didn't make the cut."

"Shane tried recruiting you?" Keesha asked.

Grantham answered, "It was miserable. He wasn't allowed to hang out with any of his old friends."

"Shane asked a bunch of questions about my friends, Silverton, and how we survived. I obviously didn't want or get the spot. I never knew who else was being interviewed."

"Was Shane trying to get Chin to be the leader of one of these secret groups?"

Jayco nodded. "If not a leader, a member."

"Then why did he transfer to a different school?" Keesha asked. "And what does this have to do with Raul?"

Grantham said, "Raul is back at school. I wonder if we could ask him."

"How would he know what Chin was doing?" Jet protested.

"Would you try talking to Raul?" Keesha pleaded.

"Not sure that's a great idea. I haven't had a real conversation with him since my birthday, a few months ago. He seems tight with Shane now. If we push it too much, Shane will know that we're looking into Chin."

Rick cleared his voice. "This is good and all, but I want more information on magic."

"Let's go in here," Jayco said. He led them through the same door he'd exited. They followed Jayco into a small conference room with a dozen chairs around a table. "This is as safe a place as we're going to find."

Jet sat down and asked, "What is it that you want to know?"

"What can you do?" Jackson smirked. "Are you immortal?"

"Don't be stupid. I can work a little Elemental magic."

Keesha asked, "How did this all start?"

"I'm pretty sure it started when Mckenzey and I survived the earthquake in Silverton. Seyanna, who isn't here, Latisha, Grantham, and Jayco were all out of town at the time. I barely managed to get out of my house. You see, I had these abilities that allowed me to survive. Mckenzey escaped as well."

Rick interrupted. "How did you learn magic?"

"Chill, bro," Grantham said. "Jet's getting there."

Rick nodded eagerly.

Jet continued, "The house was crashing down around me, and this shadow box in my room fell to the floor. Turns out, there was something hidden inside this old box that I thought was a family heirloom."

"What was it?" Rick asked, barely in control of his excitement.

"A book, unlike anything I've ever seen."

"Well, that's disappointing." Jackson leaned back in his chair. "I hate school enough; I don't want to have to worry about a stupid book."

Reaching into his backpack, Jet pulled out the leather-bound ancient book with the words *The Sorcerer's Guide* on the cover and tossed it to Jackson. "Why don't you have a look."

The book slid across the table and into the hands of Jackson, who caught it expertly. Rick and Keesha moved closer.

"Try to open it," Jet said.

Jackson smirked, tried prying open the book. His fingers gripped both edges of the cover, and he pulled. The book didn't budge. He pushed harder and harder and was soon pulling with all his strength. It remained stubbornly shut.

"Let me try." Keesha took the book, but instead of trying to open it, she methodically searched the front and back covers for a button or a way to open the book. When she found nothing, she removed a small pocket knife from her pants and pulled out the blade. Before Jet could react, she tried sliding it into the pages.

"What the?" screamed Rick.

As the blade touched the pages, it melted on contact with the side of the book. A moment later Keesha held up her destroyed knife. She whispered, "I'm a believer."

"Same," Rick shouted and pushed the book back over to Jet.

Jet, still startled, managed to say, "I've been the only one to be able to open this book. But instead of a book, we call it a tome."

"Show us," Rick said.

"I would, but something happened recently, and it's ignoring us."

Keesha said, "You talk about it like it has a mind of its own."

"It just might. It shows me what it thinks I should know."

Jackson asked, "Like what?"

"The first page is a fable that seems like a good story, but it has some bite to it. Turns out, it's probably true. The next pages have letters or words, or ways to learn magic."

Keesha stood. "Try opening it."

Jayco mumbled, "This should be interesting."

Using one finger, as he had done when he first showed his friend, he attempted to open the front cover. However, this did not work as intended. Instead, the tome opened to a page that appeared almost halfway into the book. Grantham and Latisha leaped to their feet. Jet was speechless.

CHAPTER 5

Jet was far from prepared for *The Sorcerer's Guide* to open; in fact, he was downright alarmed. He reacted and yanked the tome closer. Staring down, he read the title of this page, "A Recipe to Augmenting the Echoes."

"What does it say?" demanded Jayco.

Keesha asked quickly, "Can't you see what it says?"

"No," Jayco said coolly. "Can you?"

Jet lifted the book so everyone could see the page.

"It's blank," Keesha replied. "Is that supposed to happen?"

"Every time." Latisha added.

"No way," Jackson said.

"That's convenient," Keesha replied. "He could tell us almost anything he wanted."

"That's just the way it is," Grantham said.

As Jet pulled the book closer, Jayco said, "Read it aloud."

Parfit Inclusionem

Certain rules of Elemental magic are fixed and immovable, while others are far less understood. The ability to use magic is not found within every person or creature, and despite the attempts or desires, magic cannot be gifted to all persons.

Elemental magic is reborn through the Mikado, who governs its control but cannot change the rules to fit his or her own motives. The Mikado will govern the Occultists and Tyros.

A Mikado cannot be replaced in death but can be mimicked in duty by the five trusted Aureum.

As magic awakens, more people and creatures will be able to use magic for good. Five occultists will be chosen by the Mikado and magic to govern the affairs of each of the five elements.

Each Elemental Occultist will instruct a group of novices or Tyros. As the groups gain Tyros, additional Occultists will be chosen. New Occultists will be selected from among the Tyros. If an Occultist should die or revolt, they will be replaced by another among their Tyros. Once five clusters of five Occultists are created, the Aureum is created.

An Occultist governs and mentors their Tyros and may learn to use more than one spell. The Tyro may one day become more capable with their spell, but that doesn't invite an insurrection to overthrow the Occultist. Honor and Respect are vital to Elemental magic. Outright deception or mutiny may result in the taking away of magical prowess through atrophy or a more direct approach.

Gifting magic is the mechanism of creating Tyros. The Mikado and most Occultists can gift magic to persons and creatures, but beware, not all will be fortunate enough to absorb the capacity.

The gifting word is: Parfit Inclusionem

Once this is accomplished, the Tyro will reply:
Suscepit Parfit

This will be followed by an aura of color.
Red—Fire
Yellow—Wind
Aqua Blue—Water
Brown—Earth
White—Spirit
No color—the gift was not given

For years, the 10 Kings attempted to govern the magical world both with and without open magic. They witnessed an abundance of deception and rebellion. A Tyro trying to overpower an Occultist who uses magic to attack and kill or seriously injure an Occultist may be subject to permanently losing their gift.
A Mikado has the power to erase the gift of magic.

"Perfect timing," Jayco responded awestruck. "What are the chances that this page would open with Keesha, Rick, and Jackson here. It's a sign."

"It's something," replied Jet, unsure of what to do next.

"Let's do it right now." Jackson rushed forward.

"No!" Latisha demanded. "It's important for all of us to be here to make this decision. How can we decide without Mckenzey and Seyanna?"

Grantham said, "Maybe. It'll be weeks before we're all back together. After…"

"Let's look at this logically." Jet interrupted. "The tome has been closed since Silverton. Maybe the problem was that we were going in the wrong direction. This is a clear signal that we need to start expanding Elemental magic. With Keesha, Rick, and Jackson, it opens to a page talking about gifting magic. This has to mean something."

"Don't tell me we have to travel back to Silverton and stand in front of that cave for the magic to appear." Grantham complained.

Magic only seemed to flow through Jet at first. He had this moth-eaten rag turn into his cloak. When they'd arrived at Silverton, they found this huge cavern door. That was when magic started flowing through his friends. Their cloaks changed and some unique abilities arrived shortly thereafter. Since then each of his friends had been able to perform at least one spell.

Mckenzey could manipulate water, Jayco fire, Grantham earth, Latisha wind, and Seyanna spirit. His friends, each proficient with a different element, were Occultists. If he was correct, that meant that Jackson, Rick, and Keesha would be the first Tyros. He desperately wanted to try.

"No, we don't," Jet answered. "In fact, we could do it right now."

"Really?" Latisha questioned. "Can we trust your book?"

"It hasn't failed us before," replied Jet.

"I'm in," Rick said confidently.

Keesha asked, "Are we really ready?"

Sitting back down, Jet said, "Good point. You'll need to hear more to really understand what you are getting involved in."

Rick, Jackson, and Keesha leaned forward.

"Are we really doing this?" Jayco asked, a hint of excitement in his voice.

"Let's at least give them a summary. In the end they'll have to make their own choices."

Over the next hour, Jet and the others explained Silverton, Washington, DC, *The Sorcerer's Guide*, and most of the basics. He read the fable and was unsurprised when they kept mixing up the names. After finishing, the three students appeared exhausted.

"Sorry for the info dump," Jet said.

"There's no way I'm going to remember the difference between Leotyton and Faunal."

"Names are hard to remember," Latisha said. "When I first heard the fable, I was totally lost, and to make things worse, I didn't believe it. That changed pretty quickly. Just remember that Leotyton died to create the book, I mean, tome. Arisol is the big name to remember. He pretty much wants to escape his prison and kill everyone. We ran into Faunal in the cave in Silverton, and he's a walking, talking wolf."

Grantham added, "He's basically besties with Arisol but can't hurt us right now, at least not directly."

Keesha asked, "Does Shane want to help Arisol or control him?"

Jet answered, "Honestly, I think he wants to control Arisol, but we can't be certain."

Keesha followed up with, "And you want to kill Arisol."

"If possible." Jet shrugged. "At the least put him back in prison permanently."

Rick interjected, "What's the Rivalry?"

"Can I answer this?" asked Jayco. He continued, "The Rivalry is this ancient war that settles magical problems. It vanished for a while, and now that Arisol wants to kill us, it's back in style. It's essentially gold versus black, like in football, and we're golden."

Keesha asked, "Does that mean that Shane is on the dark side?"

Jet laughed. "Without a doubt."

Keesha smiled and gave Jet a slight wink. He tried not reacting, assuming she was just being playful. He couldn't deal with more girl problems at the moment. Continuing, he said, "We have some weapons of our own." Pulling out the three golden orbs from his pocket, he tossed them lightly into the air. "Shane has black items and weapons, and he's quite powerful. If you join us, you risk being attacked by him…"

"Or worse." Grantham finished. "It got sticky for a minute. You'll need to decide what's best for you."

"When do we have to decide?" Keesha asked.

Rick moved to the front of the room. "I'll be the first victim."

Jet scanned the faces of Latisha, Grantham, and Jayco. They all appeared as confident as he felt.

Grantham said, "Let's do this."

Everyone pushed back the chairs, and they walked to an open space at the front of the room. No one was certain what was going to happen. Jet said, "Okay. I'm going to say the word, and you'll need to answer with Suscepit Parfait. I'm pretty sure I'm giving you a gift, and by saying the words, you're accepting the gift."

"And to be clear, this could work on Rick but not me?" Jackson added.

"I think so," Jet answered. Turning to Rick, he said, "Are you ready?"

"A hundred percent."

Jet spoke, "Parfit Inclusionem."

Rick replied slowly, "Suscepit Parfait."

Instantly the air in the room warmed, and an aura on the outer edges of Rick's figure glowed red.

Jayco punched the air.

Jet said, "I think that means that Jayco is your mentor."

"What?" Rick said. "Jayco can do fire magic?"

"Chango." Jayco spoke the same word that Jet had used the night before. For Jayco, it did something slightly different.

"What the…" Rick said, and he shook his hand back and forth. "That felt like you were burning my skin."

"Just warmed it up a little, but you're right, if I wanted, I could toast your skin."

Keesha let out a long whistle. "That's some crazy stuff."

Jayco took a slight step back. "It's sobering when you realize that a single word can hurt almost anyone. You must be careful. On the bright side, I can boil water without a fire."

"My turn," Jackson said. Almost to himself, he asked, "Do I want fire or something else?"

Before anyone could react, Rick spoke, "Chango" in the direction of the bottled water on the table. Nothing happened.

"It doesn't work like that. You'll be able to do one spell. Be patient."

"Tell them all to me," Rick demanded.

Realizing their error in going too quickly, Jet said, "Jayco's right. We're going to take this really slow. Your progression in certain things will allow you to gain Jayco's confidence. He will test you and see what spell works for you. We aren't going to tell you everything today."

"Really?" Rick asked.

"That's how this is going to work," Jet explained.

Grantham added, "I think we might have a better understanding of why Shane is putting his friends into groups. Could he be doing the same thing we are?"

"You might be right," Jet said.

Latisha said, "Interesting."

Turning to Rick, Jackson, and Keesha, he said, "Keep cool. This is a gift and if you abuse it, there will be consequence."

"You would take away magic?" Keesha asked warily.

"Only if I have to." Looking to Jackson, he asked, "Ready?"

Matching Rick, he replied, "Without a doubt."

"Parfit Inclusionem."

"Suscepit Parfait." Surprisingly, the aura he produced was yellow.

"Wind," Jet said. "That means you're with Latisha. Keesha, you're up next if you want to be, but it's your choice."

"If I'm going to find out why Chin left and what Shane did to him, there's not much of a choice. Count me in."

After the words were spoken, the aura around Keesha shone a bright aqua blue.

"That's Mckenzey's color."

"Didn't you say that she left for Colorado?"

"She did."

"What am I supposed to do now?"

Jet thought about it for a moment. Finally, he said, "I'll work with you. In fact, we'll all work together tomorrow after school."

"What are we going to do?" Rick asked.

Jackson asked, "Are we going to learn magic?"

"You'll find out tomorrow."

CHAPTER 6

Ducking into the science building, Jet went through the front door, this time. He walked into his classroom expecting to see a note waiting for him, with instructions on how to prepare for this week's geology lab. Being the TA for this class had its perks. It gave him a chance to learn more about science and allowed him to find the secret room downstairs. The best part, it was a paying gig.

Autumn Bells, the main TA, worked to get the lab room prepared. Jet found stacks of papers needing to be separated.

"Glad you're here, Jet," Autumn said kindly. "I've been here for an hour already, and I feel like I've accomplished nothing. I tried calling you, but your phone went directly to voicemail. I need you to separate each pile of papers into thirty stacks."

"What is this stuff?"

"We're going to be talking about earthquakes this week. This is a handout explaining the release of stored energy, seismographs, and other things. The handouts are pretty central to Professor Blum's discussion."

"This is what I'm talking about," Jet said quickly. "I've been looking forward to this lesson all year."

"Is that because you lived through Silverton?" she asked pointedly.

Jet was momentarily distracted by her stunning looks, which hoodwinked his mind into thinking she wasn't as perceptive as she was. He hated himself because something about her caused his hormones to rage uncontrollably. He found himself blurting out the stupidest things, and his face would turn red. A few times he'd thrown caution to the wind. Thankfully he hadn't done anything too stupid. He managed to say, "I didn't know that you knew that."

"Uh…most everyone knows that all of the Silverton survivors received a full-ride scholarship. It doesn't bother me, but not everyone feels the same."

"Are we talking about Shane again?" Jet remembered back to the Halloween party, when he'd danced with Autumn. She'd given him some insight into Shane, including the fact that he'd transferred from Dillon Lake, one of the five boarding schools connected with Chadwicks.

"Not just Shane. There are others as well," Autumn said as she strode in his direction. "What was it like living through that horrible disaster?"

Jet wasn't sure what to say. "Uh. I lived outside of town. Silverton itself received most of the damage. My house was demolished, and my grandmother and I barely escaped."

"Tons of people died." She stopped near the counter's edge. Her perfectly sculpted face stared at him like he was the most important person in the room, maybe in the school.

"That's true."

"How did you escape?"

Jet's mouth felt dry. "A gully hit my house while I slept, and it woke me up. The entire house shook. I found Nana, my grandmother, and we went out the back door. The backyard was toast, and we were forced to cross a river of lava. We barely made it to our car before the entire house crumbled to the ground."

She reached out and squeezed his shoulder.

Jet shivered.

"Have you ever been back?"

"Not really. After leaving Silverton, Nana and I moved north to Portland."

Jet wasn't sure where this conversation was going. Despite his attraction to Autumn, he was starting to feel slightly apprehensive.

Autumn sat down across from him and started separating the documents for the lab. Jet busied himself. Once they'd finished half of the pile, Autumn asked, "Would it be all right if I told you a secret?"

Jet nearly fell out of his chair.

Autumn giggled.

After recovering, he said, "Depends on the secret."

"It could get me into trouble, so you would have to promise not to tell anyone."

"This sounds dangerous."

She remained quiet, staring at him, as if expecting an answer.

"Can I ask what it is about?"

"I think you already know."

"Trust me, I don't." He felt his heart racing. "How about a hint?"

"It isn't about Ariana, your ex-girlfriend, or her brother."

Jet swallowed. He knew that Ariana and Autumn had been good friends a few years ago. They were both a year older than he was. Something had happened between them, and they had stopped talking until Jet mended the bridge, in a way. "Is it about Shane or me?"

"That's a weird way to ask a question. But yes, at least I think so."

"Do I really want to know?" Jet asked, half resigned to a miserable existence.

"It's an answer to a question that you asked Professor Blum a few months ago."

Jet stared at Autumn, clueless about what she was hinting at. Professor Blum was his teacher for the geology lab class that he was preparing for. He didn't think that he'd asked Professor Blum anything that had to do with Shane.

Autumn continued, "Promise that you won't tell anyone. Especially not Professor Blum."

"I'm baffled."

"Remember when Professor Blum said that his meteorites were stolen?"

"Okay! The ones from Silverton?"

"The same."

"Do you know what happened to them?"

"Maybe."

"How would Shane have known about them?"

"I told him. In fact, I was talking to Professor Rysen, the chemistry teacher, about the meteorites, and Shane overheard. He was beyond excited when he learned they were from Silverton. Because I was with Professor Rysen, I thought it would be okay to bring them here and show them the meteorites."

"How did they react?"

"They didn't get quite as excited as you did. They didn't fall off their stools and try to play it off as if they had slipped."

"What do you mean?"

"Meteorites from Silverton. You could barely control yourself. I thought you were going to have a seizure or something."

Jet wasn't about to tell Autumn what had really happened. Seeing a vision of a cave inside of a mountain and getting a burn on his hand. Weeks later, in Silverton, he and his friends had found that same cave, but this time there were the black and golden weapons. Jet rubbed the palm of his hand where the meteorite had burned his skin. He still had a scar. The reason that Jet had been so excited in the first place was that he and Mckenzey had found a similar-looking rock in the hills north of Silverton when they were younger. He had always thought it was a special rock. Turned out, it was a meteorite. "Like you said, they were from Silverton, and I was pretty excited to see them."

Autumn added, "Shane and Professor Rysen both studied the meteorites for several minutes. After they were done, I locked them in the office."

"When did they go missing?"

After a pause, Autumn said, "The next day."

Jet let out a long whistle. "That's a pretty big coincidence. I'm betting that you didn't tell Professor Blum."

"No way. He would never understand."

"Why tell me?"

"Truthfully, I think something more happened when you touched the meteorites. They mean something to you."

"Why now?"

"I know Shane's watching you and your friends. He knows that I work with you in the lab."

"Are you warning me of something?"

"Not really. But he'll come to talk with me soon. I'm not sure if I have the willpower to not be affected by his allure."

"You could just say no."

Autumn laughed. "That does nothing. You should know him better."

"What does his allure do?"

"Do you think Ariana and Raul want to be so close to him after what he did to them? They have some ability to act on their own, but really, what choice do they have. He can do things that I've never seen before."

"When we danced back at Halloween, you said that Shane was a good guy. He watches people's backs."

"If it serves him. Like I said back then, he asked Ariana to watch Mckenzey and Raul to watch you."

"I don't understand. Why would they do that?"

"They really didn't have a choice."

"You talk like he has power over them."

"Allure," Autumn said.

But before she could say anything else, the side door flew open, and Jayco and Grantham thundered into the room.

Jet leaped to his feet. "Is something wrong?"

"Not at all," Jayco said quickly, his eyes darting to Autumn. "We thought you were alone and about to be finished."

Grantham added, "There's a bonfire starting up on the beach. We wanted to see if you want to go over. There's a girl that's interested in you."

"Really. Me?" Jet asked, feeling uncomfortable with how close Autumn was.

"Oh yes. She ran into me earlier today and said that she wanted to see you tonight."

Jet shrugged casually. "Sure. I have another thirty minutes here, but..."

Autumn's voice was loud and insistent. "We're almost done. I'll finish up the rest."

"You sure?" Jet asked, peering back at Autumn.

"No problem." She asked Grantham, "Who's the girl that wants to talk with Jet?"

"Oh. You know." Grantham mumbled a bit. "Trina Madden."

To his astonishment, Autumn's face narrowed. She said, "Before you go can you help carry these papers in the back room?"

"Sure."

Jet grabbed the stacks they'd finished while Autumn carefully arranged the rest of the papers. He followed her into the back room of the classroom; they entered a large storage room full of rocks, equipment, and more. Autumn turned left, and he followed her into a smaller space, just big enough for a few chairs and a table. Jet placed his papers on the desk.

Autumn spoke quickly, almost frantically, "Be very careful of Trina. She's also been allured."

"What are you talking about?"

"You know more than you're letting on." With both of her hands, she grabbed his hand, the same one that had touched the meteorite. Her thumbs went over the scar. "I know that you can do magic, but I bet yours is different from Shane's."

Jet pulled back his hand. "How do you know this?"

"Just a few months ago, in the classroom, I told you that when you watch things and ask the right people the right questions, you usually get the right answers."

"I don't believe you."

"It doesn't matter. I don't have the willpower to stop him the next time he tries to collect me."

"Collect you?" Jet felt the ground of uncertainty beneath him. "What does this have to do with Trina?"

"Shane has been searching for the magically inclined for years. Someone has been teaching him. Silverton is a huge part of this. He uses allure to collect people to do what he wants. He thought Trina was involved. Initially she refused to tell him anything. She became his target with the powder and the allure charm. He told Ariana that if you have been magically gifted, then allure can't affect you nearly as much."

"Why did you wait to tell me this?"

"I tried to find a way to meet up with you near Halloween."

"I thought you meant for a date."

"It was both. But now it's too late for that. Shane's going to collect me."

Jayco's voice echoed from the front room. "Hey, Jet. We need to get going."

"Almost done," Jet said quickly. "I'll try to figure a way to protect you."

"I wish." She leaned forward and kissed him on the mouth so hard that Jet felt that he was sliding into an unconscious bliss. The moment only lasted for a split second before Autumn pulled away. "Get out of here. Be very careful. Shane is after you and your friends."

Jet stumbled back into the classroom and silently followed Jayco and Grantham as they left the building. Talking with Autumn was dizzying, but she had hinted at a fair number of things. If what she had said was true, Shane could somewhat control the behaviors of others. Trina was a possible trap, and Raul and Ariana were being managed to some degree. After five minutes of walking, Jet asked, "I thought we were going to the beach?"

"We lied," Jayco replied.

Without even realizing it, they were standing at the south end of campus.

Grantham opened the door to the laundry building used by campus workers for the linens, bedding, and other items used by the school. Jet wasn't sure what was happening. He didn't know anything about this building. They crossed a large room with several big pieces of equipment and entered a doorway. After a few steps, they curved right and found another door, this time descending into the basement. "What are we doing?"

"We need to show you something."

"What about Trina?"

"There's something wrong with that girl."

"What do you mean?"

"She's been caught four or five times trying to sneak inside your dorm. Napoleon didn't want to tell you. She's been in the principal's office a few times. Latisha works over there again, and the gossip is that Trina's behavior is being pushed under the rug."

"That's a little shocking," Jet said. "Where are we really going?"

"We've been working on a side project for the last four weeks. It's time to show you."

"Did Mckenzey mention it the other night?"

"You heard that?" asked Grantham.

"Hard to miss," Jet said. "I thought you guys were using your talents to swim, make money, and do whatever you wanted."

In the basement the walls around them were concrete. The hallway was dark and damp. "Most of that's true," Grantham admitted as he led them to a large metal cabinet. "But we had a higher purpose."

"What are you talking about?"

Jayco shoved the metal cabinet, and the entire thing moved. It was as if the cabinet were on wheels. Upon closer inspection, Jet noticed the two metal tracts allowed the cabinet to glide. Behind the cabinet was another door. Jayco pulled out a key and unlocked the door. Reaching inside his pocket, he handed Jet a spare.

Shocked, Jet asked, "Where does this go?"

"We've spent the last four weeks building this tunnel."

"You built a tunnel?"

"Sort of," Grantham said.

"This is ludicrous."

"When Mckenzey's talent is working, she can not only heal, but she can also dig in dirt and rocks and rearrange them perfectly."

"No way." Jet felt slightly astonished and angry.

"I promise," Jayco said. "She gets tired easily, so it still took about a week or two."

"Where does this tunnel go?"

Grantham punched his shoulder. "That's what we're going to show you."

The door swung inward, and Jet followed his two friends into a circular concrete corridor. Jayco closed the door just as Grantham pulled out a few flashlights, handing one to Jet.

"It gets dark in here. We only have about a mile to go."

"A mile."

"We've been busy."

"How did you get the concrete down here?"

Jayco grinned. "Carefully, very carefully. They don't weigh as much as you would think."

Grantham chuckled. "For you, not the rest of us, and only when you're wearing your golden bracelets."

After a dozen steps, Jet asked, "What in the world have you guys been doing?"

Grantham and Jayco led Jet into the darkness. The corridor wasn't completely straight, and after five minutes, they curved slightly left. After another ten minutes of walking, Jet asked, "How close are we to the beach?"

"Nice one," Grantham said. "There's the other door up ahead."

"This isn't possible," Jet replied.

"You can do some pretty exceptional magic," Grantham pointed out. "This corridor is nothing but grunt work."

"Must've been expensive."

"There's a lot of gold in the ocean," Jayco said. "We're pretty much rich. All of us."

"No way," Jet said.

Jayco added, "Turns out I can see underwater and can hold my breath for about fifteen minutes. I have limitations to how deep I can go and how much I can see underwater."

Jet stopped walking. "Are you serious? Why all the secrecy?"

Both boys turned to Jet. What they said surprised him. Jayco said, "You've a ton of power—especially with magic. Imagine you were us; until Silverton, we were picking up the small pieces behind you and Mckenzey, almost an afterthought. We had nothing. This group is about all of us. Grantham and I wanted to show you and the others that we are all important."

"I never said you weren't."

"We know, bro," Grantham said, his bright teeth shining in the darkness as a huge smile spread across his face. "We've made it to the big leagues now. We can't have a small basement as our hideout. We need protection and a place to chill. We need a castle."

"How's that possible?"

"Follow us," Jayco insisted.

CHAPTER 7

Jet, partially filled with excitement and terror, reluctantly followed Grantham and Jayco as they led him to another concrete door with a lock. Producing another key, he opened the door, and passed another spare over. He thought a blinding light would attack his eyes, but instead he found that they were in a small cave. Once they stepped outside, the door was closed and locked. Debris, such as wood, rocks, and other items, was placed in front of the door. The cave was more like a narrow crevice. Light shone from the far end, only ten feet away.

"Isn't this place beautiful?" asked Jayco.

It didn't take long to exit the cave and make their way down to the beach, dodging the underbrush. This was indeed one of the most stunning beaches on the West Coast. The water was pristine blue, and on both sides, there were two giant rock walls. Boulders the size of small houses prevented most people from entering the cove from the open water. Jayco had previously found this paradise and had shared his discovery.

"Follow me." Jayco grinned, and they tore through the sand. "No one's ever going to find that entrance."

"Mckenzey's a hard worker," Grantham added. "She's got game."

"So you guys made a quicker way to the beach?" Jet asked.

"And a more secure one," said Jayco. "Remember when we went cliff jumping the first time we came?"

"I didn't jump." Jet said. "My collarbone was still broken."

"Next time," Grantham said.

They crossed the main part of the sand and stopped. Pointing into the water where the far rock wall met the sand, Jayco said, "There's a rope that's anchored to the wall. You can't see it, but it's there."

Grantham added, "If you use that rope, it will take you out into the water."

"Do I have to use the rope?"

"Not necessarily. But it's there nonetheless."

"Where are we going?" asked Jet.

Jayco nodded at the gigantic rock wall. "We're going inside the hill."

"There's a trick to getting inside," Grantham explained. "Only the six of us can know about this place. No outsiders."

"Fine," Jet said. "What kind of trick?"

Grinning even wider, Jayco said, "When you're following the rope, you have to kick a certain rock on the bottom of the ocean. It's attached to a lever that unlocks the door. After you go inside, the door closes, and the rock returns to where it started."

Grantham added, "We have to go one at a time."

"I'll go first," Jayco said. "The rock is black and it's about the size of a bowling ball."

Before diving into the water, Jayco touched the rope with his foot, and Jet saw a metal loop clamped onto the wall. Jayco swam to about a third of the way out and disappeared under the water.

"That seemed easy," Grantham said. "But Jayco always makes it look easy. I'll take your backpack this time. I'll be a step behind."

Jet wasn't the best swimmer, in fact, he had avoided water altogether for the past four years. Having a few scars on his legs and arms from when he'd escaped Silverton prevented him from getting in.

Grantham nodded, and Jet followed the rope. He walked as far as he could, then dove into the cold water. His hands grasped the rope, and he pulled himself forward. He was forced to resurface a few minutes later, still holding on to the rope. It didn't take long before he was near where Jayco had dived under. As he submerged, he found Jayco sitting on the bottom of the ocean, with his legs crossed, pointing at a black rock.

Stretching out his foot, Jet nudged the underwater stone, but nothing happened. He was forced to resurface for air and dove again. This time he pushed hard and heard a latch unlock, and to his left, the rock wall shifted, and a door opened within the rock wall. Jayco motioned for him to enter.

Jet swam through the opening, and the door closed directly behind him as the locking mechanism reengaged. He found himself in an underwater corridor with smooth edges. The first room was large, and a foot and a half of water filled up most of the room. He was able to walk to the far side and exit the small pool. Further inside was a narrow corridor. It didn't take long for Grantham and Jayco to gain entrance.

Jayco said, "You're not going to believe what we've been working on."

"This is impossible," Jet said, awestruck.

"You really thought we were just messing around?" Grantham asked from a few steps behind.

"It had crossed my mind a time or two."

"Ouch," Jayco said playfully. "That's harsh."

Jayco led them down a rock corridor for another ten feet. The space opened into a gigantic room, and there were dozens of alcoves spread about with five or six candles in each. There was plenty of light in the large chamber. A firepit, cut into the ground, was in the center, but not in use. To his left and in the space considered the back of the room were six small half rooms with only a portion of a front wall on each. There was almost no privacy, but he was astonished to see that each room had a mattress and a small cabinet. On the far side of the firepit were a generator, a stove, and a fridge. More toward the front, there was a table and several chairs. Against the far wall, twelve cubicles had been cut, and Jet thought that these would store items, weapons, and other valuables.

"What do you think?" Jayco asked.

"This place is beyond awesome." Jet stared at each of his friends. "How did you guys do this?"

Grantham answered, "It was Jayco's idea to get a more secure area, and Mckenzey used her ability. This seemed like the perfect spot, but it took a lot of work. Once we decided to use this space, we made the shortcut through the laundry."

"Am I the only one out of the loop?"

Jayco said, "Actually, Latisha and Seyanna haven't seen it. I'm not sure Seyanna knows about it at all. She has been so busy with her parents that we never get to see her."

"Is she still planning on starting classes after the Christmas break?"

"She is," answered Jayco. "I think that's why her parents have been so busy."

"When did you guys want to move the Phoenix, pyramids, and other items here?"

Grantham said, "We were thinking later tonight after we meet up with Rick, Jackson, and Keesha."

"I'm pretty speechless at how unbelievable this place looks."

Jayco strolled toward the front of the chamber. "We have some more ideas as well. This is going to be so much fun. See you guys on the beach." He leaned over and hit a button, and a hydraulic vibration sounded that could be felt through the floor. A massive piece of the front wall moved up a few feet, and lapping ocean water became visible. Jayco hit another button, and the massive rock piece moved toward its normal position. Jayco dove out into the water and disappeared.

"He's such a show-off," Grantham said, turning back to Jet.

"This place is the best."

Grantham said quickly, "I'm worried about Mckenzey. No one really wants to say anything to you, but she's still talking with Eric."

"Her old boyfriend from back in Colorado?"

"Remember when we were in Silverton, and he went to visit her family for Thanksgiving? He was there. I think her parents are really pressuring her to come back for Christmas. I'm sure Eric will be there."

Jet considered this information. He'd never met Eric, but Mckenzey had assured him that they were no longer seeing each other. Jet was mildly suspicious of Eric, but more so after learning that he attended Dillon Lake, like Shane. In fact, the two might have known each other. Jet said flatly, "I hope she's able to clear her head and figure out what she wants."

"So you're not worried?"

"I didn't say that, but she won't talk to me. She has been super distant."

"That doesn't seem like her."

"That girl is hard to read and even harder to understand."

Together Grantham and Jet made their way back down the corridor and out into the water. The tide was coming in, but they were able to hold onto the rope and drag themselves toward the shore. Jayco was already waiting for them with towels. Jet shook his head and spoke, "Chango." Within thirty seconds, they were completely dry.

"That works," Grantham commented.

Jet said, "Let's get back and find Rick, Jackson, and Keesha. Any idea where we should take them?"

Grantham responded, "We've been exploring this southern edge of campus a bit more. There's a pretty good place about a quarter of a mile south of here on College Avenue. It's a place to sit down, between some rock formations, allowing for us to talk. Does that sound good?"

"Perfect."

# # #

An hour later they zigzagged down College Avenue on their longboards with Rick, Jackson, and Keesha. It wasn't hard to convince Latisha and Seyanna to join them. Jet, always toting around his backpack with the tome and a few other items, wanted to get their first lesson out of the way. Like Jayco, he loved the idea of a more secure place for their magical items, and he wanted to get started as soon as possible. He was also curious to see what the newcomers could do.

Seyanna caught up next to him and smiled. She was tall and athletic and had been one of Jet's closest friends, despite their physical distance over the last few years. She was the only one he felt didn't judge him daily. Her strawberry blond hair swirled behind her as she rode forward. Her pale skin had developed a slight tan since she'd arrived in California a few months ago. He doubted she had worn shorts outside in three years. She was the only one in their group not to start at Chadwicks their freshman year. Instead, after Silverton she'd gone to Alaska for six months and ended up doing research and homeschooling with her parents on an island called Svalbard Island in the Arctic Ocean. It had been a once-in-a-lifetime adventure, and as far as Jet knew, she loved every moment of it.

Jet asked loudly, "What have you and your parents been working on?"

"Reviewing data from the disaster in Washington, DC."

"And?"

"They really think it was a normal phenomenon, unlike Silverton."

"What about you?"

"Not sure. I know Mckenzey had some dreams about seeing a plane crash and the blue fog, but outside of that, it seems pretty cut and dried."

"A storm that kills a hundred thousand people is never cut and dried. That storm was enormous."

"I see what you're saying, but science says that it happens."

Jet shrugged and suddenly maneuvered his longboard to avoid a pothole in the ground. When he'd recovered, Seyanna was closer to Jayco, and they were chatting. Before Silverton, he and his friends and snuck into a museum in Switzerland. That trip changed everything as the friends started paring off. He and Mckenzey, Jayco and Seyanna, and Grantham and Latisha. He wondered if any of their relationships would last.

Jayco began slowing, and Grantham soon followed. Rick and Jackson stayed close together while Keesha remained in the far back of the group.

When they came to a stop, Jayco pointed down a path, away from the beach. "There's a good spot in here for us to talk."

Rick and Jackson waited for Keesha, and the three of them walked with Jayco. Jet positioned himself in the far back to make sure that no one was following them. He moved forward slowly, even stopping a few times and listening. It soon became clear that they were alone. He hurried to catch up to the others. The farther they went forward, the denser the trees became. After another twenty minutes, they finally came to a stop. They had to continue, single file, and squirm into the area ahead. When they all had made it through, they found a semi large place, well hidden, with ten-foot rock walls on both the north and south sides. This natural formation felt like a room without a ceiling.

Jayco asked, speaking directly to Jet, "Does this look familiar?"

"I don't think so."

Jayco and Grantham shared a look. Jayco continued, "This is the end of the cliff line that continues back toward campus, where we do the rock climbing. That place holds some special memories for you."

Keesha laughed. "Isn't that where you fell and broke your arm?"

Rick and Jackson, mimicking Jet's voice, said, "Collarbone."

"Ha ha," Jet replied. "I remember."

"That was epic," Jackson said. "Are you always this klutzy?"

"Not always. Just when getting attacked by Shane and his Runic magic," replied Jet.

Keesha asked, "Are you serious? You fell because you were being attacked."

"It's a long story."

"Well," Rick pointed out. "That's why we're here. Give us the scoop."

Jet spoke, "Agni," and bright light filled the air, brighter than the sun. He followed this with "Urania," and a wind explosion knocked everyone but Jet to the ground. The last spell he spoke, "Vesta," caused an overwhelming amount of fear to ambush the group. He felt a small decrease in his energy, but he continued, allowing each spell to linger for another few seconds. Finally, he let the magic escape back into the ether.

Seyanna was the first to recover. She said, "How about a little warning next time."

Grantham added, "Totally lit. I didn't see it coming."

"What just happened?" Keesha asked, pulling herself off the ground.

Jayco said, "Jet was either pissed off or trying to impress you guys. I rarely know which one it is."

Jet continued, "Spells and magic can be powerful. But you also need to understand the context of what is happening. I wanted to show you what we're capable of, but you also need to appreciate how we got here."

"You read us the fable," Keesha pointed out. "And you talked about how your family was involved, about Shane, and a lot more. We want the good stuff."

Jet asked, "Who's Faunal? What's the Phoenix?"

Keesha shook her head. "I can't remember."

"Isn't Faunal who you guys fought inside Silverton?" Rick asked.

Latisha answered, "Close. Jet fought and killed Lucretius."

"It's so confusing," replied Jackson.

"But it's important to remember," Jet said calmly. "Faunal is the wolf beast creature that initiated the Rivalry. He's not on our side."

"Can you describe him for us?" Rick asked. "Just in case we see him again."

"He's over nine feet tall and walks and runs on his hind legs. Very similar to the Egyptian god Anubis, except he has a wolf's head. White sharp teeth and like a sword and a whip and some armor."

"Easy to miss," Jackson said calmly. "No big deal."

"He was absolutely terrifying," Latisha managed to add.

Rick said, "Sounds like he would be fun at parties."

The tension eased slightly.

Seyanna said, "Honestly, I can't remember what the Phoenix is."

"Is that the box we went to find in Switzerland?" asked Latisha.

"No," Jet answered. "The Phoenix is the tablet of power. It was broken into six pieces. We found the first piece, and we intend on finding the others."

Keesha asked, "Is Shane looking for it as well? Where do you think the other pieces are?"

"We're not completely sure," responded Jet. "We have an idea of the next location."

Keesha asked excitedly, "Where is it?"

"Let's focus on today before we get ahead of ourselves."

"You don't trust us?" Rick asked.

"If we didn't trust you, you wouldn't be here. Back in Silverton the path of the Phoenix was so hard, we barely survived. We need to make sure that you're prepared first."

"How do you plan on doing that?"

Jet nodded at Jayco, who removed three golden staffs from his bags and tossed one to each of them. "Get a feel for these," Jet encouraged them.

Rick and Jackson each caught their staffs easily, but Keesha missed hers, and it clattered to the ground. As she bent over to pick it up, she muttered, "Don't judge me on that. Usually I catch everything."

The first thing Jayco taught them was how to move their feet and keep the correct distance. He then added lunges and strikes. The golden shields and staffs could deflect some types of magic and break simple protective spells. No one had seen a shield break before the other night. The staffs were equally durable.

Within the first ten minutes, it became clear that Rick excelled with the staff. His weapon moved twice as fast as Jackson. It wasn't a slight on Jackson, who was skillful himself, but Rick was a savant. Keesha, however, fumbled the object more often than she could use it. She was slow and off target and couldn't manage to block the simplest attacks.

Keesha gasped. "What's wrong with me? I usually excel at things like this. I don't understand."

"Stop! Stop!" Jet shouted.

Rick and Jackson took another few shots at each other. On the other hand, Keesha dropped her weapon and leaned up against the wall, gasping for air. Once the golden item slipped from her fingers, she seemed to regain some energy.

"What just happened?" Keesha asked. "It felt like I'd just run a marathon, but now I'm better. Is there something wrong with me?"

"Probably not," replied Jet. "There's magic in these items. Instead of the staff helping you, like it did Rick, it was pulling energy from you. No matter how hard you try, I don't think you'll ever be talented at using the staffs."

"Well, that sucks," Keesha muttered.

"On the contrary," Seyanna said. "I bet that means that you'll be able to use something different better than the rest of us."

"Really?"

"That's how this magic thing seems to work."

"What other options do I have?"

"Nothing right now," Grantham said. "We've only got a limited number of items from our last exploits."

"Can we work on magic now?" Keesha asked.

Jet had been wondering how this was going to work. He nodded and lined each of them in front of him. He brought Jayco to stand in front of Rick and Seyanna to stand in front of Jackson. He took the position ahead of Keesha. "The three of us are going to concentrate to see if we can determine what piece of magic, you'll be able to do. We've never done this before, so we're all in for a treat."

Rick said, "When I said, 'Chango', nothing happened."

"We remember." Jet concentrated on the magic of water, seeking to know more. The spell came to his lips without any real effort. He spoke, "Abzu" and nodded.

"Is that the spell?" Keesha asked.

"Give it a try, but remember, don't speak it too forcefully; it might require a lot of energy.

Keesha opened her mouth.

Jet cut her off, adding, "Loud doesn't mean forcefully. You can whisper with extreme force."

"I got it," Keesha insisted. After a few deep breathes, she spoke, "Abzu."

Above them, lightning exploded in the early evening sky, and a gigantic spray of ice crystals burst from a cloud that abruptly appeared. The entire group, except for Keesha, was forced to crouch low to the ground. When the ice crystals landed, they accumulated for almost half an inch. She insisted, "That was not forceful."

"Did you feel any drop in your energy?" asked Jet.

"Barely."

Latisha laughed. "The golden staff is not good for our girl, but she's an ice queen."

Jackson brushed his shoulders of any ice. "I'm sort of jealous of both of you." He asked Seyanna, "Got anything for me?"

She hesitated for only an instant. "Try 'Enlil.'"

"En—what?"

She repeated the word.

Jackson widened his stance as if a hurricane were about to come crashing through the canyon. "Enlil."

Four trees on the opposite side of the open area froze completely, including the branches and leaves, even the ones falling. It was an incredible sight.

"What's this?" Jackson asked. "I calm the wind?"

"Interesting," Seyanna said. "I haven't been able to calm a paper airplane, let alone branches and leaves."

"What's the point?" asked Jackson. "How can this really help me?"

"Who knows," Jet said. "You'll find a good use. Imagine if someone throws a javelin at you; maybe you can stop it from moving."

"Because of the air?"

"Everything must travel through the air to reach its target. This could be interesting."

"My turn," Rick said. "I hope mine isn't as lame as calming the air."

"Agni," Jayco said confidently.

"Is that my word?"

"Try it."

Rick spoke, "Agni."

A small fireball of light erupted in the center of the clearing. It was bright, and Jet watched as Rick could control the movement of the ball. It was its own light source, and he could manipulate its movement. Only twenty seconds after he'd conjured the sphere, Rick was panting heavily.

Jayco shouted, "Release the spell."

"How?" Rick asked.

"Like water slipping through your fingers."

Rick fell to his knees. He managed to say, "Not working."

Jayco wasn't sure what to do. Jet shot one of his orbs, and it collided with the back of Rick's head. He collapsed forward, unconscious, and the globe of light disappeared.

CHAPTER 8

They had the next two and a half weeks off from school. It was two days before Christmas, and the airport was packed. They hoped that they wouldn't be gone for more than a week. To convince their parents, Seyanna had pretended to be a professor, and Latisha snuck some blank papers with the school's letterhead from the admin building. A letter outlining the extra credit they would receive from the community service projects was sent out. This included a brochure and several welcoming statements from local families greeting the students from Chadwick boarding school to Argentina. Reluctantly all parents agreed.

Stepping onto an airplane without Mckenzey and Seyanna felt awkward and unsettling. Jet navigated the walkway to his first-class seat disguised as a forty-something portly male. Jayco was bald and in his late fifties with a suit and tie. He sat two rows up from Jet with an aisle seat. His shoulders loomed over the petite man next to him. Grantham wore black, ripped jeans, with bright red plaid where the fabric was torn. His oversized maroon hoodie enveloped him as he slouched in his seat across the aisle. Next to Grantham sat an elegant Latisha with high heels, a beautiful white blouse, and fishnet stockings, with remarkably tasteful makeup.

In the days leading to their departure, rumors swirled

around school that Shane was heading off for a once-in-a-lifetime adventure over Christmas. Any misgivings about going without their friends was squashed. Mckenzey refused to return any phone calls, and Seyanna couldn't find a way to escape her parents.

Through a series of phone calls, Jet had told Nana that he was staying with Grantham in Los Angeles so that she wouldn't worry. He thought that she was still in Canada but couldn't be sure.

The flight to Argentina was not going to be pretty. They would first fly to Texas, then Buenos Aires, and finally onto San Miguel de Tucuman. From there they would take a bus to their destination. From the moment the plane took off, it would take nearly forty hours for them to arrive. The next two days were going to be interesting.

As the third plane landed, Jet was sick and tired of the cramped seating, terrible airplane food, and the constant pressure on his ears and his stomach. He vowed that he would personally find a way for them to travel more efficiently in the future. They each unloaded a large duffel bag from the overhead compartment and their carry-on luggage. They received a few quick glances from the other passengers, and no one could account for how these four individuals had managed to bring so much onto the planes. In truth, Jet had used his cloak to get their items through security and onto the plane.

Sweat trickled down Jet's back the instant he stepped foot out of the airport. They'd chosen to take a taxi to Catamarca and quickly found someone and negotiated the price. Latisha took center stage as she spoke Spanish the best in the group. Once the price was agreed upon, they settled in for the ride. Getting out of the city was a sight to see. The taxi driver maneuvered the car like a missile, narrowly missing other cars and accelerating down side streets. Soon they were watching the landscape pass by. Halfway there they stopped in La Cocha for some food. They found a wonderful place with empanadas and pizza. The atmosphere was like a midday party, with singing and dancing. The food was beyond amazing, and no one wanted to get back into the car. Tomorrow was Christmas Eve, and Jet assumed this was the reason for the excitement.

The next hour of the car ride was done in silence. This part of the landscape was dry, with a few mountains in the distance. Jet dozed for a few minutes feeling full and satisfied. About ten minutes before they arrived in Catamarca, the driver began explaining in good English about the mountain range on their right and several of the smaller villages. Jet stared at the gigantic mountain that overshadowed everything nearby.

"Look at the boulders on your right," the driver said. "Those weren't there five or six years ago, before part of the town was destroyed. Is that why you are here?"

"Just checking out the area," replied Jet. He noticed hundreds of boulders lay scattered away from the base of the mountain. There was a large ravine that was cut into the ground, heading away from the base. It looked eerily like the one that had smashed into his house.

The driver pointed to the mountain and transitioning to Spanish explained that it was haunted. As Latisha translated and Jet got a chill up his spine. The area was called Manchao or the Valley of Death. It was slightly northwest of town and had been designated off-limits by the government. It was part of the Andes in Argentina, and on the other side of the Andes was Chile. Most of the residents of Catamarca were moving out of the region because it was no longer safe to go out after dark.

The driver explained that a few years ago, an explosion of sorts in the region and mass flooding caused half the town of Catamarca to either wash away or run off scared. Scientists had come to the area to search for answers in the last two years, but little had been explained. Typically the scientists lasted around town for a few months before running off. The driver pointed out that the town was divided by a river. The original town had been built on the north side of the river. In the last few years, more and more buildings were built on the south side, and no one complained about the ghosts of the night on the far side of the river.

Latisha asked what "ghosts of the night" meant but got no response.

Reverting back to English, the driver said, "Make sure your hotel is on the south side of the river."

They arrived in Catamarca an hour later and went directly to their hotel. It was modern with plenty of light. They already had reservations for two rooms connecting to each other. However, when they pulled up to the curb, they were dismayed to find that it was not on the south side of the river. As the driver drove away, he shook his head knowingly.

Latisha rolled her eyes and hurried into the hotel. Five minutes later, they were making their way up to their rooms with all their bags.

As they stepped into their rooms, Jayco asked, "What's the plan?"

"Rest tonight, and we'll go for a hike tomorrow."

"What are we even looking for?" Grantham asked.

Jet sat down, feeling exhausted. "A few months ago, Seyanna and her parents came to Catamarca. They were looking into a weather disturbance like the one in DC."

"Okay," Latisha replied.

"Seyanna found that in December, nearly four years ago, the same year that Silverton was destroyed, there was a large weather system that planted itself offshore, in the South Pacific for two days, gathering energy."

"Just like the two storms that hit DC." Latisha finished the thought.

"There wasn't an increase in the temperature like we saw, but there was a dramatic drop in barometric pressure. Dark clouds circled over Catamarca, and many of the residents were scared. A medicine man from Peru was traveling through the area at the time and mistakenly hoped the day would become a sacred day. It wasn't. The oxygen was sucked up from the northern part of town, killing many people. The news inaccurately reported that there was a huge earthquake. But Seyanna explained that locals described the destruction as an explosion inside the mountain."

Latisha added, "Just like our taxi driver explained."

"Did you see all those boulders?" asked Jet

"Yes," Grantham said. "Do you think that part of the mountain crumbled?"

Jet leaned back. "I'm not sure."

"What do you think really happened?" Jayco asked.

"Nothing good."

Grantham asked, "What do you think of the driver talking about 'ghosts of the night'?"

Jet opened a bottle of cold water. "I might have an idea. I'll explain in a minute."

"We don't really have a plan," Latisha pointed out.

"Sure we do," Grantham said. "Grab our cloaks, our magic, our weapons, and find a way into that mountain."

"That's a reckless plan," Latisha hissed. "I wish the other girls were here."

"So do I," Jayco muttered.

"Any other bright ideas?" Latisha asked.

Jet hesitated. "Seyanna said that getting to the mountain was hard. There are so many boulders and other issues that it makes walking difficult. One night, before they left, she met an older and superstitious woman lurking outside their camp. When the woman was brought forward, she rambled about the clarity of the air when the dark cloud first arrived. She believed that an evil spirit had awoken, and in her anger, the mountain shook. The evil spirit couldn't be contained and visited in the form of a blue fog that had cascaded through the town of Catamarca. The blue fog went as far as the Abaucán river, but it couldn't pass beyond."

"Is that the same river that the driver spoke about?" Grantham asked.

"I think so."

"We need to move our hotel tonight," Latisha said quickly.

"We're fine," Jet said. "Everything will work out."

Silence filled the room for another minute. Jet said, his voice tense, "The women said the hills around the boulders are home for the *los diablitos* or little devils. Maybe these are the ghosts of the night. She said she'd seen several of them over the last three years. They were the protectors of the grotto, but they weren't human or animal-like, but in fact, were like walking bugs."

"Oh no. We're totally out of here," Latisha shouted. "Why in the hell didn't you tell us these things *before* we got on the plane? I refuse to go out there tomorrow. I simply refuse."

Jet said quickly, "We'll all be together. We have Iris and the other animals. We are going to be fine." He snuck a look at Grantham and Jayco, and neither of them appeared relaxed.

"Why bugs?" Grantham asked.

"No idea," Jet said. "She might be totally wrong."

Latisha gasped. "This is why Seyanna didn't come with us. She knew exactly what was happening. She's a genius for skipping out. She didn't want to get killed, dismembered, and eaten by gigantic bugs."

"Come on." Jet chuckled. "Seyanna wanted to come. She didn't ditch us."

"You don't know that."

"Bro," Grantham said, "I'm with Latisha. You should've told us more."

"Like you did with the hideout you guys were working on? We need to find out if this town relates to Silverton."

"Why didn't we go to DC?" Jayco asked.

"Because it's still partly underwater."

"That doesn't bother me," Jayco pointed out.

Jet stood and said, "I'm going to bed. I'll see you guys in the morning."

"How are we getting up there?" Jayco asked. "Tomorrow is Christmas Eve."

"Latisha rented us some motorbikes."

Jayco nodded his approval. "Sweet."

# # #

The following day, dawn light cut between the old green drapes, landing directly on Jet's face. It was only six-thirty in the morning, and he didn't think anyone else was awake. Before dressing, he arranged his items, including the pyramids, his tome, and his three golden orbs. He was going to be ready for anything today, including the heat. He packed water, a bag full of granola bars, and a headlamp. He wore breathable The North Face hiking pants and a short-sleeved shirt. He had a sun hat and his cloak. The average temperature in Argentina for this time of the year was ninety-three degrees. He was both eager and hesitant to go.

Soon Jayco and Grantham were awake and cooking breakfast. They found some cheese, eggs, and tortillas at a local market. Breakfast was delicious. Latisha sauntered in twenty minutes later ready to roll.

No one spoke more than a few words until they were ready to leave. The room was rented for the next three nights, and they would return tonight and set off again tomorrow. The sooner they headed back home, the better. They left only a few items in the room and carried most of what they needed. Each had a pyramid, their weapons, and some additional items. His friends also wore their cloaks, and remarkably they appeared natural and proper, even here. Jayco's cloak was a leather biker's cloak, while Latisha's was glossy red and shimmered when she moved. It fluttered to the ground. Grantham wore a sophisticated gray trench coat that ended at his knees with several pockets and a few buttons. All three of their cloaks were unlike any material Jet had ever seen. The cloaks had hoods that could be pulled up to enhance their Elemental magic abilities.

"Follow me," Latisha said as they exited their hotel. "The motorbike rental is a few blocks away. I have the directions."

The air was bright and getting warmer by the second. There were no clouds directly over the town, but as Jet glanced up toward the Manchao Mountain, there was a thundercloud burgeoning into existence.

The streets of Catamarca were narrow, and most of them were one-way, big enough for a single parked car and one car driving. The sidewalks were often stone, while the road was asphalt. Most of the buildings in this part of town weren't very tall but were colorful. The ambiance was quite enjoyable. Many people smiled as they passed by, and trees grew out of the sidewalks whenever possible. As they crossed town, Jet observed that many people were on mopeds, scooters, or motorcycles.

The second thing he detected was that everyone appeared to be nervous or on edge. They weren't worried about him or his friends, but rather, almost absentmindedly, they glanced northeast toward the peaks of the Manchao Mountains. This happened at every corner and during every conversation. It was as if a runaway train were heading right for them, and they didn't know how to get out of its way.

"There it is," Latisha said.

The storefront ahead of them was largely glass on the front side. Latisha and Grantham hurried inside while Jayco and Jet remained with their items. Twenty minutes later four local teenagers pushed four motorcycles out from a garage out back. Latisha and Grantham exited the front a short time later. An older man walked with them. Once they had rejoined Jet, the older man spoke in English.

"Don't lose the bikes, and don't crash them. Get on and see if you can start them."

It took Jet longer to start his bike, which seemed a bit trickier than the others. Soon they were each given a map of the area, and the old man pointed to places that they should visit. None of the sites were north of town.

The man stated, "See this line here? Don't go above this line. Many of the houses up there are destroyed—lots of problems. The rocks are hazardous, and it's hard to navigate. Too many people have gone missing up there or broken my bikes. Don't go and be careful."

"No problem," Grantham said.

Latisha added something in Spanish, and the older man nodded.

The man walked away several steps, turned back, and watched them. Latisha said, "He told me about this location down south. I think that it's the best place to start."

Jayco asked, louder than normal, "Is there a place to ride on the hills?"

"Yes. Across the river to the south. There are some beautiful places over there."

Grantham added, "Let's start here, go get something to drink, and head down south."

"I'll follow you," said Jet.

All four of them drove off, heading south, with Jet the last to follow. Glancing behind him, he noticed the old man pointing to someone. The rider was on a motorcycle with a black helmet. It became clear that they were going to be followed.

They drove south and spent the next half an hour sightseeing around the southern part of Catamarca. Soon he thought that they'd lost their follower, but they continued riding for another ten minutes. The motorcycle sent after them was likely to make sure that they weren't going to steal them.

They stopped at a local market and purchased two dozen bottles of water. They had packed other food items, but they needed to make the concoction to recover the greatest amount of their energy.

"Where to now?" Latisha asked after they finished.

Jet hadn't seen the following motorcycle in twenty minutes. He said, "Seyanna told me that they took a dirt road about a mile outside of town, directly to the west, that twisted and headed up north. That's where they had their camp positioned. That's where we need to go."

After studying the map, Jayco said, "There's a park of sorts that I think will be a perfect place to leave Catamarca and find this road. Follow me."

As they drove Jet kept looking for their tail but saw nothing. The town of Catamarca transformed significantly the farther one got from the center of town. Roads, buildings, and houses became weathered, damaged, or destroyed. The streets became dirt, and the buildings were beyond poorly preserved, if they were still standing. They saw almost no cars or motorcycles and even fewer people. The outskirts of town were a time shift back fifty years.

Ahead, Jet watched Jayco swerve into the park and kept riding along the southern border. There was a small path next to dozens of trees. The park was more like an open field. No grass or sports field could be seen. This would be more described as a garbage dump back home.

Jet gunned his motorcycle, and soon they were leaving behind all roads, buildings, or any other structures. They followed a path that had been used before by other motorcycles. The sun was moving overhead, and the temperature was scorching, especially out in the wilderness. Minutes later they crested a hill, and the town of Catamarca disappeared completely behind them.

It wasn't hard to find the road traveling north. It was slightly wider than the path they had been traveling. It appeared to have not been used in weeks. There was an overgrowth of weeds and bushes, but it was easy to follow.

Jayco stopped and waited for the others. When everyone was idling, he asked, "Are we sure we are ready to do this?"

Latisha answered first. "I'm not sure we'll ever be ready, but we aren't likely to get another chance."

"What do you mean?" Jet asked.

"The man back at the shop told me that the Argentinian military came out about three weeks ago to do some exercises in response to some missing scientists. This area was used with night-vision equipment to track the missing workers. They brought in hundreds of troops to search this area. Fifteen scientists went missing at the end of November. They didn't find much, but six soldiers disappeared during the exercise. The military is returning next week to build large fences around this area. They'll build a military station, and several soldiers will be assigned in this area. Everybody in town is spooked."

"Wasn't that around the time Seyanna was here?" Grantham asked.

"No. It was after Seyanna was here. I bet it was around the same time we were at Silverton."

"Coincidence?" wondered Jayco.

"Not sure." Jet wiped the sweat from his forehead. "Let's get going. I think this is going to turn out to be a very long day."

CHAPTER 9

The gravel road was dry, and dust cascaded up Jet's legs as they biked their way up the windy dirt road. The climb was steady rather than steep, but after just a few miles, they had rose 1000 feet in elevation. As they rounded the next bend, the boulder field came into view, still another few miles ahead. After hearing the rumors of an explosion, he could almost picture a bomb of sorts within the ground, spewing chunks of debris. Some of the boulders were the size of houses and others smaller. There was a significant number around the size of a car engine, and Jet was surprised that these were the smallest boulders around. It seemed the wreckage expanded outward from the side of the mountain.

Fifteen minutes later they found where the scientists' camp had been located. This part of the road was much flatter than the last few miles. Two vehicles had been left behind, and all that remained were burnt-out shells of a car and a van. Other debris scattered in the area was visible.

"Should we stop here?" Jayco yelled over the engine of his motorcycle.

Jet shook his head and pointed farther ahead. He remembered the gully crossing the road. That would be a better place to hide their motorcycles. He led the group forward.

The road dipped slightly, and it was clear that this gully was the one he'd seen from the road. It was now a riverbed, and a wooden bridge had been built over it, likely to allow the scientists to move further up the road. Jet maneuvered his bike up the riverbed for twenty feet and laid it down on the closer bank. The others followed suit. If any one of them stood, except for Jayco, they could just barely look out of the gully.

"Perfect spot," Grantham remarked. "Is that the mountain we're going to climb?"

Jet followed his gaze. The mountain was three times taller than what they'd found in Silverton. Jet thought that from this side they might need some gear to climb it. He wasn't entirely thrilled about the idea of using ropes and harnesses, mainly because they didn't have them. The blackness and obscurity of the clouds at the mountain's summit were eerie and concerning, as if the mountain knew what they were there for. The haze rotated ominously, sucking in any satellite cloud in the vicinity.

A whine of a motorcycle caught their attention, and they ducked out of view. Carefully they crawled forward enough to watch the road back toward Catamarca. A few minutes later, two motorcycles came into view. It was clear that the first was the one from back at the shop. Jet realized that they'd been tricked. Either they were easier to follow than he anticipated, or the bikes had trackers. He felt around his bike and found a device near the back fender.

"What do we do?" Latisha asked.

Jet stood and waved his arms. "We show ourselves and find out who is following us and why."

"Are you crazy?" Jayco asked.

"You don't think we can take them?" Jet asked

Grantham stepped forward. "Not the point."

The two motorbikes soon sped in their direction. Jet watched as Jayco slid up his golden bracelets to his biceps.

The bikes stopped ten feet from where they stood. The first driver was indeed the one from the shop. His black helmet and black jacket appeared new and expensive. He was the first to dismount. The second person was taller than the first.

"What do you want?" Jet asked. "We're just looking around. Our friend was a scientist that came here last year."

The man with the black helmet pulled it off. Long black hair tumbled out of the helmet.

"A girl," Jayco said, verbalizing Jet's thoughts.

Latisha replied, "A girl can ride a bike as well as any boy."

"Clearly," Grantham said. "That's not the point. Just a little shocking."

The second person removed their helmet, and a slightly older boy stood next to the girl.

"Then what is the point?" the girl asked in excellent English. She was as tall as Seyanna, beautiful with brown eyes and brown skin. She had high cheekbones, and her nose was slightly pointy.

Jayco said quickly, "We thought you were here to fight us. Fighting a girl is never our first choice."

The boy, whose voice was only slightly deeper, questioned, "Why did you think you would need to fight us?"

Jet answered, "You're clearly following us. I saw the old man at the garage tell you to trail us. I doubt you thought you were going to get caught. Is there a reason why you're here?"

The girl spoke. "Maybe my uncle thought you were going to steal his bikes."

"Maybe. But—" pointing back over his shoulder, Jet said, "—you have a tracker on the bike and didn't need to physically follow us. You being here means you want something."

The boy clenched both fists, but the girl placed a reassuring hand on his shoulder. "This is my brother Sebastian, and I'm Maria. You know that this part of town is off-limits."

"Like I said before. Our friend was a scientist here earlier this year."

"Did she disappear?" Sebastian interrupted him.

"No. But some of her friends did."

Sebastian scoffed. "Did you think that you could find out more than our army did? You Americans always think that you know best."

Jayco asked, "Have there been other Americans here?"

Sebastian's head tilted, and he gazed at Jayco as if for the first time. He shuddered slightly. "A week ago five or six kids borrowed bikes from another shop in town. Diego told our uncle about it. The boys came, and the bikes never came back to the shop. Diego lost a lot of money."

Jet asked, "What did they look like?"

Maria answered, "We never saw them."

Latisha asked, "Are you saying that you're following us to make sure that we don't steal your bikes?"

"I think so," Maria answered. "My uncle thinks the boys came up here, like you. They were different, though. They offered to pay some people from town to come up with them. They brought lots of money. Five people came up, and only two returned."

"Did the boys come back?"

"Yes. They partied the next night, then they left. Diego never got his bikes back, and he never got paid."

Jet said, "We aren't with them. We're not going to steal your bikes."

"Then, what are you doing here?" Sebastian demanded.

Jayco answered, "Searching for answers."

"You won't find them here. You need to leave. This place is haunted."

Jet said, "Thanks for the warning, but we're not leaving."

"What if you disappear too?" Sebastian asked, a small smile on his face.

Jayco strode forward, his hands pointing at Sebastian. "You know where the bikes are. Don't threaten us."

Sebastian retreated, slipped, and fell backward. Maria stood in front of Jayco, raising her hand. "Leave him alone."

Jayco tilted his head slightly, appraising the girl. He stopped approaching.

Jet replied, "Thanks for the warning. We're just going to look around a bit. It would be better if you two returned to town."

Sebastian jumped to his feet and inched toward his bike. "I'm going back, and I'm going to tell my uncle. He'll bring up a lot of men. You're going to get hurt."

"Nope," Jet shouted. "We can't allow that. No one else can come up here."

"Why?" Maria asked.

"Like you said," Grantham added, "this place is haunted. Let us do our thing, and we'll bring back the bikes tonight."

"We can handle ourselves," huffed Jayco, who was circling around to Sebastian, who sat on his bike.

Maria said quickly, "We can help."

"*Que?*" Sebastian asked in Spanish.

Maria spoke to him in rapid Spanish. Jet spun to Latisha, but she shrugged. "Look," Maria continued, "we've all had friends go missing in these mountains. We want to help."

Jet said quickly, "We don't need your help."

"I bet you do," she said knowingly. "We've seen what comes out at night."

Sebastian grunted. "Sister."

"No one believes us. These mountains are haunted."

"We've got this," Grantham said.

"Well," Maria huffed. "We're not leaving."

"We can make you," Jayco said, and he shifted toward Sebastian.

If Jet hadn't been watching, he wouldn't have seen a bolt of electricity zap Jayco, who yelped in displeasure.

"How did you do that?" Jet asked.

"He saw you," Sebastian said. "Why did you have to show them?"

Maria's face flushed slightly. Facing Jet, she raised both hands, preparing to attack.

Jet spoke, "Pan," and the ground around Sebastian's and Maria's feet began to shake, tossing both to the ground, along with their bikes.

Maria glared up at him. "What did *you* just do?"

"Magic. Just like you did."

Jet pulled Jayco, Grantham, and Latisha together and asked, "What should we do?"

Jayco said, "Knock them out or bring them with. But we need to get moving. It's almost noon already, and we're losing time."

"Agreed," Grantham said.

Latisha remained quiet but finally nodded.

Turning to Sebastian and Maria, Jet said, "Looks like you're coming with us."

Sebastian was furious. "You broke my bike."

"Don't attack us next time." Jet retrieved his backpack and duffel bag as the others gathered their supplies. He pulled out a knife and some food and water and placed them in his backpack.

As he was getting ready, Maria walked over. "Who are you guys?" She'd removed her bike jacket and had pulled out some water and a small bag that she'd wrapped around her waist.

"Kids who survived a disaster like what happened here but back in our country."

"Is that why I can, how do you say, shock people?"

"Maybe. Do you need to say any words to do it?"

"No. I just concentrate."

"Can Sebastian do anything?" he asked.

Shaking her head, she added, "He hates when I do it. I think I've heard of a few other kids in town that can do some weird things, but I've never seen anything."

"How is your English so good?"

"Since I was little, there have always been people speaking English in the town. They lived by us and taught at the schools. They had family that moved here as well. But when the town was vandalized, they left."

"I think you mean destroyed." Jet grinned. He noticed that Maria was stunning, but also fierce. He was confident that she'd been through a lot and gaining her trust might prove to be important. If she trusted them, Sebastian would as well.

"Oh yes. 'Vandalize' is something that you do to a building."

"How many English speakers were there?"

"Five or six."

"How old are you?"

"Seventeen, and my brother is nineteen."

Jayco shouted, "We're ready. Let's get moving."

The group exited the gully but traveled along it as they scrambled forward.

Sebastian came up to walk next to Maria, and Jet overheard them whispering. Ahead of them was a large field with more than fifty boulders. The ground rose slightly to the base of the mountain. He couldn't see any place where a portion of the mountain had broken off. He also noticed that some of the boulders were black, but the ground around them was rust-colored. It was as if the boulders had been scorched.

"Why are you carrying so many things?" Maria asked.

Jet lifted his duffel onto his shoulder. "In case we get attacked."

"By the creatures that come out at night?"

"That, or something else."

Ten minutes later they'd passed the outskirts of the boulder field. As they walked farther in, it was clear that this place was cursed or jinxed. Jet reached out and touched some of the boulders; they were cold, as if they'd been formed in ice.

Sebastian shuttered. "This is a trap. We're not going to survive."

"The boy's right," Jayco said. "This doesn't feel right."

"Are you suggesting that we turn back?" asked Grantham.

"No. But we're carrying four golden pyramids that can help protect us. We need to let them out."

"In front of Maria and Sebastian?" Latisha asked.

"What are you talking about?" Maria asked. "What is a pyramid?"

Jet stopped abruptly and directed his attention on Maria and Sebastian. "When you shock someone, that's magic. You've seen a little magic. We have a lot of magic. Can we trust you to not tell anyone?"

"What does this mean?" Sebastian asked. "Lots of magic."

"Take out the pyramids," Jet said.

"Oh yeah," Grantham said. "Lit to the max."

From his own duffel, Jet removed his golden pyramid.

"Are those gold?" Maria asked.

"This is going to get weird," Jet said. He dropped his pyramid and shouted, "Pyramis of Aurum." Before the item hit the ground, Iris, the panther, quickly transformed. The moment she touched the ground, she was tense, sniffing the ground, the hairs on her back standing on end.

"Of the devil," Sebastian screamed, and intended to run. Jayco, expecting such a reaction, picked up Sebastian with one hand and carried him into the center of the group.

"Iris, release the others," Jet said.

The majestic golden panther darted, touching her nose to each of the other three pyramids. Life-sized animals transformed before them. Soon a male lion, a barn owl, and a grizzly bear nuzzled Iris, but they were uneasy as well. Jet and his friends scratched each of the animals, and they took up positions to protect the group. As far as Jet knew, the animals were alive. They would eat, drink, breathe, and would even relieve themselves. In their golden pyramid shape, it was as if they were hibernating.

Shane also had four black animals that transformed from pyramids. A large wolf, a snake, a falcon, and a jackal.

"What are these?" Maria asked.

"These are our friends, and they protect us."

"This is crazy." Maria laughed, almost sounding bewildered. "And delightful."

Jet said, "Iris. This is Maria. Can she pet you?"

Despite her concerns about the surroundings, Iris leaped to Maria and let the girl touch her head and back.

Maria giggled with unrestrained joy. Jayco finally relented and placed Sebastian on the ground. Soon Grantham was pulling out his specialized staff. The handle was dark brown wood and at the far end of the wood was a golden half-circle. Latisha had her golden chalice with black powder tied around her waist.

Maria and Sebastian were given a golden staff and told to use them as protection. Jet and Latisha also carried one. The shields had all been left behind; they would've been too much to carry.

After another few minutes of arranging things, the group proceeded forward, cautiously. The golden animals fanned out, exploring the area.

Once again Maria came to walk next to Jet. Sebastian remained a few steps behind. "Is this all for real?" she asked.

"You can turn back at any time."

"You guys are very prepared. Why are you here?"

"We're here to see what has happened to your city, and why. We did the same thing back home."

"What did you find?"

"That staff you're holding and some of these other items."

"You've heard of the los diablitos that come out at night?"

"We have."

"Are you going to fight them?"

"Only if they attack us."

Maria was quiet for the next few minutes. They passed a boulder that was larger than a normal house. There was movement ahead, about fifty or a hundred feet up the mountain. It was still a good distance away, but Jet triggered his vision to magnify, and he was shocked at what he saw. Blending in, almost perfectly, was a medium-sized creature that caused Jet's body to recoil. Jet hissed, "Everyone. Stop."

The group gathered close as Jet explained, "I see some weird creatures. They blend in perfectly with the other rocks. I think that some are black, and some are the rust color of the sand."

"They can't be," Maria insisted. "It isn't nighttime yet."

"They're absolutely out," Jet countered.

"What are they?" Latisha asked.

"I can't tell exactly, but it seems like they're giant pill bugs."

"What are you talking about?" Jayco asked. "Those things aren't scary at all."

"Stupid comparison," Jet admitted. "But a pill bug has a shell on its back and can roll into a ball. These diablitos, or whatever, can do the same things and they look like the boulders on the mountain. They have a protective rock shell and can roll up into a ball."

Latisha pointed to the boulder next to them, shading them from the sun. "Are you telling me that this thing is a diablito?"

Jet shrugged. "I can't be certain, but I don't think so. It's too big."

Maria spoke. "I've seen one before, and I have no idea what a pill bug is. They aren't all the same. Some are quick, and some are bigger."

Grantham asked, "Where do you think they go during the day?"

"Probably hiding in the mountains." Pointing partway up the mountain, Jet said, "There's one walking on its back two legs."

"No one else can see it," Jayco said, slightly impatient. "What does it look like?"

"This one is different from the other that I saw. It might be as tall as we are. It has pinchers as claws and walks on two hind legs. The rock acts as its protective shield. It might be guarding something."

"An entrance," Grantham suggested.

Latisha asked, "How many are there?"

"Could be hundreds. There's no way to tell. Every boulder could be one hiding."

"We've passed more than thirty boulders. We could be surrounded."

Sebastian muttered, "Let's get out of here."

"Too late," Jayco replied as Iris and the other animals unleashed a frenzied wail. It was as if they had been befuddled. Iris especially was leaping around frantically but without a particular destination.

Jet yelled, "Iris! Come!"

For the first time, it appeared the golden panther was going to refuse to obey a command. Iris bent low to the ground, shook her head, and made a concentrated effort to move closer to Jet. She yowled repeatedly, which caused the other animals to follow her lead. The owl came to rest on the back of Iris.

"What's going on?" Grantham asked.

Jet said, "I think we need to be ready for an attack."

From behind them, a dozen feet away, a boulder shuddered and started to open. Soon standing before them was a six-foot-tall creature with two legs and two arms. It slightly resembled a bug, but it was more like a fantastical creature that he'd never seen before. The arms were as long as Jet's were, but instead of hands, there were pinchers. The legs were also similar to humans', but the feet ended in two forward toes and a single hind toe, likely giving it balance. The head was circular and was protected by a rock exterior. Jet was certain that the entire creature was hairless and made of rock. This one had teeth and hissed at them.

"Anyone got any ideas?" Grantham asked.

Next to Jet, Maria held out her staff as if ready to protect herself. Sebastian, on the other hand, was on the verge of running away.

Jet whispered, "Your brother is going to run."

She reacted in time by grabbing the back of his shirt. She said, in Spanish, "*No huyas*."

Sebastian nodded. Jayco bent over and picked up watermelon-sized rocks in his hands.

Another boulder, this time black and not as close, rolled open. This creature was slightly different than the first. It had four arms and two legs, and its components reminded Jet of a praying mantis. It was sleeker than the first and appeared much quicker. It had less protection, but it was deadly. Instead of pinchers at the ends of each arm, it had three razor-sharp claws. The feet were similar to the first creature's.

They waited for the creatures to attack, but they just surveyed them. The reason became clear after another two of the thicker creatures snuck behind them.

Jet said, "We've got to move, or we'll be surrounded."

Latisha asked, "Are we leaving?"

"No," Jet said quickly. "Go toward the base of the mountain."

Jet heard Sebastian groan. Together they migrated sideways and backward several steps. The animals followed. From behind a house-sized boulder, a skinny clawed creature attacked. Jayco was ready and threw a rock as hard as he could at the oncoming attacker. The rock shattered in the face of the clawed creature, and it was launched twenty feet back.

The real invasion began. Twenty creatures rushed forward, and the group sprinted toward the mountain. Jet made it a point to stay near Maria and Sebastian. His vision magnified, and his peripheral vision increased to nearly a 360-degree view.

From behind and to his right, a stocky creature approached. Jet stopped, rotated, and threw his three orbs as hard as he could. The creature slowed, intending to block the projectiles, but Jet, using his hands, guided the orbs up and around the creature's safeguard. As the orbs converged, crashing into the neck of the beast, it fell forward and moved no more.

In a quick motion, Jet brought the orbs back to his hand. They kept running.

Ahead, Grantham used the larger boulders as spring pads, and he was jumping and landing on the heads of three or four creatures. He moved flawlessly. They had difficulty protecting themselves as he used his sheath to batter them in the heads.

A pincher creature dove at Sebastian, cutting his leg and knocking him to the ground. Maria reacted swiftly and swung her staff, connecting with the back of the beast. Nothing happened, except Maria was flung backward feet over hair. She landed hard. The creature lifted its weapon to slice through Sebastian just as Jet yelled, "Aer," and a green aura could be seen.

A tornado erupted from his hand and lifted the clawed creature from off Sebastian and flung him a hundred feet in the air. It landed so hard that a crater in the ground formed. It didn't get back to its feet. Maria picked herself off the ground and dashed forward, helping her brother to his feet.

Maria said quickly, "*Gracias.*"

Jet nodded. When he focused, he found that a dozen creatures had been battered around. Grantham and Latisha were working together, and Jayco was crushing it. In fact, he held a smaller creature off the ground, its feet dangling in mid-air as he squeezed the head. The head exploded inward into a small dust cloud. Jayco tossed the body aside.

Grantham yelled, "There are two large boulders up here that we can climb and get to the rock shelf. There are a few more creatures protecting something up here. I think it is an entrance."

"Okay. Let's go. But be careful."

Grantham had not taken more than a dozen steps before the two giant boulders shifted and the entire ground shook. The boulders gave the impression that they were getting sucked into the mountain itself. From farther up the mountain, rock debris and other rubble showered down on them. If they didn't move, they were going to be buried alive.

CHAPTER 10

The terrain shook like nothing any of them had experienced. Jet wondered if it was possible they were straddling a fault line. They scattered in all different directions, even the golden animals. Part of the mountainside shifted, and it appeared they were about to be buried in a rockslide. But just as quickly, a shape grew as if something were surging out of an abyss. Jet recoiled when he realized what was happening. They weren't witnessing a natural disaster but rather a living and breathing creature so large, it took up part of the mountain.

The brute was as massive as a two-story building, and it had somehow burrowed into the side of the mountain. The two giant boulders were nothing more than the end portions of the brute's tail. The creature hissed skyward and twisted to face Jet and the others. The brute stood on four legs and was also entirely made of stone. It had external spines of raised jetted rocks that originated from behind its head and continued to its tail. The brute clamored, and its serpentine body, along with its elongated head, lowered to the ground so that it could get a better look at Jet and his friends. He was awestruck with the creature's emerald eyes while shivering fearfully.

The brute spoke, in a deep molten voice, "I do not believe that you are a Chupovana. Have you come to see the oracle?"

Jayco hissed, "Jet. Say something."

"We've come for the Phoenix," replied Jet.

The creature sprayed a fiery blue flame from between its razor-sharp teeth. The jet of hot air burned another dozen boulders to the far right of their group. It was lucky that none of them had retreated in that direction. "Then why did you attack my entertainers?" the beast demanded, shaking his head.

Jet yelled, "What are you?"

The brute must be a dragon but with a muscular, broad, and fierce body. Its frame was not long or lean, and there was no reaching neck or wings. Instead, the head matched that of a dragon with a giant jaw and jagged teeth. The neck was shorter, and the torso was wide and built for power. The front two legs were thick and splayed outward from the body, with thick shoulder and elbow joints with long and sharp claws. The back legs were twice as thick as the front and allowed this brute the ability to leap and jump. The tail was shorter and likely packed quite a punch. When not used for attack, it might help with balance.

The brute bellowed, "What are these cobwebs in my head? I can't think straight. What have you done to me?"

"Nothing," Jet replied. "We just arrived, and you woke up. We thought it was an earthquake."

The brute's head tilted slightly sideways, just as Jet had seen Iris do. It then glanced back at where it had been lying, partly inside the mountain.

"Are you part of the Rivalry?" Jet asked.

"That silly game." The brute's eyes found Jet once again. "No. I was defeated by Leotyton years ago. I became a protector of the magic. The Rivalry was reborn by Arisol in his attempt at controlling all the magic."

Jet said quickly, "You realize that Leotyton gave his life to stop Arisol, and so do we."

"It doesn't matter. Arisol will win, or he will lose, but magic will always be in danger."

Jet inched forward, "What do you mean?"

Another spray of blue flame connected with the same boulders, and soon the rocks glowed a deep red. Jet could feel the heat radiating from them.

"Magic is not a gift from an unseen god. It is a living, breathing entity, and it can be enslaved and even killed. There are those in this world that would destroy what you can do."

"Do you know who I am?" Jet asked.

"Despite your weaknesses and infirmities. If you woke me, you must be the Mikado. I see far more clearly now. These devilish creatures have beguiled me with their song and dance. But for a Mikado, you have little experience, even less confidence, and are far from whole."

Feeling self-conscious, Jet asked, "Why do you say that?"

"Do not worry, my small nipper. You may yet grow into your skin... if you can find a way to live."

"Who are you exactly?"

"I am Siwalik, the hidden herder. I was recruited by the Ten Kings to fight a war against the Chupovanas, an evil pack destined to kill and steal the magic of the world. If they can find the magical entity, they can plunder it from you. The Kings hoped to stop the Chupovanas before things became as bad as they did. Prior to becoming Leotyton, the Two Kings traveled to my homeland and bested me for the right of my services. I have made a pact to protect magic from the Chupovanas."

"How did you get here? Leotyton was years ago."

"I was placed in dormancy before Arisol and Leotyton died. I believe that something or someone has removed me and brought me here."

"Who?" Jet asked. "Why? What is the oracle?"

"Behind you," warned Siwalik.

Jet rotated quickly and found that an army of diablitos had formed. Even from here he could see a wolf-like creature, nearly ten feet tall, standing on a large boulder. Faunal was heavily protected by his armor while he held his weapons. Behind him stood nearly a hundred stocky and claw creatures, as if waiting for his orders.

"I hope he isn't with you," said Siwalik. "That's the collaborator Faunal."

"He's also not a big fan of mine," Jet said. "I didn't think he could attack us."

Jayco followed Jet's gaze, crying out. "Why the hell is he here again?"

But before anyone could speak, the voice of Faunal howled around them. "Welcome, Echoes. Glad to see you are two steps behind, as usual. You'll remember from our last encounter, I cannot attack you directly. But that doesn't mean I can't facilitate your destruction." Pointing to the creatures spitting and hissing at his feet, he added, "We have other ways. The diablitos have become our most loyal Drekavac demons. They sing and chant and have kept poor Siwalik controlled until the Mikado arrived to wake him. After they kill you, we will take possession of Siwalik for our own purposes. He's not able to fight against us."

Siwalik answered, "He speaks the truth, and I feel the power in his statement. I've somehow made a pact with these creatures. I know not how, but I cannot attack them."

"Perfect," Grantham said. "Are you on our side or theirs?"

"Neither," Siwalik answered. "I'm here only to stop the Chupovanas."

"Whatever that means," Grantham hissed. "What's happening here?"

Back down the slope, the diablitos begin spreading out in a line, preparing to attack. Jet asked Siwalik quickly, "Are you going to attack us?"

"No."

Jet replied, "What about other humans that may be here to fight us?"

"I have not made a pact with them," Siwalik answered.

"Do you think Shane is here?" Jayco asked.

Jet said, "It's the only explanation."

"Oh crap," Latisha exclaimed. "We're totally dead."

Maria asked, "What's happening? All of this can't be real."

Ignoring everyone else, Jet asked Siwalik, "Will you climb the mountain and search for other humans coming in this direction? There's a village not far away. Most of those humans shouldn't be attacking."

"How do I tell the difference?"

Grantham said pointedly, "They won't be running this way."

"I'll climb to higher ground. If my flame turns green, you have company."

"If you say so," Jet answered. He quickly added, "We have golden protectors; they have black ones."

"The Rivalry," Siwalik answered. "Elemental versus Runic. I remember."

The brute hurdled into the air, and his giant legs opened, and webbing like skin became visible. Siwalik glided more than flew to a higher level of the mountain. When he landed, he triggered a small rockslide.

At that precise moment, Faunal bellowed, and los diablitos attacked.

Jet yelled, "Keep the creatures at bay for as long as possible." Turning to Maria and Sebastian, he said, "Can you carry rocks over to Jayco?"

Maria shrugged and explained the request to Sebastian in Spanish.

Jayco asked, "What exactly do you want me to do?"

"Pelt the creatures with rocks until I figure out how to get out of here."

"That seems pointless.," Jayco said.

"Latisha," Jet said, "spread out some of your black powder to give us a little more protection."

She stared back at him skeptically. "Are you sure?"

"Trust me."

The creatures covered half the distance before Jayco was in place and began flinging rocks. It worked, and the creatures slowed considerably. The first half dozen strikes did minor damage, but quickly, his effectiveness improved. If he hit one well enough, they crumbled on contact or at least lost an arm or a leg. As Latisha lay down some cover, Jet considered his options.

The four golden animals were helpless. They danced around, clawing at their ears. If the diablitos were singing, Jet couldn't hear it.

"What about me?" Grantham asked.

"If any creatures break through our defenses, you will need to take them out."

"Roger that," Grantham said, and he rocketed to a grouping of rock that gave him a slight advantage. Several diablitos broke off in his direction.

Jet unleashed several spells at the oncoming attackers. First, he spoke, "Kali." Red stunning firebolts shot through the air. When they hit los diablitos, the creatures were knocked off their feet and stunned, but nothing else.

The larger diablitos started organizing together, and the smaller clawed creatures ducked behind. Jet couldn't stun the bigger ones and Jayco was less effective in damaging them. Jet changed tactics. He spoke, "Aer," but at this distance, the wind tornado, did little to disrupt the oncoming creatures.

Slowly the creatures marched forward, gaining confidence. Faunal bellowed, "Take the Echoes down."

Jayco hissed, "We need to get out of here. We can't hold them much longer."

Jet had an idea. "Keep firing. Slow them down and give me some time. Try adding magic to the rocks. Flip on your hoods and see what happens."

Jayco, Grantham, and Latisha all flipped on their hoods. Soon Jayco had the rocks, burning hot, but they did little damage. Latisha, being adept at wind, set off wind bombs that kicked dirt into the air. Grantham was still leaping and climbing and attacking. Between the three of them, the diablitos momentarily stopped.

Moving to the front of the group, Jet bent down. He first spoke, "Pachamana" a dozen times. Instead of a deep crevice, he pictured what he wanted. He created a crater in the ground that grew with every use of the spell. His energy level sank quickly, and he pulled bottles of mud and water from his backpack. He gulped down two. When he glanced up, he found the creatures moving again, within twenty feet of his friends. His friends, Maria, and Sebastian threw everything they had at the oncoming diablitos.

Jet next spoke, "Ogen," and a deluge of water fell from the sky directly into his hole. He repeated the spell six or seven times until the entire crater was filled. The diablitos were less than ten feet away when they recognized what was happening. They broke ranks and sprinted at Jet and the others. Maria, Sebastian, and his friends retreated behind Jet, preparing to make one last stand.

Jet yelled, "Yemoja!" and a green aura brightly illuminated the air. Jet had never imagined a good use for this spell except for attempting to find water to drink from within the ground. Instead, it doubled and tripled the amount of water he had already prepared in the gigantic crevice. Because they were on higher ground, the water overflowed, and like a dam breaking, began to surge down the slope at an alarming speed. Debris, fallen logs, small rocks, and whatever else was in its path were picked up and carried down the hill. Jet yelled the spell several more times, and the amount of water became colossal.

When the first wave of water hit, the diablitos were unable to progress further up the hill. The second and third waves crashed into them with such force that they were sent flailing backward. The pure strength of the flash flood was unstoppable. Most boulders in the water's path, even those the size of small houses, were washed down the slope. A new ravine cut into the ground, and every last diablitos was buried deep in mud and water or washed away.

The Echoes around him cheered loudly. Jet stumbled to his knees, his vision flickering. He felt more exhausted than he had ever felt before.

Maria arrived first and surprised everyone by hugging him fiercely. The rest of the gang quickly caught up.

"I did not think that you had that type of power in you," Jayco commented.

"It's all about using the elements to our advantage."

Grantham put out a hand to help Jet to his feet, but before he could react, Iris came slamming into him, giving her version of a hug, licking every part of her face.

"Why didn't Iris help?" asked Latisha.

"No idea," Jet said as he pushed himself to his feet. "Something about those creatures affects Iris and the others." Inside his backpack he found two bottles of mud water and ate some granola bars. As he gulped down the last of his energy drink, Siwalik crested an adjacent peak in the direction of Catamarca and continued closer. When the rock dragon finally came to a stop, it gawked down at them curiously. For an instant Jet feared the creature was about to attack.

Siwalik said, "The village is in an uproar. Some of the water you sent down has made its way to the town. They're forming a group to come up here."

"If they come up here, will you attack them?" asked Maria.

"They are not my enemy."

Jet asked cautiously, "Then who is?"

"The Chupovanas."

"Who are they?" Jayco asked.

"An enemy to us all."

"Will you help us?" Jet pleaded. He imagined that even Faunal would be fearful of this colossal dragon. "We've been tasked to fight against Arisol."

"This I know. You are a marked youngling. It's on your hand, your arm, and your back. You have no choice but to stop Arisol. But what I am fighting is more destructive than Arisol could ever be."

Shaking his head, Jet mumbled, "I don't understand."

"The Rivalry is what you've been called to follow. My calling is the Chupovanas. They are the leeches of magic. I cannot help you, but I'll assist if ever possible. I must go."

"Where to?"

"To search for the horde and their leader."

Pulling at Jet's arm, Jayco said, "If the town is coming, we have bigger problems."

"I know." Jet broke eye contact with Siwalik.

Before the rock dragon left, he gave a warning. "Be wise of Coso Subtrano. It is not all as it appears. Others have traveled here before, foolishly leaving behind what they came searching for. Be wise."

"What is the Coso Subtrano?"

"The next phase of your journey. Take a glimpse at what awaits you."

The group plodded forward, stopping at where Siwalik had been half-buried in the mountain wall. Jet was dumfounded at what was revealed. The hole gave a glimpse into an entirely unique ecosystem below Manchao, unlike anything he'd ever seen. The cavern mimicked the Grand Canyon with a single large valley with several offshoot ravines. It was easily one of the most beautiful canyons in the world. Somehow, it had its own light source, and the canyon stretched for dozens of miles or more. It was clear that they needed to enter this subterranean canyon rather than climb to the top.

Latisha asked, astonished, "How in the world is this possible?"

Siwalik answered. "You have been taught the rudiments of magic. You have been given but a few words. But there are realms of magic still unknown to you. Did you think that the entire magical world was governed by fifty enchanted words or fifty mythical drawings? There is much more than just Elemental and Runic magic in this world. You've been pitted together, but aren't you more like brothers?"

The group stepped away. Jet asked, "What are you saying?"

"The Rivalry is the continuation of a legendary battle that has been marching for centuries. Lady Gaea is but one of the many authors of the magical kingdom. One day you may become a powerful player, but right now, you're nothing more than a fledgling. There is much to learn. Magic may be eternal, but it is not indestructible. That's what I'm trying to prevent. You must block a war that could create unbalance. You have set out to stop Arisol at all cost, and inside Coso Subtrano, you just might find what you're looking for. But don't lose sight of the other battles raging around you."

Grantham asked, "What are other realms?"

"Time may grant you knowledge, but wisdom comes by sacrifice, truth, and choice. Even if you become lost, there is always a path back to the beginning. No mistake is too big not to learn from." The creature vaulted upward toward the highest peak of the mountain. Despite his size, he vanished after just a few minutes.

"Where does that thing think it can go? He's going to be hard to miss," replied Latisha.

"Are we going inside?" asked Grantham. "This place looks legit."

"I think we are?"

"What about Maria and Sebastian?" asked Jayco. "Should they come with us?"

"I don't think we have a choice," Jet said. "It could be a problem if they tell anyone about what has happened up here."

Maria answered, "We won't say anything. You saved our lives. But we want to follow you."

"Even after what you just saw?" Jet asked.

Maria replied calmly, "We've all been fools. I knew magic was around this area, but I was afraid. Same with my brother."

"Is your brother willing to come with us?" asked Latisha.

"I think he should go back. He can calm my town, explain what happened."

Jayco laughed. "They won't believe him."

Maria pointed to the corpse of a smaller clawed diablitos. "He will drag that with him. They would be much more likely to believe him than you. He can help."

"You should go with him," said Jet. "They'll believe both of you."

"No," she said quickly. "I'm going with you. We must hurry."

Jet glanced at the others, and Jayco shrugged. Redirecting his attention at Maria, he nodded.

Maria spoke to Sebastian in rapid Spanish. The boy appeared to have aged in the last few hours, but his eyes held more confidence and determination. Before he left Sebastian smiled at Jet and the others and said, "We bless you. Thank you for coming to our country. This is a blessed day." He gathered the head of the corpse and sprinted off down the mountain.

Taking deep breaths, they returned to the brink of the cavern. The scorching heat to their backs contrasted with the cool, humid breeze exiting the depths below. Despite the unbelievable view and the complex colors below, Jet had difficulty letting go of Siwalik's warning. He hoped they were doing the right thing.

CHAPTER 11

The water in the underground canyon of Coso Subtrano splashed and sloshed from the cavern's upper portions and collected in a large lake at the bottom of the gorge. The water was a deep green, while the earth around them was either orange or purple. If the ground rose into the air, such as in the form of a ledge or grouping of rocks or a crest, it was purple, but if the floor dropped such as with a path or ravine, the soil was orange.

Above them, which would be directly in the base of the mountain, was a sky with baby yellow and periwinkle blue clouds accumulating. The trail they stepped on to upon entering the cave was scarcely used. It wound back and forth, with other trails connecting farther down. There were trees, vegetation, undergrowth, and brushwood that were of the variety that Jet had never seen. He observed pink or silver leaves on some of the trees, dark red bushes, and many other colors arranged on the branches, trunks, ferns, shrubs, and other plants.

Bending down, he took a handful of soil into his hands and rubbed it together. It was part crystal and part crumbling rock more than soil or anything similar. The air was pungent with a muddy, musty, and earthy smell with a trace of sulfur. Any attempts to stray from the path appeared dangerous, and the footing would be nearly impossible. The likelihood of a slip and fall was significant. Grantham reached down to touch a stunning cluster of crystalline rocks just off the path and between two enormous, mauve-colored trees. The instant he brushed against the rocks, his fingers sliced open almost to the bone. The group was forced to stop for ten minutes to get the bleeding to stop.

Jet led the way, with Iris a step behind. The lion and bear positioned themselves at the back of the group. The owl stayed extremely close to the group, unwilling to stray far away.

While walking, Jet searched for the light source illuminating around them. After a half an hour, he was reasonably confident that the glow illuminated from crystalline structures in the celling. From this vantage point, they visualized three waterfalls off to their left and two dozen caves decorating the canyon walls. They were at the far end of the ravine and could only descend into the valley. In fact, that was the only direction to go.

Latisha said, "This place is magical. It's more beautiful than Disneyland."

A gigantic bull elk with four horns came galloping out of a cave two hundred feet away, to their right. The animal appeared to sense them, and it glowered as if watching their progress. The animal's fur was magenta.

Grantham asked, "How does it walk on those razor-sharp rocks?"

Jayco replied, "I think it has metal hooves."

"How's that possible?" Latisha asked.

Maria asked, in amazement, "How is *any* of this possible?"

The large bull bugled a warning as they continued forward.

"What's he pissed at?" asked Jayco.

Large beating wings erupted from above them. Jet and the others ducked, preparing for an attack. The creature was hidden in the clouds. Soon the beating of the wings faded, and a few minutes later, Jet glimpsed a ten-foot-long, skinny lizard with a long beak, climbing into a nest in the ceiling. An unsettling feeling overcame Jet.

Latisha answered, "I have no logical explanation."

"Let's move faster," Jayco advised, getting to his feet.

Over the next hour, animals that no one had ever seen darted on the land, swung in the trees, and flew above them. A horde, crossed between monkeys and skunks, scurried up a particularly large ancient tree with a deep blue trunk and silver leaves. Each animal perched on a branch and ogled at Jet and his friends. They pushed forward. At one point, the path became steeper. They stopped trying to identify the different animals.

When they reached a lower plateau, Latisha said, "Check out the waist high red grass. It's so beautiful and scary. You couldn't pay me enough to walk through that."

When they reached the bottom of the canyon, they toppled onto the ground, trying to catch their breath. The air was warmer and thicker than it had been when they started their descent. Pulling out drinking water and food they rested for thirty minutes. Iris and the other animals set up a perimeter around them. Latisha poured them water, and they drank greedily.

The valley floor was flat and extended in the direction of the ravine. It was a large gray stone slab, smooth as marble, that was nearly ice cold. It was similar to a riverbed void of any other rocks or sand. Even more peculiar, there were no stones, dirt, soil, or debris on this level. The width of this area was deceiving, twenty feet from where they sat, the emerald lake began, and it was on the same level as the valley floor, extending a good portion of the length of the ravine.

Maria was the first to recover, and she sauntered to the water's edge, staring into its depths as if mesmerized.

Jet and Jayco followed behind her a minute later. At the water's edge, Jet asked Jayco, "What do you see?"

Maria answered quickly, "It's far too dark to see the bottom."

"Jayco has an ability to see into dark and murky water," replied Jet.

Inching closer, Jayco shivered. "This is not normal water. There's not a single living thing inside the water. No bugs, no fish, or any other animals. The only thing I can see is a door at the bottom of the lake."

"Is the water toxic?" Jet wondered. "Did you say you saw a door?"

Jayco's hand reached cautiously toward the liquid. When he was mere inches away, he ran into a barrier preventing him from going further. Jet followed and found that he could not touch the water either.

"Should I try?" Maria asked.

"Be careful," Jet warned.

Maria's hand advanced slowly, and when she reached the barrier, she was unable to proceed. Pulling her hand back, a glimmer materialized on the tip of her longest finger, her fourth digit. Quickly the glow consumed Maria's entire hand, and a spark surged from her skin and cascaded onto the lake. The lake's surface vibrated once, and a deep grinding sound, like a machine turning, rumbled from the depths of the water.

"The door is opening. I see hands gripping the door, pushing it open. Something is swimming fast toward the surface. Run," Jayco shouted, and he sprinted away. Jet and Maria were a step behind.

The pristineness of the surface vanished as a purple blur burst from the water and soared several feet into the air, landing acrobatically with ease onto the ground. The animal was tall with antlers, four legs with brilliant purple fur. Jet recoiled, pulling out his orbs. Grantham and Latisha leaped to their feet as the golden animals hissed and pawed the ground. An image of an attacking deer entered Jet's mind.

"Synastasis," the creature hummed in a whispery voice an instant before Jet attacked.

His concerns and fears evaporated as quickly as they had arrived.

In a more pleasing tone, the animal said, "I can't thank you enough for releasing me. I have been stuck here far too long. Welcome to Coso Subtrano. I am Alces."

Jet studied the creature more closely. It was larger than a deer and was likely a moose, though he'd never seen one this up close. This creature was akin to the other creatures in this canyon, with beautiful but unexpected colors. This moose was varying shades of purple. It was sleek, tall, and reminded Jet of Faunal. Sure enough, the creature raised itself and could walk on its back two legs. The hands that had been his front hooves gained dexterity. The face was pleasant and kind.

Alces continued, "You do not seem surprised by my movement or by my words. Have you seen others like me?"

"Maybe," Jayco answered, glancing around he pointed to Iris and the others. "We have walking golden animals with us. We've seen your friend Faunal."

"That fiend is not my friend," Alces said quickly, her voice suddenly becoming enraged. "I am not with him, and we do not share the same attitudes or perspectives."

Jet added, "For our part, Faunal has sworn to help kill us."

Alces stared at Jet meticulously. "You must be part of the Rivalry resistance. Can you perform magic?"

"I guess."

"Are you searching for Arisol? How long have I been trapped here?"

Jet said, "I'm not sure. This is our first time in Coso Subtrano."

The moose appeared to shutter, as if riding herself of a bad thought. Wearily, she said, "You are the Mikado. I did not think that a Mikado had been born for several centuries. Have you met with Leotyton and the other allies?"

Jet shared confused glances with the others. Even Iris appeared to bow her head. The panther sidled closer to Jet, coming to rest next to him. "We've only heard stories about Leotyton. He has long since died putting Arisol back into his prison."

"The assault on the Starving Peaks worked?" Alces asked.

"I can only assume so. It has been many hundreds or thousands of years since that happened."

Alces's eyes bored into Jet. "You lie. I could not have been trapped here for that long."

Grantham pointed to where Jet and the others had entered the canyon. He said, "This canyon is far different from our world. In fact, we've never seen such colors or creatures. Our world lies beyond that opening. We are searching for something. Faunal is out there, trying to stop us from finding it. Inside this cavern, do you know where there is a cache of golden items?"

Alces's mind seemed to be spinning. "Lady Gaea entrusted me to watch over this canyon. It was Faunal who attacked but he could not retake this land. Instead, he tricked me by using a friend as bait inside of Lake Vita." It pointed to the green lake next to them. "I was trapped and ensnared. How did you free me?"

Maria took a step forward. "There was a glimmer on my finger that went into the lake and released you."

"I see," Alces said. "You must be a daughter of the Wandering Marauders."

Shrugging, Maria muttered, "Not sure what that means."

Suspicion formed on Alces's face, and it glared at each of them in turn. "Who sent you?"

Jet pulled out his tome, *The Sorcerer's Guide*, showing it to the Moose.

Alces squeaked and stepped away as if it had been struck. The golden lion and bear hustled away to avoid being trampled and settled near a cove opposite the lake. Alces hissed, "You have one of the five tomes of Terra Maleficis."

Jet replied, "You're speaking in riddles. I don't know what you mean."

"The five tomes decide who governs the land. In ancient days a representative had a seat at the table of Lexicon. You have one of the tomes and are a member of the Elementals."

"If you say so."

"How did you come into possession of this book?"

"It was given to me by my family before they died. It has helped me learn Elemental magic. It taught us about Leotyton and his fight against Arisol. Arisol tried to escape by using a powerful tablet called the Phoenix, but Leotyton sacrificed his life to put the demon back into his prison and created this book. However, the Phoenix was broken and scattered, and we are looking for its pieces. We think one of the pieces has been hidden here. Will you help us?"

"How could you have not known about the other four books?"

"I've heard of another. Someone from our school has the other book. He can perform Runic magic. He's working with Faunal, who works for Arisol."

"I'm not sure what to think," Alces responded. The moose pawed the ground, studying them. "Are you telling the truth? How am I supposed to trust you?"

"Iris," Jet said, "go to Alces and let him pet you."

Alces bristled. "I am the daughter of Queen Aurora. She commanded that I come to Coso Subtrano and prepare it for the day it was attacked. Instead, I was enslaved for thousands of years. All my friends and family are gone."

Iris loped next to the giant purple moose and rubbed up against her leg. Alces appeared to calm considerably. "This doesn't explain everything."

"We're looking for objects from the Rivalry. Can you help us?" Jet asked.

Instead of answering, Alces said, "These creatures were the champions of our world. Each of the five magical tribes had four champions. The Rivalry was first meant to keep the peace between the magics. You command the Sagitta tribe, and Iris is their leader."

Latisha scowled. "We've never heard of five magic types. We've seen a giant rock dragon, large attacking bugs, and now a talking moose. We're standing in a world inside of a world with green water and orange sand. I'm not sure how much more of this I can take. I just want to leave."

"For the first time," Jayco said, "I'm with Latisha. Spending the night here is not an option." Turning to Jet, he added, "We need to keep moving. Can this moose help us or not?"

"You are aggravating creatures," Alces scoffed. She again pawed the ground and stated, "There are five tribes of magic. Before Arisol fell, each was directed by an ancient tome. These tomes were called the Terra Maleficis, and the assembly was called the Lexicon. It had been this way for years, even centuries. Before Arisol caused a rebellion, peace had settled into the land, following heartbreak and destruction. At some point, magic began to be lost, even Elemental and Runic but not as quickly as the others. Deceit and deception always hid just under the surface, and at some point, from far west of Goth Airtha, the Chupovanas were recruited by one of the leaders of the Resitituals, the fifth form of magic."

Jayco asked, "Can you please first explain the books of magic?"

Alces replied, "You know about Elemental magic. These individuals use the elements for good. They were excellent at defending and attacking and were the workers, the military commanders, and the protectors of our leaders. Those with Runic magic were the soldiers, the laborer, the peasants. The final three magical forms are Shaman, Incrementum, and Resitituals. Shaman can influence aspects of life and death and some of the spirits in this world and the next. Incrementum helps life to grow, reproduce, and prosper. Resitituals are unique because this faction fixes unexplainable magical problems, bewitchments, and lasting incantations of death and destruction."

Grantham said, "I've never heard of the last three."

"Most of the leaders of Goth Airtha came from the Incrementum magic society. They were peaceful, wise, and filled with empathy. For centuries the five magics worked well together. There was always a small skirmish that was resolved almost immediately; if not, the Rivalry would solve the crisis."

"Why were Elemental and Runic magic forgotten?"

"For two reasons. First, advanced technology and weapons, tools, and other means gained influence, especially among those with less magic capability. Second, those with magic overstepped their authority, and restrictions were placed. Over time magic was forgotten."

"Restrictions?" Jet asked.

"Magical clarity." Alces amended her statement.

"Why did the Resitituals recruit the Chupovanas?" Latisha asked.

Alces appeared to ponder the question as if trying to find the best answer. Finally, she said, "My best guess is that the Resitituals harbored a feeling that their magic was useless. They had no power to create, attack, defend, or help anything to grow. They concluded that they were only needed after a mistake from someone with true magical powers. An idealist leader convinced them that they were being used. Most of the tribe broke away and began attacking those with magic and trying to steal their magic. They supposed that if someone stole enough magic, they would develop true magical abilities. The Resitituals spread fear throughout the land, and those with magic and sorcery became hidden. War followed.

"Arisol was the leader of the ten kings; at the time he was known as the Grey Panther. He and the other kings protected Goth Airtha from the Resitituals and the Chupovanas, but they were no match. Death and destruction followed wherever they went. Arisol sought to find and learn the expert levels of Runic magic to stop the Resitituals from killing those possessing magic. As noble as his intentions may have seemed, he became caught up in the power he found and decided to control all magic abilities. He killed Staka Arben, the leader of the Resitituals, and took over dictatorship of Goth Airtha until the other kings were forced to fight him. I imagine that you know the rest of the story."

Jet was speechless. He felt simultaneously empowered because of his anger and inept since he had no knowledge of this for so long. He had not imagined that there were other types of magic. Siwalik and Faunal had both called him young, inexperienced, and without understanding. They had been right. Hearing about the wars and contentions of the past made everything feel so foreign to him.

Jayco asked, "Do you have a magic ability?"

Alces replied, "My tribesman cannot perform magic like the Elementals or others, but we have our own talents."

Glancing at the others, Jet felt unsure what to do next. For the first time, he wondered if it was a bad thing that Elemental magic had returned to the earth?

"Are we fighting the right battle?" asked Jet. "Is magic bad? Maybe Arisol isn't as evil as we were led to believe. It seems like the Resitituals, and the Chupovanas are the real problems."

Alces laughed humorlessly. "I knew the Grey Panther when I was a child, as did my mother. He was kind and charismatic and a monster underneath, hiding and biding his time. Arisol is the real threat no matter what you've heard. You are on the right path."

Latisha's head shot up. She asked, "You really knew him?"

"Yes. He often came to my village to speak with my father and mother. He brought gifts and became a trusted friend and advisor. He was charitable to his friends but ruthless to his enemies and those friends whom he no longer trusted. I know more than most how much he changed. He is blinded by anger, distrust, and greed. He sent Faunal to entrap me, keeping me as a slave."

"But he let you live?" asked Latisha.

"He did. The cruelest punishment possible. I suffered daily because I chose to speak out about him. He took my freedom and I had no prospect of ever leaving my imprisonment, until you came." Turning to Jet, the moose said, "No matter what the Chupovanas have become, the ultimate goal must be defeating Arisol. But I foresee a battle with the Chupovanas before Arisol is released. You need to prepare."

Jet renewed his question from earlier. "Will you help us?"

Alces replied, "I will try, Mikado. We need to keep moving."

Jet and the others gathered their belongings and searched the surrounding area. Jet considered several sections of the canyon that might conceal the Phoenix, but it might take hours or days to search everywhere. If they followed the ravine, it would provide the best chance to examine each gully; it was flat and easy to travel. On the far side of the lake, to his left, were more peaks and slopes, and it would be nearly impossible to cross. There was a bend in the turn a mile ahead, and that seemed like the right direction to go.

When his friends had regrouped, Jet said, pointing forward, "Iris and I will be in front. Everyone watch your backs to make sure none of us gets ambushed."

"What's our plan?" asked Latisha.

"We're going to follow this ravine. Don't get separated, and let's get out of this alive."

"Great plan," Grantham replied sarcastically.

As the group moved forward, Jet felt anxious and stressed. He worried that Alces might be more than she appeared. She'd given them a lot of information to consider. He noticed Jayco staring into the water every ten minutes, likely searching for changes within the lake. They crossed the lake's entire length an hour later and reached the bend in the turn, except it wasn't what he expected. As they turned the corner, it became clear that the ravine morphed into more of a path, winding back and forth, disappearing as it cut through an enormous black wall with crumbling boulders strewn everywhere except on the gray stone path. The landscape immediately to their right had also changed. Fifty feet back, something had blasted away the slope, leaving behind a smooth, orange stone wall.

Latisha asked, "Do we keep going down the path?"

"Take a minute and search this area," said Jet. "Be careful, though. Something feels off."

Jayco pointed up the side of a steep hill above the wall. "There are a few caves up the rise. Grantham, Maria, and I will check them out."

"Don't split up."

After a command, Iris, the other animals, and even Alces spread out to provide protection. The animals sniffed the air, clearly a smell had caught their attention.

Jet examined the far wall but found nothing and turned his attention to the area beyond the gray stone ravine. A dozen varying sized boulders were strewn across a small stretch in front of the enormous black wall. The path was the same color and stone as the ravine, just narrower. He took five steps onto the path intending to get a closer look at the boulders. A spine-chilling sensation attacked his senses, and he quickly retreated to safer ground. Next, he drew near to where the lake ended and was surprised to find that a small dam of rocky debris blocked the movement of the water. The debris had been painstakingly placed. Staring back from whence they came, he realized that the far side of the lake had been narrowing the entire time.

"Is that something sticking out of the water?" asked Latisha.

Jet gaped at where she was pointing. A large six-inch-thick circular wooden beam jutted out of the water nearly three feet."

"What is it?" asked Latisha.

"No idea."

"We better not have to go swimming to find out."

Inching closer to the edge, Jet reached out for the piece of wood. He couldn't see into the depths of the water and wished Jayco was here for a better look. His fingers were centimeters from touching the wood when a horror filled wail burst forth from somewhere ahead of them and echoed around the cavern.

"What was that?" asked Latisha.

"Maybe a mating call."

"That's where your mind went?" she asked. "So typical and stupid."

Pulling back his arm, Jet moved to get a better look at the area dammed up. It was almost six feet high on the backside. Staring closer, he found a perfectly circular hole had been cut into the base of the debris, allowing a tiny amount of water to escape and trickle down the ditch. The water soon diverged from the stone path and headed to the left, away from the ravine path.

"Something just moved," said Jet, pointing to a small, almost enclosed spot on a ledge above the section with the boulders. The only means to get to this spot was by climbing on the dam itself. A stalactite hung down from the enclosure.

"What was it?" replied Latisha.

"Something with four long legs."

Latisha said, "I vote that we continue down the path. I hate the idea of four long legs. This whole place is creeping me out."

"What's going on?" asked Alces as she joined them.

Jet pointed to the dam and said, "Someone created this lake. The normal path goes to the right, but the water goes to the left."

"Who cares," replied Latisha as her head shot back and forth as if she were trying to look everywhere at once.

Jet said, "You build a dam because you either want to create a lake or you want to reveal something that would've otherwise been hidden."

Alces replied, "We can't follow that riverbed, it's too narrow, and I don't see another way."

Pointing back to the small area on the opposite side of the dam. "Give me a second. I want to go see what is over there."

"Other than that hanging rock. I don't see anything," replied Latisha. "That place is a waste of time."

Small clusters of rubble cascaded down from where Jayco and the others had gone to search the caves. Jet watched as Grantham, Jayco, and Maria set off a small rockslide. The instant the soil touched the gray ravine it burnt to a crisp and vanished entirely.

"That's not normal," Latisha replied. "I hate it here."

At that instant, a second wail erupted, this time far closer.

"We need to get out of here," Alces cried. "We're in danger."

The others leaped onto the ravine and hurried forward.

Jet asked, "Find anything?"

"Nothing worth mentioning," Jayco shouted. "Those caves were a bust."

Pointing at the narrow passage, Grantham asked, "Are we going to follow this route?"

"I'm not sure, but I don't think so," replied Jet.

"Does that mean we're going back?" asked Latisha.

Pointing to the dam, Jet said, "Someone went to a lot of trouble to slow this flow of water. I'd bet anything that the way is over there."

"What's happening to the rocks?" asked Maria.

Staring at the base or top of the stalactite, a dark green color was being absorbed into the rock as if it were being overtaken. Scanning around, Jet didn't see the same color anywhere else.

Alces replied, "That's an Incrementum curse. One of their beasts have been unleashed."

"What?" Latisha asked. "Is it a Chupovana?"

"No," Alces replied. "This animal doesn't steal your magic, it poisons you."

"Much better," replied Jayco. "Just what we needed."

Latisha asked, "Are you saying the rock is dying?"

"No. The rock isn't alive. Dark green is the color of poison. If it touches you, the poison is transferred to you. Proceed with caution."

Grantham playfully nudged Jet. "After you bro."

Pulling his orbs from his pocket, he shuffled across the dam for more than ten feet. Jet yelled, "Watch my back."

"No problem," shouted Jayco.

There wasn't a direct route, so he was forced to jump the last three feet. The ground was slippery, and Jet landed and almost slid into the stalactite.

Alces said, "Just so you are clear, if you touch that rock after it turns green, the enchantment will leach onto you."

"Crystal clear," Jet said.

Baby step after baby step, Jet maneuvered behind the hanging rock. As he circled around, he found no animal or person, but near the back wall was a narrow corridor where only a single person at a time could enter. Poking in his head, he could only see a dozen feet before the trail curved right.

"Bro, are you still breathing?" Grantham asked.

"Nah. My lifeless body is just hanging out. By the way there's no one here, but there's a trail. Iris, follow!"

The panther quickly joined Jet, as did the other golden animals. They had no problem avoiding the death stone.

Maria added, "If we're following you, we need to hurry."

"Hustle away. There's a symbol on the wall over here. I've seen it before."

Jayco asked, "What kind of symbol?"

"On one side of the wall is a falcon, and on the other is a snake."

"Are you saying we're going to have to fight Lucretius again?" asked Latisha.

"I doubt it. These symbols are smaller than my hand."

Grantham was the first to arrive, followed by Maria. She asked quizzically, "What's a Lucretius?"

Jayco answered, "A few months ago, we were in a cave looking for the first tablet piece. Anyway, this huge twenty-foot creature attacked us. We won, and it died."

"Jet fought it alone," Grantham added.

"We helped with moral support," retorted Jayco.

Alces arrived last. She added, her voice uneasy, "We need to get moving. This entire area is at risk. We can't stay here much longer."

"Don't need to ask me twice," Grantham said, and he darted into the narrow and winding trail.

The sides of the corridor were smooth, with yellow, gold, and red swirls unlike anything Jet had ever seen. It was as if deep water had cut a route directly through the stone. It felt like nighttime as barely any light illuminated the narrow path. There were shadows, and a chill was in the air. Jet sprinted to catch up with Grantham, with Iris and the others a step behind. The owl, instead of flying, landed on the bear's back.

"Heads up," Grantham shouted. "There's a pile of bones up here."

The trail widened slightly after rounding the next two corners, and Jet glimpsed a pile of pristine white bones tucked deep into a cove to his right. They were from animals he'd never seen before, and they were plucked clean of any meat. He yelled, "Keep moving."

"Crap," Jayco shouted. "The puke green color is leaching down the walls."

Glancing up, Jet found that the nasty green color was spreading down from taller portions.

Alces said, "It's probably the Mantador."

"Not sure what that means," Jayco shouted.

Jet picked up the pace.

"Why is it here?" asked Jayco.

"Someone clearly knows that you're here. They don't want you to escape."

Latisha asked, "I vote we leave now?"

"That's a difficult choice," Alces replied. "But remember, if you don't claim the pieces now, they won't have any magic within them after this is finished."

"Not an option," replied Jet.

Latisha said, "Just asking."

"I think we made it," Grantham announced. "It's up here."

Ten seconds later Jet emerged from the corridor onto another open space, but it was a dead end. The walls here were higher twice as high. Dark green encroached the first six feet from the top. There was still another twenty feet to go, but it was inching slowly downward. His eyes focused on the far side of the open area that was forty feet long and twenty feet wide. He saw an overhanging circular area as if it had been cut out from the wall. The rock was purple and built into the wall. Just like back in the cave in Silverton there was a niche with a dozen golden treasures.

"We're too late," Grantham said. "No wonder Shane didn't attack us. He's already been here."

It was true. Jet felt the rise of the despair deep within him. The bright yellow box, in the center, with an animal on the lid, hung open. There was not a single black item in view.

Jayco, Maria, and Latisha quickly joined Jet and Grantham.

"What does this mean?" asked Jayco.

Jet hissed. "We're going to find a way to get the second piece back from Shane."

Latisha swore loudly, and everyone turned in her direction. She said, "We've gone through hell getting here. We needed the reward."

Alces said, "We can't linger for long."

All four of them, except for Maria, acted quickly. They opened their bags and began moving forward. There were no pyramids, but several weapons and other items.

A large black tail swept down from the ledge before them. When Jet glanced up, the tail and the creature it belonged to had vanished.

"Definitely the Mantador," Alces whispered. "Before you pick up any item, can I suggest we make a plan?"

"What kind of plan?" Latisha asked.

"If we run back the way we came, none of us will make it."

"What are our options?" asked Jet.

"Put the animals back into their pyramid forms. They won't be able to help us. Once you grab the last item, you'll need to get onto my back, and I'll take you away from here."

Grantham asked, "Are you strong enough to carry all of us and the bling?"

Alces glared at Grantham.

"Stupid question," Grantham muttered.

Latisha said, "We might need Iris and the animals to protect us."

Alces shook her head. "Trust me, they can't."

The green invading color was halfway down the rock wall. Jet realized that Alces was right. He said, "Iris, turn into a pyramid."

Jet commanded Iris who touched her nose to the other three animals and they transformed. After touching Iris, he picked up the pyramid as his friends stored the others. They sprinted toward the golden items as Jet noticed five swords and five bows with a hundred golden arrows. There was a pair of Katars, small five-inch-thick blades, a circular ring sword, and several other items. Jet thought he saw Grantham pick up two or three breastplates. Jet walked to the center and stared at the empty box where he was confident a piece of the Phoenix had been held. He was handed the circular ring sword, the Katars, a golden box, and more jewelry. He quickly packed them in his bag.

Jet shouted, "Back to Alces, and let's get out of here."

His friends sprinted in the direction of the moose. An instant before he set off, something glimmered off to his left. His vision suddenly expanded, and he thought for a second that Alces had double-crossed them. He remembered Siwalik's warning. But she was not what caught his attention. Instead, there was an item that had partially fallen into a crack in the back wall. He stretched out as the thing slowly began to disappear. He dove, wrapping his hands around a golden, flat object. It was a rectangle with no obvious use.

Turning back to his friends, he could see the despair on their faces as they sat on Alces. The overhang was crumbling around him. The ground shook, and the green color had almost reached the floor. Alces began to stampede as if something was preparing to attack. The ground groaned and rattled harder than anything he had previously encountered in Coso Subtrano. The faces of Jayco, Grantham, Latisha, and even Maria peered at him with dread and dismay. Jet had made a mistake. The rock ledge above him fractured, split, and the rubble fell, burying Jet completely.

CHAPTER 12

Despair, regret, anguish, and pain became the constant companion of Jet Black as he was squeezed, suffocated, and crushed to death. His right arm was caught awkwardly behind his back, and he could feel Iris's pyramid digging into his back. He considered speaking the magic word releasing her but loathed the idea of her suffering like him. She could not help him; no one could.

How have I let this happen? he demanded of himself. Rocks continued piling on him, and he felt a sudden pressure near his left leg.

Snap.

It felt as disgusting as it sounded. Warm liquid, blood, cascaded down his skin. Over the next ten minutes, dust and earth settled into Jet's lungs, and he coughed uncontrollably. Any movement sent pain shooting in different areas of his body. His right hand broke, and a rock settled near his jaw, cutting off the airway to this throat. Blackness overwhelmed Jet, and he slipped away into darkness.

When he awoke, he was on a bus, the rain falling hard. He couldn't move a muscle. It took him a while to focus on the bus and his surroundings. The bus had twenty or so rows with an aisle down the middle. Four seats were positioned in each row, two on each side of the aisle. He wasn't sitting in any of the seats but instead drifting above four people who sat close to each other, talking.

Jet was aghast when he realized that he was staring at a younger version of himself, with his parents seated in the row in front of him. Equally shocking was that the man sitting directly next to Jet was Geb. He had first seen this man when he and his friends had landed in Munich, Germany, on their way to Bern, Switzerland. Jet had just seen the man in passing and thought nothing of it. He had dark umber skin and was dressed in an orange sweater. Days later, while trying to steal an important artifact from a museum in Bern, Geb had shown up again, this time helping Jet by running into Shane Fallon, knocking him over. This diversion had allowed Jet to switch the artifact they needed with a replica.

It was impossible to believe that Jet had known this man when he was younger. How had he forgotten? Was this image a lie?

On the bus Geb wore a black trench cloak, with a hood and a tweed flat hat.

"Why are we discussing this now?" His mother asked, and Jet's attention was brought back to his parents. Alice and Remington Black appeared just as he had remembered. They had originally named him Joshua, but he hated the name because it came from his great-uncle, who had been the drunk and clown of Silverton, or at least that was what Jet had believed. His middle name was Elbert, and Taley had been in the family as well. Joshua Elbert Taley became Jet.

"We *are* being watched. We both know this." Remington looked upset, his voice rising.

"Keep it down. Or Joshy will hear you."

Jet's heart broke. How had he forgotten his mother's nickname for him?

Alice glanced back at her son, who was drawing an item that Jet recognized. It was an amulet-like ornament that he had played with when he was younger. This trinket was one of the several items given to him by Nana a few months ago. The amulet was midnight black, with a small loop at the top that didn't close completely. Jet had to admit, the younger version of himself had drawn an almost perfect image.

Jet's mom asked, "Why does the Brotherhood want us to give our son this liquid concoction?"

Remington said sternly, "For his own good. And ours."

"I don't think I can." Tears ran down his mother's face.

Remington continued, "The chances that he is anything but a protector is quite slim. The Brotherhood believes that a family from California whose son is attending Dillon Lake is likely the next aspirant. If that's the case, do you want Joshua living his life like we are, running from one clue to the next? The Brotherhood wants us to protect him."

"How much will he forget? What will the mixture do to him?"

"It will cause him to forget everything he knows about magic, and it'll likely prevent him from being affected by conjury in the future."

"I don't know," she continued. "Can we trust the Brotherhood?"

Geb, seemingly unaware of the conversation in the seat above, visibly reacted to this comment. Neither Jet's dad nor his mom could see his reaction. The man continued to whisper into the younger Jet's ear and congratulated him on his exceptional drawing.

"Of course we can," Jet's father said. "They gave Uncle Joshua several cloaks and the book. We still don't know how to open it."

"Doesn't the Brotherhood want it back?"

"Only Geb knows that we have it. I think he's willing to have us keep it for another few years until we figure out how to open it." Jet stared anxiously as his father brought out *The Sorcerer's Guide*. He handed it to Alice, and she pulled out a wooden box that Jet also recognized. This old wooden box had been hanging on his wall, inside a shadow box, since his parents had died. This was where he'd found the tome in the first place.

"What about Nana?"

"She knows some things, but she isn't ready to hear everything."

"Fine," Alice said as she handed the box back to Remington. "When should we give Joshy the mixture?"

"Tonight. There's something special about him. People can tell that he has been around magic. We need that to disappear."

Alice placed her head in her hands and whispered, "Do it."

Remington glanced back, between seats, and nodded at Geb. From a pocket inside his cloak, Geb pulled out a stoppered vial. The liquid inside was a pale green.

The younger Joshua was so preoccupied with his drawing that he never noticed the liquid being added to his orange juice.

Geb's soothing voice said, "Joshua, you need a long drink of orange juice to stay strong and healthy. It's time for you to start growing and for you to become who you're supposed to be."

The younger Joshua shrugged and drank his entire cup of orange juice. There was no noticeable change to his face, nor a dazed look that came into his eyes. Jet wondered if anything had actually happened. The bus turned a corner and began climbing up a steep cliff. No one said anything for ten minutes, although his mother's shoulders shook. Jet watched each of them closely. His younger self just stared out the window.

Geb asked, "Joshua, what do you think of this picture?" He held up the picture of the black amulet.

"It looks all right. Not sure what it is. Who drew it?" asked the younger Joshua.

"No idea," Geb replied. "I was just wondering if you had an opinion about it."

"Nope."

His father and Geb shared a glance. Remington's hand caressed the back of his mom's neck, and she sobbed for another ten minutes.

The rain worsened as they summited the top of the hill, and Jet felt unsure about every choice he had made about magic. His parents had wanted him to forget magic, and they'd given him a drink to do so.

A bright light soared into the air, and at first Jet thought it was lightning. The red flame of a firebolt blasted into the far side of the bus and it was knocked off the road. Jet watched in horror as the driver swerved to miss one tree, only to crash into another. The bus came to a sudden stop. The younger Joshua, his parents, Geb, and many of the other passengers were jolted forward. Jet thought that they'd made it through the worst part, but he was wrong.

A second bolt hit the bus, and it began tipping to the left. It was like watching a horror movie unfold and being unable to stop a runaway train. The bus rolled at least five times before crashing into several larger trees and coming to a complete stop. They landed with the left side facing down, partly in a river. Jet's parents were crumpled together, unmoving. The younger Joshua had fared somewhat better and was trying to get Geb off from him.

Other passengers were trying to climb toward the front or back to escape the bus. When Geb had recovered, he lifted the younger Joshua, carrying him to the back of the bus. Jet remained with his parents, knowing that they only had minutes to live. Remington was injured more seriously than Alice. The bus had hit a tree at the exact point where their window was. Glass had cut his face, and his left arm was clearly broken. Alice had landed on Remington but was crawling to her purse, and Jet began to hope that she would make it out alive.

Geb reappeared, intending to help both his parents. Geb tried to lift Alice, but she was pale and weak. She hissed, "This accident wasn't a coincidence."

Geb replied, "What do you mean?"

"Someone is coming."

"Let's get out of here," Geb said. "Help me get your husband."

At that moment Jet could see the truth and despair on her face. Tears, mixed with blood, ran down her cheeks. Pulling a wooden box from her purse, she said, "My husband is dead. They are after the two of us. No one knew that you and Joshua were here." Removing two rings from her fingers and a necklace, Jet recognized both, she handed these and the wooden box to Geb.

Jet wailed. "No. Mom! You can't just give up!"

Alice continued, not hearing her son's pleas, "Get Joshua back to Nana. Hide this box until he's ready; if he's ever ready. We made a grave mistake giving him that drink tonight."

Jet tried scrambling forward but was unable to move or touch his mother. Peering at his dad, he noticed that he wasn't breathing. Jet screamed, "This is not happening."

Geb said, "Come with us. You are well enough to escape."

"If I do," she said, her voice now void of emotion, "they'll come searching for me for the rest of my life. Joshua will always be in danger. If I stay, he'll be safe."

"The Brotherhood can protect you."

Alice stared deeply at Geb. "Do you really believe that?"

"We must try."

Glass broke from a small explosion near the front of the bus. There were screams all around them. But voices, angry voices, could also be heard.

"You need to leave. Do your best to protect my son."

Geb said, "I will." He gathered up the items from Alice and disappeared toward the back of the bus.

His mother didn't stare after Geb but instead crawled back over to Remington. She bent down and kissed him on the cheek. His father's face appeared even paler than before, and Jet knew the truth. Movement at the front of the bus surprised Jet as three people walked onto the crash site. She lay down and pulled out a flask with a stoppered liquid. She removed the stopper and drank the entire contents.

Steps approached on broken glass, and Jet tore his eyes away from his parents. Three adults strode in his direction, two men and one female. They carefully searched eat seat.

The female said, pointing in their direction, "There they are. Your ingenuity, Rysen, appears a little too devastating." The older woman appeared to be in her forties. She was tall, thin, with silky clay skin and black hair. She was beautiful and menacing.

But Jet reacted to the name "Rysen". He'd only heard one other person with that name, and Jet's eyes bored into the man to the left of this woman. There was no doubt. The man was Professor Rysen, the same man who had recently transferred to Chadwicks to teach chemistry.

Rysen said, "You said you wanted them caught."

"Caught, yes, not killed. We could've learned so much from them."

The other man spoke, and Jet didn't recognize him. "The bus is partly in a river, and soon the water will cover them."

The woman asked, "Are they alive?"

Rysen bent down and checked for a pulse. "Dead."

Jet felt himself shaking.

The woman said, pointing to some debris nearby, "Bury them, and leave no doubt."

The two men piled on metal and other pieces of luggage. The bus was now empty of survivors, though there had only been a handful. Soon his parents were gone, buried with debris and covered in water. Without a conscious choice, Jet was dragged away from his parents, following the three killers. They exited the front and quickly made their way up the bank, in the direction of the road where the bus had first crashed. Jet was pulled as if he was on a leash, and he fought against it for the first minute. When he realized it was pointless, he shadowed the three assassins.

Jet heard the woman say, "Rysen. You need to accept that position at Dillon Lake and start recruiting students. I've already been accepted at Sun Valley Academy. Alex, keep a low profile at Cranbrook. We already have people at Chadwicks and San Mateo. We need to put all of our efforts into finding the two hidden books before the Brotherhood does. If we do that, we can win this war."

Rysen said, "Will the Brotherhood get involved?"

"They already have," the woman said hotly. "But they are several steps behind. They have their own agenda."

Alex said, "What about the Blacks' son?"

"Our spies in the Brotherhood report that the group thinks he has little chance of being anyone important. But we'll watch him nonetheless."

"How much time do we have before the solar calendar begins?"

"Probably within the next five years. We must have everything in place."

"How much will the killing Remington and Alice cost us?" Rysen asked.

"I'm not going to lie. It'll be a heavy price. They were close to finding the location of both books and likely the location of the first tablet piece. We can assume that the probable locations will be here in Germany, or Egypt, or even on the West Coast. I've heard that they were three months away from finding both books," she answered. "But you've solidified your position with us. I mean, for killing your best friends, there will be a huge reward. We think we know where they were headed."

The three reached the summit, and three vehicles were waiting for them. They nodded at each other, slipped inside, and drove away. Jet was left there standing, shell-shocked at everything he'd seen and learned.

Hands wrapped around his left foot, and Jet thought he was going to lose his mind. His heart raced, and thoughts of attacking spirits and seeing the dead invaded his head. The man grasping his leg was in bad shape. He wore a brown cloak that covered most of his body. The man was missing most of his lower legs and had crawled up the entire hill. Jet recognized the man, having seen him on the bus, on the opposite side, a few rows up from his parents.

The man whispered, "If you're here, then you're about to face an oracle."

"What's an oracle?" Jet asked.

"A mystical healer of Shaman magic. Like me. That's how they can make this connection."

"Okay," replied Jet.

"Remember, the cost is steep for the awareness you've been given. You're an incomplete Mikado, and only as you touch the tendrils of death can you heal. When you are weak and have lost all hope, search for Anesidora and the secrets to solemnity."

Bending down, Jet said, "Old man, you speak in riddles."

"Your time in this portal is ending. You dropped this back in the bus."

The man held up the golden rectangle item, and now hieroglyphic markings were visible on both sides.

"What is it?"

"A hoaxing key."

As he grasped the golden rectangle, the man, the rain, the mountain, the crashed bus, and his dead parents vanished into the darkness.

CHAPTER 13

Coldness, delicious coldness, was a welcomed sensation throughout Jet's entire body, but he felt empty and hollow inside. What he had just witnessed had altered his life forever, both then and now.

"Do you appreciate all that I have shown you?" A raspy and ancient voice filled with power spoke with contempt from the shadows. "Do you appreciate that it was I who saved your life?"

"Where am I?" Jet asked.

The voice continued, "In both instances, only I could have protected you."

Wearily, he asked, "Who are you?"

"Can you fathom the sacrifices I have made to ensure that someone would be here to greet you?"

Jet paused, unsure what to say. It was at this precise moment he realized his pain had vanished, and he had been strapped to a rock slab with leather cords binding him tightly. He tried to magnify his vision but was unable. He yearned to use magic, but the words melted away in his mind. In a soft, respectful voice, he responded, "I fully comprehend all that you have done. It's obvious that I owe you my life, and without your greatness, I would be nothing more than rotting flesh."

A sound, like dragging tree branches came from his right. Jet could not stop himself from shivering when the enormous frame came into view. It appeared to be a man at first sight, but the creature was hairless, and its skin was entirely white, as if void of any other colors. His skin was full of wrinkles, and its four fingers were profoundly elongated. The eyes were bright blue, but the pupils were an oval rather than a circle. It wore a thigh-length, forest-green toga with a hood. It wore no other clothing except for leather shoes.

The creature's right leg was dead weight and it dragged it uncaring. Jet did a double take as a third appendage came into view. This one exited the front of the toga near the belly and was smaller than the other two. It only had two fingers, like pinchers, and it held a large black crystal ball.

"I am Vates, the Oraculi. You have been welcomed to my humble asylum. You are the weakened Mikado, I see."

"Where am I, exactly?"

"You are in the grotto of Mugtar, the banished prison below Coso Subtrano."

"Is there a way out?"

"If you are willing to pay the price." Vates smiled, and Jet was shocked to see that its teeth were round, and it had about sixty of them, and they were the same color as its eyes. Rather unnerving and unnatural.

Jet tried fighting against his binding, but it was useless.

Vates said, "We can free you from your restraints." Pulling a maroon dagger with a black handle from within its toga, before Jet could react, the creature slashed down and cut cleanly through the leather. "Don't sit up too fast, or you will fall back into unconsciousness. We had to bind you, so you wouldn't get lost during your travels."

"What do you mean?"

"Wandering into the past and the whispers of the dead can cause you to become adrift."

"Did I see my own memory?"

"Mostly. But there must've been another of my kin. I felt him when you first arrived."

"He appeared nothing like you."

In an instant Vates's skin changed to match that of a freckle-faced, thirty-something male with brown hair standing five and a half feet tall. "We have some ability to change our appearance. We each have two or three options. This human was my favorite."

"Are you an oracle?"

"Did my kin tell you what I am?"

"No. Before I came down here, we met an imprisoned animal who said she was the daughter of Queen Aurora. She told us about oracles and Resitituals and the other tribes of magic. I was only guessing because you called him your kin."

Vates appeared unconvinced. Finally, it said, "What did you see in the memory?"

"Myself, when I was younger and on a bus. I had forgotten even being there. My parents were sitting in the seats in front of us. Something crashed into the bus, and my parents were killed."

"I saw the same."

"Could you see everything?"

"It would be easy to say yes, but I saw and sensed most of it. Impossible to explain. It answered the most critical questions about you." Vates asked, "Do you understand what your parents gave you to drink?"

Jet shook his head.

Vates answered, "It's called the forgotten shroom. There's a mushroom near the Starving Peaks, in fact, and if it is boiled, the broth can be added to snake venom, causing you to forget magic. That's what happened to you."

"Like, magic was erased from my memory?"

"Not erased but blocked. In essence, the magic was hidden."

"Why am I able to do magic, then?"

"If I'm not mistaken, your mind was attacked and invaded by an enemy. Their intent was to discover your true nature. By doing so, they removed a portion of the restraint on your mind."

"A portion?"

"You're not fully a Mikado. Of course, you are one in name, but not power. Quite weakened."

"Can it be fixed?"

"Are you willing to pay the price?"

"Can you do it?"

"No. I'm not strong enough to survive past today, especially after my realm has been poisoned. My minutes are numbered. Do you know who attacked your mind?"

"Yes. Faunal."

"He has always been most adept at striking the psyche. How did you survive?"

"To be honest, I'm not sure. He was powerful. A few different times, I thought he was really going to inflict pain, but it never came. He opened up memories that I had forgotten."

"Possibly the product of the forgotten shroom." Vates pondered for a moment. "By chance, do you remember the words he used to attempt to invade your mind?"

"Breathe in. Breathe out. Die," Jet repeated, trying to remain casual.

"How interesting." Vates said, with a note of surprise in its voice. "That makes things nearly impossible for you."

"What do you mean?"

"We will get to it in due time." Vates pointed to stone chairs facing each other. "I need you to gather your things and sit in the far seat." Vates nodded to the corner. "Your items and your tome are over there."

Jet sat up slowly, the blood racing out of his brain. He felt only slightly unsteady. When putting his foot down, he remembered the pain in both legs. "What happened to my broken legs, or was that just something in my head?"

"Oh, you broke them all right." He laughed. "I had to call down my Incrementum magic vassal, and he worked on you. You haven't been completely healed by any means, and it took hours or days, I can't remember which, to get you better."

"How long have I been here?"

"Just the right amount of time." Vates dragged himself to the closest stone chair and sat down. "Hurry over! We haven't gotten all century long."

"Yes, sir," Jet said, and he grasped his backpack and limped over. His bag was as heavy as before, and glancing inside, he found all the items accounted for.

Before he sat down, Vates asked, "What's the name of your tome?"

Jet was about to blurt out the name, but noticed Vates's face, which held a glimmer of resentment. Instead, he asked, "Don't you know?

"How would I?" Vates growled. "During my time, barely anyone knew its name. Elemental magic wielders believed themselves to be better than the rest of us. Rumors said that the book had been destroyed."

Sitting on his stone chair, Jet asked, "Is that possible?"

"Oh yes, it is. And for the book to be recreated, it requires power beyond our understanding."

Jet considered this piece of information. He wondered the history of the tome he held. "Who was the oracle that I saw in my memory?"

"In truth, I'm not sure. That was years and years after I was exiled to this world. I have less than an idea of who among my kin still remains."

Jet wasn't sure he believed Vates, and he was starting to trust this creature less and less. He asked, "What is that crystal ball that you are holding on to? Can it see into the future?"

"It is not crystal, but obsidian, and it's why you are here today."

"What are you talking about?"

Cords sprang from his stone chair and wrapped tightly around his wrist, arms, and torso. Jet demanded, "What are you doing?"

"Saving a life is a wonderful thing, but in rare circumstances, it has an expenditure associated with it. I have saved your life, and now you must make a choice. You're now left with a few different options. You can bequeath your book to me by telling me its name and releasing your control over it. What say you?"

Jet thought he had enough room to reach into his pocket, but before he could, Vates pulled something from somewhere within his own toga. A white cloth was removed and opened. Jet's three orbs lay within. "How did you get those?"

"Carefully. Very carefully."

Vates had Jet's full attention. "What do you really want?"

"To help you."

"By binding me to this chair and trying to steal my book?"

"One of two things is clear. Either you're not strong enough to use the tome as it is designed, or you need help in a way that you can't fathom. I need to find which one is the case. That is why you are bound to that chair."

"Am I supposed to try to escape?"

"No." Vates laughed. "Escape is impossible. You must be tested, but beware, the cost is high."

Jet began to form a spell on his lips, and suddenly he was shocked so hard that he lost control of every single muscle movement. The aftermath was far from pretty. When he had recovered, his foolishness led to another attempt at using magic. This time, the shock was stronger than the first, and he fell unconscious for a time.

When Jet had partly recovered, Vates hissed, "I imagine you can handle that shock again two more times before it kills you. Don't make that mistake again."

"What am I supposed to do?" He wheezed.

"You've begun the contest called the Hoyuk Crescent, designed initially as a torture device on the enemies of Goth Airtha, especially when the creatures Chupovanas were smuggled into our land. Their witchcraft is universal and complete. You sit on the Hoyuk, and it delivers the punishment based on your choices." From the ground between them, a stone checkerboard rose, held up by a stone rod. It stopped when it was waist-high, and fifty squares appeared.

Vates said, "I'm impressed. I've never seen more than thirty. Arisol is going to win, and you're going to suffer greatly if you don't counterbalance the fight."

Figurines that were perfectly sculpted appeared on the board. Jet saw one of himself land in the center. Next, he saw Mckenzey, Jayco, Grantham, Latisha, Seyanna, Keesha, Rick, Jackson, Maria, Sebastian, and others.

"Interesting," Vates replied.

On the opposite side of the board, Shane Fallon appeared. Figurines of Jessiva, Jocelyn, Vinny, Nash, Ariana, Rick, Autumn, and several others appeared. One of Jake Hurley landed, became black like dust, and blew away.

"The board is pretty full," noted Vates.

Jet asked, "What is this?"

"Watch."

Weapons appeared with Jet's friends. He could see Jayco's golden bracelets, Grantham's long sheath, and more. Many of Shane's goons held weapons as well. But not everyone. The hands of Maria, her brother, as well as Ariana, Raul, and Autumn, were empty.

Vates said, "I move first. I will attack your player with one of those of the Runic soldiers. You can move more than one, but you can't move them all."

Before Jet had time to react, he watched Nash cross the board and land next to Mckenzey. Nash held a large black club, and Vates waved his hand, and Nash swung it, hitting Mckenzey's left leg with such force that her figurine toppled to the ground, and authentic blood-curdling screams echoed around the cavern.

In Jet's mind he disappeared from the cave and was taken to a bedroom with Mckenzey sitting on her bed. There might've been someone else in the room with her, but he couldn't tell. She sat on her bed, her eyes red and puffy from crying. She seemed to be barely keeping her emotions under control. Suddenly, her left leg crumpled, and she collapsed to the floor, screaming in terror. The vision began to darken as Jet was pulled from the room. His last image was of Mckenzey lying on the floor, holding her leg, screaming uncontrollably and someone rushing to her side.

Jet's heart raced fast, and he could barely breathe. He demanded, "Did that just happen?"

"Sadly, it did."

"No way. Not possible." Jet struggled against the bonds, but couldn't move. He opened his hands to force the three orbs into his hands. They sat on the stone armrest of the stone chair and inched in his direction.

"Good," Vates said sharply. "You do have power in your bones."

Jet glared, and Vates returned the look.

Vates hissed, "Your turn to choose a move. Who do you want to be injured? Imagine breaking Shane's arm so bad that it doesn't work properly again. Or payback for Jessiva sneaking into your dorm disguised."

"How do you know these things?"

Vates shouted, "I am the Lion's Oracle. Now make a choice."

Jet stared at the board in front of him. How could he make *this* choice? It was far from easy to pick someone to unleash pain upon. He remembered what Vates had said. Most everyone could be moved. He gathered up all his friends and moved them directly behind his own figurine, which he left untouched.

Vates howled in displeasure. "You didn't follow the directions."

Another shock coursed through Jet's body, and he felt his jaw clench and his right leg break in the same place it had done so previously. This time, though, he didn't fall unconscious, but the pain was beyond anything he'd felt. The pain did not stop for several minutes or hours, he couldn't be certain which.

From a significant distance away, Vates screamed, "You still have to choose someone to suffer."

Jet thought about Shane. He hated him so badly. Or even Raul, who had been a friend but had left. Jet pointed to Jayco, who became alive and marched across the board. In front of Jayco, three weapons presented themselves, a club, an arrow, or a sword. Jet chose the arrow. He next had the option of where to shoot, the shoulder, the leg, or the abdomen. Jet watched as the small figurine of Jayco unleashed an arrow, and it landed directly in the correct spot. A delay of a few seconds, and Jet felt the searing pain of the arrow slamming into his own left shoulder. In fact, he could see the arrow sticking out of the skin.

He had never been shot by anything before and thought the pain would be the most bearable. He was dead wrong. His vision darkened slightly, and spots appeared. He screamed and screamed and screamed. His eyes found Vates, who now looked cruel and angry.

Vates hissed, "Two rounds to go. You and I both play this round. But the third one is only you."

"I'm going to kill you," Jet hissed. "I'll find a way sooner or later."

"I'm dead in less than an hour. Your revenge will not happen today."

"Why did you heal me only to force me to go through this?"

"Torture is more than just pain. It's the knowledge and the experience of the pain you cause others. Imagine a world where you felt the pain you consciously or unconsciously caused others. Would you be more careful about your choices?"

"Let me go."

Ignoring this, Vates said, "Round two is the loss of a charmed weapon. I choose for Shane and his crew, and you choose for your friends. One on each side will lose a weapon." Looking up, he added, "This has to happen. You can't escape this inevitability." Reaching out, Vates picked a brown-haired boy that Jet recognized as the boy who had tried to break into his dorm and who had been with Shane in Switzerland. The boy held a mace in his hands. Vates flicked the boy, and the mace was pulled from his grip. The mace landed on the ground, and brown-haired boy frantically tried picking it back up but was unable to do so.

"You are up. I would suggest Mckenzey because she's already leaving the group. She has a broken leg, and you're probably doing her a favor."

Jet reacted quickly and again picked his own character.

"Wrong choice again," Vates cackled. "That was probably the worst choice you could've made." Reaching over to the stone armchair, Vates picked up the three orbs, handing them to Jet. The instant they touched his skin, they burned and blistered the palm. Jet quickly dumped them onto the ground, and they made a loud thud.

"The final round," Vates hissed.

Jet could not imagine that this was going to go any better.

"One of the group needs to die, and you are forbidden to choose yourself."

Jet stared at the board, and it was an impossible choice. He could never choose to kill his friends. Killing Shane would make the most sense, but that was the coward's choice. He bent down his finger millimeters from Shane's head.

From the corner of his eye, he saw Vates smile.

Jet moved quickly and touched the top of his own head.

A jolt of shock more potent than anything imaginable slammed into Jet so hard that dozens of bones broke. The surge of pain continued, even worsening. Jet vomited once, twice, twenty times. As he drifted toward unconsciousness, he hoped he would never wake again.

Sometime later, when Jet opened his eyes, he found Vates sitting across from him.

"Wrong choice once again."

Jet wheezed, "You should've let me die in the cave-in. I refuse to choose anyone else. Sooner or later either you will die, or I will." Without warning Jet reached out and touched himself again. He stiffened his muscles, anticipating the next shock, but it never came.

Instead, the leather binds released him, and he slumped to the floor. He fell into a pool of sweat, vomit, blood, and more. Vates was next to him in an instant. Jet recoiled, fearing another attack, but instead, Vates picked him up and placed him softly back on the stone chair. Vates said, kindly, "You did it, my child. You did it."

"What are you talking about?"

"The Hoyuk Crescent tests your strength, willpower, and above all your choices. There are other ways to win. No one who has ever done this before has survived what you did. But you are now cursed."

Jet wheezed, "Why go through it in the first place?"

From another pocket, Vates produced a liquid like the one his parents had given him. He was helpless at preventing the liquid going down his throat. The liquid was lukewarm, and Jet wanted to vomit. The instant it reached his stomach, he felt long-legged bugs crawling on every portion of his skin.

Vates stated, "This will heal your bones. But it won't heal you much beyond. I doubt you'll be able to walk for several weeks."

"How am I cursed?"

"It is the way." With surprising strength Vates lifted Jet and carried him back to the stone slab.

"Was Mckenzey really attacked?"

"Yes. And you can never wield those golden orbs again."

"But why?"

"Choices have a cost. You came to Coso Subtrano searching for something."

"We got here too late. I bet Shane is laughing at us. They got here first."

Jet watched as Vates repositioned the obsidian globe in front of his eyes. Vates said, "Shane Fallon came to Coso Subtrano two weeks ago. I watched him enter and leave with all the black trinkets and the second piece of the Phoenix."

"I knew it." Jet rested his head on the stone slab.

"Partially. You see, Faunal was with him. Faunal guided him through the most difficult parts and showed him the secret location of the tablet piece."

"How can I possibly hope to get it back now?"

"You don't have to."

"What?"

"Faunal broke the authority of the Rivalry. He was attached to the first tablet piece, as I am to the second. Faunal told Shane that you were the Mikado and where to find the tablet piece. This deception allowed me to hide the true tablet piece."

The obsidian globe began melting, revealing a clear piece of rock with three jagged sides and one smooth side.

"Are you serious?" Jet asked.

Vates placed both hands on Jet's shoulders and said, "I know you don't trust me, but I'm proud of the choices that you made here today. It's time for you to leave. My time here is almost up."

"How can I leave; I can't even walk?" Jet asked.

Vates released a long, high-pitched whistle. "My Incrementum vassal will carry you out. He will become your ally in my stead."

There was movement near the ceiling, and the entire canopy shifted, and the room that Jet thought was underground was actually a room within a room. A gigantic four-legged creature stared down at both him and Vates. It could only be described as an enormous creature of bark, like a fallen tree. Its arms were long pieces of wood that bent at the crevices. Positioned off its back were an array of jagged pieces of sticks. Moss and flowers grew on the creature's back, and some of the sticks had clumps of leaves.

Vates said, "This is Pincher. He is one of the most powerful Incrementum from my time."

"Is he friendly?" Jet asked.

Vates slumped to the floor, losing his balance. Pincher lowered what Jet realized was his head toward its master. The eyes were dark green, darker than the different shading of its body. He had wooden horns, and his head was shaped like an upside-down triangle. Like a dog, the creature licked his master. Jet thought that some energy was transferred to Vates, and he stood quickly.

"You need to go," the oracle exclaimed. "Time is running out."

Jet could still not move. "But I'm cursed."

"Yes, you are." Vates glared at Jet. "Don't deny it, but my kin told you about Anesidora, didn't he?"

Jet nodded once.

"It's hidden in a most unexpected place." Vates hurriedly retrieved the three golden orbs, picking them up with the white cloth. When he returned, he placed them in a small leather pouch and inside Jet's backpack which he placed on Jet's stomach. He added, "These are no longer yours. Find Anesidora. You must travel to the island in the Arctic Ocean."

"What am I looking for?"

"Something that can restore you to what you always should have been and reverse the curse."

"Are you referring to the Svalbard Islands?"

"I've been forbidden to say, but Seyanna will know the way." Vates glanced down at his own skin, and Jet gasped at what was happening. The oracle's white skin was turning the same color as the poisoned rocks.

"May Zodiac's sign point you in the right direction."

"What does that mean?"

Vates again stumbled to the ground, knee first. He mumbled, "Anesidora is eternally fastened, and only the golden key and the king's watchword will grant entrance."

"*Okay?*" Jet replied, extremely confused.

Vates fell to the ground. Lying on his back, he gazed up at the looming creature. "Goodbye, my friend. Bring Jet to the surface and help defeat Arisol." The oracle's eyes latched onto Jet's, but he died before he could say another word. The white, leather-skinned, oracle transformed into a green reptile. The same color began spreading throughout the room.

A frog-like tongue shot out and lifted Jet to a thicket of branches on Pincher's back. He was placed carefully onto the bark, and several vines attached to him and his backpack. The creature was adept at climbing and moved with precision and power. They were deep within the mountain, and it took some time for Pincher to make its way to the surface. They exited either before dawn or after sunset, Jet couldn't be sure. Pincher continued until he was next to a nearby lake and Jet was placed on the shore. Pincher snarled and the entire ground shook.

As the creature ran off a voice entered Jet's mind, and it was even more ancient than Vates's. Pincher said solemnly,

"Travel safe and heal well. I'm sure our paths will cross again."

"What?" Jet asked but as he glanced around, the land was empty. He dozed off. The next thing he knew, there were dozens of flashlights illuminating the ground around him.

"There's someone over here," yelled a voice in the distance.

"Maybe it's a survivor."

CHAPTER 14

ootsteps, flashlights, and fingers were the only things that Jet remembered with any certainty over the next few hours. Faces swam in his vision, but then he found himself dreaming of a purple moose, a bus crash, and a marching tree.

"He's in shock and dehydrated."

"Is he stable enough to travel?"

"*Sí*. But where?"

"Airport in Varela."

"*Realmente?*"

"*Sí*"

When Jet awoke again, he lay on a soft bed, with plush covers and a soft pillow. He wanted to sit up but still couldn't move. He spotted a small window but doubted he could be on a plane. "What's going on?" he hissed, his voice dry.

Steps approached, and Maria entered his vision.

"Am I strapped to his bed?" asked Jet fiercely, his heart racing.

"No."

"Am I here against my will?"

"I don't think so," the girl responded.

"I can't seem to move."

Relief spread across her face.

Before she could respond, Jet asked, "Where am I? What happened?"

"We found you two days ago by Rincon Lake on the opposite side of the mountain. Well, it's not much of a mountain anymore. You have a lot of damage to your body."

"Damage?"

Maria flushed. "I think you say bruises and cuts." She added, "You were very dehydrated, and you've been knocked out since we found you."

Jet saw a makeshift IV pole and some fluids going into his right arm. "Where are we?"

"We are in Peru."

"Peru?"

"We're on a private plane. We stopped for fuel. We'll leave soon and land in Mexico. Then we'll fly to California."

"Are you coming with me?"

Maria nodded slowly. "My new home."

"How did you guys' escape?"

She leaned in and whispered, "Alces carried us out the mouth of that underground place. Part of it crashed down by an earthquake. My town, except the area south of Abaucán river, was destroyed. The earthquake before we found you— the rest of the mountain fell."

"And your brother?"

Maria pointed to the front of the plane. "He's sitting up there with a friend."

"I can't move my head," Jet said.

Maria whispered, "There are around twenty people on the plane."

"Who are they?"

"Survivors of Catamarca, those with magical abilities. They have nowhere to go, and Jayco said they could come to California."

"Have you talked with him?"

"A little. They stayed around for a few days searching for you. There was no way to get back into the mountain. They had no choice but to go back home."

"Whose plane is this?"

"I think it's Jayco's. We found you a few days before the rest of us were leaving."

"Unbelievable." Jet closed her eyes.

"One of the other girls with us said that she felt that you were being...how do you say it in English, *tortura*?"

"Not sure."

"It means being attacked."

"Tortured."

"Yes. That's it." She reached up and pulled a television screen and positioned it toward Jet. "She felt that you were dying. She insisted that we go search for you. And we found you."

"I'm so glad you did!" He felt guilty about how things had turned out. "What about your uncle?"

"He died, as did some cousins. My parents left us there years ago. My uncle raised us."

"I'm sorry."

Maria nodded slowly.

Jet asked, "Does Jayco know I'm on the plane?"

"No. We're forbidden to call him or anyone else."

Feeling extremely exhausted, he lay his head back on the pillow. "Thanks again."

"Want to watch a movie?"

"Sure." Jet closed his eyes and fell immediately asleep.

# # #

Hands forcefully grabbed at Jet's ankles, arms, and his neck and pulled open his eyes. He felt groggy and too tired to move.

A male voice said, in relatively good English, "I am a doctor from Argentina. This is my patient. He was hiking in Argentina when he became lost in the jungle. He was found but is very sick. He is dehydrated and needs to get back to California."

Jet opened his eyes and found that his head had been positioned to the right. A dozen military individuals had boarded the plane and two stood over him. A man tried holding them back. The teenagers were facedown with guns pointed at their backs. Two more adults were kneeling, and a gun was in their faces.

The man again insisted. "The Americans are looking for their lost student. We are trying to get him home. He is sick."

"What about these other kids?"

"They are exchange students going to school in California from Argentina. Our town and the school have been working together for some years."

"Papers!" demanded an older, high-ranking official.

A woman in her thirties nodded to Maria, who carefully rose to her feet and moved to the back of the plane. Jet heard a compartment open, but he couldn't turn his head. Maria returned with a hand full of papers and handed them to the official. The man snatched the papers and shoved Maria to the ground. Everyone remained silent.

"So, Mr. Sosa, I have your passport and that of everyone on this plane. You say that you are going to America with this sick boy and these students, yet you have no backpacks, supplies, or any books for school."

"Those will be given upon arrival."

"What school are you headed to?"

"Chadwicks boarding school in Santa Barbara, California. Jan Fletcher is the headmistress. She will accept your phone call if you want." Mr. Sosa pulled a card from his pocket and handed it to him. Attached to the card was a white envelope that appeared to have coins in them.

"You think you can bribe me?"

"No, sir. This, however, is a token of our understanding."

"What do you mean?"

"Chadwicks has some advanced technology, and they found a sunken ship south of Cabo. The school will give you the coordinates, and you can claim the find."

"Why would they do this?"

"The school sends students around the world in search of missing things. They are very good at what they do. In the future they may want to stop at this airport again. They would appreciate your help in facilitating an easy trip."

"I will call them." The official strolled to the front of the plane and descended the steps. Ten minutes later he came back with a giant smile on his face. He demanded, "Let them go."

The other soldiers quickly exited the plane. The official strolled over to Mr. Sosa. "The headmistress was very generous. I think that this will work out nicely. Come again." The official appeared to have a spring in his step as he left the plane.

As the door closed, Mr. Sosa hissed, "Lock the door and get us out of here."

The airplane's engines started immediately, and a few minutes later, it took off. Jet wasn't sure what to think. Had the man really called the principal?

Jet was thirsty but still couldn't move. He tried lifting his arm, but it was useless. He thought he could feel a few fingers moving, but that was it.

"Maria," Jet roared.

The room was abuzz, and it took a few more times calling for Maria to appear.

"What just happened?" he asked as she repositioned his head.

"I guess Jayco had been expecting something like this. I don't know how he got us out of that mess. He's pretty amazing."

"Yes, he is," Jet said, feeling slightly annoyed. "I can't move on my own. Could you help me move to a chair?"

Maria stared at him sheepishly. "The doctor is afraid to move you."

"I don't care. I need to sit up." Jet tried as hard as he could to roll over, but nothing.

"Mr. Sosa," Maria said, "Jet wants to sit in a chair. Can you help?"

The man he'd seen moments ago talking with the official came over quickly. He said politely, "I'm not sure it is a good idea."

"I'm getting to a chair, one way or another," Jet said hotly. "Can you please help me not make a fool of myself?"

"If you start getting dizzy or vomit everywhere, it's not my fault."

Jet said, "Your accent is perfect."

"I went to school in Texas and med school in Maryland. I'm approved to practice medicine in the United States."

"Do you understand what is going on?" Jet asked.

"Well enough," he said, sharing a glance with Maria. "I've lived in Catamarca for the last five years. I was helping in southern Argentina when the explosion occurred outside of town. I never thought it was anything supernatural until the scientists and military showed up and started looking around."

"How do you know Maria?"

"The town is small, Mr. Jet, and I knew her uncle fairly well. I'm just sorry that I couldn't get him out in time."

Maria added, "Mr. Sosa's oldest daughter is just twelve, and she can move water with her mind. It is pretty cool to watch." Turning to Mr. Sosa, she said, "I told you the truth about what happened. Jet can do unbelievable things with water. He can help Catalina."

Mr. Sosa peered at Jet skeptically. "I don't see how."

"Be patient." Maria encouraged him. "Let's get Jet to one of the other seats."

"Fine," Mr. Sosa replied. "Hey, Sebastian. Can you and Mateo help me move Jet?"

Sebastian ran over, saying, "Jet. Glad to see you again. Are you okay?"

"Been better," Jet said quickly. "Good to see you."

It took Mr. Sosa, Sebastian, Mateo, and Maria to transfer Jet to one of the airplane seats. He didn't feel faint or sick, but he couldn't move a single limb. He was, however, able to keep his head up without any effort. It was good to be sitting up.

Mr. Sosa and Maria sat near Jet. Mr. Sosa asked, "What's the plan?"

"You tell me. I think I've been out of it for a few days. How did all this get set up?"

Maria and Mr. Sosa exchanged looks.

Jet asked, "What's up?"

"You've been missing for almost four weeks."

"What?" Jet said.

"I tried telling you when you first woke up. Jayco and the others left over three weeks ago. My brother and I have been living with Mr. Sosa and Catalina. Jayco sent us passports, papers, and this plane."

"Jayco did all of this?" questioned Jet.

"Yes," Maria said, partly blushing. "We didn't have any other choice but to think that you were dead. What really happened?"

Jet didn't want to tell them much of anything, especially not the truth. Instead, he said, "I got trapped under some rocks. I must've been knocked out for a while. When I woke up, it took a while to get free. I started moving around some rocks, but my body didn't seem to be working right. When I was able, I crawled out from where I was trapped. I found this crevice in the rock and made my way up. I slept a lot and had no idea what day it was. I found a few springs of water," he said quickly. "I somehow made it all the way up to the surface, I guess."

"That's amazing," Maria said quickly.

"It was lucky," Jet admitted. "My flashlight worked for the first half. I also had some granola bars and water in my backpack."

Maria nodded knowingly.

Mr. Sosa said, his face unreadable, "What was inside that mountain? What were you guys hoping to find?"

Maria kept her eyes glued to the side of Mr. Sosa's face.

Jet replied, "Something or someone caused a huge weather disturbance a few years ago. The same thing happened in the town where I was born. Come to find out, it has something to do with treasure and magic."

"Magic? Is that what you think Catalina can do?"

Jet spoke, "Agni," and the briefest flicker of light appeared. He was discouraged by his lack of strength. "Where's my backpack?"

Maria stood quickly and disappeared behind the table Jet had been lying on. When she came back into view, she carried his bag. She opened it so he had a direct view inside, and there were ten wrappers of granola bars and several empty bottles of water. He quickly spotted his tome and a white, folded cloth.

Mr. Sosa stood, gazing down at Jet. "Maria and Sebastian have each told me a little about what happened. They seem intent on keeping most of it a secret. I don't like being kept in the dark. You better have a plan when we arrive in California."

"I won't," Jet said stubbornly. "I've been missing for four weeks. I'm so weak right now that I can't move on my own."

Leaning down, nearly face-to-face with Jet, Mr. Sosa whispered, "And by the looks of it, you've had half your bones broken and healed and broken and healed again. And you tell a story of climbing out of your tomb."

Jet didn't trust himself to speak.

Mr. Sosa shook his head as if he had burst Jet's bubble. A moment later he vanished from view.

In a shocking move, Maria hugged Jet fiercely. She whispered, "Thank you for saving us." When she let go of him, he was sure that his face was bright red. She added, "Don't mind him. Watching your town getting destroyed was difficult. He is worried about Catalina. He didn't want to leave, but she made him."

"I understand," Jet mumbled. "Thanks for helping me sit up."

"Do you feel better?"

"Not really," Jet admitted. Shifting his eyes downward, he noticed that he had a wrap on his arm where the IV fluids had been administered. He tried moving his arms even the tiniest bit but failed.

Maria said, "Dr. Sosa didn't want to overload your system. If you need more fluids, he can easily reattach at the IV site."

"No worries. I'm good."

The plane touched down a few hours later, and Jet wasn't sure what his next step should be. He guessed he would wait for Maria to call Jayco and the others and tell them the news. His own cell phone was long gone. Fifteen minutes later the aircraft taxied to a private garage. The outer doors swung open, and the plane drove in. When the engine turned off, Maria was the first to exit the plane. She had told Jet that she was going to look for a wheelchair.

One by one the other passengers exited the plane. Just before Mr. Sosa left, he glanced back at Jet, shaking his head. A few minutes later, Jet heard the siren of an ambulance or maybe a police car, and he felt his stomach turn.

He thought he heard running outside the plane but wasn't positioned to look out the window.

"This can't be," a voice shouted, and Jet recognized the voice. Jayco continued, "How is this freaking possible?"

"Move over," Grantham said, "Are you sure it's Jet?"

"It's me, you idiots. Who else could it be?"

"Someone trying to punk us."

Grantham and Jayco came into view, both grinning and slapping each other on the backs. Grantham dove in first and hugged Jet.

"Ouch. You're killing me," replied Jet.

Grantham let go quickly but shook his head at the broad smile on Jet's face. "It's good to see both of you."

"Can't you walk?" Jayco asked.

"I can barely move." He asked, "What are you guys doing here?"

"Everyone came to help the Catamarca clan get settled. You risked your life to save us and them, and we had to help get them to America."

A voice sounded from the front of the plane. It was Mckenzey and she sounded hysterical. "Is it really Jet? Is he all right? What's taking so long?"

"He's fine," Grantham shouted.

"Then hurry up," she added.

"Let's not keep her waiting," Jayco said. "How are we going to move you?"

"Carry me," he suggested.

Grantham said, pointing at Jayco, "That's all you."

"Fine." Jayco bent down and lifted Jet.

As they walked toward the front of the plane, Grantham asked, "Ambulance or car?"

"We don't have a choice. Jet's going to need to go to the hospital."

"What if I don't want to."

"Not a choice."

"Why?"

"Bro. You essentially dying in Argentina was not a good look for us, the school, or anybody," Grantham explained. "This is going to be a circus."

Jayco added, "The school has been asking a lot of questions."

"About the trip?"

"Yes. Plus, Nana is pissed."

"How did she find out?"

"She stopped by campus to see you."

"What in the world is going on in there?" Mckenzey demanded. "Do I need to send in Seyanna and Latisha to get you boys out here?"

"We're coming," Grantham shouted.

They turned the corner, and Mckenzey came into view. Jet flinched. She was sitting in a wheelchair with a cast on her leg from hip to ankle. She had tears rolling down her face. Behind her stood Latisha and Seyanna, both crying.

Jet, trying to remain casual, said, "Hey everyone. Long time no see."

"Can't you walk?" Mckenzey asked. "What happened?"

"Where's the extra wheelchair?" Jayco demanded.

"Is he too heavy for you?" Grantham asked.

"No. But it would look bad if I carried him the entire way."

Seyanna wiped her nose and mouth. She added, "Maria is coming with it."

Jet couldn't stop staring at his friends. He was so happy and relieved to see them. He cringed on the inside when he saw the large cast on Mckenzey's leg. He asked, "What in the world happened?"

She replied, "I'm fine. I'll explain later."

Maria arrived with the wheelchair, and Jet was set down. Mckenzey rolled close and gave him a hug. Soon all his friends had swarmed around both wheelchairs.

Once the group separated, Grantham asked, "Who's pushing the resurrected boy?"

"Can't he push himself?" asked Seyanna.

"Nope. I got pretty messed up."

Mckenzey scowled. "Explain yourself."

"No time," Grantham said. "Looks like a media van is here."

"How do they know that Jet is back?"

Jayco began pushing Jet's wheelchair as Grantham pushed Mckenzey. The ambulance was parked with both back doors open, waiting for them. Jet asked, "What are you guys talking about?"

Grantham said, "When the news broke that you were missing, the school was in a lot of hot water about letting students go on a sponsored trip to Argentina to help the locals."

"Then the news reported that you died," Latisha added.

Jayco said, "Classes started, and you weren't there. Nana showed up a few days later and went straight to Principal Fletcher, and she came directly to us. Your disappearance became front-page news everywhere. An American disappearing in Argentina after a climbing accident. We were fortunate, though; one of the teachers stepped forward and said that our group had been working with him on trying to do humanitarian work in South America."

"Professor Rysen really saved our bacon," Seyanna said, clearly relieved. "He just asked for some basic details, like where exactly you had gone missing and stuff like that. He was a lifesaver."

"I bet," Jet said coolly. They had made it halfway to the ambulance.

Latisha added, "Principal Fletcher told the school board, and it became even a bigger deal. Nana has been around with Geb. Do you remember him?"

"How could I forget him."

"We were all questioned by the police and the school board. It was a disaster," Jayco said. "Now that you're back, the media is going to go crazy, again. We need to take you directly to the hospital in Santa Barbara, call the principal, and tell Nana."

CHAPTER 15

Two paramedics stood outside with a gurney waiting for Jet and the others. Just behind the ambulance sat a yellow school bus, and most of the people from the plane were getting on board.

Jet asked, "What's the plan here?"

"Just rolling along," Jayco admitted. "Your arrival throws an excellent wrinkle in the plan. Glad you made it home. We all were so worried."

Grantham said, "Why don't the boys and Latisha go with the Argentinians to the motel, as we arranged. The girls can go with Jet to the hospital."

"Good thought," Jayco said, and Jet noticed that everyone, even Mckenzey, waited for his response. "Yes," he finally said, "Splitting up will allow us to be the most productive. I'll call Nana and Principal Fletcher on the way to the motel."

Jet's wheelchair continued to the back of the ambulance.

The first paramedic asked, "What have we got here?"

Jayco yelled, "Check you guys later."

Seyanna said, frantically, "Jet is the missing hiker in Argentina. He has some injuries, and I don't think that he can walk."

The second paramedic asked, "The same kid from the news?"

The question came at the perfect time, as two news crews' vans came to a screeching stop near the entrance to the airport.

The first paramedic asked, "How are you doing? What kind of pain are we talking about?"

Jet replied, "It's been a few days since I've had anything to eat or drink. I'm pretty weak."

"Did you break anything?"

Jet heard the question but didn't respond right away. Suddenly he recalled the snapping of his legs. He managed to say, "Not sure."

"What about her?" The second paramedic pointed to Mckenzey.

Seyanna answered, "She broke her leg skiing back near Christmas. Can we ride in the back of the ambulance?"

"One can sit up front, and one can be in the back."

Mckenzey said quickly, "Help me up front. It'll be easier." Her hand squeezed his arm, but she didn't look at him.

Jet was transferred from his wheelchair to the gurney. He felt everything they touched, and it was often painful, but he still had no control over any muscle movement. It wasn't long before he was strapped down and inside the back of the ambulance. Soon they were driving off.

"You're going to get your fifteen minutes of fame," Seyanna said. "I can't believe I'm looking at you."

The paramedic said, "Your IV access is still good. Are you okay if I run another bag of saline?"

Unable to nod, Jet said, "Sure."

Seyanna continued, "The last few weeks have been so tough."

"What happened in Argentina?"

"They found footage of you on a camera at the hotel. Jayco and Grantham could barely be seen, but it was a clear picture of you. They've been playing that screenshot for days and days."

The paramedic added, "I've seen the video. Getting lost in Argentina, and everyone thought you died. I bet it was rough."

"It was," he muttered.

The paramedic asked, "Do you need any pain medications?"

"I don't think so."

"In the days after you went missing," Seyanna continued, "there were a thousand people who arrived in Catamarca to start searching for you. Jayco and Grantham were still there. The Argentinian military arrived and quarantined the area, refusing to allow anyone the ability to go into the mountains. This initiated a small political battle that, surprisingly for all, the Argentines won. A few fanatics tried to scale a fence that had been hastily built, and they were quickly caught and taken to jail."

"I had no idea."

From the front seat, Mckenzey added, "Reporters arrived, and they tried to put pressure on the government and the military. Nothing changed. Conspiracy theorists began saying that UFOs had arrived, or something even stranger."

Seyanna continued, "Around here, and nationwide, to have a missing student that both the United States and Argentina refused to go looking for was a front-page story. Now that you've survived, you're going to be interviewed repeatedly."

"Maybe I should go missing again."

"Good luck," Mckenzey said. "We're never letting you out of our sights again."

Jet was quiet for the next minute or so. He asked, "Have you seen Nana?"

Seyanna nodded. "She came by the first few days, then stopped. I think she was shook-up. She calls and asks if we've heard anything. I think she has mostly been talking with Jayco."

"Is she still in California?"

"I don't know."

Jet asked, "Have you started school yet?"

Seyanna glanced at him questioningly.

"Right," he said. "Jayco said school started up again. How's it going for you?"

"Strangely weird. I haven't been at a normal school for years. Half the time I want to get up and leave. It'll be good to have you back."

"I'm not sure when that will be. I'm so tired, and I can barely move."

"They'll fix that," the paramedic said, her voice kind. "Cottage Hospital has some of the best doctors around."

Jet groaned.

The paramedic asked, "What? You don't like Cottage?"

"It's not that," Jet said. "I broke my collarbone a few months ago while rock climbing at school. I had surgery at Cottage."

"It seems to me that you might need to reconsider your choices of activity," the paramedic said with a half-smile.

"What do you mean?" he asked.

"Broken bones after rock climbing and getting lost for three weeks while hiking. Either you're terrible at staying out of trouble in the outdoors or you have the worst luck ever."

"A little of both," he mumbled.

The rest of the ambulance ride was done in silence. As they drove into the emergency entrance, Jet noticed police cars and several other vehicles already blocking part of the entrance. The ambulance came to a stop, the back doors were opened, and people started yelling.

"Is that Joshua Black?"

"How did he get back into the US?"

"Who helped find him?"

Several news vans were positioned in the handicapped parking, and they tried moving to a position where they could get pictures of him.

The two paramedics expertly removed the gurney from the ambulance and pushed it into the main hospital.

Jet heard Principal Fletcher's voice say, "Joshua Black arrived back in California thirty minutes ago on a private airplane. A doctor was on board the flight to monitor him. Joshua is in good spirits and is thankful to those who helped search for him. Turns out, he was found in a different area than originally thought. He is dehydrated and…"

The rest of her words were cut off as they entered Cottage Hospital. Seyanna pushed Mckenzey.

Mckenzey said, "That was fast. Jayco must've called her right away. That was smooth, almost like it was planned."

They bypassed the ER and went directly to a room on the third floor. Jet thought that the girls were behind him for most of the time, but when they reached the third floor, he could only hear the two paramedics.

A female doctor, one that Jet recognized, was waiting in the hall. She said, "In here." She was the same doctor who had treated Trina Madden when she had been covered in a sunburn that turned out to have nothing to do with the sun.

"I'm Dr. Destiny Descartes, no relation to the French philosopher." She said this so casually, Jet knew that this was a common question for her. "You are Jet Black, a survivor of three weeks missing in Argentina. How do you feel?"

# # #

"Exhaustion" could not adequately describe what Jet felt. He was finally alone after two days of prodding and poking and every test imaginable. The questions had been relentless. A few hours ago, at the behest of Principal Fletcher, he had allowed two different camera crews to enter his room for a quick interview. He repeated the same story each time. It was also the same story he had told the countless doctors that had paraded into his room.

"We were in a cave with our guides near Catamarca. There was a rockslide, and I was separated from the rest of the group. I tried finding a way back and started moving rock. There must've been an earthquake or something. I was lucky to survive. It was dark, and trying to move that much rock was hard. I had some supplies such as food, water, a headlamp, and some other things."

At this point in the interview, Jet nodded to a torn-up backpack in his lap, with drops of dried blood, a broken zipper, and fabric tears. It still held *The Sorcerer's Guide*, the weapons, a golden rectangle, his three orbs, and the clear tablet piece wrapped up in a shirt. But Jet never let this item away from his bedside.

He continued, "Inside the cave, I lost track of time entirely and started to get pretty worried. At some point I was buried again by more rocks. I've no idea how long it took to dig myself out. It was clear that I needed to find a way out. I found a crevice and began climbing. Sometimes it got so narrow that I thought I was stuck.

I admit, there were a few times that I started to lose hope. It was dark all the time, and there were snakes, spiders, and a bunch more things. I ran out of food after several days, and I found some small pockets of water. I became more and more tired and slept for hours.

"I first noticed some light a few days before I made it out. It was faint, and I barely realized that it was light from the surface. At the end I barely had enough energy to crawl out of the crevice. It was dark, and I could see a small lake nearby. I had to drag myself, inch by inch, toward the water. I must've passed out. The next thing I knew, I was being saved."

# # #

When he awoke next, Nana sat next to the bed. She smiled, and Jet's entire mood improved. He couldn't remember a time when she looked happier. She burst into tears and came over and hugged him.

"Good to see you too, Nana!"

"You scared this old lady. What were you thinking?"

His grandmother refused to call him anything but Joshua or Joshy. It wasn't that she hated the name Jet, but she wouldn't change her mind.

He wheezed, "How long have you been here?"

"Ever since Jayco called me, saying that you were safe. They wouldn't let me see you until this morning."

"What day is it?"

"Wednesday."

"Has school started?" asked Jet.

"Last week."

"How long have I been in the hospital?"

"Three nights and four days. You look different."

He tried sitting up but the weight on his chest was astronomical. He registered what Nana had said, and asked, "What do you mean?"

"You lost a lot of weight, but your eyes are different, shadowed almost. Dr. Descartes said that all your scans came back normal. No broken bones or other injuries. She thinks that another few days, and you wouldn't have made it."

"I'm so tired. Why can't I move?"

"The doctor thinks that you suffered a trauma. She wants to remain in the hospital for a few weeks."

"A few weeks?"

"She has your best interests in mind."

"Have you seen Mckenzey and the others?"

"I saw them in the waiting room last night. The hospital and the school won't let them come up during the day."

"Any other problems?" asked Jet.

Nana shifted her head, almost imperceptibly. "Nope. Just worried about you." She added quickly, "There are so many *strange* people that come in and out of your room. I'm not used to so many people, compared to Portland."

Jet caught himself immediately. Nana had emphasized the word "strange". This was code that they couldn't talk about anything meaningful. He forced out a wheezy laugh. "California can be so busy."

"Are you hungry?"

He replied, "My mouth is dry."

Nana stood quickly. "I'll get you a drink." She walked out of his view and yelled down the hall, "My grandson is awake. Can someone get him a drink?"

Suddenly, two nurses and Dr. Descartes bustled into the room. His monitors were checked, and an EKG was performed. They pulled open his mouth and shone a light in both eyes. They propped him up, and he was bombarded with questions about how he was feeling and what parts of his body he could move—which was none.

One of the nurses reached for his backpack, placed between his legs while he was sleeping. Jet yelled, "Nana, can hold on to that. It saved my life. I'm going to keep that thing forever."

"Sure thing."

Dr. Descartes glanced at Jet and back at Nana. A third nurse came into the room with a glass of water and a straw. Nana helped position it so that he could drink.

Dr. Descartes's authoritative voice said, "Dinner is in a few hours. Your grandmother or one of my nurses can help you eat."

"Okay."

Dr. Descartes announced, "Before the food arrives though, you'll need to take a bath."

"How?" Nana asked. "He can't move."

She said, reassuringly, "We can wheel him into a seated bath and fill it with water. He can soak there for as long as he needs to. It will do him some good."

Jet remained in the elaborate medical bath for well over an hour. The nurse wheeled him in, and after he was undressed, the water slowly moved up to the right height. Some buttons could be pushed to start the jets and plenty of soothing music. The bad part, the older female nurse couldn't leave. If he slid in, he didn't have the strength to get out. She remained far enough back to give him some privacy, and he had a lot to think about. Vates, his pending death, and the loss of the three orbs were shocking enough. But finding an actual tablet piece after Faunal had violated some sort of agreement was significant. But what concerned Jet the most was his own health. The Hoyuk had affected both his mind and his body. He wasn't sure he was ever going to recover.

Dr. Descartes was waiting for him when he returned to his room. Nana sat in the corner, and there were two other doctors in white lab coats. Dr. Descartes said, "We've been studying the scans of your bones and have noticed a few unusual things."

"Like what?"

"You are healthy, but you've lost a lot of weight and muscle mass. But that doesn't explain why you can't move. We ran a DEXA scan and found something unexplainable."

Nana asked, "What's a DEXA scan?"

"It can be used to detect weak or brittle bones. It can help predict risk of future fractures."

"I'm confused," Jet said slowly.

"Your scan that almost your entire skeletal system is trying to recover. You're regenerating most of your bone cells."

"Is that why I'm so tired?" asked Jet.

"Partially," the female doctor replied. "It's likely that you damaged most of your bones and your body is trying to recover."

"Wouldn't broken bones be seen on X-rays?" Nana asked.

"Normally. But I don't think that there's anything normal about what's happening to Jet. Can you explain?"

Jet was back in his bed, lying down, hoping his face didn't reveal anything. He asked, "Like what?"

"No one on my team has seen anything like this before."

"I told you what happened."

"Did you? Can you?" Dr. Descartes walked to the edge of his bed. Glancing at the two other men in the room, she said, "This is Dr. Cummings. He specializes in hypnotherapy, and we would like to try a form of psychotherapy that uses relaxation and extreme concentration to achieve a state of consciousness."

Nana said quickly, "Why do you think Joshua needs this?"

"I think he might have experienced some sort of extreme trauma and may be unconsciously blocking what really happened. Nasty chemicals or an extreme change in pressure might explain his condition. We need to understand what really happened."

"Is that necessary?" Nana stood, almost protecting Jet.

"As his doctor, I am aiming to provide Jet the best treatment available. Hypnotherapy has allowed breakthroughs in trauma patients. This is a wonderful option."

Nana considered the statement. She made furtive glances at Jet.

"Honestly, I'm good," replied Jet. "I appreciate the option of hypnotherapy, but if I've forgotten some trauma or a fall or even a spider bite, I don't think that I want to relive it again. I'm just happy to be alive."

"Your future self might disagree." Dr. Cummings spoke for the first time. "You see, trauma like yours doesn't manifest for weeks, months, and years. You can't walk now, and your body may be slow in healing during that process. But suddenly, weeks later, what happens if you can't sleep, or your dreams overwhelm you? Down the road, you might be needlessly suffering."

Nana asked, "If Joshua agrees, when would we start? How soon could he start walking again?"

Dr. Descartes said, "We could start as soon as tomorrow. But really, we need to know what we are dealing with. I'm positive that we will figure this out."

Nana spun toward Jet. "This sounds like a good option to me. We should strongly consider it."

"If you say so, Nana," Jet said. "But for now, I'm dead tired. Can I get some sleep?"

Nana place a hand on Jet's leg. "Okay. I'll be here first thing in the morning." Turning to Dr. Descartes and Dr. Cummings, she said, "Will this really help Joshua get better?"

"I promise," Dr. Cummings said. "We will do everything in our power to make sure he gets better."

CHAPTER 16

Strong hands wrapped around Jet's mouth, preventing him from breathing or opening his mouth. His eyes flew open, and he stared into the face of a masked man. His hospital room was dark, and he couldn't see clearly who was attacking him. The man wore a black shirt, pants, and a black ski mask. Now it was partially pulled up, revealing a face. It was Geb.

"Stay calm," Geb hissed into his ear. "We're trying to help you."

Jet screamed but the sound he made was that of a masked mummy.

Geb motioned at someone near the door. He said, "Can you come calm him? He should've seen your face first. He's making too much noise."

A figure dressed like Geb stepped closer and pulled up their mask. It was an older woman. The hand released its pressure from his mouth.

"Nana? Is that you?"

"Joshua, relax!" She smiled.

"What are you guys doing?"

Geb said, "We need to get you out of the hospital and back to school."

"You're breaking me out of the hospital?"

Nana's voice was much more urgent. "And we need to leave right now."

A third figure stepped into the room. With a Spanish accent, the girl said, "Okay. The charge nurse and the assistant are asleep. We can go now."

"Is that Maria? What's she doing here?"

Geb lifted Jet as Nana pulled a wheelchair close to his bed. He said, "Your friends are being watched and couldn't make it tonight. Maria has a talent with her voice causing the susceptible to sleep. It's just the three of us."

Nana grabbed his backpack and placed it on his lap. Then she started hurrying around the room, gathering the rest of his items.

"How can I know that it's really you?"

Geb replied, "We don't have time to discuss this right now."

"When I was younger, what color was the liquid you had me drink? What type of juice did you put it in?"

"What type of question is that?" asked Nana, as she poked her head in from the bathroom.

Geb's back stiffened, and the look on his face was that of someone getting caught in the act of doing something he shouldn't have. After a small pause, Geb replied, "Light green. Orange juice."

"We can go now."

"What was that about?" asked Nana as she and Geb lowered their ski masks.

"I'll tell you later,"

"Shhh," Maria hissed.

A door on the far wall opened softly, as if someone was trying to hide their movements.

Nana placed a full Halloween mask over Jet's head. He could see through the slits in the mask, but barely. He thought he wore an older man's face. He was pushed forward silently. They turned right and continued down the corridor.

From ahead he heard Maria's voice. "The staff elevator is not working."

"Where to now?" asked Nana.

"There's a small elevator in the supply room. I think it goes directly to the basement. From there we can make it over to the parking lot."

"Are you sure?" asked Nana, clearly nervous.

"We will only need to carry Jet up two floors."

"Where's the supply room?"

"Three doors down on the right."

Jet was able to only see directly ahead of the group. He watched as Maria sprinted forward, opening the door. She didn't turn on the light, and soon he was backed into the room. Maria kept the door open slightly. Jet asked, "Why are we doing this?"

"The Azurites are coming for you," Geb said. "You need to get back to the school as soon as possible."

"Who are the Azurites?"

Geb spoke quickly as he hit the button for the supply elevator. "I don't know how you know about the orange juice. When you were young, the Brotherhood sent me to work with your parents. I became friends with them. The four of us were on a bus…"

"We don't have time for this," Nana hissed.

The elevator chimed behind him.

Geb continued, "The Azurites came for you and your parents."

"How do you know this?" asked Nana.

Another chime of the elevator sounded as Geb's head fixated on Jet.

Before anyone could say anything, Maria whispered, "Three men are heading in this direction. I think they heard the elevator." She closed the door and stepped toward them.

"You guys need to go." Geb traded places with Maria. "I'll distract them."

Nana said quickly, "No. We need your help. How are we going to carry Jet?"

Geb smiled mischievously as if he were going to do something reckless. "I'll be down there soon enough."

The elevator door opened, and Nana pulled Jet into the elevator. The handle on the outer door began to turn. It was clear that Geb wasn't ready to fight, and there was no way he was going to win.

Jet spoke, "Ignisnaeth," and just like in the museum in Switzerland, a fireball shot from him and connected with the outer door, just as it was starting to open. The energy pull was too overwhelming, and the corners of his vision became dark, and he fell unconscious.

# # #

The next thing that registered in Jet's mind was the chime of an elevator. Opening his eyes, he found himself at the front door of his dorm, back on campus. Ahead of him Geb knocked on his door three times. When the door opened, he saw both of his roommates staring back at him, smiles unfolding across their faces.

Rick said, "Welcome home."

"But hurry up inside," Jackson countered.

Jet was led into his dorm by Nana, followed by Geb. "Where's Maria?" he asked, his voice distant and weak.

Geb insisted, "She got a ride back to the hotel. She's safe."

Jet said, "Into the entertainment room, please."

"Why?" Nana asked.

"I need answers," Jet said calmly.

"Can't this wait until tomorrow?" Geb asked. "It's two in the morning."

"You guys decided when to break me out. I won't be able to sleep until I understand what's really going on."

Rick and Jackson waved their hands, saying, "We're off to bed."

"Don't dream of it," Jet said hotly. "I have plenty of questions for you."

Geb said, "You might not want them hearing everything."

Rick nodded.

"I'll start with them."

After everyone was settled, including Nana, Jet asked, "What's going on? What has Shane been up to?"

"Honestly," Jackson said, "We don't have a clue. I don't think he went home during Christmas. He has been spending a lot of time at the perimeter of the school. Raul, Ariana, and a bunch more students have been helping him."

Jet's eyes bore into Geb and Nana. "Do you guys understand why Shane would be acting in this way?"

"Is Shane the kid from the museum in Switzerland?" Geb asked.

"Yes." Jet remembered back to when Geb had crashed into Shane on purpose to give him and Mckenzey a few more minutes as they switched out a fake box for the real one on display.

"All right," Geb continued. "He knows Runic magic and is likely in possession of the second book. It's called *The Mage's Letters.*"

"I know the name of his book."

"I can't guess why he would be at the perimeter of the school or what he's doing. But you must understand that this school is special. There are five schools total that were designed to teach magic. Each of them is in the United States."

Jet said, "Dillon Lake in New York. Others in Connecticut, Florida, and Texas."

"Good. You've heard of these," said Geb.

Jackson said, "I didn't know that."

Ignoring this, Jet asked, "What is so special about the schools?"

"I don't know everything," Geb explained. "But your energy was being drained slowly at the hospital. You would have only gotten worse. The school should allow you to start to heal."

"Will I ever be back to normal?"

Sharing a glance with Nana, he said, "That depends on what happened in Argentina."

Rick and Jackson leaned closer.

Jet said, "I really was buried by a lot of rock. I have no idea how long I was trapped. It was like I was being tortured under all that weight. Just to move a few inches took so much energy. When I finally got free, it took forever to find a way out."

"You will probably get back to normal." Geb cleared his throat. "About Shane, I think he's trying to protect the school for some reason."

"Protect the school?" Rick asked. "That doesn't seem like his personality."

"Just my guess."

Jet asked Rick and Jackson, "What has been going on since I left?"

Jackson let out a long whistle. "When we learned that you had died, though, we're glad that you didn't, things started to fall apart. Grantham and Jayco got into this huge fight. Grantham almost quit school. Jayco took control of the group and used Seyanna, Keesha, Rick, and me to start working on some things."

"Like what?"

Rick continued, "Jayco gave me a list of students that went to Silverton and Chadwicks. I met and talked with them. If they were friends with Shane, I reported back what I learned."

"Why?"

"Jayco thinks that those from Silverton might have magic abilities, like Jackson, Keesha, and me," explained Rick.

"What did you find out?"

"Most of them wanted nothing to do with Shane. There's a girl, Trina Madden, who meets with Shane a lot." Jackson asked, "Do you remember her?"

"I do."

"She's definitely spying for Shane. She also has a few friends from Silverton helping her."

"Spying on what?"

"They've been watching the science building very closely."

"Oh crap," Jet said, and he rubbed his forehead. He was starting to get a massive headache.

"How did Jayco get a plane?"

Rick answered, "Believe it or not, he has a talent for finding treasure in the ocean."

"What are you talking about?" Nana asked.

Jet said, "Jayco and the rest of us have magical abilities. He can swim underwater for a long time."

"He has found so much money in the ocean," stated Jackson.

"At first he was finding rings, watches, sunglasses, and everyday items lost to swimmers and snorkelers along the California coastline," added Rick. "He told us that he's been doing this since you guys came back from Silverton. It clears his mind."

"And?" Jet questioned.

"He says he found some treasure from lost ships," Rick said, trying to remain casual.

"That makes more sense," Jet said, remembering what Mr. Sosa had told the men on the plane. "How did Grantham and Jayco resolve their issues?"

"I think it was Grantham's idea to help the kids from the town in Argentina. Jayco gave him the go-ahead to get things arranged."

"Good thinking." Jet pondered the responses from his roommate. Jayco had taken charge of the Echoes. The uneasiness in his stomach returned. Pushing down his own insecurities, Jet added, "Thanks, guys. I think that's everything."

Rick said, "Glad to see you bro. Things haven't been the same around here without you."

"Good to see you too."

After his roommates had left the room, Jet said, "Geb. Just one question. What was the tonic that you gave me?"

Nana asked, "What tonic? When?"

Geb leaned back into the couch and considered what he should say. "Years ago I was sent out by the Brotherhood to search for someone near Silverton who might have found a cave. Despite the lack of magic, the Brotherhood has a part to play in Arisol, Elemental magic, and most of your initial items. I found your parents and learned that they were searching for the two magical books, the one that you have and the one that Shane has. When I met them, I didn't know that they had found one of the books already."

"Okay," Jet said.

"There were six families that were being considered as protectors. Each of them had knowledge of the Brotherhood and had met someone who helped them along the path."

"The path to what?" Nana asked.

"The path for the Brotherhood to become the mentor of the next Mikado."

"They want to help Jet?" asked Nana.

Geb nodded. "They want to help shape the fight against Arisol. It's a noble cause, but there's a fair number of politics involved, and not everyone thinks we should be so involved. Regardless, the Brotherhood sent me and five others to instruct and help the families. About a year after I arrived, I received a transmission that they had chosen a boy from Los Angeles who was attending school at Dillon Lake."

"Shane," Jet said harshly.

"Yes. When your parents found out, they began to worry what would happen to you. You probably knew more than any other boy or girl around. They'd spoken German with you and had a few items already. Plus, the cave outside of Silverton. They felt you were in danger."

Nana asked, "From the Brotherhood?"

"Maybe. But I think more from the Azurites. If they found Jet, they could learn secrets and even hurt you."

"But why the tonic?"

"Three of the other kids were killed within a month of each other. They had let slip that they knew about magic and precious items. Your parents didn't want that. In fact, I didn't want that."

"You gave my grandson a tonic? What did it do?"

"It essentially erased magic from his mind. It trapped the thoughts of magic, and anything related. Several Azurites watched you, Jet, after your parents died. They noticed nothing, and soon you were nothing but a distant memory. It saved your life."

"But magic slipped through when Silverton was destroyed."

"Elemental magic is very powerful. It helped save you, but I bet you forgot about it after that."

"I did," Jet agreed. "A few months ago, I was attacked by a creature. It searched my memories and released my magic abilities."

Geb said calmly, "I would've never thought that possible. I was told that tonic was unbreakable."

"Good thing it wasn't."

"Maybe," Geb said. "I'm not sure you're strong enough to beat Shane and the Azurites."

"I'm not alone."

"You're going to need more than just your friends. To win, you'll need the Brotherhood."

Jet exploded. "I knew you were going to say that."

"The Brotherhood will help. But for now, you need to remain at school and regain your strength."

"How long is that going to take?"

"My guess, a year or more."

CHAPTER 17

A compulsion overcame Jet as he lay comfortably in his bed, staring at the ceiling, feeling better than he had felt since he escaped Coso Subtrano. He had slept for twelve hours, and it was almost three in the afternoon. When the overwhelming sensation first started, Jet feared that he would end up lying there all day, unable to move, with this gnawing feeling pressing down upon him. He was shocked when his arm moved slowly to where his bag had been placed. With some effort, he unzipped the opening and pulled out *The Sorcerer's Guide*. As he held it up, the next page, page 10, turned, and the indiscriminate face of Wier stared back at him.

"Welcome back, Mikado." His voice still held a musical quality, and it was deep and enthralling.

A few pages ago, he had learned that Wier was a spirit of sorts that was sent into his book to combat the dispelling of misinformation and to be his mentor. The face of Wier was a nondescript image, like an inkblot seen in psychiatry, as much a blob as a face. It moved when he spoke.

"Deception and duplicity have been on a rampage, and to my senses, it has been jarring. What, you ask, is Wier of the Hearthstone Plains referring to? The fact is simple. Someone or something has been let into my pages. They found a way around the barriers meant to keep this tome safe. It was impossible for them to change the spells, the incantations, the messages. Instead, they were bold and placed a single page that added information rather than changed the message. In doing so, I was ruined for weeks, searching for the intruder. You can thank my genius for correcting the problem. All is back to normal.

"That page had two purposes. The first, to discourage you. The second, far more dangerous, was to prevent this tome from ever opening again. Over the next few pages, you will learn about Mimics, Allies, some Enemies, and Protection. Do not get overconfident, especially with the vulnerability that now runs through your veins. I can sense that you have suffered far more than what is acceptable. In your current state, you could never defeat Arisol and his allies. We must modify our expectations and alter the trajectory of your progression. You are not currently competent or qualified to be the Mikado."

Jet was shocked at the frankness of the tome. Wier had previously only given preplanned explanations. He wondered if the being inside the book could really sense Jet's loss.

His eyes were drawn to the opposite page. Creatures of all shapes and forms began to appear and disappear on the page. They would flash into existence in one second and vanish a moment later. He watched as a wingless dragon exploded onto the page, followed by a snake with wings, and he even noticed a silver deer and other flying creatures. Many of the other animals he didn't recognize.

The lettering that appeared on the page was larger than on any previous page:

Mimics

The Magic of the Elements and Runes is far from simple. While we scarcely understand how to wield its power, we often fail to remember that magic is not born in our bodies but given as a gift. The Original bestowers are shrouded in confusion, and their intentions are far from known. Undeniably, there are legions of those who seek to control the sorcery.

Not all enchantments are well understood. Mimicry is an area where the purpose is far more hidden than revealed. Over the centuries nobles, peasants, and kings alike have witnessed the most bewildering reaction to a death. As seldom as a complete alignment of the planets, when a conscript creature or a human dies in certain circumstances, their bodies can be returned to their normal appearance but with a different energy and conscience. This creature is no longer who they were before, and they become a Mimic.

Two thousand years ago, the beloved commander of the Ralshbistine Army died in battle by a beheading from a bewitched sword by a rebellious servant. The commander's name was Langsuir. Two days later he reappeared as a cruel and deadly dictator and found a way to kill the entire army. It was believed that he was converted into a death omen spirit.

Prior to this experience, only 6 known creatures had ever been mimicked. Each of them came back as a kinder and more friendly version of themselves.

The wizardry surrounding the Mimic has thus changed, and now in most situations, the good becomes bad, and the bad becomes worse. Since the death of Langsuir, there have been 14 cases of Mimicry, and all but one of the vessels became eviler and more depraved than they were before they died. It is believed that Lucretius the Avad, was created in the likeness of Erpofalco, but became something different. He has a specific purpose to fulfill along the path of the Phoenix.

It is doubtful that Arisol created the Avad, but it was drawn to the demon and pledged its alliance, and therefore it guarded the Thrantos Grotto. That creature was powerful and constructed for a specific purpose—to guard the doors of the Grotto and the Phoenix.

The cause for concern is that Mimicry magic is evolving. It is no longer a random circumstance that allows for the magic to be effective but has become a deliberate decision to unhinge the balance. Chaos has greater control than ever before. Arisol is unlikely to be behind the changes, but he has undoubtedly benefited the most. Beware of the Mimics.

More Allies and Enemies to follow.

Hatred for this page swelled in Jet from the very instant the writing became visible. It was as if the words were revealed in a spirit of corruption, evil, and shady deals. The first thought entering his mind was that this tome had indeed been corrupted. He noticed the moment he stopped reading the words, the feeling went away.

In that precise moment, Wier's voice filled the air. "Don't be foolish. Mimic magic is not unholy, but it leaves an atmosphere of distrust whenever the words on this topic are spoken or read. Over the years this sensation has worsened, as if someone has poisoned the magic. Do not fear that this has anything to do with the deception and duplicity that were placed inside this tome. A thorough search has found that this tome is now without dishonesty."

As Jet clutched the tome, he did not feel comforted by Wier's words. Closing the cover, he found that his energy had been spent. Reaching down, he tucked the tome under his bed and quickly fell asleep.

CHAPTER 18

ana stopped by the next day with some soup, and they sat and talked. It was good to see that she had been safe and sound after leaving Portland and running off to Canada. They talked and laughed and regained a measure of comfort between them. After she left, he watched a movie on Netflix on his computer, alone in his room. As the sun started to drop, a cool sensation trickled down the back of Jet's neck as if he'd just finished showering at the same time the air-conditioner kicked on. Turning back to his tome, he was hesitant about what he was going to find.

As the next page turned, a phrase appeared:

"Say these words aloud: Benhi Visionaeth."

Jet wasn't sure he really wanted to continue. He felt indecisive, but the disagreeable feeling from before had almost vanished. The intensity of the compulsion heightened until he spoke the words out loud.

"Benhi Visionaeth."

The light in his dorm faded away, just like some of the other visions he'd seen. Jet was propelled headfirst into the tome, landing on the streets of a busy city. The year must've been more than fifty years ago, but the skyscrapers and busyness of the roads were noticeable. He strongly believed he was standing in New York and thought he could see Central Park between two buildings more than two blocks away.

The sounds, smells, and air felt different from his present day, or maybe it was just the city. He soaked in the old cars, clothing, and the bearing of each person walking past him. Some were dressed as if they were going to church, yet many others were headed in the direction of Central Park. He caught snatches of conversations but was unsure what anyone was saying. It was as if he wasn't being allowed to hear their words. He jumped out of the way of a hoard of young boys and girls about his age scurrying past, searching for something fun to do. They chatted to each other in loud voices.

Everything changed with the next voice he heard, the words were unmistakable. "What makes you think I'm going to continue to follow the orders from the Brotherhood?"

Spinning around, Jet spotted a burly man, in his mid-twenties, with a long black coat and a suit. He wore a noticeable black hat that seemed to be part of men's fashion as several men wore something similar. There was a glow about this man and the one standing next to him.

"They have picked our family for a reason."

"There's no way this is a good thing."

A smaller and thinner man, almost wiry, replied, "Keep your voice down. You never know who's listening to our conversation."

"Do you think that people just sulk around trying to gather information?" the burly man asked.

"You mean, like the fact that your sister has gone missing?"

The burly man stopped in his tracks. "How could you possibly know that?"

"You talk too loudly when you've had a few drinks, especially at McSorley's."

"I never…"

"Don't lie to me, Lester." The wiry man shoved a finger into the chest of the burly man. "My father is not happy with your family, and I don't think Grandfather is either. You need to be more careful."

"Relax," Lester said. "Why don't we head inside for this special meeting. The others are probably waiting."

"I don't trust a single one of them."

"Do we have a choice?" Lester asked. "They are family, after all."

"Right. Grandfather Middlesex has decided to start a bunch of schools because the Brotherhood told him how important it was."

Lester shrugged, and he and the wiry man walked another two blocks, turning right into an alley. Jet followed, quite sure that he couldn't be seen. At the end of the passage, Lester stepped into an Italian restaurant called Vinny's. Jet caught up just as the door closed.

"Lester," a voice shouted from the third table inside the door. "Cutting it close enough?"

"No problem, Cousin Johnny. We're fine, thanks for asking. I ran into Ricky just before getting here."

As Ricky stepped into the building, Lester touched his shoulder and said, "Family is family, don't forget. And if your dad is here, this could turn out good for you."

"Don't be tricked like the rest of them," Ricky said, admonishing him. "I trust my dad least of all." The boy continued to the far side of the room, hugging a man that closely resembled Ricky. The man kept a tight gaze on Lester but said nothing.

There were nearly twenty people in the restaurant, and five tables were placed next to each other. A sixth, smaller table was tucked into an alcove near the front, and someone sat at the table, smoking a cigar and watching the group. Unfortunately, Jet couldn't get a good look at who it was.

The aroma of the restaurant was so mind-boggling that Jet made a mental note to travel to Italy as soon as possible.

At the far table with Ricky and his father was another younger boy that kept to himself. That was when Jet noticed that only men were in the room. Lester took a seat at the table closest to the door, next to an older man. The other three tables had more than four people each.

The person in the alcove shifted purposefully, and the entire room fell silent. The same man clapped his hands, and eight servants streamed in from the kitchen with platters of food, salads, and drinks. Besides these men, the entire restaurant was empty, and all the curtains had been tightly closed.

Once the food was placed and the servants had disappeared, the man in the alcove stepped forward. He was tall and in his eighties. He was dressed in a blue suit and used a cane. He had gray hair, tanned skin, and a complex-appearing face, as if he knew more than the rest in the room and doubled their experience. He was easily the tallest man at nearly six-feet-eight.

"Lock the door," the older man said.

Jet had been mostly right. Two ginormous men, nearly the same height as the older man, stepped from a hidden area, locking the kitchen door and standing as sentinels.

Bodyguards? Jet thought to himself

The older man continued, his voice booming, "Sons and grandsons. We are on the precipice of a new world, and high standards of trust, secrecy, determination, skill, and a bit of Irish luck. Our time is limited, but feel free to eat."

Ricky's father stood and saluted. "Thank you, father, for inviting us."

The gray-haired man nodded at his oldest son, who sat and began eating.

A second man, previously unseen, stepped out from the same hidden area as the bodyguards had and made his way to the front of the restaurant. This man was far shorter, and his skin was bronze, and Jet guessed he was from somewhere in the Mediterranean.

The gray-haired man said, his voice commanding, "This is Christos Filo from Greece and the American representative of the Brotherhood."

Christos's pale blue eyes took in each man in the room. He came to stand next to the older man, who began speaking. "I, Karl Middlesex, do commence this Council of the Eonian and acknowledge Christos Filo as the Brotherhood's mouthpiece. He has assured me that magic will be reawakened, and we will play a role in its instruction."

"Here! Here!" shouted the men.

Christos said, his English proper and well enunciated, "The Brotherhood gives glad tidings to the Middlesex family. We commend you for your willingness to serve as our diplomats in this undertaking. We've provided enough money and the talismans to ensure future success."

Ricky's dad asked eagerly, "What type of talismans are we talking about?"

Mr. Middlesex silenced his son with a glance.

Christos continued, "As you may know, the Azurites recently tried to steal these valuables as they were shipped from England to Boston, the location for our initial meeting.

We were forced to change locations. We have spoken with the Müller family, and they have told the Azurites to stand down. But I don't trust that they won't try to stop you in the future. Once the talismans have been put in place, our scholars insist that they can never be removed again. Choose the locations wisely." Christos gave a half bend at the waist, as if he was bowing. He stepped five feet away from the elder Middlesex and surveyed the room, as if on alert.

Jet remembered Geb mentioned the Azurites last night.

Mr. Middlesex boasted. "I was gifted with three sons and two daughters. My two daughters have chosen wisely, and I now have two new sons." Pointing to the far table, he continued, "My youngest son, Dexter Middlesex, and his son Lester will travel to California and choose a location for their school."

There was jeering and laughter from the other tables. Dexter appeared to wilt slightly at the laughter, but only for a split second. "Thank you, father, for this blessing."

Pointing to the second table, he said, "Dicky Dart, my youngest daughter's husband, and his three sons will be sent to Texas."

There was less laughter than with Dexter, and Dicky nodded without a reply.

Pointing at the middle table, he added, "My eldest daughters' husband, Stanley Bishop, and their children will be assigned to Florida."

Stanley stood. "You will not be disappointed."

Ricky's father hissed, "Kiss-up."

The Elder Middlesex added, "Bernard, my middle son, and his three sons will supervise the school in Connecticut, and Kenneth, my eldest, will direct the school in New York."

In a soft but confident voice, Bernard replied, "Our school will become one of the top high schools in the country."

Kenneth added, "Second to Dillon Lake."

Elder Middlesex laughed. "I should've known that you would already have a name."

"It pays to be informed," Kenneth said, glancing at Dexter and Lester from across the room.

Christos Filo promptly strode toward the same doors the servants had gone through and where the bodyguards stood. For the first time, Jet noticed five small tables with an item on each table, covered by a cloth. Quickly the fabric was removed from each item.

"These are the Maleficis talismans."

A statue of sorts, two feet tall, stood on each table. None of them were exactly the same, but at the base of each sculpture were five slender columns of the same thickness, and each column was represented by a different color: gold, black, silver, brown, and white. As the columns traveled upward, this was where the changes occurred. The columns twisted and turned and created breathtaking pieces of art.

Christos continued, "These talismans must be arranged on location in the next four weeks. Each tenant will be accompanied by a member of the Brotherhood who will remain at the school until they die. There will be routine inspections to ensure the school is preparing for when magic returns."

Kenneth asked, "Will we have an opportunity to learn magic?"

"The Brotherhood is uncertain when the time will come, but we are on the cusp of a revolutionary change in history, and the Middlesex family will forever be known as its pioneers."

Bernard asked, "What is the purpose of the talisman?"

Christos returned to stand next to Karl Middlesex. "What I will tell you is one of the most tightly guarded secrets of the Brotherhood. Our scholars have confirmed that a creature, a demon, will one day leave a hidden prison intending to destroy the world. Two decades ago an ancient artifact was found that originally helped to put the demon in his prison. As a result, it was broken into six pieces. Somehow, those pieces were hidden around the world. Other artifacts were found, including books, clothing, treasures, and much more. It took over ten years to collect these talismans. Magic will be essential in finding those hidden pieces and stopping the monster. Whoever controls the demon will control the world, and the tablet pieces are the tools in controlling the beast. Don't be overzealous and think that magic alone will save you. The talismans will help create and protect a school that will allow the development of magical talents. The Azurites, our enemies, want to stop the creation of the schools."

The youngest brother, Dexter, cleared his voice. "Is that why you have been watching my family so closely? Do you think we're helping the Azurites? Have we lost favor with you, father?"

With distaste in his voice, Karl Middlesex said, "You know the Müller family better than any of us. Rebecca is a distant cousin, and despite my protests, you married her. I warned you that they were not to be trusted."

"Rebecca does not stand with her family. They've been detached since even before she was born. She has no part in this."

Christos added, "The Müllers and the Azurites deceived many in the Brotherhood to leave us and join their ranks. Your father wonders if Rebecca could have been sent as a spy. The Azurites will do whatever it takes to stop us from achieving what we want to."

"Had I another son," Karl Middlesex blurted, "we would not require your involvement in creating these schools, but without you, I have been warned that we cannot succeed."

Nearly shaking with anger, Dexter hissed, "Rebecca did not join the Azurites. She was kidnapped by them."

Kenneth demanded, "Then why is your daughter, Josephine, trying to locate Galron, the Azurite healer?"

"She isn't," Lester said defiantly as he stood next to his father. The glow from when Jet had first seen him resurfaced. "I faked drunkenness during my time at McSorley's to see who was listening. I was not disappointed."

"Doubtful," Kenneth replied. "She was spotted in Pakistan and India searching for the fortress of the Azurites."

Dexter laughed humorlessly. Turning to Christos, he said, "Tell my older brother where the stronghold of the Azurites is actually located."

Christos replied calmly, "Even we don't know its location."

"Interesting," Dexter replied.

"What does it matter?" Kenneth replied. "Your family has lost the confidence of the Brotherhood and our father. You'll be lucky to survive when all this is finished."

"Then why am I here?" demanded Dexter.

Lifting both hands in the air, trying to calm the situation, Christos replied, "You will not be harmed. I assure you. The Brotherhood will watch your school like everyone else, but there's nothing to indicate that you have joined forces with the Azurites."

"And my daughter, will you keep hunting her?"

"Son," Karl Middlesex said, "Josephine was in India just last week. I received the telegram personally."

"Is that so, Grandfather?" A female voice echoed from the back of the room.

Jet was shocked at the turn of events. A figure, dressed entirely in black approached, unfolding some fabric around her head and neck. The girl was beautiful girl and around the same age as Jet. She had rich, dark black hair with soft skin and a kind face, but she moved like a predator.

"What's the meaning of this?" Karl Middlesex demanded.

The girl held up two daggers in each hand. Ignoring her grandfather's question, she turned to Christos and nodded, "You were right, master. The Azurites have learned of this meeting. They will be here in twenty minutes."

The elder Middlesex twisted to Christos and asked, "You know my granddaughter?"

Christos said impatiently, "Rebecca Middlesex was kidnapped by the Azurites. I tried convincing you of her loyalty, but you were blinded. Josephine has been helping the Brotherhood at great peril to herself. We have discovered quite a bit about them because of her."

Dexter asked, "Josephine, why did you not tell me?"

"We don't have time for this," Christos shouted as he sprinted to the tables. Using the fabric, he handed a talisman to each family. Once he was finished, he added, "Only five schools can be built. The talismans cannot be used for anything other than education and protection."

Suddenly Karl Middlesex appeared wary of what was being said. "Why have you involved my family?"

Christos replied, "You are descendants of Hector Fontaine, while the Müllers are descendants of Garvis Cummings. These were the two gatekeepers of the talismans. Only a descendant or someone who married into the family can wield and place the talismans. That's why it must be your family."

Josephine interrupted. "Darsil Müller is here in New York. I killed two of his assassins, but they'll be here in minutes."

"Tewapa," Christos shouted.

The two bodyguards unlocked and opened the doors to the kitchen. Five women in brown cloaks entered the main hall.

Kenneth pulled out an impressive blade, and many of the other men in the room did as well.

Christos shouted, "These women will be your headmasters. It's required that the headmaster will always be someone from the Brotherhood. However, someone from your family must continually be part of the school. These are the requirements. Additionally, no one but those related can touch the talismans without the fabric," explained Christos. "Even I am unable to touch them. The Müllers are the only other family on the face of the planet with the power to use the talismans. But they will do so to the destruction of us all. Be swift and be safe."

Karl Middlesex, more subdued than when he first spoke, said, "Go forward with speed, prosperity, and affluence. Make our family proud. The serpent is always at the back door."

Glass shattered, and the Middlesex family scattered.

The vision ended abruptly, and Jet was pulled back from the darkness and found himself back in his bed, covered with sweat.

CHAPTER 19

There was a knock on Jet's bedroom door around noon the following day. He was tired and hadn't slept as well as he expected or needed.

"Come in," shouted Jet.

The door opened, and Principal Jan Fletcher stood in the doorway with Jackson standing sheepishly in the background. He shrugged timidly as if trying to apologize before disappearing before Jet could say anything.

"How are you feeling?" she asked as she stepped into the room, closing the door.

"Not great but can't really complain." Jet tried sitting up but struggled.

Principal Fletcher hurried over and helped arrange some pillows behind his back and head. She said, "I spoke with your grandmother, and she says that you had minimal mobility before coming to school. I guess it's a good thing you are here." Before sitting, she opened the door and said, "Hey Jackson, why don't you and Rick head over to Porters and get the hamburger, fries, and shakes that I ordered for the two of you. Grab Jet's milkshake on the way back."

"Okay," shouted Jackson.

Jet watched Principal Fletcher with curiosity and apprehension as she closed the door. "Is it okay if I sit down?"

"It's your school."

She had a worn-out look on her face, but she smiled anyway. "Only time will tell how long that remains to hold true."

"What's that supposed to mean?"

"You and your friends have really pushed the limit. With everything else that has been going on the last few months, the board of directors is going to seriously look at my managerial skills."

"Who's on the board of directors?"

She tilted her head and stared at him for a long moment. "I think you know."

"The Brotherhood?" Jet asked, and he was surprised he was so candid with her.

Her answer was not as direct as he would have liked. She said, "When the five boarding schools first started, the Brotherhood had a much more hands-on approach. They directly picked the headmasters, all females. They were called headmistresses until about twenty years ago. Now we're chosen by a Brotherhood committee."

Jet asked, "Are you a member of the Brotherhood?"

"Not exactly. My late husband was, and I've been here for eight years. The previous headmasters often were here for either five, ten, or fifteen years. Every five years there's a comprehensive review of your time as headmaster."

Jet nodded but remained silent.

"Why were you really in Argentina?" Principal Fletcher asked.

Jet was at a loss as to what to say. Finally, he mumbled, "How do I know I can trust you?"

"You can't, really." She said this more to herself than to him. "I've been blinded by so much. Two of the books at my school at the same time—it's unheard of."

"What do you mean?"

"Don't act coy with me. I know that this is, first and foremost, a magical school. I've known that many of those from Silverton were exposed and some were even attacked. You and I both know that Trina Madden was ambushed. I have my guesses about who it could be."

"But you told that doctor that she got a sunburn."

"You were in the hospital at the same time. It's not surprising that you overheard that." She stared out his window. "At the time I had no idea that it was anything but a sunburn. I gave my report to the Brotherhood, and they became curious. They sent someone to the school to investigate. She wasn't getting any better, but the priest brought a tonic that helped relieve much of the burn. He explained that someone was searching for those with magical potential."

"The Brotherhood has priests?"

"Not clergymen. But they have specific responsibilities."

"Interesting."

Principal Fletcher continued, "The day of the memorial, there was another attack. Several students turned red, just not as bad as Trina." She focused on him. "The Brotherhood was certain that you and some of your friends might be affected. But that didn't happen, and they changed their minds."

"I went redder than Trina. Just found an antidote."

"I want to believe you. That would make things better for the school and for me, but it's awfully hard to prove."

"Just saying," Jet replied. "It felt like I was being burned alive." He watched her closely, still unsure if he should trust her.

An awkward silence fell between them. She asked, "Do you know Kevin McCormick?"

Jet was taken aback by the change in topic and the name.

Trying to remain calm, he said, "He was a year older than I was in school. He also lived in Silverton. I haven't seen him for a few months."

"Kevin changed colors, not severely, at the memorial. The Brotherhood interceded and has been helping him learn about magic. They don't have *The Sorcerer's Guide*, but they have a fair amount of knowledge. They were hoping he could be more than the Mikado. If he becomes powerful, the Brotherhood will have a much larger part to play in all of this."

"How?" Jet mumbled. "How do you know these words?"

Principal Fletcher stood and said, "More importantly, how do you?"

Jet had been tricked, but he hadn't given anything away. He yawned and stretched and said, "Sorry, Principal Fletcher. I'm getting so tired again. I think I need some more sleep."

"I'm not here to use you or take advantage of you. But I need leverage with the Brotherhood."

"I don't really know who the Brotherhood is. If you will excuse me."

"I'll tell you what I know," Principal Fletcher replied, almost pleading. "The Brotherhood is a good thing, and for many years, they've kept the knowledge of magic alive and prepared a way for those of us willing to fight. Silverton was likely the first, and no one knew the location of the second disaster. Now that you've been to Argentina, I'm guessing that is where the second one was. That means there are four more to discover. Maybe some have already happened, maybe they haven't. The priest who visited believes DC was likely the latest in the series of disasters."

"Sounds about right," Jet replied.

"But the Brotherhood is flawed too. They are a nonmagical group of people with somewhat similar desires, trying to prepare and maybe control the groups who arise with magical proficiency. They helped create schools that can help teach those who are gifted. Over the last twenty years, political jurisdiction has been altered by a select number of people. I don't know who they are. Don't ever underestimate the Brotherhood. They might not have magic themselves, but they have amulets, weapons, words, and knowledge beyond any sixteen-year-old."

"Why would they confront a sixteen-year-old?"

"Simple, really. Magic is alluring, like power. If they can't have magic itself, they'll want the power over it. They might not trust you to do the right thing. Why do you think they sent a priest to oversee the healing of one of our students? Why did they take Kevin out of school?"

"Does the Brotherhood want to help?" Jet couldn't help but think of Geb.

"Yes, most of them do. But not all of them can be trusted."

"Why are you telling me this?"

Principal Fletcher blew out a long breath. "This could ruin me forever. You understand this?"

"Not really."

Tapping her finger against the chair absentmindedly, she said, "The Brotherhood will work with Shane or you and your friends to control the hidden demon, maybe both. I don't know his name. If they think Shane is an easier candidate to control, and he sides with Dillon Lake, they'll put their support behind him. They will fire all the teachers, including me, and essentially close Chadwicks."

"You think Shane is involved?"

"He is a likely contender. He also has been trying to protect the school from an attack. The Brotherhood is watching Chadwicks closely."

"An attack from whom?"

"I've only been told that Shane calls them 'Magicae furantur,' or stealers of magic. I don't know if the Brotherhood knows what's going on."

"Is the Brotherhood at Chadwicks?"

"Not directly."

"What are the goals of Chadwicks?"

"There are about ten teachers, including me, that have knowledge of magic. Most of them were recruited by the Brotherhood in one way or another. They are family members, friends, and such. They're here to help facilitate magical learning."

"What do you suggest I do?"

"Work with Shane to help protect Chadwicks."

Jet shook his head. "I don't know if I can work with him."

"He didn't think that you would be able to."

"You've already talked with him?"

"Just before I came here."

He added, "He tried to kill me."

"Shane is complicated. He is divided by his upbringing at Dillon Lake and his current situation."

"What does Dillon Lake have to do with this?"

"Chadwicks was always an afterthought of the other four boarding schools. Truthfully, because Silverton is so close, it changed the entire game plan for the Brotherhood. Dillon Lake was and is still the most important of all the boarding schools. About 70 percent of their school is already learning about magic and being prepared for the upcoming war."

"What about the other thirty or forty percent?"

Principal Fletcher appeared uncomfortable. "What I've heard is only a rumor."

"Go on."

"The Brotherhood has created this drink. It's a complicated world at Dillon Lake, and if you don't meet the standard and have an aptitude for magic, you're given the drink, and it prevents you from learning magic, especially retaining magic. It's like the idea of magic washing away and it being impossible to catch in your hands."

Jet felt coldness settle inside his chest.

Principal Fletcher continued, "If you agree to work with me and distantly with Shane, the Brotherhood will have no choice but keep Chadwicks open, and we can really develop these students into a strong force."

"I'll think about it."

"How many students can use magic?"

Ignoring this question, Jet asked a question of his own that had been burning with him for a long time. "Does Professor Rysen know about magic?"

"I don't think so."

"But he came from Dillon Lake?"

"That's true. But the priest used some of the red powder on Professor Rysen, and he didn't turn colors."

"Did Shane turn red?"

"No," she said, appearing slightly perplexed.

"I don't know everything about that powder, but I don't think it affects everyone."

"Do you know something about Professor Rysen that I should know about?"

"Not necessarily."

"What about Professor Blum?"

A flash of sadness crossed the principal's face. She said, her voice choked, "I don't think that he did."

"Past tense?" Jet questioned.

"Professor Blum was killed in an automobile accident in Texas five days after Christmas. There was a group of deer in the road, and he couldn't stop. It was all on his dash camera."

Jet sat back, shocked. He mumbled, "Not possible" a few times. A few minutes later, he asked, his voice flat, "Who's teaching his classes now?"

"Professor Rysen."

CHAPTER 20

Before Principal Fletcher left, she made Jet promise that he would get back to her in the next day with an answer about working alongside Shane. Closing the door, she added, "The Brotherhood is sending their committee here next Friday. We need a plan and some definitive reasons to keep the school open."

As he sat and waited for his roommates to return, it dawned on him that she never asked why he was here at the school rather than the hospital. It was curious that after less than two days, he felt better than he had the entire time in the hospital. Ten minutes later the door opened, and he was given a Butterfinger shake.

Enjoying the shake, he listened to Rick and Jackson as they filled him in on their accomplishments. Rick had perfected fire, and he could create small little light bombs. He had practiced creating light when it was pitch black and using the light as a weapon by causing temporary blindness. Jackson was proficient at freezing items, as if time had stopped. He almost had enough control to stop a rolling car.

"How's Keesha?" asked Jet after his roommates demonstrated their magical talents.

"She is taking some AP classes this year and has been super busy. We've seen her practicing like once a week."

"What do you mean practicing?"

Rick answered, "Jayco has created a schedule for those who have magical talents to be able to practice. Something has been going on almost nightly for the last two weeks."

"Is Jayco the only leader that goes?"

"No," Jackson answered. "All the Echoes but you have been down there. I've only seen Mckenzey a few times."

"You're calling us Echoes?"

"Jayco asked us to refer to the leaders as Echoes. He said it'll be easier to help everyone understand the group."

"I see," Jet said, wondering what else he needed to learn. He was just about to ask how many people on campus could perform magic when there was a knock at the door.

Rick retreated from Jet's room. A moment later he heard Rick say, "I was wondering when you were going to stop by."

Jet wasn't sure who it could be. He thought of Nana, Geb, Autumn, or even Mckenzey. When the scooter came rolling in with Mckenzey, Jet's heart ached.

"Hey, guys," she said, staring at his roommates. "Are you heading down to practice sword fighting?"

Rick said, "We still have a few classes left this afternoon. Will we see you there?"

"You bet," Mckenzey replied.

As of yet she had not glanced at Jet.

Rick said, "I guess we better get going. Take it easy, guys." His two roommates left, closing the bedroom door, leaving the two of them behind.

Mckenzey peered over at Jet for the first time. She seemed hurt, sad, scared, and mad all at the same time.

"Hey," Jet said.

"Glad to see you're moving," Mckenzey replied as she transferred to the same chair principal Fletcher had been sitting in.

"Now that I'm back on campus, I have a bit more energy."

"Nana told us that might happen."

"When?"

"The night she came and got you. I couldn't be of any help," she insisted as she glanced down at her own leg. The cast was thick and covered her foot, ankle and continued to just below her knee. She moved quickly to his bed, and he scooted to the wall, giving her room. She leaned in and hugged him. Soon she was crying, and Jet tried to comfort her the best he could. Mckenzey refused to move for several minutes. When she finally broke apart, she shifted her weight and eased back onto the chair.

Jet asked, "What's the story with your leg?"

Mckenzey laughed with a runny nose while trying to wipe her face dry. "Of course, that's what you want to talk about first?"

"That cast is impressive. Did you get in a snowboarding accident?" Anxiety ran freely up and down his spine, but he refused to let it take hold.

"I wish my story were as cool as getting injured doing something fun."

"When did it happen?"

She considered the question. "A few weeks ago. Maybe more. It was still during Christmas break."

"Looks like it is painful. Are you okay?"

"Mostly. The doctor said he hasn't seen a break like this. It happened when I was just sitting in my room. They had to do a bunch of testing to make sure I don't have brittle bones."

"Is that a real thing?" asked Jet.

"It is. But they didn't find anything abnormal."

"Weird," Jet said, and he tried to keep the revulsion from his voice.

Mckenzey said, "Your turn. What really happened to you?"

He wondered how much he should tell his friends. How much should he tell Mckenzey? Telling them the complete truth would be the right thing to do, wouldn't it? Was it harder being the one who died or the one thinking that a close friend had died?

He began, "It was the worst thing I've ever been through. I was trapped alive under the rocks for days. The constant pressure on my legs, back, and arms felt like torture. I had to make hard choices with impossible consequences. I can't explain, but it felt like my body was being healed and broken again. I really don't know how I came out of it alive."

"Your body was broken and healed again?"

"Not sure how else to explain it."

"How did you get out?"

Honestly, I'm not sure. I crawled as far as I could, but then I didn't have the energy to keep moving. It was like something carried me out the rest of the way."

"Like a person?"

"No." Jet shook his head. "Like a creature."

"Iris?"

"She was stuck in my bag the entire time. I'm not even sure how my bag made it out with me. Was I dreaming?"

"I don't know," whispered Mckenzey. She remained silent for the longest time. It was as if she were wrestling with something.

Jet asked, "What is it?"

"Latisha was working in the admin office like she did freshman year, and the female doctor from Cottage Hospital stormed into the principal's office this morning and demanded to know if you were back on campus."

"What did the principal say?"

"That she had heard you were back on campus to restart your classes."

"Really?" said Jet, slightly surprised.

"The doctor said that you were in no shape to be back doing strenuous things like studying and walking around campus. Principal Fletcher said that the teachers were well aware of your injuries. You'll be taking classes online for the next few weeks, until you're feeling better."

"I really don't understand her."

"The doctor insisted that you need another CT and DEXA scan in the next two days."

"Probably not going to happen."

"Why?" Mckenzey asked.

"Remember hearing about the Brotherhood?"

"Sure."

"Geb said that there's another group, called the Azurites. Apparently some of them broke away from the Brotherhood. They want to use magic in a way that is different than the Brotherhood."

"The Azurites," Mckenzey repeated.

"That's what he called them."

"Should I tell the others?"

"I think so." Jet asked, "Can they stop by and see me?"

"There's some tight security outside your dorm. Jayco is really busy right now with those from Argentina and keeping the group together."

"Really?" asked Jet.

"There has been a teacher here twenty-four hours a day since you came back. They have an area set up in the common room. Only your roommates, Nana, and me can be let in."

"Seriously."

"What else has been going on?" Mckenzey asked.

"After I survived, I couldn't move a muscle. It felt like I was paralyzed, even at the hospital. It wasn't until I was back on campus that I was able to move."

"You couldn't move the entire time in the hospital?"

"No."

"Why?"

"Geb also said that there's something special about the schools and they can help us and protect us."

"How's that possible?" she asked.

Jet was tempted to tell her about the talismans, but her face changed so quickly, he wasn't sure what was happening. "What's wrong?" he asked.

"I'm just at my wit's end."

"With what?"

"Everything." Tears, again, began sliding down Mckenzey's face, and she forced out a long breath. When she stared at him again, her golden eyes revealed a girl who was lost and confused. She said, "I need to tell you something. I feel horrible that I ditched you and the others before you headed off to Argentina. I was so upset and felt lost and confused."

"I know, and I—"

"Let me finish," Mckenzey insisted. "We've been searching for Kevin, and so many crazy things have happened since Silverton. I was starting to feel that my own thoughts were no longer mine. I felt attached to this path we were going down and that I had lost my freedom. So I headed home to regroup and determine what *I* wanted."

Jet wasn't sure if he should speak, and so he remained quiet.

A moment later she said, "Eric was there, and I bounced some things off him."

"Please tell me that you didn't mention what we're doing." he exclaimed.

For the first time in his life, the look Mckenzey gave him was pure annoyance and frustration. She covered it quickly by saying, "Sorry. I wasn't sure what you were asking, but no, I didn't tell him about what we're searching for. Can I continue?"

"Sure," Jet said quickly.

Her voice was unsteady when she said, "Eric was a good friend. One day, a few days before Christmas, I considered going to Dillon Lake. I guess the option was still on the table."

This time Jet kept his mouth shut.

"The day after Christmas, Jayco called and said that you were missing in Argentina. I lost it."

Jet didn't like where this conversation was going. He felt guilty. Mckenzey had slowly moved as far away from him as possible. In his mind it was a symbol.

"I cried on and off for the next few days, blaming myself. When Jayco gave me the full description of the crumbling rocks and the entire mountain shifting, I truly thought you were dead. Eric never left my side. He and my parents helped me through the darkest time in my life. He was in my room one day when I had mostly come to terms with things. He told me that he would transfer to Chadwicks and help me with whatever I was doing. I was so very grateful. I wasn't sure I could come back here without..." Her voice trailed off. When she spoke again, her voice was cold and distant, "That was when, while I was sitting on my bed, my leg suddenly broke, out of nowhere. I fell to the ground; the pain was horrible."

"Oh, my word," Jet said quickly.

"The doctor doesn't know what happened. He says that it isn't a normal break. My parents and Eric's parents came to California before school started. They've been very supportive. Eric was able to transfer to Chadwicks, and somehow, I was going to find a way to get through the rest of the school year. We still had to figure out what to do with Shane and locate the rest of the pieces to the Phoenix."

"Okay."

She glanced up again at him, "Then I got the news that Jet Black is alive."

"I'm sorry. I don't know what to say."

"It's not your fault," she said quickly. "But so much has changed."

"What do you mean?"

She reached for her scooter. "We can talk more in a few days. I need to think about things before I say anything more." She shifted to her scooter and sat for a moment.

Jet hated what she was saying, but something more pressing entered his mind. "How much does Eric know?"

"Why are you asking this?"

"It's not what you think. I'm glad he was there for you during these hard times. It was difficult that you left our group before Argentina, but I get that you were confused."

"Are you trying to guilt me?"

"Not at all. At one point, you were planning on moving in with Eric and he attends Dillon Lake."

"Not any longer," She retorted quickly. "And your ex-girlfriend is here at Chadwicks."

"That's not the point."

"Then what is?"

"Dillon Lake is another school like Chadwicks. They teach about magic at that school. Shane went to school in Dillon

Lake up until his freshman year. Professor Rysen came from Dillon Lake. These are not coincidences."

"Are you saying Eric has an ulterior motive?"

"Who knows. I just want to understand how much he knows."

Mckenzey wobbled unsteadily on her scooter, clearly upset. "I get that you almost died, but have some compassion for the rest of us?"

"I do have compassion."

Her head twitched slightly. "He knows everything. Jayco is planning on using 'Parfit Inclusionem' on him tonight after the sword training."

Using his hands, Jet moved to the side of his bed. "All of this is crazy."

"What's that supposed to mean?"

"We're moving too quickly. We need to better understand what's going on around us."

"Jayco was right about you."

"What's that supposed to mean?"

"Things go good for the group when they suit *your* needs. But once someone else has a problem or something they want to suggest, it's a no-go, unless Jet agrees."

"That's not fair."

"Prove me wrong."

"Did you know that the Brotherhood is coming to Chadwicks? Did you know that Kevin McCormick was never taken by Shane, but rather he has been helping the Brotherhood? Dillon Lake has been teaching about magic since it opened. Principal Fletcher is close with the Brotherhood, and she has asked me to work with Shane. There's a bunch more. I wonder if Eric was surprised to learn about magic or he already knew."

She mumbled, "He admitted he had heard a few things."

"You actually are probably right, though. From what Latisha told me, Eric was living there long before you did. I think he had an older brother who went to Dillon Lake."

"You know about that?" she asked.

"I know that you care about him. I just wanted to be careful. That's all."

"Why's this so important?"

"My real concern is Professor Rysen. He taught at Dillon Lake."

"You've told me that like five times."

Jet bit his lip. He was angry and hurt. He pictured Rysen, a former friend to his father, standing over the bodies of his parents. Tears were now in Jet's eyes as he said, "Professor Rysen was there the night my parents were killed. In fact, he helped kill them."

"Are you sure?" Mckenzey stood. "This seems to be much more about Eric coming to school and Jayco making decisions while you weren't here. Are you jealous?"

"I'm just asking you to slow down."

"It's not up to me what happens tonight. And for the record, I think Eric would be a perfect fit for our group. I wish you could open your eyes and see what's right in front of you."

"I'll try, but you should probably go. It was really good to see you. Thanks for stopping by. I hope your leg heals up. I'll see you around."

## PART II

THE HIDDEN PATH

CHAPTER 21

For a sixteen-year-old, Chadwicks felt much more like a small college than a high school. He had his own apartment of sorts since he didn't have a roommate. Having a car gave him freedoms that he could never have dreamed of. The problem was, he barely had the energy to walk out of his room and onto the couch to watch some television. His car sat unused over the last several weeks, and if he could drive, he didn't know where he would go. In reality the last few days had felt like this school was more like a prison than anything else.

Things between him and his friends were unfavorable. Mckenzey made it clear enough that she and Jayco thought he was controlling and unmovable. It had been two days since Mckenzey had stopped by, and they were giving him a wide berth. That was probably best for both sides. After surviving his ordeal under Coso Subtrano, he pictured coming back to school as a refuge and seeing his friends would reassure him, but the opposite had happened. His decision to grab a golden rectangle was the first piece in a cascade of events.

Reaching into his backpack, he pulled out the golden pyramid, the cloth with the three golden orbs, the tome, and the other weapons, placing them on the desk across from his bed. He moved aside some homework he was working on. Most of his teachers had accommodated his assignments and had even given him top marks for things he hadn't been there for.

He heard the main door close and assumed that his roommates were sneaking out for another round of instruction by Jayco and the others. He rubbed his left hand and the burnt marking on the palm from when he had touched the meteorite. He next glanced at his forearms at the two small tattoos of daggers. On his right forearm, near the crease in his elbow, was a completely black dagger, while on the right forearm sat a blade of majestic blue with a black handle. These reminded him of his fight with Lucretius.

Pulling up his shirt, he used the mirror and stared at the tattoo of four elements on his back. It was as pristine and incredible as ever. In the center of his back was a campfire with smoke, a glacier lake, an immense and ancient tree growing from a hill, and a descending sun behind a mountain that was surrounded by clouds.

These reminders kept Jet strong. Whatever self-doubt or anxiety he felt was squashed by these tokens of his magic.

Cutting through his thoughts was a deep pull of compulsion. Surprised, Jet pulled the tome closer to him. The next page turned with ease, and he stared down at a letter on the page with distinctive handwriting. It was as if a melody were being written on paper. The lettering was flowing with intricate swirls.

Sorcerer,

I am Donvalian, a protector of magic and the leader of my people. I am part of a group called the Wandering Nomads and decedent kin of the Brown Owl, a former commander in the Council. It has been nearly ten years since we lost Leotyton in battle, and most surprising, our knowledge of magic and the words necessary to bring forth growth, gain, and prosperity is continuing to dwindle. If the wisdom of our elders is correct, soon magic will disappear entirely from the world as we know it.

Many years ago a shrewd member of the Shaman magic shared a belief that there may never be a restoration of magic entirely back on the earth. Magic is not as equal and fair as it once was. Hundreds of years ago, there was a time when all forms of magic were of the same value, but in recent years, the conviction of a hierarchy has taken hold in the hearts of the people of the land. Runic and Elemental magic have been the guardians of our culture and our people, but it may turn out that they will be our jailers as well. Those who follow Runic magic, spawned by Arisol himself, have change and started believing that they are more worthy of being the rulers of the land.

Despite this, we have had recent discoveries that are somewhat incomplete and confusing.

A few months back, Queen Aurora and her two daughters launched an expedition to search for a possible explanation for the decline of magical abilities and competence. A similar thing happened years before Arisol attempted to take the throne of the Kings. He found and used Runic magic to try to control the Phoenix. But now he has been locked away in prison. The Rivalry was formed, but magic is nearly nothing more than a memory.

The two sisters tracked down a few laborers and soldiers who had escaped the bloodshed at the Starving Peaks, and they insist that the Rivalry will bring back magic, but it may take more for equality to return. Arisol was blinded by greed and a lust for power.

There is a clear picture of the involvement of the Chupovanas, who pleasure in the destruction of all magic. Aurora's daughters attempted to uncover the exact plan and learned of an obscure tribe that may have formed an alliance with these foul creatures. The Chupovanas have ravaged the magical communities and caused the loss of the Lexicon's governing power.

Rumors continue that point to Arisol or one of his spies creating a secret pact with the Resitituals to dismantle the other types of magic, or he may have taken advantage of the chaos of the situation. The truth of this judgment is impossible to prove. He found Runic magic and caused chaos and destruction. Only Leotyton and Lady Gaea were able to temporarily stop Arisol. The demon used Runic magic during his first escape and initiated the Rivalry.

My latest information tells me that Aurora and her daughters will soon start searching for the location of the Starving Peaks in hopes to better understand the sickness in our lands. They believe that magic can be saved if they find the two books and keep them safe. Thus far they have been unsuccessful.

If you, Sorcerer, are reading this letter soon after it was written, then I hope we have found the two books, and the Rivalry is at an end, and magic is finding strength again. But I fear that you are reading this letter many years in the future and that the spells have been concealed.

This letter is designed to forewarn you of the power and tenacity of the Chupovanas. They will never stop until they have gathered enough magic for themselves. Once they take magic, it is unknown if they can hide it in a reservoir or if they have another goal in mind. Beware of the tribe governing the Chupovanas. They have an evil disposition, and their desires are unfamiliar.

One day I hope that magic will be equal and balanced.

It has been several weeks since I finished my first letter, and I have gained some clarity that I felt I must share. Aurora's oldest daughter arranged a meeting with a surviving soldier, and the man insisted that magic is only sleeping and will reawaken in a whirlwind. But no matter what is done, Arisol will be awakened from his slumber. The Mikado will need to be empowered with Confusion and Deceit.

Additional instructions are as follows:

First: You must intricately understand all five different types of magic, not just your own.

Second: You must appreciate the enemies of the land. If and when magic is reawakened, so will these monsters be. The Chupovanas are but one of the foes of alchemy and bewitchment.

Third: Intelligence and aptitude are the ingredients to the recipe of success only if found in the hands of a humble and willing gardener of the fruits of humanity.

Fourth: Aurora's oldest daughter went missing six months ago after receiving insight on the location of the Starving Peaks.

Fifth: Aurora's youngest daughter went missing after trying to find the nest of the Chupovanas.

Sorcerer,

It has been two years since I first penned this letter. Magic has vanished from the land, and I will die before morning.

Never forget these words: My last perils of grief. I pray all is not already lost.

CHAPTER 22

Jet spent the next hour trying to wrap his mind around Donvalian's letter. The information felt incomplete, an intuition told him that only a tiny amount of the material had been allowed to enter *The Sorcerer's Guide*. The book was almost as infuriating as his friends sometimes.

After a day of homework and now this letter, Jet was exhausted. Flickers, like flames of anger lapped at his awareness. The tome had a mind of its own, and he couldn't help but thinking that there was an easier way to get information. This letter seemed to have a deeper meaning, but if so, Jet wasn't getting it.

He reread the fable entitled the Legendary Battle on the first few pages. He studied the words about the Council of the 10 Kings and the dissent of Arisol. After Arisol was forced back into his prison, a battle, the Rivalry, was initiated. For the last few months, he'd assumed that there were only two types of magic. Alces had educated him about the other three types. Could that mean that the Rivalry was something between all five types of magic or just between the Elemental and Runic ones? There were still far more questions than answers.

Recently, he'd witnessed a wingless dragon, fought the diablitos, and experienced an underground world. But meeting two Oracles, seeing how his parents died, and especially being tortured had transformed him profoundly. The choices he made during the Hoyuk Crescent were beyond hard. He would let Jayco take the reins for now, but he would help the others see how things had changed when he was better.

Jet felt the urge to turn another page. This time he recognized Wier's handwriting.

In the beginning, Magic was unstable, unusable, and dangerous. The Five Goddesses of the Four Realms of Earth began to formulate a plan to find a way to control magic. They formed the Lexicon, an agreement, and an advocate, and by cutting down the oldest tree in the land, they created five books of creation, later called the Five Books of Terra Maleficis.

Lady Gaea, Atmos Geni, Ella Dastria, Aqua Felis, Bio Vita reigned over the Four Realms, and Atmos Geni discovered Elemental magic and called on it to come to the earth. It took centuries for magic to be wrangled and disciplined, and when it was finished, five tomes of divine workmanship were produced. I showed you the thirteen priests who used Atmos Geni's instructions to finalize Spirit, and the Cloaks of Armandour were shaped.

Mikado, you wear one of the Cloaks of Armandour, as do your friends.

These five tomes allowed for writings, words, songs, and spells to be understood by the chosen. In essence, the tomes were indestructible, but the words and meanings could be lost or forgotten. All five books were named, and a leader was chosen. When Atmos Geni left to entice the final pieces of Elemental magic, he never returned. Lady Gaea, Aqua Felis, and Bio Vita became the gatekeepers of the Phoenix and other hidden relics.

Created in Goth Airtha, the five types of magic, their tome's name, and the position of their leader as well as the chosen are as follows:

Elemental magic—The Sorcerer's Guide—the Mikado and Occultists
Runic magic—The Mage's Letters—the Czaric and Mages
Shaman magic—The Book of Shadows—the Flamanis and Spirituum

Incrementum magic—The Recipes of Life—the Aedificum and Dabant

Resitituals magic—The Adaptation Guide—the Ficher and Mutatio

As with all things in the world, there is good and evil, balance and decay. Somehow evil found a way to prevail, and despite the love and unity that comes with magic, also born were jealousy, chaos, pride, and hatred. Spawned creatures of hate were formed from a union of lava and earth's destruction. Beasts of the underworld slithered out of the shadows. Soon magic became corruptible.

The first enemy to the wielders of magic were the Drekavac Demons. These twisted souls desired nothing more than to eradicate the chosen from the earth. But despite their hatred, they can be tricked or bargained with to provide a service. They will stand by their oaths only if their rewards meet their demands. Four different creatures comprise the Drekavac Demons. For centuries they attacked, killed, and conspired against all types of magic. Later, in specific battles, it appeared that they joined one or more factions of magic to kill the others. Their souls have been misguided for centuries, and they seek retribution from the living.

The second enemy was an unintended consequence of life's unexpected trials. Legend has it that the Chupovanas were born without magic, and they lived in peace and harmony with Mother Earth for years, centuries, and millennia. One day they found a dying Occultist, Mage, or similar, and attempting to save a life, they brought it to their den. The dying being, believing it was about to be attacked, lashed out. To protect themselves, the Chupovanas killed the person and became influenced by magic, and soon they were intoxicated with its aroma. Somehow the magic was transferred to the Chupovanas, though they still couldn't use it, but began to greedily thirst for its contact.

After the contact with magic, the Chupovanas initiated a war with all magical beings. After years and years of fighting, bewitchment departed Goth Airtha, and wars and combat followed for many years. The five tomes became lost or hidden. The 10 Kings were chosen to protect the land. They each were given a domain to oversee. All the Kings were just and protective of their lands, communities, and flocks.

Rumors hinted that conjuring had once again been revealed. Deadly mistakes could now be healed, and life became more plentiful than in preceding years. It was also rumored that the Chupovanas were free to roam outside their boundaries.

Some of the Kings traveled to distant lands to find rogue beasts that would protect the people against the Chupovanas. Other Kings approached the Wandering Marauders, Queen Aurora and her people, and other tribes. Most pledged a measure of support.

Because of the Council and its allies, there was peace in the land for centuries. Magic began to take root and thrive in the land once again. The Grey Panther, later known as Arisol, searched specifically for Runic magic and its tome, still lost and hidden. He desired to control the Council. The Legendary Battle was born. Staka Arben, the leader of the Resitituals, was killed by Arisol in his quest to find Runic magic.

Lastly, although unfounded as far as I know, there is a rumor that the Resitituals made a pact with the Chupovanas. It is unknown if this was as retribution for the death of Staka Arben or because Arisol was part of the takeover. Queen Aurora developed strong feelings that it might be true, and her people broke their treaty with the Council for fear that she would be the next who was attacked.

CHAPTER 23

Jet had no time to consider what the previous page meant as the next page turned without him touching the page. The handwriting was still that of Wier.

Sorcerer, you must better understand the enemies who pose the greatest threat to magic, including the Drekavac Demons and the Chupovanas. By now it must be crystal clear that I have limitations, and you can't ask direct questions, but I can sense the progression you are making or the lack thereof. Forgive me if any of this information is a duplicate.

The four kinds of Drekavac Demons emerged following the Combat of Dire Creek, three centuries before Arisol welcomed chaos and greed into his life. These demons were birthed from within the earth and slithered out to find more victims. They have unrelenting willpower but on occasions they can be bargained with. Often they will follow their own agenda. They sense magic and can lay dormant for years when magic is hidden.

These demons are divided into two categories. There are the Diablitos and the Vicerants. Within the Diablitos there are the Razors and the Ratas, and within the Vicerants there are the Pepracons and Scorepos. All Drekavac demons can swim, climb, and run. They survive in the hottest and coldest climates in the world, though they thrive and reproduce in the warmth.

Below is an abbreviated outline of all four creatures.

Drekavac Demons: Diablitos

Razors are thin and fast, and they stand over six feet tall. They have two long legs and four arms that end with small sharp claws. They are remnants of ancient bugs and can adapt to their surroundings using camouflage. Razors primarily walk on their back two legs. They can jump, are agile and deadly. These beasts communicate with their voices and croon a high-pitched song, causing some ancient creatures to sleep. Wind can move these smaller demons. Lightning, Fire, and Fear have no effect. They tend to unite with those who use Runic magic. They are almost made entirely of rock and are hairless.

Ratas have a thicker, almost stonelike protective outer skin. They do not jump and are slower than Razors but incredibly strong. They have two hind legs and two massive arms. They are slightly shorter than Razors but three times thicker. They have a protective back layer of rock, which enables them to roll themselves up and become almost indestructible. Their claws are like pinchers, like that of a crab. They are less adept at camouflage while moving but resemble rocks when curled up. They give off a low-pitched grumbling that keeps unwanted visitors from coming too close. Magic such as Fire, Wind, Earth, Lightning, and Fear have little effect on these demons.

Drekavac Demons: Vicerants

Pepracons are animals that use the sky to attack and kill. They are winged beasts, larger than a wolf, with four legs with two arms attached to wings. Most often, they sprint along the ground with ease and take flight into the air when attacking. They are entirely black with thick, matted fur. Their hind legs are thicker than their front legs. They have paws like a feline with razor-sharp claws. The wings are muscular, allowing for quick attacks with acrobatic movements, and they can remain in the sky for up to an hour. They live and sleep on the ground, under snow, in caves, or tucked away in trees. They use the air to escape, attack, forage for food or watchmen for the other Drekavac Demons. They skillfully kill with their powerful jaws and sharp claws. They are a combination of a gigantic bat and a feline. Pepracons have solid jaws and the ability to ambush, and they see perfectly in the dark. Fire, Lightning, and Fear have no effect on them.

Scorepos are diggers and movers through the ground, including rock and clay. They attack secretly from below. They have narrow heads, which are nearly unbreakable. From there, the body enlarges, giving it the ability to maneuver through the ground faster than it can run. They have retractable pinchers inside their mouths to break apart rock. They are wingless and prefer to remain subterranean. They have six short legs with a large tail like a scorpion. Their body is segmented and long but muscular. They have no pinchers, and instead, their hands have claws with the ability to grip. The tail is thicker and used for balance when above ground. The venom they unleash is a powerful sleep agent. When Scorepos are above ground, they use their hind four legs to propel the rest of their body into the air. They are intelligent and move with a hive-like mentality. They communicate with their queen, who has almost never been seen. They can hold weapons, such as bows and arrows, along with swords. They stand nearly five feet tall when up to their full height. Earth, Water, Wind, and Fire have little effect.

By contrast, the Chupovanas are enemies to all those who wield magic. They are not from Gotha Airtha, but once were peaceful and tame. They have become an evil pack destined to kill and steal the magic of the world. It is historically held that there are between five and seven Chupovanas, but to our knowledge, only three have ever been seen. They are led by an unknown ancient being that rarely shows itself to anyone, and they are shepherded by a female tribe. Chupovanas are incredibly fast and unique to themselves. They are distinguishable by having one set of large horns with a third smaller horn that grows according to the amount of magic they have stolen.

The Three Witnessed Chupovanas:

Kee-Faux

Kee-Faux is an antlered deer that is proficient at killing others. He moves as fast as any other creature who has ever lived. He stands nearly ten feet tall, with long dangling arms, and he can fight and attack on his back two legs. Black fur covers its entire body. For even faster speed during far travels, the creature runs on all four legs. Kee-Faux is second in command.

He has fanged teeth like that of a shark, with two or three rows. His head resembles that of a deer. The creature can detect movement but appears blind; his eyes are fully white without a pupil. He has one set of large deer antlers and a smaller single antler between the two. Legend states that this creature can shapeshift after it has engulfed a measure of magic, likely from two or more victims. More advanced than the others in the pack, Kee-Faux can communicate with words. He is immune to magic from Fear, Earth, and Water, but the other types of magic are chiefly ineffective.

Taraqeu

Taraqeu is a female feline beast that is impressive to behold. She is bigger than a lion, with an enormous head of jagged teeth. Her horns are thick, mostly smooth, and curve back towards her tail. There are dozens of tiny, sharp, thornlike pieces spread out on her horns. It would be impossible to sit on her back and grasp her horns. She has a massive chest and a long torso. Her four legs allow for quick movement, but the most impressive part is that she can climb most anything. She dives and lunges at her prey. Her fur is brown and gray and longer, like that of a raccoon.

Taraqeu stalks with silence, stealth, and speed. She will sink in her teeth and never let go. She has flawless balance thanks to a long tail with spikes that release like a porcupine's. The tail whips back and forth and can be used to injure, damage, and confuse her prey. Taraqeu has a fear of Water but is completely immune to Wind. She does well against magic involving Fire, Ice, and Confusion.

Dalkiate

Dalkiate is the most elusive of the three known Chupovanas, and the reason is unclear. This creature has rarely been glimpsed. His horns are thick with a large diameter. Each horn divides and wraps around the upper and lower portion of its head. This gives the appearance of four sharp points pointing forward. There are two that arise from above the eyes and two from below and adjacent to the chin. The lower two are farther away from the head than the upper two points. The creature is all muscle, with two massive front legs and four back legs. The back legs are unique, as there is an outer leg and an inner leg, and the outer leg is three times as large as the inner leg. This creature tends to run you over before doing anything else. It has surprising speed for its size but is substantially slower than Kee-Faux and Taraqeu, but it generates far more power.

Dalkiate is not subtle, and his skin is almost impenetrable. He is five times as large as a rhino, and the body is very much similar, though stronger and more muscular. The head is far different and resembles that of a hairless bear. Absent of sharp teeth, except the two canines. The other teeth are flat and large. The canines extend when magic is stolen. Along with stealing magic, this creature also drinks the blood of its victims. Dalkiate is immune to Fire, Wind, Water, Lightning, Fear, Confusion, and more.

This information should not be treated lightly, and do not underestimate these demons or the Chupovanas.

Three things are clear. First, you have secured two pieces of the Phoenix. Second, the Chupovanas are hunting you and the other wielders of magic. They are on your doorstep. Third, some of the Drekavac Demons may have come to an agreement with Arisol and are enemies to you and all of those with Elemental magic.

CHAPTER 24

For the two days Jet remained a prisoner only leaving his room to use the bathroom and shower. He refused all visitors and avoided his roommates. By Thursday, he was able to slowly walk around his room, but only for a few minutes at a time. He was eager and excited about the new information. Having names and descriptions of some of his enemies felt good. He could hate them actively. The idea of working with Shane still caused him some anxiety.

In Argentina Jet and his friends had witnessed some of the Drekavac Demons, both the Razors and Ratas. Looking back, he realized that the entire thing had been a disaster. It was more than being unprepared; they had walked blindly into Faunal's trap, and he had made one wrong decision after another.

A vision swam in his mind of the wingless dragon outside Coso Subtrano. Its voice reverberated. "I am Siwalik, the hidden herder. I was recruited by the Ten Kings to fight a war against the Chupovanas, an evil pack destined to kill and steal the magic of the world. If they can find the magical entity, they can plunder it from you. The Kings hoped to stop the Chupovanas before things became as bad as they did. Prior to becoming Leotyton, the Two Kings traveled to my homeland and bested me for the right of my services. I have made a pact to protect magic from the Chupovanas."

Those words made more sense now. Siwalik was on his side if that was what it could be called. Another image appeared. This time he was back in the alley with Vinny Estes in Los Angeles. A creature was rushing into the alley, attacking Vinny. It was a lanky deer, standing on his back legs, with exceptional speed—Kee-Faux.

Jet spent Friday through Sunday working on studying and homework. He found a note from Autumn explaining that they had found another student to fill in for him in setting up the geology lab but that he was welcome to retake the position when he was feeling better. There were notes from all his teachers, even Professor Rysen.

Professor Rysen's note read, "Joshua Black. Thank goodness you made it back safely. I know your friends have been worried. Terrible news about Professor Blum; he taught me so much. I hope that I can match his unmistakable joy and excitement in teaching his class. He will be forever missed. Joshua, get better, and we will see you soon enough."

Jet crumpled the note and threw it into the trash.

His roommates tried unsuccessfully to get him to come out of his room. Nana brought over meals, but Jet refused to talk or see her. He hoped she understood the distance he needed.

Monday morning arrived, and for the first time in several days, he sat next to his roommates as they ate breakfast before starting their first class of the day. Before either of them could ask how he was doing, he posed a question. "How has it been working with Jayco and the others?"

"Pretty awesome. But all that changed last week; everything has been cancelled."

"What about the night you guys were scheduled to practice with the sword?"

"That was the first night things were cancelled," replied Rick.

"Because of me?" asked Jet.

Nodding, Jackson said smugly, "Probably."

"What's been going on since I left?"

Jackson and Rick shared a quick glance.

"Have you been asked not to tell me?" Jet asked, slightly surprised.

Rick shook his head. "Not really. It's just that it's been complicated."

Jackson motioned to Jet with his spoon after taking a bite of cereal. "Seyanna has been a pal. She helped us while you were rogue and helped expand our abilities. Jayco is more of a 'tell you how it's done' type. He was mad that you disappeared but also irate about everything. There's been a fair amount of tension between Seyanna and Jayco and Grantham and Jayco. I'm pretty sure he and Seyanna haven't spoken in more than a week or two."

"How many other have been brought into our group?"

"Around fifty, I think," Jackson said.

Rick added, "Jayco totally flipped out when you—uh—died. He felt responsible and worried that Shane would attack to get the tablet piece."

"Who told you about that?"

"Remember that place where you first taught us about our magic abilities?"

"Yeah."

"That place has changed. It's more like a hideout and a training facility. We meet there all the time. Jayco has created a system for kids to be on protective duty every night. Sometimes we eat dinner down there before or after practice. Jayco wanted more people involved, and he told us about some of the weapons, the magical abilities, and things you guys have been through. We added fifteen more kids the next day. Some people are very eager."

"This is crazy," Jet said. "Have you met Eric?"

"Once. He seems like a good guy. He's almost as tall as Jayco, just not as burly."

"Mckenzey told me that he was going to be added to the group last week. Did that happen?"

"No," Rick said bluntly. "No one has been added, and everything has been put on hold."

"Did anyone tell you why?"

"It's based on your recovery. Except for us, people only know your strength by the stories that have been told. They want to see what you can do."

"That might take a while."

"That's what we said. Jayco wants to meet and talk with you first."

"Maybe. I should call him today."

Rick laughed. "That would be nice. He's stopped by twice a day for the last two days. He's pretty distressed."

"I did hear something," Jackson said quietly.

"Don't tell him that," Rick replied. "You don't know what took place. It's just rumors."

"He should know."

"Know what?" asked Jet.

"On Friday, Jayco, Grantham, Seyanna, Mckenzey, and Latisha all came together for the first time. I heard they were talking about working with Shane. I didn't know what to think."

"Really?" Jet asked.

Jackson pounced. "I knew that it would make you mad. There was no way you would approve of helping Shane."

Jet remained quiet, and Rick took this as an answer.

Rick said, "We won't tell anyone. What do you want us to do?"

"Nothing for now," Jet said hastily. "I need to sort some things out."

"No problem." Rick stood, taking both his and Jackson's empty bowels to the sink in the hallway near the front door.

Jackson whispered, "Don't tell anyone that we told you."

"No problem."

Rick asked, "Are you planning on getting out of the dorm today?"

"Should I?"

"Let us know if you need some protection or an escape plan."

Jet laughed. "I'll let you know." After his roommates left, Jet found something to eat, a large muffin that Nana had dropped off. He took it back to his room and thought about what Rick and Jackson had said.

At four o'clock, there was a knock at the door, and Jet was surprised that when he opened it, Keesha stood there, staring back at him.

She said, "You really are alive. The rumors weren't a lie."

"Thankfully."

She sized him up, making him feel uncomfortable.

"You've changed," she insisted. "And I mean more than the thirty pounds you lost. What's wrong with you?"

"Can't seem to catch my energy. I'm tired all the time."

"Nah." She dismissed him. "Have you been cursed?"

Jet almost fell over, coughing. When he recovered, he asked, "A curse?"

"Just calling it how I see it."

"Not cursed, just exhausted."

"If you say so."

"I'm fine."

"Whatever." Keesha leaned in and said, "Can I give you a suggestion?"

"Depends," Jet said. For the first time, he noticed that the sitting area outside his dorm was full of people. Jet could see a teacher or two that he recognized but didn't know. He was shocked to see Seyanna seated in a chair, her head down, reading a book.

Keesha's voice reverberated as she said, "Get out of this dorm. Go downstairs. The campus is crazy to see you."

"What do you mean?" Jet asked.

"The entire school has been dropping by, sending texts, and trying to catch a glimpse of you. You need to go downstairs and say hi."

"I don't have a ton of energy."

"Seyanna and your friends are in the building. They'll help you, and so will I."

"But why?"

"You're kind of a celebrity. You can't hide in here forever."

"Are you sure?"

"Let's go," she insisted.

"I haven't taken a shower today."

"I can tell. But don't worry about it."

Seyanna leaped to her feet and pulled out a wheelchair, as if having been waiting for the right moment. Quickly, she helped him into a seated position. Kindly, she said, "You're looking better. Good to see you." She appeared genuinely concerned about him. She smiled, but it didn't spread across her entire face.

Suddenly the rest of the people, including the teachers, stood and started clapping. Jet was taken aback by their reactions. He nodded but had no idea what to say. Seyanna pushed him as Keesha stepped to his left side. The first person to rush to his other side was Autumn Bells, but it seemed like she hadn't slept or showered in days. Her typical bounce, brightness, and allure were gone. Jet asked, concerned, "Autumn, are you okay?"

She leaned in and hugged him as hard as anyone had ever hugged him. To his surprise, he found that she was crying. He couldn't hug her back tightly, and after a minute, she seemed to notice. She let go almost immediately and asked, "Oh, suck it. Did I hurt you?"

"I'm fine. I just don't have a lot of strength. What's wrong?"

She rubbed furiously at her eyes as if trying to wipe away her makeup. A smile spread across her face that was as fake as anything he'd ever seen. She gushed, "I'm fine. I was just so worried about you. I can't believe…" Tears formed in her eyes again.

Seyanna shouted, "Everyone, head on downstairs."

"You're not going downstairs, are you?" Autumn asked.

"Just to say hi," Jet said, feeling the outlandishness of the situation.

The group behind Autumn cheered, and someone asked, "Can we come with you?"

Seyanna said loudly, "We're taking the elevator. The rest of you can use the stairs."

The group stampeded to the stairs just as the chime from the elevator indicated that it was ascending to their floor.

Autumn whispered, "We need to talk."

Seyanna hesitantly said, "Maybe tomorrow."

"No, now," demanded Autumn.

"What's wrong?" replied Jet.

Another beep of the elevator, and the door down the stairs closed; they were alone.

Autumn replied quickly, "Be wary of Shane."

"What do you mean?"

"Rumors are that you're going to work with him. He isn't a fan of you, especially after you beat him outside Silverton."

There was another chime of the elevator as Seyanna asked, "How did you hear that?"

"I can't say. I'm forbidden by magic."

"Magic?" asked Jet.

"Runic magic," Autumn replied, her eyes unwavering.

Jet was shocked.

Autumn added, "Raul, Ariana, me, and some other kids are subject to Shane. We're trapped in a way. You need to find a way to help us."

With the last chime, the elevator arrived at their floor, the doors opening.

Jet gasped as he recognized who stood in the elevator. Shane Fallon smiled broadly and stepped partly out of the elevator. "Glad to see you survived, Black. Sorry you were second best."

Keesha tensed as Seyanna pulled the wheelchair back a foot or so. Jet searched for Autumn, but she had vanished.

Glancing around, Shane found the area empty. "I won't stay long, but we're on even ground now. You have a piece, and I have a piece. We'll forget about the little duel we had in the bubble. There are more important things going on. Something is preparing to attack the school. Nash thinks he senses it, and I'm wondering if Latisha has felt anything. I've heard that she has a special ability with animals."

"What are you saying?" Jet asked.

Shane must've seen the confusion on his face. "The Echoes are really the stupidest group that can do Elemental magic that has ever lived. I have no idea how you guys beat us outside of Silverton. How did you survive in Argentina?"

"What do you want?" Jet hissed.

Shane said quickly, "Look. I'm pretty sure you were in Los Angeles before you went to Argentina. Jessiva said she saw you. Things are going to get crazy here on campus. Vinny was killed or is missing. Jake is already dead. More people are going to die."

"What?" Keesha replied. "Principal Fletcher said that Vinny transferred to a different school."

"That's what she's telling everyone," Shane said coolly.

Making a decision, Jet said, "I was there, searching for Kevin. I left and have no idea what happened to Vinny."

"Well, he was attacked in an alley by something strange. Nash thinks that this creature, and possibly others, are periodically testing the boundaries of the school, searching for weaknesses."

"What kind of weaknesses?" asked Jet.

"I don't know more than that."

"What do you want from us?"

"Principal Fletcher spoke with you. You realize the Brotherhood will be here on Friday. We need to have a plan on how to protect the campus."

"Why do you want to protect the campus?"

"Where else do I have to go?" Shane asked. A high-pitched sound erupted from the elevator since it had not closed. "With Kevin becoming the star at Dillon Lake, this is my home now. We need to find a way to both be here."

"What do you mean about Kevin?" Seyanna asked.

"Didn't Jet tell you? Kevin wasn't kidnapped. He was taken by the Brotherhood and given special powers."

"Jet told us that the Brotherhood is interested in Kevin, but we didn't know more than that."

"Kevin's coming on Friday. We need to stop whatever is trying to topple the school."

"Fine," Jet said. "We'll work together. We'll be in touch."

"That's all I needed to hear," responded Shane. "Let's meet in a few days."

"Fantastic," Jet said.

Stepping back into the elevator, Shane said, "Argentina was a piece of cake. Why was it so hard for you?" The elevator door closed before Jet could come up with a retort.

"What was that?" Keesha asked. "Why are we working with Shane? Sounds like you are saying an enemy of our enemy is our friend."

"Nope. An enemy of our enemy is our untrustable adversary that we're being forced to work with."

They were silent until the elevator arrived a few minutes later. As Jet was pushed inside, he said, "That was the most normal conversation I've ever had with Shane."

"He's an idiot," Keesha said.

"I'll second that," added Seyanna.

When they reached the bottom floor, nearly two hundred students were waiting for him. Word must've spread quickly. Jet was pushed to the center of a huge common area, and people started dragging over chairs and tables. Soon Jet felt like a storyteller with seated children all around him.

"Well," he started, catching a glimpse of Mckenzey and Jayco near the front door, "I would highly recommend not traveling to Argentina."

Laughter and cheers erupted. For the next hour, Jet repeated the same exact story he had told the doctor in the hospital. He answered a bunch of questions. He downright lied about half the things, such as why he had been there. It seemed that many people knew most of the details already. They knew about Jayco, Grantham, Latisha, and even knew the names of Maria and Sebastian. It turned out to be one of the craziest experiences Jet had ever had. At one point it felt that he was watching himself outside his own body.

CHAPTER 25

Jet was pleased to see Nana Tuesday, around noon, when she and Geb stopped by to see him. It took him a few minutes to get from his room to the front door, which was frustrating. As he wobbled along, he mused at his initial thoughts that he would be out of school only a week or so after returning from the hospital. But he had begun to plateau after the first few days; it was as if his body refused to improve beyond the bare minimum. He had been outside twice but only for ten minutes. He was forced to be with Keesha, Rick, or Jackson at all times. Upon returning, he required a two-hour nap.

"We come bearing gifts," said Nana. She took out snacks, drinks, and a new cell phone. She added, "You look exhausted."

"Feeling better. I just woke up."

Geb put some of the food on the counter and asked, "If I needed you to run a mile, could you?"

"Sure." Jet lied. "Maybe two. In fact, I was getting some exercise this morning, and that's probably why I look tired." He wasn't sure why he felt the need to exaggerate his abilities, but he was happy his roommates were at their classes and couldn't contradict the statement.

"We need to talk," Nana said, and she motioned toward the couch.

Jet managed to walk as normally as possible. "About what?"

"Things," replied Geb.

Jet sat. "How did you know that the school would make me feel better?"

"I think you already know the answer to that question."

"I've heard of a talisman, but I don't know what that means."

"When magic was more common, legend said that the training of magic was done in safe zones. It was done in something called a coliseum, but not like the ones in ancient Greece. These arenas and their associated buildings were like small cities, heavily protected. They were often in the middle of larger towns. Weapons, relics, and much of what you've seen were accessible in these coliseums. They learned different types of fighting. Thieves and those who were power-hungry often attempted to break in and steal the valuables. Also, there were attacks on those who could perform magic. That's when they discovered the use of the talismans. It was also discovered that an injured person who was brought within the boundaries of the talisman saw a giant improvement. The Brotherhood used the talismans to build the five boarding schools, including Chadwicks."

This explanation fit with what Jet had seen, and he was intrigued by the idea of a coliseum. He asked, "How do you know so much?"

"Before I was assigned to your family, I was interviewed for a position as professor for a school in Texas."

"San Mateo."

"You know more than you tell."

"It keeps me safe."

"Maybe," Geb said thoughtfully. "I had influence, but I chose a different route."

"What did you need to talk with me about?"

"Argentina," Nana said.

"What about it?"

She said, "Soldiers stationed around the Manchao Mountains have uncovered animals that they can't explain. Others saw a moving tree and trailed the creature south to Chile until it disappeared into the water."

"I don't know what to say."

"Before you came back, we spoke with Jayco, and he told us about the bug-like creatures that you fought and the underground world. Could these be the same animals that they can't explain?"

"It's possible. There were a lot of weird things in Argentina."

Geb and Nana shared a glance.

"What is it?"

"Did you fight anyone else? Did Shane and his friends see you?"

"We didn't see Shane at all and didn't fight anyone else." Jet stared at each of them, perplexed. "Why are you asking this?"

"Before coming here, we were summoned to the principal's office. She received word that six other Americans, high school students, were found dead in Argentina a week ago. It's going to hit the news today."

"You mean since I arrived back in California?"

"It looks like it."

"What does this have to do with anything?"

Geb said cryptically, "The Brotherhood is aware of the deaths, but they aren't saying much."

"Okay?" Jet said, puzzled.

"I've never seen the Brotherhood act like this. They know something. Is it possible that you could know something about these deaths?"

"How would I?" replied Jet emphatically.

Geb tilted his head as if watching Jet closely. Finally, he said, "Two of the kids who died were students at Dillon Lake. Two at Cranbrook in Connecticut, and the last two were from Valley Sun Academy in Florida."

Shocked, Jet muttered, "All six were from the other boarding schools with talismans?"

"It appears so."

"How can you possibly know these details?"

"I'm still close to someone on the council for the Brotherhood. They passed me the information last night, and I confirmed it today with Principal Fletcher."

"What does this mean for me?"

"That someone might be coming for you. All six were tortured. We're asking you not to leave campus until we figure out what is happening."

"At all?" asked Jet. "Even to Santa Barbara?"

"If you need anything, ask your friends, or we'll help if we can. Principal Fletcher is completely on board."

Jet asked. "Anything else?"

After a minute Geb asked, "How did you know I gave you a tonic?"

"My magic ability and many of my memories were tampered with. *The Sorcerer's Guide* described a tonic, and it matched with what I was experiencing. I suspected it was you or someone you know since you're part of the Brotherhood."

Geb shook his head as if he didn't believe Jet but said nothing.

Nana added, "We've heard that the Brotherhood will be here at the end of the week. What do they want?"

"I've been told that I need to work with Shane, or the school risks being closed."

"They won't," Geb interrupted. "They want to test both of you—to see how proficient you are with magic. The return of magic is a big thing for them, and it's not like either of you guys are turning out to be what they wanted in the first place. Shane has been known to use violence to get what he wants, and you're more of a wild card."

"I don't get it," Jet said.

"Imagine that you've had information for years and years that magic will reappear and that a demon will be released to destroy the earth."

"I get that," said Jet.

Geb continued, "The Brotherhood knows ten times more than you think they do. They had the talismans, the cloaks, and they even had both books at one time. They had the keywords to open them, and all they needed was for magic to reappear."

"I still don't see your point."

"The Brotherhood believes that the Mikado and Czaric are destined to fail if they don't work together. This was the basis of much of what they have done. They don't like the Rivalry and even learned things along the way to bypass magic."

"Like what?"

"There are jewels and a dozen locations on the earth where magic has no effect. They have found about five and are searching for more."

"What?" Jet asked. "Why?"

"Essentially, they fear that if you and Shane don't work together, Arisol will win."

Jet said flatly, "Seriously?"

"They have a plan B, and I'm not entirely sure exactly what it is, but it has to do with Kevin McCormick?"

"This is totally crazy." Jet asked, "Why come to Chadwicks at all?"

"About sixty years ago, both books were stolen or hidden, depending on who you talk to. This really disrupted the Brotherhood's plans. They still had to open five schools, having lost the two most important books."

"What does that have to do with Chadwicks?"

"When the six of us were sent to you, Shane and the others, the Brotherhood felt it was close to reacquiring the books. Back then Shane was always their first pick for *The Sorcerer's Guide*. They had chosen a girl for Runic magic. At the time he wasn't more than twelve years old. His parents attended San Mateo when they were younger. That's where they likely met and where the Brotherhood first took notice of them. I was sent to your parents, as I explained before, and my sister, in fact, was sent to protect Shane. For two years, while I created a relationship with you and your parents, my sister was doing the same with Shane and his family. Another four students were being considered, but I don't know who they were. At some point Shane was sent to Dillon Lake, and about a month later, my sister went missing. This must've been when Shane was in sixth or seventh grade."

"Do you think Shane had something to do with your sister's disappearance?" asked Jet.

"I don't think so."

"Then what?"

"I didn't think the truth hit me until the last few days. I should've seen it before this."

Nana asked, turning to Geb, "What are you talking about?"

Instead of answering, Geb stared intently at Jet. "Can you do something for me?"

276

He was curious but unsure how to answer.

"Somehow, you found out that I was close to your family and that I gave you a tonic. It shouldn't have been possible. You know more than you're willing to tell me. How well do you know that day your parents died?"

Tapping his fingers on the table, Jet considered his options. He wanted to keep what he knew a secret, yet he wasn't entirely convinced that what he'd seen was the truth. Could a vision be manipulated? "Why don't you tell me why my parents were on the bus."

Geb said, his voice filled with anguish. "About sixty years ago, there was a division in some of the leadership. Different ideas about how to move forward were introduced. Some twenty members left and created a group called the Azurites. The Brotherhood had found this keyword that opened both books. They began adding information, letters, and such to the books. Around the same time as the Azurites were formed, both books went missing by a man named Jstor Farish. Even to this day, I have no idea if he was on one side or another. He was hunted by the Azurites and tortured for the locations of both books. They got partial information about the places and began searching. One was a man named Gamal, who was the historical leader in Asyut, Egypt, and a friend to the Brotherhood. The other was someone in Germany, and that's why your parents were on that bus. We only had a location but not a name."

"In my book," Jet said, "there's a letter that was sent to my great uncle from Gamal. He said that people were speaking with him. He sent some of the other items as well."

Nana added, "A lot of those items were in the storage unit."

"It's making more sense. Your parents hid, very well, I might add, that they had one book. I didn't know until the end."

Nana asked, "Where did the Brotherhood get the books?"

"That's a story for another time."

Jet asked, "What about the other book?"

"Vanished. Or at least until it showed up with none other than Shane Fallon at Dillon Lake. My sister had been missing for months, and Shane had a new book, just not the one that the Brotherhood thought he should have."

"Why my parents?"

"They had been gathering items and artifacts and were skilled at uncovering information and tracking down the next clue or location to follow."

"What happened?" asked Nana.

Geb traded a glance with Jet. Geb continued, "The information must've been leaked, or Remington and Alice were being followed. I don't know which. On the bus to the town where the book was supposedly hidden, Jet was given a tonic that caused him to lose his magical memories. The bus crashed, and his parents died."

"Makes sense," said Jet, slightly distracted.

Jet felt Geb's eyes on him. Glancing up, he asked, "What do you want to know?"

Geb said, "The truth. You knew the tonic was in orange juice. It's time to come clean."

"Wait," Nana roared. "You gave Jet the tonic and you were with his parents when they died."

Ignoring this, Jet asked, "Why was I traveling with them?"

"Parents traveling with children are less suspicious. And you had this ability to identify traces of magic even when it was invisible. Had I not seen it, I would've never believed it.

Magic relics leave hints, and you can follow them better than anyone I've ever known."

"I can't do that," he protested.

"Because of the tonic, you probably can't now. It's actually remarkable that you can use magic at all." Geb asked bluntly, "Who killed your parents?"

"How would Jet know?" asked Nana.

Geb stood quickly. "This is very important for me. Will you tell me the truth?"

"Why?" asked Jet.

"It might be a clue to what happened to my sister."

Jet pictured the three people in his mind. He had always focused on Rysen, but he knew who he was. But this time he focused on the other two. "Oh! My! Word!" Jet hissed as he put his hands on his head.

"What's wrong, Joshua?" Nana demanded.

"This is just crazy," he replied. "Part of the truth was staring at me all along."

"Who was there?" asked Geb.

Jet answered flatly, "Two men and a woman. I only focused on one of the men before today. I recognized him. He's a professor here at Chadwicks. His name is Professor Rysen, and he transferred from Dillon Lake last year. The other man was named Alex, and the woman is a perfect match to Dr. Descartes."

Nana growled, "Dalf Rysen, Remington's college roommate, is part of this? And now he's teaching here at Chadwicks."

Geb replied, "So Dalf has been working with the Azurites. This is unbelievable. I never got a good look at your doctor in the hospital. If what you are saying is correct, she was a council member of the Azurites."

"This is all too crazy," said Nana.

Geb asked, "What did Alex look like?"

"Um…" After a moment, he said, "He was like six-two, black hair and a mustache."

Geb said, "Sounds like Alexander Wozniak. He was a leader of the Brotherhood at one time. Everyone thought he'd been killed by the Azurites. He most likely found *The Mage's Letters* in Germany and gave them to Rysen while at Dillon Lake. I bet you that's where Shane got the book from."

Nana asked, "How did Dalf get involved?"

"My guess, jealousy and power," replied Geb. "The Azurites came to believe that Arisol wasn't the one responsible for the loss of magic on the earth. They've accepted that one of the Ten Kings didn't die and has become the being controlling the creatures called the Chupovanas. The Azurites want to control Arisol in order to restore magical balance and defeat the Chupovanas."

Nana, clearly confused, asked, "What are the Chupo things?"

Jet proceeded to give a general description, and Geb nodded in agreement.

"Does that mean that Shane is working with the Azurites?"

"Maybe," Geb replied.

Jet asked, "Does the Brotherhood know any of this?"

"Doubtful."

"Can you tell them?"

"Since I've decided to help your grandmother, I've been exiled from the Brotherhood. I'm like an outsider. I can ask for some basic resources, but I've lost my place within them."

"Well," Jet said, "they'll be here later this week; we can just tell them then."

"It's certainly something we should consider. But we also need to be mindful of Dr. Descartes. If she was involved in the death of your parents and now, she's close by; the Azurites have more influence than we ever thought possible."

CHAPTER 26

After a long nap, Jet pieced through the statements made by Geb. It was a lot to handle. By four in the afternoon, he felt that it was time to meet with his friends and figure out what they should do next. As long as he stayed on campus, Jet was pretty sure he would continue to improve. He still hadn't heard from any of his friends. They only had three days until the Brotherhood arrived, and there was so much to discuss.

An hour later Rick and Jackson stepped in from dinner. Jet immediately assaulted them with questions. "Where is everyone? Is there a meeting tonight? What has Jayco been up to?"

Rick said, "Everything is suspended until tomorrow. Why don't we enjoy a little Xbox?"

"Nope. We're heading out."

"When you say *we…*"

"The four of us. Call Keesha."

Keesha arrived fifteen minutes later, and none of them were happy about the prospect of searching for Jayco or any of the Echoes. Keesha protested by saying, "Jayco gave strict orders. You were not to leave the dorm, and you were never to be alone."

"I'm leaving in five minutes," replied Jet. "You can accompany me, or you can taste my dust."

Jackson pointed out, "You're moving so slow. I bet that you can't make any dust."

"Where do you want to go?" Keesha asked.

"Let's start by heading down to the updated teaching grounds."

Keesha shook her head. "You're crazy. A downright bonehead."

"How do you want us to get there?" Jackson asked.

"Let's take Napoleon's golf cart."

"We're screwed," lamented Rick.

Five minutes later he said, "Let's go." He wore his backpack with the golden pyramid, the tome, the second piece of the tablet, and the other items.

Finding and commandeering Napoleon's golf cart turned out to be easier than expected. The four of them headed out, and no one gave them a second glance. It took but a few minutes to get onto the main road heading south. They passed all the buildings and found a small trail heading off, away from the beach.

Jet said, "That is far more noticeable than it was before I left for Argentina."

Rick said, "Lots of people travel here. It's not a huge secret."

"I see," said Jet.

As before, the trail wound back and forth. The cart made it most of the way. It had taken twenty minutes to walk, but with the cart, just over five minutes. They parked the cart under a tree and began walking. This time speed was not part of Jet's plan.

It took another five minutes to cover the small distance to the natural area he'd seen before. It was still narrow at the front, but they had built up a defense of the site. Rock had been crafted as if naturally built, very similar to the narrow passages of Coso Subtrano. As Jet stepped through the narrow gate, the area opened into an arena five times larger than before. The space was completely empty of anyone. This part had been built like a dome, with smooth rock as the walls and the floor and a partial ceiling for the three-fourths of the space to his left. The small natural opening was still there, taking up the remaining fourth.

"Jet. Is that you?" cried Seyanna from a doorway in the rock wall to the right. Jet had completely missed this before. Yelling behind her, she screamed, "Hey, everyone, Jet's here."

"Not possible," Jayco shouted. "I told his roommate to not let him go anywhere."

Rick shouted back, "We aren't babysitters. He's quite stubborn, you know."

The rest of his friends piled out, and Mckenzey and a tall boy Jet assumed was Eric were the last ones. Mckenzey still had a cast on her leg, but she was using crutches.

Grantham yelled, "Get over here and come sit down."

"Where?" asked Jet as he moved forward.

Latisha pointed to where they had come from. "We built a sweet room back here."

Jet nodded and continued walking as calmly as possible toward his friends.

Rick whispered, "What should we do?"

"We're all going together." Halfway to his friends, Jet was surprised to see Maria and Sebastian were here.

Maria asked, "Is that really Jet?"

"Hey, Maria. How are you and Sebastian?"

"We're fine. Thank you. Looks like you are doing better too."

"I am," Jet said, though he was already starting to feel the pull and his energy.

"In here," Jayco said, and Jet was led down a small corridor that opened into a large room. There was a large table and plenty of chairs.

When everyone was inside, Jet asked, "Did Mckenzey make this?"

It was Eric who replied. "She sure did. It's amazing."

"You must be Eric," Jet said, and he held out his hand.

Eric shook it as the rest of his friends tried staring at anything but the awkwardness between them.

"What's your last name?"

"It's Callaway."

"Nice to finally meet you." Jet moved to the closest chair and took a seat.

The rest of his friends quickly found chairs around him. Eric sat next to Mckenzey across the table and to his right. Keesha sat on Jet's right, while Rick and Jackson sat to his left.

Jet said, "Jayco. You look like you've lost a few pounds."

Jayco chuckled. "It's been complicated the last few weeks. Not enough time in the weight room, I guess."

Latisha unleashed a disapproving click of her mouth.

"What?" Jet responded.

"Jet. You know that you look all skin and bones. You've lost like half your weight and you're asking Jayco about his."

"They didn't have a weight room in Argentina either," Jet said, but no one laughed.

Silence fell between everyone. Finally, Jet asked, "What's been going on?"

Jayco let out a deep breath. "We have around forty-eight students who have been divided into each Elemental magic group. There were another ten that didn't transform, but eight of them still wanted to be involved. We made a sixth group and called them the Aspsum. These guys keep a lookout and are pretty good with some of the other weapons."

"Great idea," Jet said. He noticed that some of the pent-up tension evaporated when he said this, as if his approval relaxed them.

Jayco added, "We hope that Maria and her group will be able to start coming to school next week. We haven't started with them yet."

Peering at Maria, he added, "That's good news."

Sebastian huffed.

"What does that mean?"

"He's just been, how do you say, cooped up. He feels like he's in a prison."

Jayco said quickly, "Like I said yesterday, we're waiting on Principal Fletcher."

"Maybe I can talk with her," replied Jet. "She owes me a favor or two."

"That would be wonderful," Maria said. "It has been a hard transition."

"I bet," said Jet.

"We need to talk," Jayco said, his voice strangely aggressive. "Things have changed around here."

The tension swam back into the room like a flood of rainwater.

"Naturally," Jet said. He felt an odd sensation, and he smiled wistfully, as if the inconceivable explanation of life had just aligned itself, if only for a moment.

"What's so funny?" Jayco asked defensively. "You don't approve of what we've done?"

"I've no idea what not to approve of. I'm clueless about what you're doing."

"You were dead," Jayco explained. "Tough decisions had to be made."

Jet's eyes fluttered to Eric, and Mckenzey glanced away. For the first time, he noticed several weapons in the corner of the room. He recognized some golden shields, swords, bows and arrows, a whip, and two hand axes. "What's this?"

Grantham spoke softly, "We decided to allow Maria and Sebastian to try and see if any of the weapons chose them."

An awareness that Jet had never felt before, the unnatural tingling of his fingers, almost overwhelmed him. Jet balled his hands into fists and pulled both hands to his chest.

"What's wrong?" Mckenzey blurted.

"Nothing," Jet managed to say, and with effort, he unlocked his fingers. "Did it work?"

"We haven't yet started," Seyanna said, her voice calm.

"I guess we arrived at the perfect time." Jet smiled. "Go ahead."

Jayco hesitated for a moment, then he pulled out all the weapons and laid them on the table. There were three golden swords, three bows and arrows, and the other two items. Jet watched as Maria stood and asked, "What do I do?"

"Try picking up each weapon," Jayco said. "It should be clear if you can or cannot."

Maria reached for the first sword but was unable to get closer than an inch to the grip. The same thing happened with the following two swords and the bows. By the time she reached for the whip, Jet felt an immense surge of tingling in his fingers. He knew that she wasn't going to be able to pick up a single item before her. Afterwards she sat down dejected.

"Can I try?" asked Sebastian.

"Sure," Jayco said.

The second sword glowed red, and Sebastian was able to pick it up without hesitation. He beamed as he closely inspected the blade.

"What about us?" Rick asked.

Jayco glanced at Jet, who refused to answer.

"Sure."

Neither Rick nor Jackson were able to pick up anything, but one of the bows glowed red as Keesha touched it. Latisha gave her ten golden arrows.

"This sucks," Jackson said.

Maria mumbled, "I had the strongest feeling that something was going to choose me."

Jet choked down a swallow. "I felt it too."

"Really," Mckenzey asked.

"He's just mocking us," Jayco said. "Screw you."

Ignoring this, Jet reached inside his backpack and removed the two Katars and the circular ring blade, placing them on the table.

"Do you think that one of these is for me?" asked Maria.

"No. They are not." Jet removed the white cloth and held it out to Maria. "These are yours. Take good care of them. They saved my life a time or two."

"What do you mean?" demanded Mckenzey as she jumped to her feet.

Maria accepted the white cloth and opened it to find three dazzling golden orbs.

"No way," Grantham said. "Those are yours."

"Not anymore."

A red glow flashed through the room as Maria touched the orbs. "Oh, my," she hissed. "These are beautiful."

Rick and Jackson both reached for the newly added weapons but came up empty.

Jet said, "Sorry boys."

"Stupid," Jackson seethed. "Idiotically stupid."

Jet asked, "Where are the rest of the weapons, items, and other treasures?"

"We moved them out of the science building to *a safer location*." Jayco winked at Jet knowingly.

Turning his attention to Eric, Jet asked, "Which Elemental magic group did you get chosen for?"

"No," Mckenzey said quickly. "We haven't gotten around to it."

"What are we waiting for?"

"You want this to happen?" asked Jayco. "Mckenzey said you had some concerns."

Eric stood, placing both hands on the table. "I'm right here, man."

Jet stood and stared directly at Eric. "Are you willing to join our magical fight to stop Arisol?"

Eric nodded eagerly. "I am."

"Then let's do this." Jet pointed to an area behind the table. "How about over there?"

"Perfect," Eric hissed.

"I should do this," Jayco said.

"It would be my honor."

"Holly hells," Mckenzey screamed. "Stop the male flexing show already. What are we really doing here?"

Jet said swiftly, "The Brotherhood is going to be here in a few days to determine if the school stays open. There were six students killed in Argentina after we left. I just heard the news from Geb." Pointing to Eric, he added, "Dillon Lake has been teaching about magic for the last ten years. I bet he knows a lot about the theory of magic, so let's give him a firsthand demonstration."

Jayco walked back to the table, glaring at Eric. "Did you know about Arisol before we talked to you?"

"Yes," Eric said fearlessly.

"You did?" Mckenzey asked.

"Like Jet said, it's an open topic at our school. We know a lot about the Brotherhood, and they come to the school often. We've had one of your students, Kevin McCormick, for the last few months. I don't personally know him, but he's well on his way to having more power than Jet. I mean, look at Jet; he can hardly stand. You need all the help you can get."

Mckenzey asked, "Why didn't you tell us sooner?"

"I couldn't. And when your leg broke, it told me that something weird was happening with you. It was the first time I thought magic could be involved. I mean, Chadwicks was the least likely of all the schools to find magic. But trust me, no one's leg breaks like that all of a sudden."

Grantham asked, "What are you saying?"

"Chadwicks, Jet, and the rest of you are in danger. You think you have things figured out, but you don't. I think someone attacked Mckenzey."

Latisha reacted. "Are you serious?"

"Is that why you wanted me to go to Dillon Lake?" Mckenzey asked. "To get away from Chadwicks. Why didn't you tell me the truth?"

Eric replied, "I was forbidden. Look, the Brotherhood has these different drinks. When you agree to learn about magic, you have to drink a yellow tonic. You become forbidden to talk about magic with any outsiders. Before I came here with you, Mckenzey, I couldn't have said a single word to you."

"And after you arrived?" asked Jet.

"The school and everyone's involvement allowed me to talk about it with you."

Seyanna asked, "Why didn't you?"

"Honestly, my concern is for Kenz."

"Eric," Mckenzey hissed.

"Oh, sorry. Mckenzey. I needed to know that she was safe. I wanted to know that you have her best interests in mind, like I do."

Mckenzey's face reddened.

"Unbelievable," Jayco said. "What have we done?"

Seyanna asked, "Anyone have an idea what these tonics are?"

Eric replied, "The Brotherhood may be limited on true magic, but they've been studying the art of spells and enchantments for years. They've found some pretty powerful concoctions."

Grantham replied, "This doesn't even sound possible. What do we do now?"

Jet cleared his voice. "Add him to our Elemental group. He knows things."

Mckenzey asked, "Are you saying you want Eric here?"

"He's told us things we didn't know before. This could be good." To Eric, he asked, "What do you know about Kevin?"

"He gets preferential treatment and special classes with some of the younger Brotherhood teachers. He walks around the school like he owns the place. He has rubbed a bunch of the upperclassmen the wrong way, but it's like he is protected or something."

"Kevin is at Dillon Lake," Seyanna repeated. "I can't wrap my mind around that."

"After Eric becomes part of the team, we can talk about this more. We all need to be on the same page. Who's going to do the honors?" Jet felt that he was hemorrhaging energy, and he sat on the table.

No one moved for a long time.

Mckenzey stood and pushed Eric. "You're here because of me. I got you all into this mess."

"Kenz. Don't say it like that. I don't have to be here if you don't want to."

Mckenzey replied, "Jet's right. We need your help. Let's get this over with."

Eric moved to the empty chair. The room was silent.

Standing over Eric, an instant before she said anything, Mckenzey glanced quickly in Jet's direction. He saw it but was purposefully staring at Eric. Mckenzey said, "Parfit Inclusionem."

Eric responded as if he'd already been told what to say, "Suscepit Parfit."

At first there was no response. After a moment a faint aqua blue aura appeared, and a groan escaped half the group.

Jet said, "Guess you're with Mckenzey."

CHAPTER 27

After everyone was seated around the table, Jayco asked, "What's the plan here? What really happened in Argentina?"

Jet said, "This war that we find ourselves in is so much more complicated than we ever thought."

"I got that," Jayco said, "from Alces back in Coso Subtrano."

"Where is that magnificent moose?" asked Jet.

"She left us right after we escaped," Grantham said.

"What is Coso Subtrano?" Eric asked.

Rubbing his hands together, Jet glanced around the table. "First we need to come to some sort of agreement in the leadership of this group. Things are a little out of control."

"Things are fine," Jayco said. "But we cannot have one person in charge. This needs to be a group effort."

"It seems like we touched on this subject before, back in the science building."

"Well, we're no longer in the science building," Jayco said. "Since we came back from Silverton, I've made a lot of changes, increased the followers of Elemental magic, and rescued several items, including you. If the six original members of the Echoes aren't the leaders, then it should be a partnership, me and Jet."

"Dude," Grantham groaned.

This was followed by, "Holly hells," from Mckenzey.

Jayco said, clearly angry, "Mckenzey, I don't think you mean what you're saying."

She said quickly, "I meant it exactly how it came out."

"That makes no sense," he retorted.

Mckenzey laughed humorlessly. "Don't you remember how much my mom hated me swearing. So I made up my own words and, if you remember, said, 'Holly bells.' I've just changed the second word."

Eric interjected, "I've heard it like a hundred times."

"Not helpful," Jayco countered.

"*Stop!*" Seyanna shouted. "None of this is helping. If we don't figure this out, I'm gone."

"Why?" Jayco said. "Because you don't like how I do things?"

"No. We've talked about this before. I told you that you're going too fast. Before Jet returned, Mckenzey had a foot halfway out of the group. Latisha is sick of not knowing what's going on, and I can only imagine what Jet is feeling after surviving his ordeal."

"Do you think you can do better?" Jayco asked.

Seyanna rubbed her lips. "The point is that the book opens for Jet. He's the Mikado. We should be following his lead."

"His lead almost got him killed, and where would that put the rest of us?"

"Sorry," Jet said. "We're not making any changes."

"Why won't you listen to anyone else's ideas?" Jayco demanded.

"We need to treat *The Sorcerer's Guide* like our mentor. We get information through the book that helps each and every one of us. Sure, I'm the only one that can read the pages, but the ideas and words are for all of us. Each of the original five, not including me, is in charge of their tyros. You are the leaders of your magical area. That's what the tome wanted, and that's what we're going to do. We don't have time to argue about who has done what. We've all sacrificed, and each of you is vital to the success of what we're trying to do."

"What about the rest of us?" Keesha asked.

Jet said, "There are twelve of us here. We can be the Elemental Council, and if there's something big to discuss, we can call you six up, and we can vote on whatever the issues are. Does this work?"

"If it doesn't," Jayco said. "I'll recommend more drastic changes."

Muttering under his breath, Jet added, "I'm sure you will." To the group, he said, "Now, to more pressing concerns. How much do the newcomers know about the Rivalry?"

They spent the next hour ensuring everyone was on the next page.

Once finished, Jet said, "I've been approached by Principal Fletcher, Geb, and Shane over the last few days. Turns out that there are members of the Brotherhood at each of the five schools. The leadership of the Brotherhood will be here on Friday, and we've been asked to work with Shane. I'm not sure we really have a choice."

"Unbelievable," Jayco said. "How are they going to stop us?"

"Kevin McCormick," Eric said. "That's how. Along with all the amulets, tonics, and other mechanisms that they have. They could close the school and tear up each of your scholarships or acceptance letters. They are much more powerful than you can imagine."

"What are they going to want?" asked Mckenzey.

"Have you ever heard of the Azurites?" Jet asked Eric.

"I don't think so."

Jet said, "We're fairly familiar with the Brotherhood, and they are protectors of magic, and they want to stop Arisol. Years ago, they possessed both *The Sorcerer's Guide* and *The Mage's Letters*, the book that Shane has. All along, the Brotherhood felt that the two groups should work together to defeat Arisol. Several members, with different ideas, broke away and formed the Azurites. Somewhere along the way both books were lost. Now Shane and I have the books and I'm not sure how the Brotherhood feels about this."

"But they need you," Mckenzey said quickly.

Grantham asked, "Can he perform magic?"

Eric answered, "Not like you can, but he's being taught ways to use magic nonetheless."

"No one has actually given him the keys to magic," Seyanna said.

"I don't think so," replied Jet. "We need to walk carefully with the Brotherhood."

"Are we actually going to work with Shane or just say that we are?" Grantham asked.

"Probably both. Shane came to my dorm a few nights ago. He says that he's protecting the school against something. Shane is worried. He specifically wants to talk with Latisha."

"Why me?"

"He heard a rumor that you can sense animals and that you've been edgy about a few things."

"I only said that to a few members of my magic group. How would he know?"

"I think he has spies in our group," Jet concluded. "What have you felt?"

Latisha licked her lips. When she spoke, her voice partially shook. "There's something evil roaming near the school. I've no idea what it is. It's an animal of some sort, and it has hatred and desire like nothing I've ever felt."

"You never said anything to me about this," said Grantham.

"I didn't want you to think I was overreacting."

Jet replied, "It's called a Chupovanas."

"What?" Jayco said. "What's that?"

"Siwalik told us about them, at least partially."

"Who's Siwalik?" Mckenzey asked.

Jet opened the tome and read the descriptions of the Drekavac demons and the Chupovanas. Jayco, Grantham, and Latisha all explained what they'd seen. Jet described Siwalik, and there was a healthy discussion about the creatures who take pleasure in stealing magic.

Once they were finished, Seyanna asked, "Why have they come here?"

"My guess," Jet said, "there hasn't been much magic on the earth since Goth Airtha. We've been adding loads of people to our magical groups. The Chupovanas are attracted by the allure that the school is giving off."

"It sounds like the school is protected," Mckenzey said.

"There's a talisman at each of the schools." Jet shared his vision of the Middlesex family and the lunch in the Italian restaurant. He finished by saying, "I have no idea if the talisman can stop the Chupovanas permanently, but I bet we'll need to work with Shane to stop them."

"What if we don't?" Rick asked.

"What?" Seyanna asked. "Work with Shane, or these weird devils find a way into the school?"

"The latter," answered Rick.

Jet said, "I'm confident that I saw one of the Chupovanas attack Vinny back in the alley in Los Angeles when Mckenzey and I were looking for Kevin. It was not a pretty sight. The creature devoured Vinny and his magic. It was one of the most gruesome things I've ever seen."

"Should I be surprised that things feel more complicated than ever?" asked Latisha.

"What else have you got for us?" Jayco asked.

"A bunch of stuff, but I don't have the energy right now. I'll be lucky to get back to my dorm without crashing. Let's plan on meeting tomorrow to prepare for the Brotherhood. We'll need to find time to work in a meeting with Shane."

"Does he know that you are the Mikado?" Grantham asked.

"Yes. He mentioned our little encounter back at Silverton."

The group dispersed. Rick and Jackson each tried all of the weapons again to see if there had been a mistake. Mckenzey pulled Eric into the corner, and they began whispering.

To his surprise, Maria sat in the chair next to him. She held out the three orbs. "I don't think that I understood half of what was said today." Her ability to speak English was remarkable. "But I'm pretty sure I understood that these are yours. I can't take them."

Jet laughed. "It's not like I have all the power. They *were* mine for a short time, but I can't even hold them anymore."

"What does that mean?"

"Watch." Pointing at the orbs, he said, "Drop them into my hand."

Placing his palm upwards, Maria released the orbs, and they fell as if they were going to land in his palm. An inch from the skin, they veered away, scattering across the floor. An instant later they were flying back into Maria's hand.

"That's crazy." She gasped.

Others in the room watched the interaction. He thought he saw Seyanna shaking her head. Jet stood, ready to leave. Grabbing his backpack, he picked up the tome. When he had set out this afternoon, he intended to give back the second tablet piece, the golden rectangle, and Iris's pyramid. Instead, he kept each of them, unwilling to share all his secrets with the newest members of their group.

Mckenzey's voice was slightly amplified. "I need to talk with him for a moment."

Jet was reasonably sure this was about him, but he didn't want to stick around to find out. He made his way out of the stone room, down the hallway, and into the open area. Again, he was astonished at this section; it would be a great practice arena.

Without a word Jet stumbled to the far corner in search of the golf cart. Rick, Jackson, and Keesha caught up as he sat in the passenger seat. Keesha started the engine, and they headed back to campus.

Halfway there, Jet asked, "Anyone up for hamburgers?"

"Oh, yes!" Rick agreed. "I'm starving. Nothing to eat all day."

"Didn't you guys go to the cafeteria before we left?"

Rick amended his statement. "*Feels* like I haven't eaten all day."

The group hooted, and Jet felt an increasing level of comfort with these friends. Sitting outside of Porters with Keesha, he watched his roommates head inside for food and shakes. Several students recognized him, and while some pointed fingers, others came up and introduced themselves or asked how he was doing. Jet met people that he'd never seen before. Despite feeling worn out, he tried being as friendly as possible.

During a break in the celebrity onrush, Keesha asked, "What are your thoughts on Eric? He's as good looking as they come. So tall and mysterious."

"That's a loaded question," Jet said, trying hard not to smile. "He seems nice enough."

"How can you trust him, coming from Dillon Lake?"

"Oh. I don't trust him."

"You allowed him to become one of the council. Seems like a big deal."

He said flatly, "I did that for Mckenzey and Mckenzey alone. She's in a tough spot.

"You didn't let Jayco off so easily."

"It has never sat well with Jayco that I was chosen, and he wasn't. He desperately wants to be leading the group. His actions, though, could be detrimental. He's already put all of us at risk."

"Seems like a double standard to me."

"It's not easy to gain trust around here. Eric will have to prove he is trustworthy. You, Rick, and Jackson have impressed all of us. Keep up the hard work. I have a feeling that we're going to need your help in the upcoming weeks and months. Things seem to be getting more and more complicated every day."

"What if I don't agree with you?"

"Be bold and communicate your thoughts."

After a short silence, Keesha added, "I do actually agree with you about Eric. I just wanted to understand your reasoning."

"We'll need to watch him closely."

"Why do you say that?"

Jet didn't explain everything but enough about Professor Rysen for Keesha to understand that the professor had come from Dillon Lake as well. "He's mixed up with the Azurites and teaching at our school. I bet he has some tricks up his sleeve. If Eric communicates with him at all, we'll know something is up."

"Good to know. Should I tell Rick and Jackson?"

"I think you can handle watching Eric for now. Are you in?"

"Without a doubt. I got this."

Rick and Jackson returned with food five minutes later. They sat and talked while enjoying the cool January night. It was already dark, but it felt so enjoyable to be outside. Jet breathed in a deep breath, trying to release some of his darker inner thoughts.

Keesha headed home as he, Rick, and Jackson returned the golf cart and strolled into their dorm building at a snail's pace. As they stepped out of the elevator and neared their door, Rick retrieved a folded note taped to the door, handing it to Jet. It read:

Jet,

Meet me tomorrow, 8 pm, at the place you almost fell to your death.
Bring your closest friends and no one else.

Shane

CHAPTER 28

At seven thirty Jet and the Echoes left Kelci Halls and travelled eastward. As they crossed campus in the direction of the CeU building, no one spoke. Soon Jet slowed behind the pace of the others, feeling tired and frustrated.

As they crossed College Avenue, Jayco joked, "Jet, I think a dead man is healing faster than you are."

"I'm good," Jet wheezed. "Went for a walk this morning. Must've gone too far."

Mckenzey, still using a scooter for her leg, whispered, "You haven't left your dorm all day. What's going on?"

Jet rolled his eyes but tried sounding casual. "I'm good. Were you assigned to babysit me today?"

"Nana and Principal Fletcher are worried about you."

Seyanna added, "That's why we have a ride to the cliffs waiting for us ahead."

"I was whispering. How did you hear what I said?" asked Jet.

"Gifted," Seyanna replied.

"I can't keep all the talents straight," Jet said, but the building ahead was starting to spin, and he closed his eyes tight. A hand touched his shoulder and helped direct him.

They found two off-road vehicles near the back of the parking lot. Jayco drove the first with Grantham and

Mckenzey, and Seyanna steered the second, with Latisha up front and Jet in the back. It was ironic traveling in the exact vehicle that had transported him after he nearly fell to his death at the beginning of the school year. His own talents had prevented his death. Turned out, Shane had used Runic magic to cut his rope, and now he was expected to work with him.

They crossed over the first ridge with Jayco in the lead and driving and hollering as if he were having the time of his life. Jet gazed back at Chadwicks and the picturesque ocean and, for the first time in months, wondered if he was handling this like he should.

Seyanna interrupted his thoughts when she asked, "What should we expect with Shane?"

"Honestly, I'm not sure," Jet said. "I don't trust him at all."

"None of us do."

"What did the others say?" he asked.

"That it is downright crazy for Principal Fletcher and the Brotherhood to ask you to work with him. No one is happy."

Jet nodded but said nothing.

Grantham yelled from the other vehicle, "Shane is already here. And it looks like he brought a few friends."

Sitting on several rocks near where Jet had fallen were a dozen people, including Shane. He recognized the clothing of the Light Riders on five of the students. They wore white shirts with a unique insignia of an unbalanced triangle next to an uneven star; the two objects never touched. They also had on red jeans and white loafers. Vinny, Jake, and Jocelyn had worn the same clothing before Vinny and Jake were killed. Jocelyn was still part of the group, but four others that were new. Clyde, a boy that Jet had met earlier in the school year, seemed to be the new leader or a paramount. Clyde had knocked Jet off his feet when he and Mckenzey had been ambushed. The other three he didn't know.

Another group stood further back, as if an afterthought, and it included Ariana, Autumn, Raul, and six others. Jet was surprised to see them here. He wondered if they had been placed into their own group as they all wore a black shirt with a white insignia of a bench with a single line. Above the bench was a circle, divided into four, and a single dot in each triangle. They all wore black pants and black shoes.

The Dark Angels were the last group, and this was Shane's group. Each of them wore black leather jackets, a black undershirt, and black pants. Jessiva and Nash were still part of this group. She wasn't nearly as menacing as she had been on the first day they had met. Nash had recovered from his broken leg, and he stood near Shane, smirking at Jet.

Grantham whispered, "We should have brought more people."

"If they attack, we have our gear in the back of the four wheelers," hissed Jayco. Any tension between the Echoes had evaporated the moment Shane came into view.

Shane yelled, "That's far enough."

Jet and the others lined up next to each other. Mckenzey, still using her scooter was in the center.

Jayco yelled, "You brought a small army. Where is that brown-haired guy that we saw at the museum?"

"Do you mean Martin?"

"I guess."

"That's interesting you should ask about him. He can still use magic, but he's sort of lost his mind. You see, it was as if he was attacked and suddenly, he lost the ability to use a black mace he was given from Silverton. He can't come within a few inches from touching it. He sort of went crazy for a few days. He's helping with another project."

Grantham asked, "When did this happen?"

"A few days after Christmas."

"What time in the day?" Mckenzey asked.

"Just after lunch."

Mckenzey whispered, "That was the same day and time that my leg broke."

"And," Jayco hissed, "Jet can no longer use his orbs."

"What was that?" Shane asked loudly. "Don't hold back secrets now."

Pointing to her leg, Mckenzey said, "That's the same day and time that my leg spontaneously broke."

Jayco added, "Jet also lost the ability to use a weapon."

The expression that appeared on Shane's face was contrary to what Jet expected. There was fear and confusion. The arrogance in his voice was gone. Shane pointed to Ariana, Raul, Autumn, and the others. "Like you, sort of. I have a rune that I can draw on the back shoulder of someone, and they'll be placed into one of the forms of Runic magic. Motion, Life, Darkness, Matter, and Mixture. I doubt that will mean anything to you. The transformation didn't occur with these individuals, but I've found a way to use them to benefit both of us."

"What are you talking about?" Jet asked.

Shane said pointedly, "The school is under attack."

"By whom?"

Tapping his leg, Shane appeared to be considering what he should say. "With the help of Faunal, I was able to strike a bargain with the diablitos of the Drekavac demons. They were the ones that attacked part of your group in Argentina."

Jayco's voice flared, "You sent those things to kill us."

"Maim and injure, I'll agree to that," Shane said, though his voice held no contempt. "When I first started reading *The Mage's Letters*, I came to believe that Elemental magic would be my enemy. I thought that either your group would control Arisol or mine. But lately my eyes have been opened to the idea of us working together. I'm guessing that we have similar plans and ideas. Working against each other will cause us both to fail."

"What's your point?" Grantham yelled. "We don't have all day."

"Faunal helped me, Jessiva, Nash, and a few others to find the second piece of the Phoenix. We went in and missed the second most important piece, Siwalik. I had no idea he was even there. Faunal later helped me make a deal with the diablitos. It took time, but they revealed a superior creature that had been found in Argentina that could help fight against the magic stealers."

"What are you talking about?" Seyanna asked.

"I think you know. The Chupovanas. They're at our doorstep, trying to sneak inside Chadwicks and kill all of us."

With anger and hurt in her words, Latisha screamed, "You killed those people back at the museum! You just murdered them."

This time Shane's voice became powerful and angry. "You know very little, Latisha. You're just as helpless as a tadpole in a lake with sharks and killer whales. Don't judge me on how little Jet has told you. I'm not as naive or ignorant as you."

"What do you mean?" Jayco demanded. "We know about the Chupovanas. We know about the diablitos and much more."

"But has Jet told you about the Tribe of the Khalicaans?"

"The who?" Seyanna asked.

"They are the wind whispers who control the Chupovanas. They are the walking sinners of times past. As far as I can tell, they have dominion over the Chupovanas. The Khalicaans have palish skin, red eyes, and blackness around their eyes that seeps into their faces. They are those who have died for their sins, but their bodies can't rest. In some cases the Khalicaans can control humans, like back at the museum in Switzerland. They were either tracking you or one of us. The four people I killed were essentially already dead. They weren't as pale, but they still had red eyes and darkness below their eyes. I killed them to save us all. Your ignorance will eventually get you slaughtered."

"Why have you called us here?" demanded Jet.

Lifting two fingers dramatically, he said, "The Brotherhood will be here on Friday. We'll meet them in a building that is hidden on the school's property. We'll show you the way."

Mckenzey countered, "Why?"

"A show of unity."

"Can we bring anyone else? You have nearly fifteen here."

"You can bring your council if you want." Shane sneered.

Jayco asked defensively, "How do you know about our council?"

"Please. Don't be foolish. I may not be able to see inside your little arena, but don't think that I don't have ears everywhere."

"What's the second reason?" asked Grantham calmly.

Pointing to Ariana and the others, Shane said, "In Runic magic these are Operai. They cannot do Runic magic, but they can handle the Claustra."

"What are Claustra?" asked Jet.

"You guys are like newborns. You know nothing. Each school is given seven Claustra to be used if attacked by Chupovanas. They must be buried in the correct location to form a barrier against the Chupovanas. We've buried five, but only two have worked. We can't bury them without your help, and they won't work correctly until the Khalicaan that is attached to one of us is killed."

"What are you saying?"

Shane shook his head. "It's not that hard to understand. There's a Khalicaan near campus, hiding somewhere, controlling a Chupovana. We need to find and kill the Khalicaan."

"Why us?"

"There are some things that you should know about this tribe. In fact, one of *you* likely spotted the Khalicaan the night that Vinny disappeared. Whoever glimpsed the girl is the only one who can see the enchantress going forward and will have the best chance of killing her. Now that she has been seen, she's nearly invisible to the rest of us. If we work together, we can defeat her. On the plus side, the enchantress cannot kill the rest of us until she kills the person who viewed her, but the Chupovanas can. Jet has been gone for weeks, lost in Argentina, and the rest of us have lived. The chances that Jet saw the Khalicaan are astronomically high, and it's up to him to die or kill the Khalicaan."

"Are you freaking serious?" Mckenzey lashed out, shouting, "Abzu!" A thunderstorm erupted, and shards of ice torpedoed down from the sky. Shane and all his cronies ducked for cover. Some tried to draw runes of protection, but none of them did so fast enough. The ice storm lasted for half a minute. Mckenzey was breathing hard when it was done, and all of Shane's friends were on the ground, some injured.

Shane stood and asked, "What was that for?"

"You could have told us sooner, you prick. We've left Jet open for an attack. We could've sent him somewhere else."

"You're not the only ones watching him," seethed Shane. "He has been closely protected while he's been at the school."

"Thanks for sharing the details," said Grantham.

"It's important that you know about the enchantress."

Jet asked calmly, "How do you kill a Khalicaan?"

"With an enchanted blade," Shane replied.

Sarcastically Jet said, "Have any extra ones lying around?"

"I'm sure you'll come up with something."

"What about the Brotherhood?" Jayco asked. "Are they in danger?"

"Only if Jet is killed between now and Friday."

Seyanna asked, "Do you know what the Brotherhood wants?"

"They want assurances that we're working together. They'll ask us what we are doing. We'll need to tell them about the Khalicaan, the Chupovanas, and what each of our magical groups are doing individually."

"So, basically, you want us to lie," replied Seyanna.

"Hey, new girl, I'm here so that we can start working together. Chill out with all the hostility." After a long pause, Shane added, "Look. It's in both of our interests to work together."

"What do you want from us?" Jet asked.

"We need to get the Claustra working as soon as possible. The school's protections are succeeding at keeping one Chupovana out, but the school's defenses might fail if more come. The Khalicaan has been disrupting our process, and it's impossible to have someone guard the zones each day. Your team can help us."

"Can the Khalicaan get onto campus?"

"Yes. I'm not sure if you noticed, but magical fighting between us is limited, and I don't get the feeling that the tribe can kill Jet on campus. If he leaves, he'll be fair game."

"Where are the Claustra, now?"

"We tried burying some near the baseball fields. The two that are working are near the beach and by the bookstore."

Grantham asked, "Where did you get these protective items?"

"Not important."

"What happens if we kill the Khalicaan?" Mckenzey asked. "Will we still work together then?"

"I believe so," Shane said slowly. "Working together is far more effective than working separately. But killing the Khalicaan is going to be a real challenge."

Jet began laughing; he couldn't help himself. When he recovered, he added, "There's no way you're telling us the whole story."

Shane's eyes narrowed. "Why do you say that?"

"If only I can kill or see the Khalicaan, what would be the point of standing guard and protecting me? If the Khalicaan can walk wherever it wants and not be seen, it could walk into my dorm while I was sleeping and kill me without anyone being the wiser. You don't actually know if it can or can't hurt me on campus."

Shane rubbed his forehead. "We might not be able to see it, but we'll be able to feel it. The Khalicaan doesn't want to kill you, but the reason why it latches on to one person is that it wants to use you to get inside the school and kill everyone else. It's hiding somewhere, preparing a ritual, to force you to allow the Chupovanas into the school. The talisman prevents outside attacks, but there's a way around it. The Khalicaan will use you to allow the Chupovanas into the school. Your death would actually be a blessing to all of us."

"That's the Shane Fallon we all know and love," Jet hissed. "Why are Ariana and the others here?"

"Protection and power. You never know what's coming around the next corner."

"You're unbelievable," replied Jayco.

"Don't act like you aren't trying to prepare for war yourself, Jayco Carter. I know that you've introduced more than thirty tyros into your circles. Why wouldn't you after I found the second piece of the Phoenix? We've been pitted like dogs in a fight by someone above our paygrade. If we work together on this and more, we can actually win this war."

"We'll think about it," replied Grantham.

"No. I need an answer today," Shane said.

Jayco turned his back on Shane and added, "You'll have it."

"Hey, Jet, the Mikado," Shane shouted, "you really don't understand the essentials of this, do you?"

"Understand what?"

"We are in the minority. It's a tale older than time. Those without the power will want the power. The Khalicaan is only the beginning of those who will come searching for what you and I have. Whether you have Runic or Elemental magic, we're being hunted right now. Let's hope Jet makes the right decision, or the rest of you will suffer the consequences."

"I hear you."

"The Brotherhood is another group wanting for a place at the table. They've used Kevin to create that place. I think there's something wrong with him. Keep up your guard with the Brotherhood."

Grantham headed toward the four wheelers and the rest followed.

"One more thing," shouted Shane. "The boundary of the campus is shrinking every day. It's something that, no matter what we do, continues to happen. We think there's a Chupovana near Moon's Landing. Maybe Latisha can get a better idea of where it could be hiding."

"That cliff is twice the size of Devil's Landing," pointed out Jayco. "The forest is thick back there, with some great hiding places."

"Exactly what we were thinking. Head there tonight, after midnight."

"After midnight is breaking the curfew," Latish said. "What happens if I get caught?"

"You won't. Bring Mckenzey and her new boyfriend as lookouts. I think I remember Eric from my time back at Dillon Lake. He's grown up quite a bit."

"Thanks for your advice," Grantham shouted.

They sped away without saying another word. They went to Porters and pushed together two tables. After everyone was seated, Jayco asked, "What do you think?"

"He's probably lying," Grantham said.

"There was a figure outside the alley before I went searching for Kevin," Jet said. "I thought it was a homeless girl. She had red eyes and black smudges on her face. I'm not sure why I didn't think anything of it sooner."

"Are you saying we need to work with him?" Latisha asked.

"Until the Brotherhood and the Khalicaans are no longer here. After that, who knows."

"I loathe the idea of working with Shane, but Jet's right," Jayco said.

Everyone nodded in agreement. They ordered food and spent time planning the next few days.

Once they'd finished, Mckenzey asked, "Did you get a look at Ariana and Raul? Is there something we can do to help them?"

Jayco replied, "Let's worry about that once the Brotherhood is long gone."

CHAPTER 29

Thirty yellow school buses drove onto College Avenue around three-thirty, and the entire campus was loaded onto one of the buses. Principal Fletcher had ordered the entire school to attend a late-night field trip to the zoo. This was a once-a-year field trip, and the message was sent out Friday morning. The students had been buzzing with excitement all day. The zoo was an hour away and would be shut down to facilitate the adventure. Unique animals would be on display, and most of the students would have a chance to ride or pet several animals. A dozen food trucks would be called in to cater the evening.

Rick, Jackson, Eric, and Keesha glared out the window, clearly upset that they hadn't been asked to stay behind to meet with the Brotherhood. These four friends sat in the second to the last bus, searching the second story of the CeU building for where Jet and the others were hiding.

Seyanna whispered, "Did I hear that Nana and Geb were ordered by the Brotherhood to leave?"

Pulling his eyes from the buses, Jet stared at Seyanna. He said, "They've been ordered to return to Silverton. There has been a lot of activity around the small mountain south of town."

"The same one we got into looking for the Phoenix?" asked Grantham.

314

"The same."

Jayco asked, "But why?"

"Geb learned through Nana about the bones, crystals, and those weird looking alligator creatures. The Brotherhood sent someone to see if they could sneak inside and look around. They found kids lurking about, trying to get inside. Geb and Nana are being sent to meet up with the Brotherhood and report back if they find anything."

"Will Nana go hiking?" asked Mckenzey

"I doubt it. I really think they were just sending them away from California."

Jayco stated, "The Brotherhood meddles in everything."

"Very true."

Once the campus was deserted, Jet and the others walked down to find Shane, Nash, Clyde, Jessiva, and two others that hadn't been up the canyon. Each of his friends wore their cloaks and brought their golden weapons.

Shane quickly introduced the two students. "This is Trudi Veeshing from Toronto and Asher Enzo, born in Singapore but living in California. Both are new to our groups, students at Chadwicks, but they have interesting things to say."

This unexpected twist from Shane didn't sit well with Jet. Trudi was more than husky and was considerably overweight. She was confident, social, and had a kind smile. Asher was short, nearly five feet tall and was someone that stood unnoticed, blending into the background. They were far from what Jet was expecting from Shane's magical group.

"Couldn't you have said something yesterday?" asked Jet as he took up position in the back seat of the same off-road vehicle.

Shane hissed, "You guys were practically running away."

Jayco asked, "Why the new friends?"

"You'll see."

It took twenty minutes to head south, even further south than the turnoff to their practicing facility. Shane stopped his vehicle, and Clyde removed a branch acting as a gate to a hidden road. The gravel road wound back and forth for a few miles. Jet wasn't sure how they could still be on campus. At one point they drove through a one-way tunnel. When they exited the opposite side, they found a large and spacious building in a valley completely hidden only a mile or so away from the outskirts of Santa Barbara.

Three black SUVs were already parked at the back of the building as Jet and his friends drove up. This building was newer and more sophisticated than the other buildings on campus. It had a similar style, with cobblestone walkways and gigantic trees. The exterior of the building was a dazzling sight of columns, stone inlays, and an expensive combination of metal and wood. Only a drone would've been able to find this building.

Principal Jan Fletcher, Professor Dickerson, and Mr. Smuin stood near the front doors, waiting for Jet, Shane, and the others to arrive. After parking, Shane confidently strolled to the doors, and they were ushered inside. Jet ambled forward, trying to retain his energy and avoid appearing weak.

The building felt like a lodge, and the entrance was massive and elegantly decorated. Ahead there was another set of large doors and a hallway that shot off to the left. In this section the heads of animals hung on the walls, from this country and others. The large doors further on opened, and four teachers, including Professor Rysen, stood there, awaiting their entrance. Upon seeing Professor Rysen, Jet's blood ran hot, and he wanted nothing more than to attack Rysen where he stood.

A hand gripped his shoulder, and he found Mckenzey pulling him forward. Jet regained control over his emotions and nodded to Professor Rysen and the others. He and his friends were escorted into the next room. It was a small auditorium, and Jet observed a built-in stage with elongated tables like something you would see at the Capitol building. Behind each table were cushy chairs, and two dozen people sat, almost perched as they scrutinized the group entering. The doors slammed, and Latisha flinched.

Principal Fletcher instructed, "Please sit in the first two rows. Runics on the far side and Elementals in the chairs closer to this side." But she didn't need to show them where to sit. One set of benches was entirely black, while the other was golden. Jayco led the group to the closest set of seats. In the middle seat, Jet sat quickly, with Mckenzey on his right and Jayco next to her. Seyanna sat to his left, followed by Latisha then Grantham.

"Welcome Sorcerers and Mages!" a voice boomed from an older man, who appeared to be Chinese, with long white hair and a long white beard.

The other delegates around the older man began clapping, all except someone on the far right. Jet's mouth fell open as he recognized Kevin McCormick.

The older man continued, "I am Li Wei, and I'm the commander of the Brotherhood."

Again the other delegates began clapping. This time Kevin joined them.

Li Wei continued, "Two my left are chiefs Lara Brancoff and Ahmed Saeed, and to my right are chiefs Ethan Davenport and Junjie Su. We are the chamber electees that govern the decisions made by the Brotherhood. The other delegates are divided among our leadership." Each person nodded slightly at the mention of their name.

Jet eyed each of the chiefs carefully. The woman, Lara, to Li Wei's left, was dazzling, beautiful, and the youngest. Junjie Su was older and quite diminutive. Ethan was broad-shouldered and in his sixties. Ahmed was thin with a long black beard that he kept playing with. None of the five stared down with any type of kindness; it was all business.

Principal Fletcher broke the silence by saying, "We thank you for your visit, High Praefectus. Chadwicks is thankful for your generosity." The principal and all the teachers sat in the middle of the room, several feet from Jet and Shane.

Li Wei tore his eyes from the students and spoke directly to the staff. "Chadwicks has exceeded our expectations. We are both delighted and made uneasy by the state of affairs. We are at a loss as to what should be done."

Glancing around, Jet found Jessiva staring at him from the second row with contempt and anger.

"What is the status of the Phoenix?" demanded Li. "Who has found the first piece? Do we know where the next piece might be?"

Grantham held a black decorative box with Egyptian carvings they had found in Switzerland before the Brotherhood. All eyes, even Kevin's, stared hungrily down at the box.

"We know not how you found that before we did," Li Wei said as he nodded slightly while he spoke. "But we are glad that magic has been reawakened. Without it, finding the Phoenix was impossible."

Shane replied quickly, holding up his own findings from Coso Subtrano, "I present the second piece from Argentina. We found this long before Jet and his friends."

"Incredible." Lara Brancoff cheered; her voice was sweet and high-pitched. "Two different types of magics at

Chadwicks, and they're both going after the Phoenix. We never would've imagined Chadwicks to play such a vital role. Turning her attention to Principal Fletcher. "You must be proud. When we agreed that you would remain at Chadwicks after the passing of your husband, we never would have foreseen this incredible outcome."

"Thank you, Chief Brancoff," Principal Fletcher said in a soft tone.

"Enough pleasantries." Li Wei cut through the conversation. "We want to see *The Mage's Letter* and *The Sorcerer's Guide*. Present them to the Delegates.

Grantham reached into a bag at his side and pulled out *The Sorcerer's Guide*. He approached and placed the open book on the table before them. The gasps from the room were evident. Shane did the same with *The Mage's Letters*. Jet knew that he was not the only one impatient to see the other book. Jet was certain that Shane and his friends had tried to steal his a few months ago. *The Mage's Letters* did not appear like any book that he'd ever seen. From his seat, he noticed that there were dozens and dozens of letters, kept together by a leather cord stretching from top to bottom. Shane kept his book closed.

"Extraordinary," Chief Saeed replied, awe in his voice. "To be in the presence of two of the oldest and most important books in our lifetime is inspirational."

"Do you know why we are here?" asked Li Wei; the thickness of his accent was far more pronounced with this question.

Shane said, "To examine our aptitude and determine how we can better serve the Brotherhood."

Li Wei laughed throatily. "How long did it take you to come up with that reply? Very diplomatic. Duly noted." The

High Praefectus stood, appearing intimidating and insightful as he stared down at Jet, Shane, and the rest. He was tall, lean, and there was something impressive about how he held the room. "We've decided on only two options as we move forward to prepare for the eventual release of Arisol. His rebirth nears like an avalanche approaching the base of the mountain. It is inevitable. For decades the Brotherhood has anticipated this moment, to defend humankind from the sleeping devil. We hoped that the Brotherhood would create a magical army to rival those of ancient times. We selected likely candidates. All of our plans have been for naught as the two divination tomes lay before us, in the hands of the unexpected."

"Have we disappointed you?" ask Principal Fletcher.

"Not completely," Li Wei answered. After a long pause, the High Praefectus began pacing, and words spilled from his mouth. "The Brotherhood was born at the Starving Peaks. Criminals entered the hidden cavern desiring to control the magic within. It's always about controlling the magic. They brought slaves and servants only to become slaves themselves. Many died but not my ancestors nor the ancestors of many in this room. The slaves emerged with hordes of treasures along with the two books that lay before us—*The Mage's Letters* and *The Sorcerer's Guide*."

Li Wei continued, "We kept these items hidden for decades, but evil came circling back, and we were forced to send many items abroad, or the books were stolen from us. How these treasures fell into your hands, we know not. But the rumors of their uses have led us to believe that you can't be trusted."

Peering over at Shane and his friends, he saw they were preparing for an attack. For the first time, he noticed that they wore protective breastplates. Shane would defend himself from whatever might come.

Jet's words were loud and clear. "We're learning and following the guidance of the mentors inside our tome. We understand how dangerous Arisol is and we're gathering information to stop him. Elemental magic is powerful, but we don't know everything. We need more time."

Junjie Su spoke for the first time. Her voice was diminished but steady. "Are you saying that you can read the book? It appears blank to me."

"Yes, it does, but it has provided much information, but does so in its own time."

She asked Shane, "Does your book speak to you?"

"*The Mage's Letters* cannot be opened. It is forbidden. The words become visible on the back of the book." Shane, pointing to the knot, added, "If this knot is ever broken, all would be lost."

"You only reveal this information because you recently learned that we had found the truth," replied Li Wei coldly.

Jet, Jayco, and Grantham exchanged a quick glance.

"You mistrust us," Shane acknowledged in a kinder voice than Jet had ever heard, "but you also misunderstand. We've been called into the Rivalry by the Ten Kings. Even if you wanted to, you could not stop what is going to happen."

"What are you saying, boy?" demanded Chief Ethan Davenport.

Shane stood. "The Rivalry is why our benches are black and theirs are golden." Pulling out his remaining Katana, he added, "This is black because of our ties to the Rivalry. No one else can touch these items except us." Pointing to Grantham, he added, "Grantham has that long sheath with a half circle. If you notice, it is golden."

"Each of you, place your weapons on the table next to your book."

Hesitantly Shane and Grantham followed the command.

Li Wei demanded, "Kevin. See which of the two weapons you can pick up. Try reading from both books. *The Sorcerer's Guide* will turn page by page, while *The Mage's Letters* has a piece on the back that will reproduce the letters inside."

From the far-right corner, Kevin McCormick stood and walked to the edge of the stage. The fall was about two or three feet. Instead of casually lowering himself, Kevin jumped and flipped in the air several times before landing. He whispered words that Jet had never heard before. He landed and moved lightning fast to the table before anyone could react. His hand movement was fast as he tried to lift both items.

A force field prevented Kevin from grasping either weapon. Kevin's hands shook as he attempted to break past the protective barrier. After a full minute, he released his effort, but Jet was impressed with Kevin's strength. Even though he couldn't break through, Jet thought he saw Kevin's hands inching closer. Kevin snatched up The Sorcerer's Guide, and Jet watched in horror as Kevin tried turning the pages. To his relief, Kevin grunted and said, in a cold voice, "The pages are blank, and I can't turn them."

He wordlessly dropped the book so that it closed on the table. Reaching for *The Mage's Letters*, Kevin was partially blocked by Shane, who drew a rune and tried knocking Kevin across the room. Kevin was not anticipating the attack, but he barely traveled a few feet. Kevin reacted, and Jet thought that he touched a stone embedded in his hands. In the next instant, powerful flames and wind slammed into Shane. There was no time to construct a shield rune, and

Shane and his friends were gripped with fire and wind. While distracted, Kevin picked up *The Mage's Letters* and immediately stopped his attack.

Within the span of a few seconds, the fire and wind stopped. *The Mage's Letters* was back in its place, and Kevin was seated back in his chair, looking bored. Kevin muttered, "Can't see anything, Praefectus."

Shane and the others glanced at each other, unsure what to do.

"My apprentice," Li Wei replied, "is far more advanced than you are. He and his disciples will remain at Chadwicks to oversee the planning of the remaining four Phoenix pieces. He will decide strategy and any attack planning. Both pieces will be given to Kevin for safekeeping. The Brotherhood will not allow Arisol to be released or any deceit to undermine our preparation."

Shane faced the chamber electees. "High Praefectus. If you will, all is not well at Chadwicks. In fact, you need to leave as soon as possible. You are in danger."

"What is the meaning of this?" asked Chief Brancoff.

Shane nodded at Trudi Veeshing, who stood and replied hesitantly, "Chupovanas have been awakened by our magic. They're attacking Chadwicks and as we speak, they are searching to find a weakness. The outside protective border is weakening and growing smaller each day."

Li responded, "How would these creatures know where to find you? They haven't been seen in centuries."

"They track magic like any animal who tracks prey."

"How can you know this?" asked Chief Davenport.

"If you will allow me to perform a rune, I can show you."

Li Wei nodded hesitantly, and from the corner of his eye, Jet saw Kevin tense.

As she drew in the air, Trudi spoke. "I am a motion conjurer, and I can track large animals or compelling magical events." Trudi's hands drew a right and left single claw facing each other. She then placed a circle completely around the two pieces. From a pouch at her hip, she pulled out gray powder. She sprinkled a light dusting on the rune, and the whole room went dark for Jet and everyone.

Jet could see a light igniting the entire room as he looked inside the rune. He was awestruck as his eyes adjusted, and quickly realized that he was staring at the building they were currently occupying, but from a short distance away.

Shane's voice spoke. "I brought Trudi so you could understand. Jet and I are working together against a common enemy here and now. Arisol is a serious threat, but so are the Chupovanas. They're here to kill everyone at this school."

A deer-antlered beast stepped into view, but it was shrouded in blackness with only white eyes and three deer antlers clearly visible. The creature bellowed and ran full force forward. It crashed into an invisible barrier fifty feet from the building, but a piece of his right antler passed through the barrier.

In a raspy, cruel voice, the creature bellowed, "Your cherished magic will soon be worthless. I will massacre the lot of you." The mostly hidden creature sprinted away amused. His speed was unimaginable.

The vision ended, and Trudi sat in her chair, breathing hard.

"Was that real?" demanded Chief Brancoff.

Shane pointed to Asher Enzo, who stood and drew a rune of his own. He drew a large image of pi. Around the image, he drew a three-sided triangle, then he sketched another triangle upside down on the first triangle. Enzo said, "At the precise rate of decay, without the successful placement of the Claustra, the barrier to Chadwicks will be destroyed in nineteen days. Chadwicks will be overrun in a matter of hours." Where the rune had been there was now a complex mathematical equation that gave a countdown for eighteen days, sixteen hours, and seven minutes.

"Li Wei asked, "How can this be stopped?"

Shane responded, "Let Jet and I continue working together. We will find a way."

"Who has seen the Khalicaan?" asked Junjie Su.

Shane continued, "We do not know. But we'll find out in the next day or two."

Li Wei stood. "If the barrier at Chadwicks falls, then all the schools will be at risk."

Jet said, "Our thoughts exactly. We could use Kevin's help."

"No," Li Wei shouted. "Kevin cannot remain at Chadwicks. Our presence here will be catastrophic if the Chupovanas steal his magic or disrupt our plans. Both of you must work together and stop the Chupovanas from finding a foothold." Pointing at Principal Fletcher, he added, "How could you have allowed us to come into this danger? You will be reprimanded."

Jet, feeling slightly bad about how this had turned out, added, "High Praefectus. I alone knew about the Khalicaan and the Chupovanas. I informed Shane, and we've only revealed the truth to those who can help stop them from entering the school. Principal Fletcher was not made aware."

Li Wei asked, "Will you work with the Czaric to help stop the Chupovanas?"

Jet replied, "Already happening."

Another loud crash erupted from the east side of the boundary; this time the entire building shook.

Li Wei exclaimed, "We must leave. Chadwicks will continue as before. Fletcher, keep us apprised of the conditions here."

The entire entourage of the Brotherhood was gone in minutes. As the group left, Chief Junjie Su stared at Jet as if trying to communicate something. For the first time, she had a look of kindness on her face. He had no idea what she was trying to say, but all too quickly, she and the others vanished. Soon the sounds of cars tearing out of the parking lot reached their ears.

Shane and his friends left almost as quickly. The other teachers had vanished.

CHAPTER 30

Sweat poured down Jet's face as he tried using a hand shovel to dig another hole. He was exhausted and took a moment to catch his breath. A week had passed since the Brotherhood had left, with very little development. He was too weak to be of much use, and sometimes he felt so dizzy that he could barely stand. They were near the campus bookstore, reaching the northern boundary of campus. He had worked on two and a half holes, while each person in the group had created ten, at a minimum. The moon was just rising; it was a full moon tonight. This was apparently a requirement for the placement of the Claustra.

There was a movement to his right, and Ariana and her brother Raul inched into view. They pretended to work on another hole as Ariana asked, "Why are you helping Shane and his friends?"

"I'm not helping him," Jet wheezed.

"Why are you doing the grunt work? You're the leader of the Elementals!"

"These creatures are coming after all of us. I've got to do something to stop them from attacking the school."

Raul said, "I just would've never guessed *you* would help him."

Jet's laugh sounded more like a cough. "I'm as surprised as you are. It's like we're allies until he stabs me in the back.

I'm relieved this is the last Claustra to put into the ground. This better work." To Ariana, he added, "At the beginning of the year, I thought you and Shane were dating."

"Sometimes you're so clueless. It's not all about kissing and snuggling."

Raul interjected, "I don't need to hear this."

Jet's eyebrows raised slightly. "So not dating?"

"No way in hell."

"Then what's the deal?" asked Jet.

Ariana, scanning around, found Jessiva pulling out a small wooden crate nearby. She whispered, "Autumn tried to warn you, but I don't think you got the point."

"Warn me?"

"Shhh," Ariana hissed. "You see, I overstated why Shane came over to our house during the summer. He can draw a rune that can identify those with an ability to perform runes. If you don't pass the test, he draws another rune of subjection. Neither of us had much of a choice."

"What?" Jet mouthed. "Are you serious?"

"Completely." Ariana groaned.

Raul hissed, "Don't get us in trouble."

Staring at his old roommate, Jet asked, "Raul, when did Shane do this to you?"

"Last year."

"Why didn't you tell me?" Jet felt like his mind was blown.

"I couldn't."

"Why did he draw this rune on you?"

"He knew that you were from Silverton, and he wanted me to keep an eye on you. I didn't find anything that made him think that you could do magic. Suddenly this year, you've surprised everyone."

"Things have been crazy."

"Understatement of the year," Ariana said. "No offense, but you look terrible. You've lost weight, and you can barely walk."

"It's been rough."

They chatted quietly as they continued working. Jet barely managed to finish a fourth hole before he was worn out. Raul and Ariana both helped him, and he was grateful. As they said their goodbyes, Jet felt an overwhelming sense of compulsion. Latisha arrived at that precise moment to give him a ride, and they also chatted casually back to his dorm. He said nothing about the book and headed straight into the bathroom to shower. Turning on the water provided him a few minutes to read what *The Sorcerer's Guide* wanted to show him.

Claustra

Claustra is the first combination of magic and machinery created in our society. We knew that something needed to change following the decades of sudden attacks by demons, Chupovanas, and other creatures, especially at our sacred locations.

Two Sorcerers set off to uncover different possibilities, and the Claustra were created. They are remarkable magical machines that allow a small area to become impenetrable and protected. For years our tribes would stand guard only to succumb to a missing person, a killing, or the disappearance of an entire village. The attacks often began from within the underbelly of the earth.

Sorcerer Gelaki from Elemental Fire and Sorcerer Mifdye from Elemental Earth created seven clusters of seven Claustra. It took ten years to be completed. Once done, they were sent out to the seven kingdoms to be used appropriately.

Warning: It is direly important that they are to be used as they were intended. If you do not set them into the ground as instructed, they will not work. If they are set up in a certain order that is incorrect, they will signal the Chupovanas and allow them into the area, despite other enchantments or protections.

Each Claustra has been given a number. To find the number, you must use Elemental Fire. To place them, you must use Elemental Earth. The Claustra can only be placed within three days of a full moon. The first Claustra placed must be number 7. They must be placed outside of the area you want protected. Water, Rocks, Oceans, or Rivers do not count as barriers.

These instructions seem simple enough but dire consequences for those unwilling to follow.

Jet burst from the bathroom in only his underwear, screaming, "Call Shane or Jessiva *right now* and tell them to stop whatever they're doing. Get the Echoes and Shane over here."

"What are you talking about?" Latisha asked.

"Make sure they don't put the last Claustra into the ground."

Latisha quickly dialed Shane's number, and he heard her say, "Jet insists that you must stop any further placement of the Claustra. He has new information. Get over to his dorm as soon as possible."

The swear words through the phone were unmistakable.

Shane added, "I'll call Jessiva, and we'll be there in ten minutes."

Latisha's next call was to Jayco, and he promised that he would hurry over.

Returning to the bathroom to shower, Jet hoped that they had just prevented a disaster.

Fifteen minutes later, Jet finished dressing and exited his room to a packed entertainment room. Shane, Jessiva, Nash, Clyde, Rick, and Jackson stood at the far wall. Jayco, Mckenzey, Eric, Latisha, and Grantham were along the opposite corner.

Stepping in, and all eyes focused on Jet. He had purposely left his tome in his bedroom. He noticed Seyanna's absence but said nothing.

"What's the deal, Black?" Shane hissed. "We've been working too hard to start over. You better have some pretty good—"

Jet interrupted, "Where did you get your information about the Claustra?"

Shane hesitated. Finally, he said, "What does it matter?"

"Tell us about them."

"I already did. They'll prevent the Chupovanas from entering the campus."

"But we already have the protection from the talisman on campus."

"I don't know," Shane admitted bitterly. "I was told that the talisman protects the school and limits the damage we can do to each other but that eventually the Chupovanas will find a way inside."

"Where did you get the Claustra?"

"From the same source."

There were cries of frustration.

"My source," Jet roared, "informs me that upon putting the last Claustra into the ground near a full moon, if it's the wrong direction, it will call the Chupovanas and other creatures to the school, nullifying the talisman."

"My source said nothing of this."

"Interesting." To the group, he added, "The claustra are magical machines, and you need to use Elemental Fire to see what number they are, and Elemental Earth to dig the spot, all within three days of a full moon."

"What?" Jessiva responded. "We are within that window, but we probably need to get them into the ground tomorrow. Who is your source?"

"My book."

"I want to see it," Shane demanded.

"Not happening," replied Jet. "Tomorrow we'll use magic to see if the numbers are there. After that, we will put them in the ground."

Jayco asked, "How close were we to putting the last one in the ground?"

"Jet and the others finished the last few holes," explained Jessiva. "I was just about to place the last one when Shane called."

"If Black were right, we would've been dead in a few hours," replied Shane. Any composure that Shane might have lost was back within seconds. In a commanding voice, he said, "Everyone, meet tomorrow at the cliffs, and we'll test Jet's theory." He and Jessiva hurried from the dorm.

After the door closed, and Grantham said, "We're screwed if we have to keep following Shane's lead. I'm not sure he has half the answers he thinks he does."

"Where's Seyanna?"

A few eyes fluttered to Jayco. After a moment, he said, "We had a small fight earlier. She went to dinner with her parents."

"A fight over what?" asked Latisha, who had clearly been caught off guard to the same extent as Jet.

"No big deal. It's already resolved. She just texted me that she's almost back on campus. No worries." Jayco smiled, and he and Grantham left.

Mckenzey whispered, "Jet. Can we talk?"

Before he could answer, Eric peeked inside the dorm and asked, "Kenz. Is everything all right?"

Mckenzey replied quickly, "Fine. I'll fill you in. Let's go." With enthusiasm she said, "See everybody tomorrow." She refused to look at Jet, who felt his stomach drop into a frozen abyss.

Shouting erupted from the hallway, and Shane, Jessiva, Jayco, and Grantham bolted back into Jet's dorm. The door ricocheted open, nearly hitting Eric and Mckenzey.

"What's wrong?" cried Jet.

She exclaimed, "You were right. Trudi just called, and Jessiva admitted to burying the last Claustra. The Chupovanas are going to attack in the next few hours."

"What did Trudi see?" asked Jet.

"More than one Chupovana heading in the direction of the school."

"How long do we have?" asked Jayco.

"Maybe an hour or two."

"What do we do?" asked Mckenzey, and all eyes, including Shane's, turned to Jet.

"I need Seyanna and Jessiva to dig up all of the Claustra and bring them to the quad outside. We need to bury the Claustra in order. We also need a plan to defend the school. We don't have much time before these beasts are going to come to steal our magic. Everyone else meet back outside this dorm in fifteen minutes ready for battle."

Shane insisted, "We can have some surprises waiting for them."

"So can we," Jayco replied. "I'll call Seyanna. Where do you want to meet her?"

Jessiva replied, "Near the bookstore."

"Let's get going!" Jet screamed.

The dorm emptied quickly, and Rick and Jackson sprinted out as excited as Jet had ever seen them. They were finally going to see some action.

Grabbing his cloak, Jet wore it for the first time in weeks, and the material felt flawless in every way. It was dark gray and was perfectly fitting; the material was nothing like anything he knew. He remembered the spinning wheel of colors when he first put it on, and a small smile crept across his face.

The moment slipped away as he realized that he had no weapon, and the reality was, he had very little energy to sustain him. He had some magical rings that could provide a slight boost in energy, at least he hoped so. Jet clutched his backpack with his tome, Iris's pyramid, and the remaining magical items hoping he would have enough strength and ingenuity to survive tonight.

Two minutes later he stood in the open quad outside his dorm building. Using some rocks, he began drawing a rough outline of the school. He knew there were seven Claustra that needed to be arranged correctly. He drew a 7 near the CeU building but farther out in the field. He placed a 6 near the sports fields and a few hundred feet south of the CeU buildings. The number 5 was even further south, while 4 was placed directly south of campus, but more centrally. The number 3 was placed near the boardwalk on the beach side of campus, and 2 was two hundred feet further north. The last Claustra, 1, was destined to be placed in line with 3 but at as far north as possible. An attack from the east seemed the most likely.

Rick and Jackson were the first to arrive and Keesha was not far behind. They watched him as he worked. More people began to arrive as he finished the diagram. Looking up, he found nearly fifty people. The weapon of choice for the Runics was a black club. Those chosen for defense wore wrist guards or a chest protector. Everything they carried was black. The Elementals had golden objects for their offense, such as staffs, swords, and bows and arrows. A few held a shield as a defensive item. Jet only recognized a few students. The Elementals and Runics began practicing their magic on each other, though they didn't try anything on someone of the opposite magical discipline.

Mckenzey and Eric were the first to arrive from the Echoes. Another ten minutes later, Seyanna and Jessiva appeared with a handful of red objects three feet long. He hadn't ever seen the things before. They were spiked on one end and round on the other. Jayco, Grantham, Shane, Nash, and several others arrived minutes later.

Trudi joined the central group, gasping. She managed to mutter, "We should expect two or three Chupovanas. They'll be here in less than sixty minutes. Probably more like forty."

Shane demanded, "What's the plan?"

Pointing to the rocks, Jet said, "I need Jayco and Seyanna to accompany me to each spot. We'll bury the Claustra. Send groups of Runics and Elementals along each border. Once the Claustra are placed, less protection will be required. Remember the Chupovanas can attack from land or water."

Jayco asked Grantham, "Can you get everything arranged?"

"I think so," Grantham responded.

"Don't forget about the Khalicaan," Shane reminded the group. "She can't kill any of us until she kills Jet. Or she's killed. No offense."

"None taken."

He continued, "You need a special sword or knife to kill her. Do you have one yet?"

"Let's see if we can find a way around killing her tonight. I don't know if it is possible, but what we want to do is protect the school."

Shane rolled his eyes. He then added, "When she attacks, she should become visible again."

"Should?" Mckenzey questioned.

"Doesn't matter," Jet replied. "We need the Claustra in place before the Chupovanas arrive. Once a Claustra has been placed into the ground, we need only minimal protection in that area. The final one to be buried at northernmost point on campus. That's where we'll all meet…if we make it that far.""

"Lit," replied Grantham. "We'll be ready with a few surprises up our cloaks."

A hoard of bellows erupted from several different directions. The sounds were petrifying and menacing.

Shane replied, "We'll be lucky if we don't die tonight."

CHAPTER 31

Shane, Grantham, and several Runics and Elementals rushed off to the north. Turning to Rick and Jackson, he said, "Help Grantham organize everyone. Afterward, split up with one of you going to the east side and one to the west."

"Roger that." Rick and Jackson grinned and sprinted after Shane.

"What about me?" Keesha asked.

Jet whispered, "Watch and follow Shane. Make sure he doesn't do something that's going to get all of us killed."

"What?" she gushed. "You don't trust him?"

"Get going." Turning to his friends, he asked, "Anyone have some energy rings or drinks?"

"I do," Mckenzey said. She handed him three rings, and five bottles of mud water. Other refreshments were handed out.

"Thanks," Jet replied.

"What do you want us to do?" asked Mckenzey.

Scanning around, Jet said, "Honestly, they could attack from anywhere. Either go north or south and warn us if anything happens."

Latisha said, "I'll go with Grantham. We'll head south."

Eric replied, "That leaves the north for us."

Jet nodded, and he, Seyanna, and Jayco began heading north but away from the beach. Jet sprinted five steps before tumbling to the ground. Jayco, carrying the Claustra, still managed to catch Jet before he slammed into the ground.

Seyanna said insistently, "Jayco, you're going to have to carry him."

"Seriously?" Jayco asked. He pushed up golden bands from his wrist to his biceps and smiled. With ease, Jayco lifted Jet and carried the Claustra.

They sprinted near the CeU building and continued past it, into the fields beyond. Seyanna easily outpaced them and reached the spot first. A few minutes later, Jet and Jayco arrived.

"Should I start digging?" Seyanna asked.

"No. It has to be done with magic." Jet fell to his knees, gasping for breath. He noticed Jayco and Seyanna sharing a quick glance. The Claustra were dropped on the ground. Jet began arranging them, side by side.

"What now?" asked Seyanna.

Jet spoke, "Chango," and the air around them grew warm. The instant the warm air touched the Claustra, a number became visible.

"Oh my word," Seyanna said. "That was cool."

"I could've done that," replied Jayco.

Jet reached down and found the machine that was marked with a 7.

"Why number seven first?" Seyanna asked.

Jet said quickly, "Those are the rules." Without hesitation Jet spoke, "Pan," and the ground shook, and a hole opened. He shoved the tip into the dirt, and the earth mysteriously buried the Claustra. A bright, light-blue circle shone in the ground, and a small filmlike barrier sprung up in the air. The film didn't last long, and Jet assumed it was because only one machine had been buried correctly.

Speaking into his phone, Jayco said, "First one's done."

They set off for the next, with Jayco carrying Jet. They were starting to feel pretty good about themselves by the time they reached the fourth location. Only twenty had passed. This time they needed to make sure they went far enough south to protect their hidden hideout. Jet opened up a hole and was about to throw in the Claustra when an explosion rocked the air. It came from their right, back toward Santa Barbara, and the night sky became illuminated by an eerie orange glow. A large flame of fire shot into the air as if something had collided with a gas station or a semitruck.

Seyanna cried, "Not good!"

Jet tossed in the Claustra, and the hole sealed itself. The protective film was more evident on the east and south sides of campus now.

"Three left," Jayco said as he hoisted Jet up and ran forward.

As they finished placing number three, Seyanna screamed, "There's something ginormous coming out of the water."

Studying the water, Jet was spellbound as a mountain of a creature emerged from nowhere in the middle of the ocean. He shouted, "The Chupovanas are here."

The beast's tough skin glowed in the moonlight. It stood twenty feet tall and twenty feet in length. It was even more impressive than Jet had imagined. Screams and shouts and Elemental magic such as fireballs and wind were hurled at the creature. It made no difference as the rhino creature's skin was too thick, and it rumbled toward the beach and the school unfazed.

Without hesitating, Jayco picked up speed. They reached the next spot, the second to the last, and Jet landed awkwardly on the ground as Seyanna fumbled with Claustra number 2. Jet spoke, "Pan," once again, and the ground shook.

Jayco commented, "That brute is less than ten feet from shore."

"Not helping," replied Jet.

Screams and cries blanketed the night and students retreated.

Seyanna gripped the Claustra and tossed it to Jet. He caught it and stabbed it into the ground. The hole closed, and an instant later, the film vaulted into the place. The tremendous concussion of sound and air detonated around them. Jet was thrown face forward onto the ground, as were several others around him. Dalkiate was knocked back twenty feet, and a deep crater changed the beachfront shoreline.

"It worked!" Seyanna bellowed, and she quickly stood up and did a happy dance.

"One more," Jayco shouted, and he picked up Jet from the waist.

Dalkiate didn't attempt to bash the school a second time, nor did it seem injured. Instead, it veered north as if sensing the last open area from which to attack the school. They dashed past the bookstore and onto College Avenue and continued up a small hill. Shane, Jessiva, Mckenzey, Eric, and dozens of other kids stood prepared to defend the school. There was fear and panic on everyone's faces. Dalkiate would tear everyone to pieces.

Jayco bellowed, "Move aside!"

The students parted, and Jayco rushed through the opening. Seyanna had taken a different route and was well ahead of Jet. She was at the northernmost point possible, and most of the students knew what this meant. A cheer burst from the crowd as Jayco neared the spot.

Jet was placed on the ground, and he spoke, "Pan," and the ground shook, and before them, a small opening in the earth uncovered itself. Seyanna smiled triumphantly and began to toss the Claustra to Jet. Before she could, vicelike hands plucked Seyanna from the ground and lifted her into the air. The creature hissed, and Jet glimpsed the deerlike antlers.

"Kee-Faux!" bellowed Jet.

The head of the deer, with its fanged teeth, twisted in his direction. Jet knew that he had only the strength for a single spell. When the nudging within him arrived, he was surprised by the thought but didn't hesitate. With as much power as he could, he spoke, "Agni!" A green aura materialized in Jet's vision.

A flash of light so bright that the entire night was turned to day exploded from Jet. The consequence was astounding. The deer was inches from tasting Seyanna and stealing her magic when it threw her, trying to protect its own eyes, and retreated dozens of steps. A feline that had been stealthily advancing toward Mckenzey and Eric was knocked aside by the brightness. Maybe the greatest effect was on Dalkiate, who was running full speed along the beach and was sent sprawling, causing a small earthquake as he slid more than a dozen feet.

Jet dropped to the ground, heading towards unconsciousness.

Seyanna was flung, landing hard, and the Claustra was pitched into the air; end over end, veering away from Jet.

Shane Fallon stepped out from a shadow and caught it.

Dread and fear coursed through Jet. From the ground he wheezed, "What are you doing?" In the back of his mind, he wondered if the time had come for Shane to double-cross them.

"Remember," Shane shouted, "The last one can't be set until you kill the Khalicaan. The only way to protect the school is to kill the Khalicaan."

Jayco shouted. "How are we going to find the enchantress?"

"She's here," Shane barked. "These creatures wouldn't be here without her."

"What are we supposed to do?" Jayco asked. "Look at Jet. He is barely conscious."

"The other option is that he can die."

Jet tried standing, but he didn't have the strength. "What happens if I die?"

"Then the last Claustra can be placed without a problem." Shane smiled coldly. "Either way, it's a win-win for me. You look pathetic. That last spell took all your energy. You don't really think you can win?"

Pointing to an open area north of campus, Latisha said, "The Chupovanas are starting to recover."

"I'm going to puke," Seyanna said, and all eyes turned to her.

"Did that thing hurt you?" Jayco asked, clearly worried.

"That deer thing squeezed me so tight, I think I broke a rib. This is not going to be pretty."

Shane, appearing almost delighted, took a step forward to watch. Bending down, Seyanna started dry heaving, and a smile crossed Shane's lips. With lightning-fast speed, Seyanna punched Shane in the face, so hard that he was knocked back a few feet, staggering to the ground. The Claustra tumbled out of his hand, and Mckenzey reached down and picked it up.

Standing over Shane, Seyanna said, "A girl just kicked your ass. Get the rest of your Runics up here to protect this opening until Jet finds a way to kill the Khalicaan. Where are your black animals?"

From the ground Shane hissed, "Where are your golden ones?"

"Right here," Grantham said, and he presented Jet with the three golden pyramids.

Hands helped Jet to stand. First, he drank some mud water and placed two rings onto his fingers. Next, he pulled out his own pyramid and whispered, "Pyramis of Aurum." Iris transformed and leapt from his hands, landing gracefully. She nudged the other pyramids, and they quickly transformed. Iris returned and licked Jet's face. Surprisingly, this gave him a wave of energy. He whispered, "Protect me as best as you can."

Shane shouted, "Hey, Black...if we're doing this, don't go getting yourself killed."

Before he could respond, Nash hollered "Something's coming!" Jessiva helped Shane to his feet. Clyde and a dozen Runics were close by, all prepared to fight.

From behind the CeU building, a majestic purple moose galloped fast into a clearing. She wove between rocks and trees, heading northward.

"It's Alces," Latisha screamed.

Shane asked, "Is that purple moose friendly?"

Jayco acknowledged, "She's with us."

"She's not alone," replied Jet. Thirty feet back, but gaining speed, a hooded figure rode a saber-toothed tiger of sorts, with dark green fur and two large tusks at the front with several thorns on the back.

Shane asked, "Is someone chasing her?"

"Yes. She's riding a tiger."

"That must be the Khalicaan," Shane answered. "The rest of us can't see anything."

"We've got to protect her."

"How far behind the moose is the tiger?"

"Ten feet and moving fast."

Jayco and Shane passed along the information, and suddenly magic, both Runic and Elemental, was unleashed at the assailant. The Khalicaan had covered half the distance, but the onslaught of strikes caused her to veer off and halt her attack. A minute later Alces galloped through the only remaining open area for the school.

"Alces," Latisha squealed, "why are you here?"

Alces, in her musical tone, replied, "Because you all are about to die. I tried finding Siwalik, but he won't make it here in time. If you think that this is over, you have no idea. Another five Khalicaans are waiting for my sister to kill Jet."

CHAPTER 32

It took several long beats of Jet's heart for him to understand what Alces was saying. By the time his lips moved, he wasn't sure he'd heard correctly. "Your sister?"

"What's going on here?" Grantham demanded, and he lifted his long crescent-shaped weapon directly at Alces.

Latisha asked, "Are you with them?"

"I'm here to defend and help Jet. I departed from my sister long ago."

Shane countered, "How can we trust you?"

"Quiet," Eric shouted. "Those big, nasty creatures are gathering. Who are they talking with?"

Jet took his eyes off Alces momentarily and recognized the hooded creature still astride the tiger in an open area three hundred feet ahead. "That is the Khalicaan. I see her." Turning back to Alces, he said, "If she's your sister, I can't just kill her."

"Why?" Alces said quickly. "You don't have a choice. I will help you."

"I don't have an enchanted blade. I don't have the energy; I can barely do magic."

"We're dead," Shane said, only half-disheartened. "Or at least you are." To Jessiva, he said, "Release the Death Pack, and we'll protect the school, or what's left of it."

"They're over here." Jessiva pointed to where Nash and several other Relics were situated.

Grantham asked, "Is Faunal coming to fight?"

Without a further explanation, Shane said, "He's busy," and walked off.

Alces, her eyes never leaving Jet, asked, "What's wrong with you? Where's your magic?"

"Lost it in Coso Subtrano."

"What about those orbs you had?"

"Gone."

"And" —Alces shuddered as if realizing something—"no other weapons?"

"None."

Alces bristled. "How many humans know magic?"

"We have fifty Elementals," Jayco said. "Shane told us before that they have around forty Runics."

"We're going to need every weapon and person to help at this location," Alces howled. "Call everyone here!"

Jet pulled out some sludge water and drank. Jayco started relaying information and commands to those around him.

Iris rubbed up against his leg as if reassuring him that nothing terrible was going to happen today.

Organized chaos ensued. Rick, Jackson, and Keesha arrived on his left and began organizing Elementals into groups. Jet watched as Maria, Sebastian, and several others from Argentina came forward as more weapons were passed out. Shane, Jessiva Clyde, and Nash directed their groups far to his right.

Alces asked, "What if I said…Hoyuk Crescent?"

"I would say…sucked, badly."

"Oh my," Alces replied.

"What do those words mean?" Mckenzey asked.

"More importantly," Jayco said, "why is your sister here to kill Jet? How can she be a Khalicaan?"

"My boy, no one is born into the tribe of enchantresses known as the Khalicaans. They are thieves, criminals, and occasionally stolen from other families. They have died for their sins but are caught up purposefully before the afterlife. Kaya was snatched years ago. I do not know when she first died."

Grantham asked, "If she's already died, how do we kill her again?"

"That's why you need an enchanted blade."

"Is she also a moose, like you?" Latisha asked.

"Kaya has chosen her human form, forever. I believe it was a consequence of taking an oath as a Khalicaan." Almost to herself, she whispered, "She was a gazelle, as fast as the wind."

"You have a human form?" asked Jayco.

Alces's transformation was swift and incredible. Her skin became a golden tan, and her purple fir transformed into a long and beautiful cloak. Her hair remained purple, and her skin was soft and lush. She was beautiful and young, maybe seventeen or eighteen. She said, "No matter how many years pass, this is the age I transform into as a human."

"Was your sister trying to kill you?" asked Jet.

"We have become sworn enemies. There's no going back, for either of us."

Eric interrupted. "Chat time is over. Here comes the attack."

The three Chupovanas stalked into positions in the field, facing the school. They began to trot slowly forward and spreading out.

Jet screamed to his friends, "Go help the other Elementals."

"We're staying with you," Mckenzey replied defiantly.

Jet heard screams of fear, but these were outnumbered by a war cry that penetrated the air from both Runics and Elementals. This time rocks and boulders were set afire and launched at the creatures. Holes in the ground, and ice storms pelted down. Some of these pieces of magic slowed the oncoming Chupovanas, who were clearly fighting through an Elemental storm. From the Runics, invisible wires were pulled around the legs of the oncoming creatures, invisible barriers smashed into the legs, and much more to place. Dozens and dozens of hands scribbled things in the air. Jet had no idea about everything that was happening, but it was clear that the students were not going to allow the school to be overrun.

Immediately to his right, Mckenzey hobbled forward. Jet also saw Latisha and Seyanna draw up next to Mckenzey. To his left, Jayco and Grantham readied themselves.

Mckenzey hollered, "We're stronger together."

Eric bellowed his war cry and began using magic.

Jayco lifted a car and hurled it at Taraqeu. The feline creature did not react in time and was knocked aside, but it recovered quickly and reset its course toward the Runics.

Alces said, with powerful emotion in her voice, "You are truly aggravating creatures. You can't help Jet in this fight. You must prevent the Chupovanas from getting into the school, but Jet is the only one who can fight Kaya. He might be able to use Iris and the Sagitta tribe for help if she's forgotten the word. But honestly, this is *his* fight."

The golden creatures were just feet behind Jet, waiting for any command.

Angrily, Jet seethed, "I still don't have an enchanted blade."

"How did you kill Lucretius the Avad? Killing him required a similar blade."

"I was able to use a dagger that came from my skin." He pointed to the two tattoos, like emblems, on each forearm. The majestic blue dagger glimmered in the moonlight.

"That's an enchanted blade," Alces replied. "You only have one left, so be careful. When Kaya attacks, use that weapon."

"We can help," Mckenzey insisted. "I'm not leaving Jet."

"You must," Alces said. "I can perceive from here... your heart is full of doubt but be clear about this—you stay; you will get Jet killed."

Mckenzey glared at Alces.

"We've got to go," Jayco said, placing a hand on Mckenzey's shoulder. "Let Jet go."

"Bye, guys!" said Jet. "Good luck."

"See you on the flip side, bro," replied Grantham with a high five.

Seyanna whispered, "You can kill her. I know it. Be safe." She touched his back and he shivered.

His friends tore into the fray as pandemonium and destruction encompassed the entire school.

Alces pulled Jet back a few feet, and it felt as if he were abandoning his friends and everyone. He struggled to free himself, torn with what he should do, but he had almost no energy. There was no way he was going to be able to wield a weapon to kill a Khalicaan.

"They're retreating," a voice bellowed.

"Just regrouping," another voice answered.

From her pocket, Alces pulled out a ring, unlike anything Jet had ever seen. It was a semi-thick, with a gray band and dark red stone in the middle. She said, "This is an Imnolo stone, one of three crafted by my kinsman. The other two are lost, but this is for you."

"It's mesmerizing." The stone held depths and mysteries that Jet couldn't explain. He thought there were swirls of a hidden place.

Alces bowed slightly. "This stone has a unique purpose. It allows the owner, which will be you, to hide things, like in a closet. Only you will have the key to open it."

"How's that possible?"

"Magic, of course." She added, "You'll need a keyword that you'll say out loud when you first place the ring on your finger. This will open and close the closet door. You'll be able to put things on the shelf and always carry them around with you. The closet is limited in size, but you'll be able to arrange them as needed.

"Incredible." He asked, "What type of keyword?"

"The stone will never open for someone else, and it's nearly unbreakable. It opens only to the correct keyword and your voice."

"What if I die and someone needs what is inside?"

"It can be broken, and the contents removed only at the Archelos Lagoon."

"Never heard of it."

"That's the point. It's virtually impossible to find." Holding the stone out to him, she said, "The word needs to be full of wisdom, excitement, and cunning, enough that it will be nearly impossible to discover."

Jet thought for a second. When he held the ring, he quickly placed it on his finger and whispered, "Bookshelf." As the ring slipped onto his right hand, pointer finger, he beheld a small closet. He placed his backpack on the shelf and closed the door. He was shocked to find his bag had vanished. He repeated the word and found the item just where he'd placed it.

Alces repeated, "The closet is limited in size, but you have your own protected hiding place."

"Thank you," replied Jet. "This is one of the best gifts I've ever been given."

"You can't fight my sister with a bag on your back."

"Good point."

For the next few minutes, silence overcame almost every other sound as people stood in anticipation of the next attack.

A voice bellowed, "The Chupovanas are starting to glow orange?"

Alces said, "They're using the magic they've stolen to enrage themselves. Prepare yourselves."

Jayco yelled, "Jet, do you know what's happening?"

Jet repeated Alces's warning. He added, "Probably a good time to show them something amazing."

"Working on it," replied Jayco.

In a low voice, Alces asked, "Did Mckenzey's leg get broken during the Hoyuk Crescent?"

Jet's shoulders jerked at the question. "How did you know?" He quickly added, "But not by me."

Alces replied, "Her broken leg will take far longer to heal than you can imagine."

Jet felt pity, guilt, and regret boil together. He was suddenly distracted as the three Chupovanas bayed their own warning. Directly ahead of him was Kee-Faux. To his left was Dalkiate, and to his right was the feline creature Taraqeu. Despite everything they had already thrown at these creatures, they didn't appear injured in the slightest. Their orange glow was terrifying.

Jet yelled; his voice boomed. "The creatures from left to right are Dalkiate, Kee-Faux, and Taraqeu. They are here to steal your magic, and to do so, they will kill you. Dalkiate has skin that is hard to penetrate. Kee-Faux is as fast as they come, and Taraqeu is agile and difficult to trap. Killing them will be hard, but our goal is to prevent them from destroying you and Chadwicks."

A cheer surprisingly broke out from both groups that quickly turned into a chant. From his left, from somewhere among the Elementals, someone yelled:

Creatures! Creatures!

Creatures of the night must die!

Monsters! Monsters!

Monsters, you'll feel the pain tonight!

The chant was repeated over and over as the Chupovanas approached, this time more cautiously.

Alces asked, "Who did you choose to kill?"

"Myself," Jet whispered.

Jet watched as Alces closed her eyes, as if pained by his response.

Defensively he said, "I couldn't choose anyone else."

"Not even your worst enemy?"

The chanting continued, growing louder.

"I'm not afraid to kill someone," Jet said, hoping to sound confident. "But not like that."

"Can you kill my sister?" Alces asked.

"You know that I can't."

Shane shouted, "Everyone, to your places."

Jet was intrigued by what he saw next, especially at the command of Shane Fallon. Suddenly, eight students, all dressed in black, stepped forward, each six feet away from each other. They held Y-shaped weapons that Jet recognized; in fact, he and his friends had had the misfortune of being on the opposite side of that attack. The Y-shaped weapon would shoot a specialized blue rope that was nearly impossible to escape from.

Jayco bellowed, "Elementals, throw out the corn."

Though momentarily confused, the reality became clear when hundreds of corn kernels fell onto the ground, and hundreds of replicas of students sprang into place. The Chupovanas hesitated moving forward as the number they were facing tripled.

The next set of orders came from Latisha, and she commanded Jackson to move nine full balloons, the size of an orange, into the air. Every student watched the balloons rise about twenty feet over the heads of Kee-Faux and Taraqeu, but only a few feet over Dalkiate.

"Steady, "Latisha shouted.

In a loud voice, Eric shouted, "Aperir."

Jet asked, "What does that mean?"

Alces replied, "Open."

To his amazement, dozens of thick sharp wooden spikes exploded out of the ground, near the feet of the three Chupovanas. Taraqeu and Kee-Faux barely avoided the tips, but the back left paw of Dalkiate suffered a cut that went directly through the skin. The creature bent over, and with teeth Jet hadn't known it had, it grasped the stake and pulled it free.

Alces replied, "It appears that your friends have a plan for now."

A bugle sounded, and the concentration of the Chupovanas turned to the school.

"That was my sister. The attack has begun."

"Now," Shane shouted, and the blue ropes were shot across the field. Each Chupovanas was hit several times. The blue ropes caused the creatures quite a bit of irritation, but they did no damage other than slow them down. Spells and other items, including arrows and such, were shot when the creatures were tethered. The goal was clear; it was easier to hit a still target than a moving one.

Alces clutched at Jet's arm, and he turned toward her. She said, "If you survive this attack, and if you kill my sister, you must go find Anesidora."

"I don't know what that is. I've heard of it before."

Alces pointed to Seyanna. "She does. I think she also knows where it can be found."

"How?"

"It isn't clear to me, but I believe that she found an entrance when she lived on the island."

"Why is Anesidora so important?"

The young girl's mouth tightened, and she said, full of tears, "Today, I can only save you so much. If I help you, you will live a little longer. If not, you won't be alive in the next few days."

"How's that possible?"

"When I first met you, you were already weakened. You are far worse now."

Jet nodded. "The Brotherhood gave me a drink when I was younger that erased much of my memories of magic."

"That drink plus the torture that came with the Hoyuk Crescent are killing you."

"What can I do?"

Alces whispered, "In the legend of the battle between Leotyton and Arisol, it talks about Lady Gaea giving up her lifeforce. It's a true gift for someone worthy to receive it.

The fact that you have gone through the Hoyuk Crescent and are still standing here today is astonishing."

"I didn't tell them what happened."

"And you might never tell them," she added. "But then again…"

"It feels like I failed. Mckenzey still got injured. Now we have a war on our campus."

"What did you get as your reward?"

"The second piece of the Phoenix."

"I see," she said, contemplating.

Jet glanced up just as the Chupovanas were cutting through the first line of defense. Latisha shouted, "Now!"

Arrows shot through the air and connected with the nine balloons. Black powder dropped, and the Chupovanas were caught in darkness. They did not know which way to turn.

Alces pulled him back several more steps. She said, "Mikado Jet, I choose to give you my lifeforce. Use it wisely."

Before he could react, the adolescent girl opened her mouth and pulled out a circular sphere that was, incredibly, white and glowing. She held it for him to take.

Appalled and shocked, Jet pleaded, "I don't want this."

She dropped it into his hands. "It's my choice to give it to you." The sphere felt both warm and heavy.

"If I take it, will you die?"

"No. It will give you the energy you need and will temporarily prevent you from dying."

"What about you? Don't you need the energy?"

"I have plenty."

"I can't," Jet said quickly, and he tried shoving the sphere back to her but found that he couldn't.

She smiled sadly. "If it is my time to die, so shall it be. But one thing is certain—you can't die today."

A howl from a wolf sliced through the air. Jet wasn't sure what was happening, but soon Iris was roaring back as if answering. The golden panther rubbed up against his leg, her hairs raised.

Alces said, her voice steady and strong, "My sister is coming. Use my lifeforce or die."

CHAPTER 33

Kee-Faux launched forward and collided with a thick haze of powder. It suddenly teetered back and forth, acting as if it were temporarily dazed. Bellows of determination and excitement came from the students as they hoped they were holding the creatures at bay.

Alces crushed their hopes, "All of this is temporary. We can't close the barrier until my sister is dead. What is your choice?"

Jet held the white sphere higher. He whispered, "What do I do?"

She said quickly, "To give your lifeforce, you say 'Dare Vim Vitalem.' And to receive the lifeforce, you reply, 'Vitalem.' It's pretty straightforward."

Jet felt something he couldn't explain. Somehow, he felt Kaya sneaking onto campus, searching for him. *Is it because I'm holding Alces's lifeforce?* he wondered to himself. Out loud, he said, "Vitalem."

Quicker than the speed of light, the sphere was inhaled into Jet's body. The relief was beyond stunning, as if he had been in pain for weeks only to have it totally vanish. It was impossible to understand how weak and fragile he had been and equally frightening to know how close to death he was.

Without Alces speaking, her voice entered his mind. "I will always be with you now, in one form or another, but

I am not Lady Gaea, and my energy will only sustain you tonight. Is that clear?"

Jet's mind immediately communicated with Alces, without spoken words, like telepathy. "You bet."

"It's time."

Jet spoke. "Iris, follow. The rest stay and fight." The golden panther followed his command. He left the fighting and sauntered toward the CeU building, traveling down College Avenue. The street was deserted. Those who knew magic were fighting, while the rest hid until this mess was over. They reached the CeU building but needed to go farther. Alces remained silent.

The darkness of this portion of campus made this area perfect. After passing two buildings, Jet noticed that the clamor of battle had escalated in a bad way, but he couldn't turn back. A chill crept up his spine; she was watching him. He pushed, and his vision expanded around him and found Kaya crouching at the back bricks of the CeU building. She pulled an arrow from her quiver and shot it at him. At the last moment, he moved his head an inch, and it passed by harmlessly. He kept moving forward, and she followed. Near the baseball fields, Jet stopped and waited for Alces's sister.

Words reached them from the shadows. "You choose to protect this magic wielder? I am your sister, and you know why I was taken." A hooded figure stepped into view. When she pulled down her hood, Jet saw a pale face, with a sickness of black around her red eyes. She only slightly resembled the human form of Alces.

"Jet was not there when our tribe was attacked," Alces explained. "He is not one of the murderers."

"How do you know?"

"Search your heart and his, and you will see."

Kaya hissed, her lips tight, "I no longer have that ability."

"What have they done to you?" Alces asked.

Jet's finger went to the skin of his arm, but he found he couldn't remove the dagger.

"After my first death, I swore an oath of revenge," Kaya screamed. "After what the magic wielders did to our home and family, how could you have ever sided with them?"

"So instead," Alces demanded, "you chose to leave your family and shepherd these killers."

"They will destroy magic. Most of our family left this earth years ago; so did the ideals of our mother. Don't lecture me."

"Things are different now," Jet said calmly. Iris remained just off to his side.

"That is of no consequence, Elemental. The magic will corrupt you, eventually."

"That's not what happened." Alces beseeched him. "I believed that you had been taken."

"I joined the Khalicaans feely, and that's why I'm one of their Narvarcs."

"You're a chieftain?" exclaimed Alces, apparent surprise on her face. "You can help change their ways."

"I've sworn an oath to kill this Elemental."

Alces replied, "You don't have to. Join us. Join me."

Kaya exposed a black blade that curved twice, back and forth, like a snake. Even from here, the point was incredibly sharp. Using the sword, she pointed it at Jet and said, "He will die tonight, and soon magic will be destroyed on earth forever."

Guilt, sadness, and regret crashed into Jet like a tsunami, and he stumbled back two steps. Alces's emotions were on full display, but she stepped in front of Jet protectively. When she spoke, her voice barely trembled. "I won't let that happen."

"Move, sister. This doesn't involve you."

"No." Alces took two steps forward.

"Stop," Jet and Kaya said together, but Alces continued moving.

"Don't let hatred destroy you," Alces pleaded, and he felt warmth and love wrestle her other emotions into a slight submission.

"It empowers me," Kaya screamed. "It makes me see the truth."

"That's not truth but chaos's distraction of your senses. That path leads to destruction."

"You know nothing, enemy." Kaya's voice was cold, and Jet's left arm began to tingle.

Alces stopped suddenly.

"I can feel her thoughts," Jet said. "She intends to kill you."

"I know." Alces's voice was sweet and serene. "Make my family proud." Alces rushed at Kaya, who lifted her unusual sword and, slashing downward, cut her sister across the chest, killing her instantly.

Something flared within his body, and more power and energy flooded into his body. He felt at least as strong as before his torture.

"What just happened?" Kaya asked, and she wobbled slightly. "Did Alces give you her lifeforce? I can't kill her twice."

Jet wasn't sure what to say.

After a few seconds, the Khalicaan steadied. "Give it to me," she demanded.

"No."

"Why would she give you her lifeforce? Have you any idea what your kind has done to our family?"

"I don't, actually. But I do know what you're trying to do to mine."

"Your friends are already dead."

"You've done enough damage already." Glancing down at Alces's body, he said, "Leave, and let this be the last we see of you."

The Khalicaan opened her stance. He sensed her hatred and her intentions. His arms burned, but before he could remove the dagger, Kaye said, "Immogelida."

From the corners of his eyes, he watched as Iris became petrified.

"What have you done?"

"The Sagitta tribe were once free to delight the world with their mysticism. Then they were enslaved to the magicians, just like my family was. Did you think that I had forgotten, sister?"

Jet wondered if something in her mind had snapped.

"The Sagitta tribe will be a good addition to the Khalicaans once you've been killed."

Like before, it was as if he was pulling a sticker off a wall; he removed a single blade with a black obsidian handle. The blade itself was sea blue, ten inches in length, and the handle another eight.

"That's not possible," Kaya sputtered. "Where did you get that?"

"Does it really matter?" He pointed to the darkened tattoo. "They've worked for me before."

Kaya's red eyes burned bright with bitterness and hate. With her black blade, she circled to his right. After a short time, she circled back to his left.

"Checking my footwork?" muttered Jet.

"Finding the best way to kill you. There are so many."

She bent her knees and stalked forward gracefully. There was something hypnotic to the way she moved, and it triggered a memory of a forgotten dance. Wisps of recollection escaped, and Jet's body moved contrary to gravity, and he blocked her attack in the exact moment his legs split apart impossibly. He had done the splits, but his legs were partially angled behind his back. He wasn't this limber. Next, he was gracefully parrying her subsequent five attacks with unusual and impossible moves. He wondered if it could be Alces's lifeforce, but the thought felt wrong.

Concentrating on Kaya, he perceived that she knew some amount of magic. After her next attack, he said, "It's pretty ironic that you've been given magic and are using it to kill those with magic." The truth dawned on him at once. "When I'm dead, magic won't be gone forever unless the Chupovanas turn on you."

"They can't," she replied quickly as she tensed for the next attack. She covered half the distance between them and tried stabbing. Jet performed a backflip, landing again in the splits, but with one leg forward and one behind. The move was perfect as Kaya unleashed an arrow that sailed harmlessly over his head.

Kaya recovered and said, "My beauties won't attack me." The enchantress's outline dimmed slightly as she transformed into a blur and attacked.

A gust of wind knocked the hood of Jet's cloak onto his head, and Kaya reappeared. Using his blade, he parried her attacks with ease. At one point, he pushed the flat end of his blade out and kicked his left foot at the ground. His body went end over end gracefully, three times, and he landed well out of reach of the Khalicaan.

Having been in the midst of a move, Kaya had no one to attack, and she crashed headfirst onto the ground. She slapped the dirt and shouted, "Have you studied Capocea?"

"Not lately," replied Jet. He was stunned at his movements. They could be described as a martial art with a concentration in acrobatics, yoga, dancing, and quick sword movements. When fighting, he spent minimal time in one place.

Jumping to her feet, she shouted, "Plathera," and cords burst from the ground, intending to wrap around his feet.

Jet was faster. He leaped into the air with poise while somersaulting to his left. At the same time, he spoke, "Kali," and a small firebolt shot to the ground and disintegrated the cords.

"You're not what I expected," Kaya said. "Terrible attack, only defense."

Jet answered, "You've become your enemy. Magic wielders came and attacked your family and now you're doing the same. Here and now you can break the cycle."

"If I don't fulfill my oath, I die."

"There has to be another way."

"Why do you care?"

"Because Alces did."

Kaya reached for a red whip from around her waist that dripped with magic. She held this weapon in her right hand, and Alces's sentiments told him to be very careful.

"This is one of the five missing Chalua," Kaya explained. "It will tear through your cloak and burn you to the bone."

"Delightful."

She moved both quickly, and it was clear that she was an expert in both weapons. The whip exploded out about four feet. It snapped and sailed back behind Kaya's head. She shifted and danced, and Jet wished he could shoot her with something from a safe distance. That was when he realized that her movements were getting faster. There was a slight red glow near her neck, and he caught a glimpse of a small imp creature next to Kaya's ear. It was like a lizard with wings, and its long tail, like a tendril, wrapped around her neck. It was barely noticeable, but Jet was pretty sure that its claws were stuck under her skin.

Kaya attacked Jet with her blade and the whip for the next several minutes. She would fire off a spell or two that Jet had never heard of. She lunged, attacked, and one time used the wall of one of the buildings to run up one part only to leap and kick out at Jet. Her leg slammed into Jet's shoulder, but he used the spell, "Aer" and was able to get out of the way of her attack. Despite his vision and his quickness, she had him cornered.

A death scream echoed in the distance, and the imp brightened considerably.

"Have enough of my friends been killed tonight?"

Kaya hissed, "Not enough. But soon."

"You're gaining strength through their deaths." It was not a question but a statement.

She retorted, "So do the Chupovanas. Soon no one will be able to stop them."

Jet howled, "This isn't about eliminating magic but stealing it and using it for your own purposes."

"That's what your kind did to my family," Kaya screamed. "It's about time someone had the courage to pay back the gesture in kind."

"Alces would never have understood this," Jet replied. "You're stomping on her memory."

"Alces's worries are over. She was such a perfect big sister—until she wasn't. Magic divided and separated us, and magic is what got her killed."

"No," Jet replied. "She knew death was coming. She had been trapped for so long in Coso Subtrano."

"What a fool."

"She was free in the end. Unlike you, with that imp latched onto your neck. It's your real master."

"I'll kill you," Kaya screamed, and she lunged with a speed that could rival Kee-Faux's.

He should've been killed, as her attack was perfectly placed. The whip's cord sailed at his neck, and her sword would've gutted him, except for some unspoken magic. Dirt and rocks from the ground around him formed a protective layer, encircling his body. Kaya's whip became entrapped in the dirt, and the blade couldn't penetrate the wall.

Both of Jet's arms exploded outward, pulsating the dirt with enough force that a portion of the building next to him caved it. Kaya was belted to the ground. Jet's anger engulfed him. The death of Alces, his friends, and the attack on the school only fueled a portion of his anger. The change in Mckenzey's friendship, the Brotherhood's treatment of him, and especially the death of his parents enraged him. Using magic, he battered Kaya. He buried her, froze her, and burned her. He slashed out with his weapon and cut Kaya across the back as she whimpered and tried to escape.

Jet spoke, "Ea," and a confused look crossed the enchantress's face, and he stabbed his blade deep into her shoulder. Having sensed that Kaya had lost, the imp unlatched itself from her neck and tried to escape in the commotion. Jet spoke, "Kali," and a firebolt flew straight through the demon, burning it severely. The screams and cries from the other Khalicaans nearby told Jet that they were interconnected and felt the attack.

Instead of killing her, he used the hilt of his dagger to knock her unconscious. He bent over the exposed imp and demanded, "Stop the attack. It's finished." He thought he heard cheers, and he assumed the Chupovanas were retreating.

An explosion diverted his attention, and he watched as a fireball bounced off Dalkiate and careened into the upper level of the CeU building. From the periphery he glimpsed, far too late, as the imp took advantage of the moment, opening its mouth and biting into the sword. The blade cracked, and it started turning black as if it had been poisoned, just like the sickness that had spread in Coso Subtrano.

The Chupovanas reengaged their attacks, and the imp pulled itself away from Jet. It flew quickly to the unconscious Kaya and latched around her neck once again. She was jolted from her sleep, and anger, hatred, and the desire to kill everyone shone brightly on the Khalicaan's face. She would never stop until he was dead.

Jet sprinted faster than he'd ever run before. As Kaya prepared to attack, Jet swung the disintegrating blade, cutting through Kaya's neck and slicing the imp in half. That black curved blade and the red whip dropped from her hands, and she was dead before her body hit the ground.

The Chupovanas bellowed in fury and withdrew. Jet let go of his own sword, and before it hit the ground, a blaze of pain shot through his arm as the blackened dagger became an image on his skin. Most of Alces's energy disintegrated with the sword.

In the distance he heard Shane scream, "The Khalicaan is dead. Place the last Claustra."

Seyanna answered, "We need Jet."

Jet slogged in the direction of his friends and felt something rub up against his leg. He instantly recoiled until he realized it was Iris. She licked his face and lent him some strength.

The Chupovanas were regrouping near where Kaya had first spoken with them. Five more Khalicaans slipped into view, discussing their options. It seemed clear that they were going to attack again.

Jet sluggishly clambered ahead, and he noticed that everyone's faces were blurred, as if in a dream. There were both cheers and chants and some excitement. He also recognized agony and tears as students stood next to dead bodies.

The last few steps up the incline were nearly impossible. He had to place the final Claustra to protect the campus. A movement caught his attention, but it was far too late, and he was far too slow. A green saber-toothed tiger leaped at him from his right, and there was nothing he could do to stop the collision. A golden blur latched onto the back of the tiger and bit down on its neck. The next few seconds were intense as the fight between Iris and the tiger was ferocious.

"We're under attack," screamed Keesha.

Jet crawled the last few feet as his energy evaporated. The Chupovanas had regrouped and were once again racing at the campus. A different Khalicaan sat firmly placed on each of the Chupovanas. The last two were riding green saber-tooth tigers.

A voice inside Jet's mind whispered, "I am truly free." Alces's friendship felt warm and inviting.

Seyanna slammed into Jet, half hugging him and lifting him up. She handed him the last Claustra, and he drove it into the last hole and collapsed unconscious.

CHAPTER 34

For the first time in nearly a decade, it felt like he was going *home*. Every bone ached to feel the summer breeze, the brook running between his hooves, and the pure love he felt from his tribesman, his family, and especially his mother, the matriarch. He hurried so fast that every tendon and muscle ached with pure joy. He was an unstoppable force.

Rounding the next corner, he found heaven on earth, Illustina, the sole place of the realm where clouds touched the ocean while mixing with mountain peaks. He didn't know how the sea could reached this high in altitude, but legend whispered that it was a gift from his grandmother. Illustina was the most stunning and colorful place in the entire magical kingdom. The flowers were twice as large, the grass greener than a gem, and the forest was vibrant and alive.

Picking up his pace he suddenly became worried that he would be late for the summer solstice feast, the feast of fortune. Kaya would never forgive him and would tease him unceasingly. She was the kindest sister in the world. Oh, how he loved her. She shared his love of nature, desire for peace, and ambition for all the magical realms to respect and work together to help each other, despite their differences.

Up ahead a stranger in a cloak was passing through the front gates. Where were the sentinels? He didn't think that they were expecting any guests. Who could have requested an audience with his mother? The gate had not completely closed when he passed through, but the stranger had vanished. He sprinted toward the queen's quarters, but every building was empty. An eerie sense of unease spread across his back. Hurrying to the palace, he was tempted to push open the gigantic golden doors to understand what was happening. Instead, he went to the back of the palace and found a hidden stairway to a shielded room. Once inside he found a perch and gazed out on the expansive open chamber. His tribesman filled the spectator seats, staring at the queen's throne in disbelief. Indignant gasps and screams echoed around the chamber.

He could not comprehend what he was seeing. A magical glass cage had been positioned around his mother's throne, trapping the queen in the form of a caribou. More than a dozen magical guards surrounded her with emblems of the Elementals and the Runics on their clothing. His mother pressed against the glass.

There was a howl so powerful that it caused many in their seats to bend over and hide. A tall, intimidating wolf with a long sword in his claws stepped into view. Faunal strode to the end of the glass, glaring at the queen.

His hackles raised in volume, and he desired nothing more than to leap down and free his mother and kill the wolf.

Faunal spoke to the queen, "Where are your two daughters? Why were they not invited for this feast?"

The queen spoke, "Kaya has been trying to locate the magic stealers, and Alces has been helping the Kings search for Arisol."

"Don't say his name," seethed the wolf.

Ignoring this, Aurora asked, "Why are you here, and why have you brought the Czaric and the Mikado with you? Are you planning an attack?"

"I am here just to ask you some questions. Rumor has it that your tribe knows the location of the other three tomes of Terra Maleficis."

"That's a lie," the queen said almost too quickly. "We are only aware of the tomes for Elemental and Runic magic. The other three tomes are lost and hidden."

Faunal asked, "Did you send them with Kaya and Alces?"

In a spectacular voice, Aurora answered, "Faunal of the Ravencats and guard of the Runics. We are not part of the magical war, but we have chosen to help the remaining Kings. We don't know why magic is losing its luster, nor why your books won't open, and we don't know where the other tomes may be hidden. My daughters have nothing to do with any of this."

Faunal sauntered back and forth as if contemplating his response. "You have two choices, my queen. Help me find the missing tomes, or I will hunt down your daughters. There are consequences to violating the law of treason. Either you must suffer, or they will."

Trying to get a better view of his mother, he moved to a different position. He passed in front of a mirror, and as he did so the reflection revealed a large purple moose. He was Alces. Wanting to scream but unable, he moved to a better vantage point.

Seven gray and brown wolves surrounded Faunal. The Czaric and Mikado, wearing cloaks full of gems and gold, also stepped forward.

Aurora defiantly answered, "We nomads are peaceful and have no ill will toward the magical races. Leave us alone, and we will help you find the missing tomes."

Faunal glanced at the Mikado and nodded. The man, nearly seven feet tall, spoke a word that Alces couldn't understand. After a pause, the Mikado answered, "She really doesn't know where they are."

"A pity," Faunal replied. "She has no use to us."

The Czaric hand moved in a blur. Queen Aurora began choking. It was clear that she couldn't breathe, and her body began to convulse. She transitioned into a fifty-year-old elegant woman, but the result was the same."

Alces screamed, "Leave the queen alone, and come get me."

Faunal bellowed back, "Where are you hiding, Alces? What does your human form look like? Come down here, or I'll kill everyone."

The Czaric didn't stop his attack, and Queen Aurora crashed into the glass. Faunal held up a hand, and the Runic leader slowly stopped his attack.

Queen Aurora screamed, "Run, Alces, and don't ever come back. Never let them find you." A bright glow originated from the inner circle of the glass barrier, and Alces watched as Queen Aurora gave her lifeforce to the land around her. Illustina would force Alces, Faunal, the wolves, and all those with magic to depart from this land forever.

"Why?" sobbed Alces.

"An unseen voice, her mothers, emanated around Alces, "To protect you, the magic, the tomes, and to stop Arisol's most trusted commander from enslaving our people. Now run!"

Faunal howled his displeasure and swore, "Alces, I will find you or your sister sooner than you can imagine."

Alces did not answer but ran as fast as she could.

Faunal commanded, "Find her!"

# # #

A door opened and closed, but it was far too dark for Jet to see anything. He waited for what seemed like hours for light to come into his vision. The room felt as if it were spinning as he kept replaying images of Faunal, the choking Aurora, and the lands of Illustina and the lifeforce used to expel Faunal and the others. He had been Alces herself as she raced home, only to find that her mother had been deceived and essentially killed. He tasted the despair on his own lips and thought little of anything else.

Sometime later a door opened again, and an unfamiliar voice said, "Welcome back, Mrs. Taley."

Jet thought his heart would pick up knowing Nana was so close.

"Thank you" was the quick reply, and the door closed.

Footsteps patted across the floor, and someone sat in the chair next to where he lay. He still couldn't open his eyes or turn his head. For the next hour, Jet tried every conceivable attempt to move his body, flick his finger, or breathe faster. The only sounds in the room were the slow respirations from Nana and the gasps of the medical machines.

He must've drifted to sleep. The next time he woke, he was in no better shape than before. If it was possible, the room was darker, and he deduced it was nighttime. The silence was unnatural.

This continued for the next few days, and only Nana visited. Jet's mind began to wander, and he lost track of whether it was day or night, and he really didn't care. As the hours passed, he heard snatches of conversations here and there and thought he overheard Mckenzey's voice once but wasn't sure.

Later a door slammed, and Jet awoke quickly. "This is getting old," said Jayco hotly. "The doctors insist that there's nothing wrong with you. You're breathing and are hooked up to a minimal number of machines. The only reason you have an IV is for food. We need your help."

Jayco sat in the chair usually occupied by Nana. He continued, "There were a few dozen students killed the other night, almost a week ago now, but the Runics are threatening to take over the school. We need you to wake up and talk with Shane. Can't you help us out?"

Jayco kicked the bed and stood. As he walked away, he said, "Get better, bro." His voice became muffled for a moment, but then Jet heard, "Hope you have better luck."

The door closed softly, and steps crossed the room. "Sounds like he was pissed." The words came from his friend Seyanna. "I don't think he has any idea what to do." She spoke far more calmly but still with a slight edge. "They found the bodies of Alces and her sister. The Brotherhood arrived with Kevin and took both of their bodies away from here. We told them that you were severely injured, and they seemed pleased. Five hundred students dropped out the next day, but we've had a steady stream of others wanting to join both the Runics and Elementals. There were eleven damaged buildings, including the CeU building."

"More bad news," she continued, "Principal Fletcher was killed, along with Professor Dickerson. Mr. Smuin has been promoted to the new principal. He has definitely been the shining moment in all of this. He acted quickly and allowed you and some of the other injured students to be moved to the basement of the CeU building. I didn't even know this place existed, but it's like a small hospital.

"Latisha was captured by Kee-Faux and was nearly killed. It seems that she has lost most of her magical abilities. She can no longer use the black powder, see in the darkness, or use any of the golden weapons. She can still wear her cloak and has wind spell capability, but it's far weaker than before. Surprisingly, after all her melodrama about not believing in it, she's not taking it well. Grantham is trying to help."

Jet sat in disbelief.

There was a pause in the conversation. When Seyanna spoke again, her voice shook slightly. "Nash and a few more of Shane's friends were killed. Shane was injured severely, but he'll make a full recovery. Sebastian and five kids from Argentina were killed. Maria is distraught. During the attack several huge explosions came from Santa Barbara, and they're blaming an earthquake for causing a gas pocket under the surface that ignited. The story is crazy, but it's holding up right now."

Seyanna cleared her voice and continued, "The Chupovanas and the Khalicaans crashed into the barrier after you placed the Claustra and were incapacitated, but we couldn't get to them before they woke up and retreated. Siwalik arrived and has been guarding the school, but I don't think the Chupovanas are going to return any time soon. Iris is outside this room, protecting you fiercely. She wouldn't let Mckenzey, Jayco, or me approach you for the longest time. The other three golden animals are currently living in the gym, and no one is sure what to do with them. Get better soon. We really need you."

Seyanna fell silent. After a while she squeezed his hand and left.

When he woke again, someone was already in the room talking with him. Mckenzey's voice was easy to recognize. She held his hand and was sobbing. "I'm so sorry."

When Mckenzey next spoke, she said, "Jet, I love you, and I think that I have for a long time despite how young we are. But we might have missed our chance earlier this year. Why did I move to Colorado and meet Eric? Then, this year, you and I found something special. I ruined it when I got cold feet after Silverton. I wanted to be so close to you, but after seeing you kill that boy, I got cold feet."

Mckenzey blew her nose. "I left to go home, get my head on straight, and there was Eric, and I enjoyed the time I spent with him. There was no pressure, no magic, and no responsibilities. Then you died, and everything changed for real. Now it's like you've died all over again. I can't handle this back and forth. I've tasted happiness and love from two different amazing boys. I'm not sure if you can hear me, but I wanted to tell you that even if you come back, I'm with Eric now. Please understand and respect my feelings."

Jet's heart was removed from his chest, cut in half, burned, and placed back where it had always been.

Mckenzey whispered, "Eric and I are transferring to Dillon Lake. We'll be gone in a few days. If I stay around here any longer, I'm going to lose my mind." Her tears landed on his face. She kissed his cheek, his mouth as her two hands gripped his hair, and it felt like she was trying to pull out each piece at once. Then she was gone.

Jet slept and woke and slept for an endless amount of time. He didn't care what happened and was so racked with guilt and sadness, he became convinced that he would remain in this state for the rest of his life. Nana returned often, Jayco popped in, and Seyanna stopped by once or twice.

Once he heard voices talking about the upcoming visit from some of the Brotherhood. They wanted an update on him, but he didn't care. He tried blocking out all thoughts of his friends, magic, and the life he once had.

A melody of pure innocence began in a spot behind his left eye. It was something that dragged at hidden memories, unwilling to resurface. The tune was full of melancholy and spoke of death, regret, sadness, and sacrifice. Jet soaked in the feelings underneath the music. He allowed his own sorrow and guilt to mix with the song, and he hoped that this was a death serenade to take him away.

Alces's words weren't angry or sharp, but they weren't soft or forgiving. From a depth he did not know, she said, "If you are a decent person, you are bound to feel regret and anguish when you experience loss and death. That is the price of life and love and friendship. Years ago two twin brothers were the Mikado and the Czaric, and together they traveled to the land of my parents. They came bearing gifts, kindness, and promises of collaboration. Our people knew magic in a different way than with words or written signs. It was in our music, commands, friendship, love, and even death. Faunal explained that the Elementals and Runics feared the Nomads for our unusual form of magic. We did not need a book or even words to display Mother Earth's pleasure to those around us. For the first time in thousands of years, jealousy and fear created a divide between the two magic types. They also hungered after the other three tomes.

"During the feast of fortune, in our holy lands, our people were slaughtered. My mother, Aurora, became a slave, and my father, Ajax, was killed. Many other tribesmen were killed, enslaved, or worse. Illustina transformed from paradise to a forsaken land. I think Kaya watched the attack from somewhere hidden. She became corrupt through her own emotions and allowed the grief to destroy her. She would never understand why I am helping you, with my lifeforce, to bring magic back to what it once was. Don't let your guilt and anguish win. That's why you're trapped here today."

Jet replied, "I killed your family to save my friends."

Alces continued, "I did not have the strength to kill Kaya, but she needed to die. You've gained and lost much. You've killed and protected and suffered more than anyone can know. You chose yourself in the Hoyuk Crescent, and now you're dying. My lifeforce gives you no more strength. If you don't leave to find Anesidora in the next few days, you will not survive. If you think things are bad now, just imagine life without a Mikado. The Brotherhood, Shane Fallon, Kevin McCormick, the Azurites, and Arisol, along with all his followers, won't be stopped. Chaos and world destruction will transpire. You're the only one that can bring symmetry to this situation."

Hope and desire inched into his soul. "What can I do?"

"You must accept your responsibility. The coma you are in is a product of your own fight against accepting your place in this war."

His voice, slightly stronger, said, "I've accepted my place."

"No. You've accepted that you've been called, not that you must freely choose to be part of this war."

"Is that what you did when you gave me your lifeforce?" asked Jet.

"No. That was a decision I made many years before you were born. I was taken from my family, trapped in prison, and eventually released by a wielder of the same magic that destroyed my tribe. Do you know how ironic that is?"

"What happened to the two brothers?"

"They slaughtered on sacred ground. Lady Gaea hid the Phoenix and confined both Runic Magic and Elemental Magic to a limited number of words and shapes. They set forth their own destruction."

"Are you saying that Elemental magic is more than just the limited number of words that I have learned?"

"Far more than you can ever imagine."

"How can I have access to that?"

"I doubt you ever will. So much destruction and bloodshed happened on sacred ground; be happy and true to what you've been given. Magic was lost from that time forward until Arisol and the other kings went searching for the hidden books."

"Is Elemental magic unholy?"

"It can be used for good and bad, like anything else," replied Alces.

"Do you know how I can be released?"

"I do, and so do you."

Jet said, "I wish that you didn't have to die, and your sister."

"I know. This was meant to be. You must walk the path that uplifts the soul and refreshes the dead."

"What does that mean?"

"Khalicaans are women tribesman, enchantresses that have given their souls to those imps in exchange for the chance to kill and do things that they wouldn't have otherwise been able to do. All those that are part of chaos and destruction are subject to an imp, real or not, that's been embedded in their hearts. You must free them of their anger, or you must end their lives. It's as simple as that."

"So simple that it's not simple at all."

"Choose your path."

Inside his own head, Jet found the large stone barrier, preventing him from waking. Ever since the first day, whether he admitted it to himself or not, the stone barrier was only partially open. But it now sat closed. This was the river of his will, and it was partially always blocked. He felt the coldness of the barrier in his own mind. His fingers wrapped around the edges, and with all his might, muscle, and willpower, he tried moving the rock. He gave a 100 percent of himself, everything he had, to move the stone barrier, but it would not budge.

Alces voice, fading away, added, "Try the words 'Libertas Animamea.'"

Without hesitation, Jet repeated "Libertas Animamea."

The stone block disintegrated as if it had never existed.

CHAPTER 35

Jet's eyes fluttered open, and he felt freedom, the ability to move, and was confident in his choices. Swirling around him was his Elemental magic, whispers of the fable, and a quiet happiness emanating from Alces's thoughts.

Sitting up, he felt he would be whole again. Yet, he could only move his fingers and both hands, and it took a considerable amount of effort to turn his head from side to side. The walls and ceiling were concrete, but there were lights, medical equipment, and IV lines, electrodes running from his body, along with a nasal tube.

"Is this a damn joke?" Grantham asked from the only chair in the room. "Are you actually awake?"

"Barely," Jet whispered, his throat dry.

"Let me go get the others."

"No," Jet said. "Did Mckenzey already leave?"

"Like three and a half weeks ago."

"Is the Brotherhood here?"

"They've come and gone too. Sounds like you heard a few things while you were on vacation."

"I don't remember you coming to tell me your deep, dark secrets."

Grantham laughed. "You were probably sleeping when I stopped by."

"Doubtful, bro."

"What do you want me to do?"

"Find Seyanna."

"What?" Grantham said. "If anything happened, I was supposed to report it to Jayco immediately."

Jet raised his eyebrows as much as he could. He also tried to create a facial expression of surprise, but he wasn't sure he appeared any different than being constipated.

"It's just the way it is," Grantham said. "I don't make the rules."

"Neither does Jayco."

"The Brotherhood and Principal Smuin say differently."

"Trust me. This is bigger than all of us."

"How so?"

"If you don't get Seyanna, I'll be dead in a few days."

Grantham stuttered slightly. "How sure are you about this?"

"Beyond sure."

"And Seyanna can help?"

"Don't tell *anyone*."

"What about your doctors?"

"Definitely don't tell them."

Grantham stepped toward the door. Jet added quickly, "Before you go, can you move my head back into the position it was in before?"

"Seriously?" Grantham said. "The things I do for my friends."

Four doctors or nurses came in over the next hour. Jet remained perfectly still, except when he allowed his eyelids to open slightly. They were so preoccupied with their regular routine they didn't notice.

A woman in a lab coat said something downright alarming. "I'm still shocked that we've been feeding him for almost seven weeks, and he still hasn't had a bowel movement."

This hurt Jet on so many levels.

Seyanna arrived two hours later. She was thrilled that he was awake but kept asking, "Why am I here?"

"It's probably best that I only talk with Seyanna. Wouldn't want to get Grantham in trouble."

Grantham shot him a look. "Are you playing me? I'm going to hear what you've got to say."

"Jet might be right. Jayco has been unbending. He is relentless with how he wants things and slightly ruthless to all of us."

"I'm staying."

Seyanna continued, "He hasn't found a replacement for Mckenzey, and he's trying to get each element with around fifty people. He has banished and imprisoned others. Things are getting out of control, and he has some heavy backers."

"How does Jayco have so much power?"

"The Brotherhood gave him some weird amulet, just like they did with Kevin. The power has gone to his head."

"Well, finding a replacement for Mckenzey isn't his area to control." Jet asked, "What about Shane?"

Grantham said, "He's gone underground. He won't share any ideas with Jayco or the rest of us. Jayco is worried he's planning on attacking the Elementals to get the first piece of the Phoenix."

"I need to get out of here." Jet tried sitting up. "And no one else can know."

"Wait a minute," Grantham said. "I thought you said you were dying. Was that a joke?"

"Dying?" Seyanna gasped.

Jet blew out a long breath. "Things are seriously bad for me. I haven't been entirely honest with you guys."

"About what?"

"What really happened when I was in Coso Subtrano."

"We all knew that you didn't really just get swallowed by the mountain," replied Seyanna.

Jet said, "I had a vision of when my parents died."

"Is that it?" Grantham said hotly. "Look. My best friend has gone psycho, but that's not enough for me to go behind his back and all. I think you've tricked me enough for today."

"Just listen," Jet pleaded.

"You have like five seconds."

Jet said, "Geb was with my parents when they died, and Professor Rysen helped kill them." He paused to see the look on their faces.

"I'm intrigued," Grantham admitted.

"Before they died, Geb gave me a tonic that removes magical memories from my mind. When Faunal first attacked me, he dislodged some of those memories, including Silverton and some other things. But I'm not as strong as I could be."

"Less interested," Grantham stated.

"Inside the mountain, after the vision of my parents, I met an oracle that tortured me."

"Heating up."

"Shut up," Seyanna said as she punched Grantham. "Let Jet talk."

"The game was almost like chess. He moved, then I moved, etcetera."

"What was the point?" Grantham asked.

"All choices have consequences."

Hesitantly Seyanna asked, "What type of consequences?"

"Round one, the oracle sent Nash to break Mckenzey's leg. Then it was my turn."

"Did you pick Shane?" asked Grantham.

"I couldn't reasonably choose anyone, so I chose myself."

"Why?" Grantham asked, rolling his eyes.

"Because I didn't choose someone, I was tortured. Round two, and the oracle chose someone to lose the ability of their weapons, and that brown-haired guy, Lawrence, I think, used to be able to use a mace. He can't now."

Seyanna asked, "Who did you pick?"

"Myself again. I lost the ability to use my orbs, and I was tortured."

"I don't like where this is going," replied Seyanna. "What happened after that?"

"Round three. Only one choice to make…I had to choose who died."

"Oh, crap," Grantham said. "I'm guessing you chose Vinny."

"He was already dead. I had to choose myself."

"What?" Seyanna asked. "Why?"

"How could I choose someone?"

Grantham moved closer, fully drawn in by the story. "Not even Shane?"

"Not even Shane, not like that." He continued, "Somehow, because of the tonic and the torture game, I'm dying, and I can't heal without help."

Tears slid down Seyanna's face, and she asked, "Why are you telling us now?"

"The oracle and Alces told me of a way to survive."

The intensity of the moment was shattered by Grantham's cell phone. "Jayco's calling me right now. What should I say?"

Jet hissed, "That you couldn't get in to see me and you will stop by later."

"That might not work."

"It's our best bet."

As Grantham spoke to Jayco, Seyanna asked, "Why did you ask Grantham to come find me?"

"The oracle and Alces said that you'd know the way."

"Me?" Seyanna shook her head. "That's impossible."

Jet whispered, "It has something to do with Anesidora and something you found in Svalbard."

Seyanna's face paled. "You can't possibly know about that. How do you know about the Soul of Anesidora?"

"Only from them. What do you mean, 'soul'?"

Before Seyanna could respond, Grantham stepped into the room. "Well, I told Jayco that Jet is awake. That was probably not the best idea. He's pissed. He wants to meet with me to find out what you said. He asked if anyone else knows. I said no, and he wants me to go to the hideout near the beach. What should I do?"

"Tell him I asked about the others. You explained that Mckenzey has left and that the Brotherhood has put him in charge of the school."

"That's what you want me to say. Anything about the other stuff? About the fact that you might be dying?"

"Not yet. Give me until tomorrow to gather my strength, and we'll tell him together. We'll figure out a plan at that point. You need to feel him out, see how you think he'll take things."

"Okay," Grantham said. "I can do that."

"Perfect."

"Should I go with you?" Seyanna asked.

"No," Grantham said quickly. "He shouldn't know that you've been to see Jet."

"Good idea," Jet said.

"You leave first," Seyanna said. "I'll slip away in ten minutes."

Grantham nodded, and he tilted his head back and forth as if preparing for a long-distance run. Grantham was a great runner, and this was his routine before the big races. He muttered to himself, "I've got this." Without another glance, Grantham left the room.

The instant he was gone, Seyanna turned to Jet. "What now?"

"We need to be on a plane to Svalbard in the next few hours."

"That's going to be nearly impossible. How am I supposed to get you out of this hospital? How do we get teenagers on a plane? Where's your passport? You can barely walk."

Jet considered his options. He said, "I need some clothes and a wheelchair. I think we should leave now, and you can run into my dorm."

"What about your book? Don't you need weapons?"

"I have some. You should grab whatever you think you might need."

"Seriously. We're just going to run off to the Arctic Ocean?"

"That's exactly what we are going to do."

"How am I supposed to get a plane?"

"Ask your parents."

Seyanna rolled her eyes and bit her lower lip as if holding back a response. "I hate you right now, Jet. I hope you know that." She glanced around the room. "It'll take me a moment to find a wheelchair."

Five minutes later she was back. "I can't believe you're serious about this." She pulled up his sleeve and quickly unattached the IV. Jet was surprised at how easily she was able to accomplish this. Before he said anything, she said, "No. I don't know what I'm doing, but I'm going to enjoy this." She reached over and tilted back his head. Jet gagged as the flexible cord was pulled out of his stomach, through his nose. He felt every inch and fell into a coughing fit once the tube was removed.

"What about these electrodes on my chest?"

"Those will be the last thing. I'm pretty sure they're going to signal something, and the nurses will come running."

Seyanna moved to the side of the bed and drew forward the wheelchair. She yanked up the sheets and took a few steps back. "How long has it been since you've showered?"

"Weeks, I bet. But they were probably doing bird-baths."

She plugged her nose. "Not very well." She found his cloak hanging up and tried wrapping it around his shoulders and arms. "You might have to disappear if we see someone."

With a fair amount of tugging, Jet was finally wrenched and stretched into the wheelchair. There was a faint smell of something comforting and delightful when she was near. Over the years he imagined that he'd smelled it a time or two, but other than the last few months, they hadn't been this close in years.

"You suck," Seyanna hissed, clearly out of breath. In the next second, she was removing all the equipment attached to his chest. There was no ringing bell or anything similar as Jet was pushed from the medical room. "Flip on your hood," barked Seyanna.

As he did so, there was a light draft that gusted down the hallway. Seyanna turned right and headed down the hall.

Jet whispered, "Iris, follow," and the golden panther followed soundlessly.

The path was clear until their second turn as Principal Smuin stepped out of the elevator with the older female from the Brotherhood. Jet thought her name was Junjie Su. Principal Smuin asked, "Do you work here, or are you friends with Jet Black? We heard that he woke up."

"Just putting away some of the supplies," Seyanna answered. "I haven't heard anything about Black waking up."

"Good," Principal Smuin said as he turned to walk down the hall. "We have that information contained. This entire thing is going to cause a serious commotion."

The elevator door closed, and Seyanna said, "The other golden animals are two stories up. What's your plan?"

"Get out of town without getting caught."

The elevator opened, and they found the other three golden animals housed in a small area. Jet commanded, "Go to the forest and protect the school. Stay there until we get back." The three golden animals followed Seyanna and Jet to the door. Once it opened, they took off to the east of school.

Seyanna used a car that was parked in the CeU lot, and she helped him into the passenger seat, putting the wheelchair in the trunk. It was a quick drive to his dorm. She was gone for ten minutes but returned with a duffel bag. She said, "Your roommates were nowhere to be seen."

"Even better."

They drove north out of campus and in the direction of Santa Barbara. Using her cell phone, Seyanna called her parents, but Jet didn't hear the conversation. The instant they left campus, Jet's already depleted energy took a hit. He slept the entire way to the local airport.

When he awoke, the car was parked next to a hanger. "What's going on?"

"My parents will be here in a few minutes. We'll use the same airplane you used to come back from Argentina."

"Is this your car?"

"Uh..." She hesitated. "I guess."

"I had no idea you had a ten-year-old Volvo."

"It's a long story."

"We've got the time."

"I had three escape plans from Chadwicks if something goes bad."

"And by 'going bad', you mean?"

"My story doesn't have anything to do with magic or the rest of you."

"All right."

When she didn't elaborate, he said, "Care to explain?"

She took a deep breath and said, "You have to promise not to tell anyone, ever."

"Not sure what that means?"

"It's a huge secret, and no one can know."

"Who knows about this secret?"

"Just me and my parents and a few other people, I think."

"This is about the weirdest conversation I've ever had."

Seyanna smirked, and the stupidness of the statement hit him like a wall of water while surfboarding.

"Point taken," he replied.

"My parents aren't actually my parents."

Whatever Jet had thought could have been the answer to his question, this wasn't it. "What are you talking about?"

"I moved to Silverton in third or fourth grade."

"I remember."

"You were one of my first friends. I've almost told you the truth a few different times."

"Does Jayco know?"

"No way."

"My parents kidnapped me from my real parents. Of course, I don't look at it like a kidnapping."

"Wait? What?"

"I was really born in Boston. My birth parents and my current parents knew each other. My parents were busy doing drugs, and for a few years, I was homeless. My current parents were professors at Boston University, and they helped with the homeless. One day my birth mom overdosed, and my dad left me at a local church. I was taken in by the Motick family, and they have raised me as one of their own. In fact, I see them as my parents."

"Why not tell us?"

"Six months after my parents found me, my dad reported me missing. He went to the police and said that I was kidnapped. He blamed the family of my birth mom. He got lost in the criminal world. My parents feared that if I went back to him, I would be in danger. I guess he has been looking for me since, but now he's part of something more sinister. He spent four years in prison and was released a few years ago. He's still looking for me."

"Why?"

"No clue. But he's sobered up and has made some money with his crew."

"That's why you have a getaway car?"

"And why we've been in Alaska and on Svalbard Island. My parents think that I'm related to someone important, and my father wants to use me somehow."

"Do you want to meet him?"

"Not a chance," Seyanna said quickly.

Jet mulled over what he had learned. The truth about Seyanna was shocking.

In a soft voice, she asked, "Am I still one of the Echoes?"

"As much as I am. I guess we'll see if the Echoes really exist after we get back."

Mr. and Mrs. Motick arrived five minutes later. They gave hugs to Seyanna and helped Jet into the wheelchair.

Mr. Motick said, "The plane is ready, and the pilot is on his way. Good luck in Svalbard. Wish we could go."

Jet whispered, "You told your parents?"

"They know everything," Seyanna said. "I don't really hide anything from them." To her parents, she said, "Jet knows about *before* Silverton."

Jet watched as Seyanna's mother, whose house he had gone over to dozens of times, pursed her lips together. "It's fine, Mrs. M.," said Jet, using the name he'd called her when he was younger. "If you knew everything, you'd know that my secrets are much bigger than yours. You've got nothing to worry about."

Surprisingly this seemed to have been the right thing to say.

Mr. M asked, "What are you looking for?"

Seyanna's face reddened. "Truthfully, I haven't told you everything."

"What does that mean, dear?" her mom asked.

"When we lived there, I didn't know about magic. I made a trip on my own and was scaling down an ice crevice, and I came to this stone door of sorts with a ton of hieroglyphics. Afterward I researched what I had found. I didn't tell anyone, but I learned a lot about Egyptian history."

"That's why you are going?" her mother asked.

"Jet really needs to get there, and it seems that I'm the only one that can go with him."

Seyanna's father said sternly, "This doesn't sound like a well thought out plan. What parents let their sixteen-year-old daughter leave the country? Can't someone else go?"

"No, Dad. I told you. Jayco is going to come looking for me. You need to keep to the script. I know we are only sixteen, but we are strong."

"You want me to tell Jayco that you're heartbroken over your breakup. You think he'll buy that? And that you left on a flight to Washington, DC, to try to get a better look at what caused the disaster?"

"Let's hope. I've been talking to him about it for days."

"But you never even liked him," her mom insisted.

Seyanna's eyes flashed at her mom, and she whispered, "We need to be going."

"Sure. Call us when you arrive."

"We can't," Seyanna said. She handed her parents her phone. "Tell Jayco that I left these with you. He'll also believe that."

"If you say so." To Jet, he said, "You had better keep my daughter safe."

"I'll try."

Seyanna huffed. "He's the one who's hurt, Dad. I'm going to keep *him* safe. Help me get him onto the plane."

Seyanna and her father carried Jet onto the plane and into one of the seats. Seyanna took the time to sit down and quickly scribbled out a note. She handed it to her mom and added, "Give this to Jayco when he stops by. Hide the car so I can use it again."

"No problem."

Seyanna's father walked to the front of the plane and spoke to the pilots, who had just arrived. Mrs. M gave Jet a hug and said, "Take care. Good to see you again."

"You too, Mrs. M."

Seyanna walked with her parents out the door, and they talked for a few minutes. Jet couldn't hear what was happening, and he didn't really care. His body felt useless, and he was pretty sure that is was going to take a miracle for him to survive the trip.

CHAPTER 36

Jet slept, woke for a few minutes, and slept again. Seyanna asked him some questions, but he didn't understand what she was saying. He assumed that they'd landed a few times, probably for refueling, but he didn't really come out of his brain fog until many hours into the flight. When he stirred, the plane's main cabin was dark, except for a light over one of the seats. Seyanna was studying a piece of cloth in her hand.

He asked, "What are you looking at?"

Seyanna jerked slightly, placed the fabric on the chair, and came to stand next to his seat. "Are you hungry?"

"I think so."

She grabbed a few blankets and helped him into a more reclined position. After he was settled, she left and came back with a gourmet sandwich, some coffee, and a doughnut. "I wasn't sure what you were in the mood for."

"It all smells good." He ate slowly and noticed it was dusk outside the windows. "Where are we?"

"We just left Iceland for Svalbard."

"What?"

"You've been asleep for twelve hours or more. We landed in New York and Iceland. We were able to refuel and leave pretty quickly."

"How long until we're there?"

"We'll land at Spitsbergen in about three hours."

"Wow. You got us here. That's incredible."

"How do you feel?"

"The sleep helped. I was delirious for most of the flight, but I'm doing better. I'm not sure that I can stand on my own."

"How well are you going to be able to walk across the snow?"

"It'll be close to impossible."

"My parents and I have a lot of friends here. We should be able to get a helicopter that can get us closer to where we need to go. After that, we'll use a snowcat."

"A snowcat?" he questioned.

"A large snowmobile that can fit several people inside the back."

"If you say so," Jet said, and after a few bites of the sandwich, he moved on to the coffee and doughnut. "Can I ask you a question?"

"Is it about my past?"

Nodding, he asked, "What's your given name?"

"The name my parents gave me?"

"Yes."

"Rainbow," she said, without the slightest bit of humor. "It's actually going to be my next tattoo."

"Seriously."

"The name is part of me. Just not one I want everyone knowing."

"Interesting."

"My turn to ask a question," said Seyanna.

"What do you want to know?"

"How in the world did you screw this up so badly?"

"Not sure I would call it a screwup. Things are more complicated than we thought, and some of it was out of my control. Terrible things have happened because I was too naive to know better."

"Why did you have to be the hero again and get caught inside the mountain?"

"Bad luck."

"No, seriously."

"The reward for my torturing was the second piece of the Phoenix."

"Are you sure? Jayco said that Shane got there first, retrieving the first piece."

"Shane cheated and only thought he did." Jet muttered softly, "Bookcase." And from the hidden compartment that only he could see, he pulled out the second piece of the Phoenix. Jet handed the fragment to Seyanna, and she inspected it.

"It looks like the first tablet piece," she said. "It's clear and about the same size. It has two smooth sides and two jagged sides. The only way we'll really know is to match it against the first piece."

"We will. When we get back."

Seyanna stood so quickly that Jet almost dropped his doughnut. She went to where she had been sitting, grabbed the cloth piece and a wooden box. When she sat down again, she opened a small wooden box and pulled out a crystal fragment.

"Where did you get that?" asked Jet.

"I didn't trust that Shane wasn't going to try to steal it. I've been hiding it since the fight at school." Taking the second fragment, she matched the right sides and pushed them together. A deep yellow glow brightened the cabin, and it was clear that the two pieces were the top two of the tablet.

"Satisfied?" asked Jet.

"I am now."

Jet took a sip, and when he was finished, he asked, "Tell me more about the Soul of Anesidora."

"How much do you already know?"

"Not much. I was just told that it was in Svalbard."

"Interesting." Seyanna placed the cloth on her lap. "Remember the crate that Nana sent you with your cloak, the pyramid, and the other things?"

"Of course."

"Do you remember seeing a piece of cloth?"

"Vaguely."

"This piece of cloth is a doozy. I mean a really scary thing." She held it up, and it was old, worn, and slightly yellow. As she turned the cloth over, he saw that hieroglyphic markings were woven into one side. "I noticed this piece of cloth right away. For a few days, I thought I was losing my mind."

"What is it?" Jet asked.

"This particular cloth has been missing for decades. It's a lost treasure originally found in the tomb of one of the kings in Egypt in the late 1920s. It was found, studied, and was sent to the Louvre to be on display. That was back in the fifties or sixties. During transport it was stolen and has been lost for fifty years."

Jet mumbled, "What does it have to do with Arisol?"

"I don't think it does, at least not directly. There's a strong connection with mysticism, relic treasures, and something far more important...to you."

"Me?"

"Over the years scholars began to theorize about what the cloth revealed. It depicts an angel appearing before gods and mortals and presenting the gift of life. Another theory, the most reliable, is that the Soul of Anesidora is an important object, an otherworldly artifact, untouchable by men. It could be that she offered magic or something else entirely."

"So it could really be nothing at all. Just a wild goose chase."

"This cloth was found in an Egyptian tomb, but it contains Greek history as well."

Jet took another drink of his coffee. "The fable and the box we found have a close connection with Egypt. There are hieroglyphics on the box itself."

"That's why this cloth caught my eye. And there's more."

"Like what?"

Seyanna appeared uneasy. "A pharaoh dreamed about an object that was hidden under a mountain. He envisioned a sizable scarab beetle as a hieroglyph on a door under the mountain. It was his tomb where they found the cloth. Rough translation of his dream is—the fountain of youth. But Anesidora is another name for Pandora. She's the angel in the story that sends a gift."

"Didn't she unleash evil on the world?"

"Maybe, but not in this story. In this story the gift of life is given."

"What does Svalbard have to do with all of this?"

"Three months before I left, I was drawn to a portion of Svalbard that I had never been to before. I found a carving of a hieroglyphic scarab beetle on a stone door, a perfect match to the one on this cloth."

"Didn't the box in Switzerland have a scarab beetle as well?"

"It sure did."

Jet said, "You're full of secrets, Seyanna Motick."

Pointing to the cloth, Seyanna continued, "There's a person, or a god, depicted on the cloth with both arms outstretched. On the ground there are two items, almost like weapons."

Jet looked more closely. He'd never seen such weapons before, if that's what they were. There was a trident with three long prongs, but the handle was oriented sideways rather than long. It looked almost like a toothbrush with three prongs. The second weapon also had three points, but the outer two were curved, almost like something to bail hay with.

A second figure stood next to a shining box. A scarab was depicted on the lid. A bird hung in midair next to the box, holding a large tablet in its claws.

"What do you see?" Seyanna asked.

"This weird bird holding a tablet," Jet answered.

"That's where the translation came from—the Soul of Anesidora."

Jet said, "Why Anesidora and not Pandora?"

"It's the blending of two cultures. But on the tablet, held by the bird, is the hieroglyph for Anesidora. She is the goddess being worshipped by the other figure." Seyanna leaned back in her chair. "I really don't understand everything. I had to read several books on this topic." Pointing to the cloth, she continued, "The bird with a human head and human arms is called Ba. It has a bunch of different meanings. Ba is an ancient Egyptian concept of the soul. With the name Anesidora on the tablet and Ba, experts have called this the Soul of Anesidora.

Pointing to the scarab beetle in the background, Jet added, "This scarab on the door is telling you that the Soul of Anesidora is on Svalbard Island?"

"It's a guess."

"Let's hope you're right."

"What did Alces say about it?"

"She believed that Anesidora was essential for me to survive. She hinted that you knew where it could be found. That's it."

"It confirms our destination."

"I guess it does."

Seyanna asked, "Where's your book and the other items you brought? I don't see your backpack."

Jet explained about the ring and showed her the basics of how it worked.

"That's sweet and totally useful," she replied. "Can you store this piece of cloth?

"No problem. They fell into silence. After a moment, he asked, "What if I can't walk or perform magic? I'll put both of us at risk."

"We don't have much of a choice, do we? I think I'll be able to handle most things."

Their plane touched down at Longyearbyen on the only runway of the airport about an hour later. This was the primary airport of this large island under the flag of Norway and the northernmost airport in the world. Around 150,000 people flew through the airport per year. The pilot and Seyanna helped Jet off the plane and into a wheelchair. It was a grand total of two degrees Fahrenheit. The bitter cold railed on Jet despite his cloak and the blankets.

They didn't stay at the airport for very long. After collecting their luggage, they boarded a helicopter to take them to Ny-Alesund, the research center on the island. It was nearly eight o'clock at night when they passed over some of the most beautiful glaciers in the world. Seyanna explained that for about half of February, the sun didn't show itself at all. Now that it was the first week into March, the sun would only be up a few hours each day.

"It's very weird being back here," Seyanna said as she stared out the window.

"What do you mean?"

"I left here as a scientist and am returning as a Sorcerer."

"You're still a scientist. You've just added some additional skills."

"I guess," she said absentmindedly as she pointed to lights in the distance. "That's Ny-Alesund. We'll rest there tonight and try to get some sleep. We'll head out in the morning."

"How was living at the camp?"

"About ten countries have permanent research facilities operated by Kings Bay. In the summertime up to a hundred and fifty people come in and out of the town. Right now there probably aren't more than fifty. We are on the Broggerhalvoya Peninsula. It can get frigid, but I absolutely loved it. I've always been okay with the solitude."

"How cold is it going to be?"

"You'll think that Longyearbyen was a heatwave."

"I'm going to need a lot of blankets tonight."

"We'll find you some."

The helicopter landed, and Seyanna threw out the luggage and helped Jet away from the overhead blade. Two heavily dressed men darted over to the chopper and appeared to recognize Seyanna almost immediately. Her strawberry blond hair, her height, and good looks were impossible to overlook. They helped with the luggage, and soon Jet and Seyanna were loaded in the back of a truck with covering over the back. They rode for two minutes to the closest five-star hotel, which turned out to be inside one of the research buildings. He was taken to a smaller room with four beds. He and his luggage were placed in one of the beds. Seyanna unpacked a few of her items on an adjacent bed. Jet, thoroughly exhausted, fell asleep, fully clothed, before another word was spoken.

He awoke, hours later, unsure of where he was. It took several minutes longer than it should for him to realize where he was. He felt warm and found five heaters surrounding him. Seyanna was nowhere to be seen, but a few packages of food, akin to military rations sat on a table next to him. The food was better than expected and still slightly warm. He ate spaghetti noodles with a red sauce, crackers, and some cookies.

After dinner he struggled to get to the bathroom. There was a shower, and he placed a plastic chair in it to avoid falling. For the first time in weeks, he sighed as the warm water soaked him. Once finished, and after toweling off, he crawled back to his bed. He lay in just his towel for several minutes, too tired to get dressed.

"Why didn't you call for me?" asked Seyanna as she entered the room.

He muttered, "How?"

She picked up a handheld radio next to his bed. "You push the button and say, 'Hey Seyanna.'"

His teeth chattered as he said, "I'll remember that for next time."

"Can you get dressed?"

"I don't think so."

She unpacked his clothes, including his underwear. Jet felt mortified. She arranged them around his feet and pulled them up to the height of the towel. "I hope you can get the rest from there."

He spent the next few minutes awkwardly getting his underwear into place. Seyanna helped with his shorts and a T-shirt. When finished, she said, "We'll be leaving in a few hours. We have some specialized gear to help you stay warm."

"Why not put it on now?"

"You don't want to get too hot and start sweating. This is the best way."

"Whatever you say." Despite the heaters and the blankets, Jet shivered.

Seyanna pushed him over a few inches, laying down next to him and started rubbing his back and his legs. "Just trying to help you get warm. Don't get any grand ideas."

Jet laughed for the first time in a long time. "Not that I could do anything about it."

A few minutes later, she whispered, "Do you miss Mckenzey?"

After recovering from a yawn, he asked, "What do you mean?"

"Never mind. I made myself promise that I wouldn't ask about her."

"About Mckenzey?"

"I bet you wish Mckenzey were here in my place."

"Why do you say that?" Jet asked. "There isn't anyone else I wish were here but you. With you, I don't have to pretend to be someone else. I haven't thought of Mckenzey once."

"Really?" replied Seyanna.

"I heard you, Jayco, and Mckenzey each talking to me back when I was in the coma."

"Seriously?"

"A few times."

"Like what?"

"Jayco was livid that I was still injured. You told me about all the students killed and what happened to Alces's and Kaya's bodies."

"Anything else?"

"Mckenzey came and told me that she was leaving for Dillion Lake. She said that we had missed our chance and that she was now with Eric. I've come to accept that and I'm okay with it."

"Mckenzey is a mess right now. Latisha and I have talked with her. Dillon Lake is different than she expected. She and Eric have been promoted to student body members. Kevin is the student president. She says it's weird there."

"I bet." Jet yawned again. "I feel awful for Mckenzey and the rest of you, believing that I had died in Argentina. Things seem so crazy. I hope finding Anesidora fixes everything."

"I hope it does."

After a moment he asked, "What about you and Jayco? Your mom said something—"

"I think it was more like an inevitable encounter."

"That's a weird way to look at it."

"You've always had a thing for Mckenzey, and Grantham and Latisha are like soulmates. I could tell Jayco was catching the feels for me, so I decided to see where it went. It just didn't work out."

"When?"

"A few days after we got back from Switzerland."

"Seriously?"

"A hundred and ten percent."

"I had no idea," he said. "I feel like an idiot."

"Don't worry. You were too busy to see the truth."

"I guess. What's the deal with Jayco these days?"

"He's power-hungry. He can be a pretty good leader, but he gets nasty when someone has more power than he does."

"You said that he was given some amulets."

"I just overheard him talking one time. He met with the Brotherhood alone. Kevin was there. I think they're teaming up for something. I think they want to attack Shane and take the fake second piece. What a predicament that would be."

"Why Kevin?" Jet was starting to feel better, but he didn't want Seyanna to move away.

"He seems like he's the puppet of the Brotherhood, and they gave Jayco the rule over the school. The amulets are embedded into the palm of your hand. They give energy and some level of magical abilities."

"He already has power."

"Latisha told me about Siwalik. I guess when the kings defeated him, and he became their servant, he gave them sixteen stones from his belly. These stones are the amulets. They each have a different function."

"I've never heard of this." Jet asked, "What can I do to fix things back home?"

Seyanna said, "You should concentrate on Grantham and Latisha first. Then try to mend things with Mckenzey. Lastly, Jayco. You'll have to show each of them what they mean to you."

"That's a good idea." He asked, "What about you? Are you on my side?" Jet thought the answer was obvious since she had traveled this far with him. But he was surprised by the pained sound in her voice.

"Life has been ironic and unfair for most of my life. You know the story about my parents. You've always been a good and close friend, but at arm's length. Mckenzey has always come first. I didn't hear about magic from you. You and

Mckenzey shared this sort of connection, and I was left on the outside. I pretended that it didn't bother me, but it does. I was so excited when you asked to fly with me to Svalbard, but I worried I was the second choice."

Trying to explain, he said, "It's not like that at all."

Seyanna sat up quickly. Her voice was emotional when she said, "I realize that you're injured and possibly dying. I didn't mean to dump this on you. I'm tired and I need some sleep."

"Seyanna…" Jet said.

"I'm going to get a quick shower. Good night." She went to her bed, retrieved her clothes and shower supplies, and set off for the bathroom.

Trying to stay awake, he pulled out his tome, hoping the next page would turn. It required most of his energy to retrieve the book, and he rested it on his chest to catch his breath. Minutes later his legs jerked, and he rubbed his eyes furiously, but it didn't matter; he couldn't stay awake any longer. As he rolled over, something crashed to the floor. An instant before falling asleep, he heard a snarl from miles away that sent shivers down his spine. Somewhere in the icy wilderness, a creature felt his magic and stirred.

CHAPTER 37

The following morning Jet woke before the sun was up, which was far from surprising. Seyanna's bags were packed, and he was alone. Needing to use the restroom, Jet attempted to stand, only to find that he couldn't feel his legs. Using his hands, he lifted his feet and placed them on the side of his bed. His foot scraped against *The Sorcerer's Guide*, lying face down, semi opened. Reaching out, he picked it up, noticing the title was one he'd never seen before.

The Soul of Anesidora

Five Ancient Matrons of Goth Airtha and the lands beyond built and protected the kingdoms with such precision that they believed they would live endlessly. The western winds blew a vessel of corruption, chaos, and greed to the salty shores, and life changed evermore.

To combat evil, the Matrons began to teach about diversity, love, magic, sacrifice, and hope. These became part of the recipe of preventing the annihilation of all creatures and inhabitants.

Lady Gaea, Bio Vita, and Aqua Felis were three sisters born of Earth, Water, and Air. Another two sisters, Atmos Geni and Ella Dastria, had been birthed of Fire and Spirit. And for many seasons, they brought forth plenitude and life while keeping evil and chaos at bay.

Years later Ella lost her heart to a boy named Tigerus. She was full of happiness and hope, and their love was widely acclaimed to be the purest in the land. Tigerus courted her, and they were soon married. As a condition of her marriage, she lost her power as Matron and became mortal. Lifetimes passed, and they were blessed with a single daughter.

As life does, through heartbreak and sorrow, things became difficult, and Tigerus fell into entanglement with mischief and later with wickedness. Betraying Ella, he divulged hallowed secrets to veiled shadows, guidelines to protecting the Matrons. Every dishonest and terrible thing that happened from that time forth was blamed on Ella and her lustful heart.

Folk songs began depicting Ella harshly, and she couldn't outrun her past. Finding herself alone and feeling unrelenting guilt and shame, she exiled herself to a hidden tomb. She took upon her the name of Anesidora and lived the remainder of her days in banishment. She accepted the punishment of the scarab with optimism that one day she would find a way to redeem her past.

The only daughter of Ella and Tigerus was embraced and educated by Lady Gaea. Aurora became a distinguished leader of the Nomads. Magic flows freely in the kindred of the Queen.

Urgently closing his tome, Jet strained to stand but couldn't. "Seyanna," he hollered into the handheld radio.

She sprinted into the room. "What is it?"

Pointing to the book, he said, "*The Sorcerer's Guide* has given us some backstory on Anesidora."

"It's got to wait. We have a blizzard hurricane heading toward us. We have to leave now, or we'll never get there."

"I didn't know that existed."

"It didn't before today."

"I can't feel my legs." Jet placed his tome into his bookshelf.

She reached over and pinched his thigh. "Do you feel this?"

"No."

Moving up, she pinched his waist. "What about this?"

"Barely."

Her next pinch was near his ribs. Screaming, he replied, "Yep, I can definitely feel that."

"Lie down. We need to get you dressed."

"Bathroom first."

She groaned but helped him into the bathroom. Once finished he was brought back to his bed. She pulled off his shirt, her eyes fixating on a scar near his shoulder. "What's this?"

Shivering, Jet said, "During my torture I was supposed to injure someone else. I picked myself, and Jayco shot me with an arrow. This is how it healed."

Seyanna's face tightened. "Jayco told me that he dreamed about shooting you. He became convinced that you deserved to be shot. He became fixated on it, and it fueled his energy in questioning every choice you've ever made."

"That's...odd."

Pulling out thermal underwear, she lifted his head and shoved in his arms. Next, she outfitted both legs. It was harder to pull up the thermals to his waist. He became a rag doll and was unable to stop any movement she made. This was followed by a breathable base layer of merino wool. She focused on a liner for his feet and wool socks, then a mid-layer with a specialized coat. The last two layers were his cloak and an outer jacket with a hood. His boots were the final items.

After finishing, Jet asked, "How's this going to work? I can't even sit up."

"We've made a bed for you in the snowcat."

"We?"

"I had to get some help. I can't carry you on my own. Two friends of mine from before will help us. They're trustworthy."

"No complaints here."

"Good," Seyanna said and stood, sweat rolling down her face. She yelled, "Okay, boys. We're ready."

Two boys in their early twenties, fully dressed in outer gear, stepped into the room. They were introduced as Donovan and Lars and seemed eager and excited. Jet presumed that had something to do with hanging out with Seyanna. They picked Jet up and carried him outside. The air was bitter cold, somehow far worse than it had been yesterday. In the distance Jet could see that the snow was being tossed around, and visibility was only a few hundred feet. Ahead of them was a large orange vehicle with large belts instead of tires. There were large front windows and smaller side ones. All in all it was a tin can moving through snow. He was hoisted into the back and onto a plastic, square bed. Gear was packed inside and on top of the snowcat.

Noticing his gaping mouth, Lars said, "Out there, you can never be too careful."

The boys continued working. Ten minutes later Seyanna joined him, as heavily dressed as he was. "We've got some food, water, drinks, tents, heaters, a few sleds, and a bunch more things. We were thinking of pulling a few snowmobiles, but the wind is too strong."

"Are we sure this is a good idea?" asked Jet.

"It's definitely *not* a good idea, but we don't have another choice. You look like you're dying, no joke."

"Thanks for the vote of confidence."

"Here is some food to store just in case. I have some things as well."

Soon the snowcat's engines started, and they left camp. The view outside the two side windows was breathtaking, despite the swirling snow and the darkness. As they traveled,

Seyanna pointed out a few glaciers and several large mountains, and sometimes he thought he could see them.

She said, "We need to get on the backside of that mountain. That's where I was before."

"Are you sure we're going to find it?"

"I was led to it before; it'll happen again.

The numbness continued moving slowly up his body. By mid-day the area below his belly button was entirely numb. It was like death was creeping up from his toes.

He slept on and off for the next few hours. The sun even came up for a time. Every so often, Seyanna would crawl up to the cab and open a door and talk with Donovan and Lars. She would return, but each time she appeared worried. The next time he woke up, he found the back area empty, and they weren't moving. Several long minutes later there were scrapes at the back door, and it opened. A frosted and snow-covered Seyanna pulled herself inside.

"We're about ten minutes from where we need to be. Things are getting bad out there. It's cold, windy as hell, getting darker, and there are these flying cats that are as large as a miniature horse. They're making life very difficult. The boys aren't sure if we can keep going."

"Is their fur black, with nasty claws?"

"Friends of yours?"

"Vicerants. A type of Drekavac Demon."

"Gotta go." A voice boomed from outside. "Those flying furballs are the least of our problems. There's something else hunting us, and it's in the middle of that frozen hurricane."

Seyanna stood at the back window as the snowcat rumbled forward. "Do you know what else is following us?"

"Only a guess," Jet muttered to himself.

"What should we do?"

"First, let's let Iris out and she can help us. Do we have any other weapons?"

"We have a lot of guns."

Shaking unsteadily, Jet barely managed to pull out the golden pyramid. He said the right words, and Iris transformed. The panther paced back and forth inside the cramped space.

"Can you see what is following us?" asked Jet.

"It comes in and out of focus. It seems like a gigantic white fury polar bear."

"That doesn't sound horrible," conceded Jet.

Rotating back to face Jet, Seyanna's face drained of any remaining color. "It has three horns and it's half the size of Dalkiate."

Jet remembered the snarl from last night. "A Chupovana."

"How's that possible?"

"No idea. Why would the Vicerants and the Chupovanas be working together?"

A voice yelled from the front cabin. "There's a huge swarm up ahead. What should we do?"

A feeling of hopeless overwhelmed Jet. He had no strength, couldn't walk, had no weapons, and couldn't use magic against those creatures.

"Keep going," replied Seyanna. "And let's try shooting those flying cats."

Moments later, gunfire erupted as either Donovan or Lars was trying to hold back the Vicerants. Seyanna opened a case and pulled out her own gun. Without a single hint of apprehension, she pocketed a fistful of shells and loaded the gun. The back door swung open, and she began firing.

After reloading a dozen times, she yelled to the driver, "We're close. I can feel it. Take a slight right turn."

The vehicle veered to the right.

She added, "Stop the snowcat in two minutes."

Donovan answered, "I hope you're right."

Jet had the same thought. "How did you ever find this place?"

"When I came here before, the northern lights brought me here."

A wonderful and warm sensation gushed through Jet and his anxiety and hopelessness vanished. Whatever it was, did not coming from him. His mind thought of Alces.

The vehicle began to slow. Seyanna yelled, "Whatever you do, don't shoot at the golden animal.

"A golden what?" asked Lars.

"You'll see."

Iris did not wait for the vehicle to stop. She leaped out the back door and began mauling every fury flying creature that came within her reach. The wind and snow had minimal effect on her. Above them Jet heard scraping sounds and thought something had perched on the top. Soon he noticed items were being tossed off the roof.

Seyanna said, "While Donovan is unpacking, let's get you ready to move." She pulled him close and wrapped some rope around his chest, just under his armpits, and expertly tied a knot.

"What's that for?" asked Jet.

"Just in case," she replied coolly.

Lars arrived at the back door shooting whenever he could. He said, "That golden beauty is deadly. She's killed a dozen of the those flying cats. Where can I get one of those?"

"Move it," shouted Seyanna.

Lars winked and jumped inside to help Seyanna pull Jet from the snowcat. They transferred him onto a large sled outside. The temperature was glacial, and snow swirled everywhere.

Taking the shotgun from Seyanna, Donovan took aim and shot three Vicerants out of the skies. Iris soon killed another six, but it didn't appear that they were making any real dent in the horde. Seyanna busied herself as she packed food, water, tents, and more clothing. She wore her white cloak and would be almost entirely camouflaged without her boots, backpack, and black beanie.

Between the two shotguns and Iris, it seemed the flying creatures were being kept at bay.

"That polar bear is going to be here soon," remarked Lars.

"We're ready. Let's go," said Seyanna.

The sun had only gone partly above the horizon during their adventure so far. It had since disappeared, and nighttime had arrived. There was still some light from the northern stars illuminating the snow.

Jet said, "I can see the stars but it's snowing."

Lars replied, "The snow is coming from that large polar bear."

Donovan tossed the shotgun back to Seyanna, and he reached for the cord to the sled. It took several steps to gain momentum, but Donovan sprinted faster than Jet expected. Lars kept ahead of the group, shooting any flying animals. It took precious seconds to reload, but it didn't appear they would be running out of ammo anytime soon. As dusk became darkness, Jet noticed that the Vicerants glowed a dark purple and were easy to spot. The Chupovana was now less than two miles away, and its majestic white fur held a slight glow of its own.

"Save your ammo," Seyanna screamed. "We just need to move faster. Let the golden panther protect us."

"We can't fight that polar bear and win. It's ten times bigger than a normal bear," said Lars.

"Where are we going?" asked Donovan.

"There's a crevice around here somewhere."

Seyanna pulled out her golden bow and arrows, dropping the shotgun into the sled next to Jet.

Lars took over for Donovan. A Vicerant glided by Donovan during the exchange and could have easily clawed him in the back.

Jet yelled, "They flying cats aren't even attacking. Ignore them."

"Over there," Seyanna screamed, and she sprinted to their right. It took longer for Lars to change the direction of the sled. When they reached Seyanna, she was staring down at the ground. She had placed two flares to highlight the area. The sled laid parallel to a gigantic crevice. Jet struggled to move to a point where he could gaze into the crevice. It was the largest he'd ever seen. Far below, he thought there was water, and noticed rock cliffs and slabs of ice. The wind howled.

"Is that water down there?" asked Jet.

"Probably the ocean," Lars said as he broke a flare and dropped it into the gap.

Jet asked, "Are we standing on a glacier?"

"Maybe." Lars shook his head. "We could be standing on the tops of mountains. If there was no ice, we'd be shocked at what was below us."

Donovan added, "I've never seen anything like this."

"Totally mind-boggling," agreed Jet.

"Over here," Seyanna yelled.

"What now?" asked Donovan.

"We need to anchor this rope and go over the edge."

"Say what?" asked Jet.

"There's a ledge down there. Don't worry."

Jet pointed at the oncoming mammoth polar bear. "We don't have time. It'll be here in less than a minute."

"Get moving," Seyanna screamed.

Iris was transformed back into a pyramid and placed inside the hidden compartment in his ring. Donovan quickly began hammering something into the ground. Lars put spiked ice climbing gear onto his feet. After finishing, he took over as Lars did the same. Before he could protest, Jet was nudged unceremoniously over the edge. He fell for the first ten feet before a strong yank in his shoulders stopped his descent. Luckily, he had lost most of the feeling below his neck.

"Don't drop me!" Jet screamed. He started hyperventilating at the prospect of falling to his death. Far below, the water was more like a river, cutting through mountain terrain into an unseen river or portion of the ocean. Ice covered most of the walls. Fifteen more feet down there was a ledge.

The Vicerants dove into the crevice, trying to knock Lars and Seyanna off the side of the mountain. They were climbing down the crevice, each wearing a backpack, while Donovan remained at the top. The echoes of pounding feet intensified as the Chupovana approached.

Jet swayed and fell another seven feet before jerking to a stop. Soon, Donovan, from above, using the rope, began to swing Jet back and forth. As he approached the cliff, he dropped the last several feet and landed hard on the ledge. This time, Jet's breath was knocked out of him, and he began coughing.

Donovan bellowed and launched himself off the top without a rope. The gigantic polar bear reached the crevice an instant later, hot air shooting out of its nostrils. Its head and half its body stretched over the edge as the magic-stealer stared down at him. The Chupovana was gigantic, with enormous claws and large icicles as spikes on its back. Its horns were white in color and were large, sharp, and pointed directly forward, like a bull. They curved from the top of its head. There were so many spikes on the creature's back that Jet was unsure if it could be ridden. The creature opened its mouth and bellowed a pulsating wave that shook the ice around them. His bright green eyes bore down on Jet.

At long last Jet could breathe again. His head ached, and he understood that he was the Chupovana's prey. Death approached, and if he wasn't careful, his magic was on the verge of being thieved.

"He's trying to cause an avalanche," Seyanna screamed.

Donovan pulled a cord and a small parachute unhitched, and he glided down to the lower ledge. Lars and Seyanna, having dodged the Vicerants, arrived a few minutes later.

Lars said, "Well, we made it. Now what?"

Jet could barely use his arm, but he pulled out Iris and she transformed into a panther. She glowed and illuminated a circular ice tunnel that led into the mountain.

Seyanna pointed. "The doorway is down there."

A Vicerant dove at the ledge, trying to reach Jet. Donovan pulled him to safety, and the flying cat hammered at the ice, making a large piece break away. A second Vicerant was far stealthier, having climbed on the overhand behind the group. The creature sunk its claws deep into Donovan's shoulders. With a swipe, the boy was flung from the ledge. A golden arrow flew through the air, embedding itself into the flying feline's neck. The creature squawked before it fell from view.

"Donovan!" Lars shouted and ran forward to the edge.

A bellow erupted from above, and a large shadow danced on the opposite rock wall as the Chupovana leaped across the ravine, more than twenty-five feet away, landing on an outcropping on the opposite side.

"Retreat," cried Seyanna.

Lars and Iris gripped Jet's cloak and pulled him backward.

Staring into the green eyes of the Chupovana he understood that it was a killing machine, and it thirsted after his magic. Relief flooded through Jet as the walls of the tunnel narrowed. The Chupovana was too large to crawl after them. The creature howled its displeasure and soared to the ledge they were on. The creature commenced clawing at the ground as they began to disappear from its view. With raw power, it would make a path to reach them soon enough.

"Here's the door," Seyanna bellowed.

Jet couldn't turn his head, but after a few feet, he came to rest on the frozen ground.

"We're screwed," Lars replied. "Is it possible that these creatures been on this island the entire time?"

"No idea," replied Seyanna, clearly traumatized.

The sound of the ripping and gashing of rocks was overwhelming. It was the most daunting thing Jet had ever heard.

Lars asked, "Can we get that door open, like now?"

Pulling out a flashlight, Seyanna illuminated a gigantic scarab beetle carved into the door. The details were enchanting.

"Pull me closer," said Jet.

Seyanna said, "I can't see a way in."

Jet replied, "Look for a dial or a keyhole, or something like that."

"There's a lot of ice and rock."

"Keep looking."

Small rocks and debris flung into the tunnel, rattling around. The Chupovana was moving faster than Jet had thought possible.

"Found something," yelled Seyanna. "There's a place in the door for a flat rock or similar."

"That's it," replied Jet. Using two unsteady fingers, he pulled out a golden rectangle and hissed, "Pull me closer." Once he was in place, he lifted the golden item to Seyanna, and she took it and shoved it into the hole in the door.

A golden dial appeared to the right, and ten small slots opened, each allowing a single number.

Seyanna cried, "We need a ten-digit number."

"What kind of number?" Lars asked as he moved closer to Seyanna.

The head of the Chupovana came into view and roared its fury, its claws cutting through more rock and ice. It was now only fifteen feet away, and its green eyes were filled with rage.

"Anything written around the dial?"

Seyanna brushed away a layer of grime and dust. Words must've come into view. She said, "The Renowned Crusade Has All The Answers."

"What's that supposed to mean?" cried Lars.

Jet replied, "Roll me onto my side."

Lars did, just in time for Jet to vomit everything he'd eaten. Lars reacted by moving back. He slipped on a piece of ice, stumbling to the ground. A claw landed on Lars' lower legs, and he was pulled mercilessly toward the Chupovanas. In one quick movement, the boy was flung behind the creature and out into the abyss.

Seyanna let out a scream, her face filling with tears. "I'm not ready to die."

Refusing to think about what had just happened, Jet mumbled to himself, "The renowned crusade has all the answers." He closed his eyes, thinking, despite the scraping sounds from behind him growing ever closer. Iris had no room and hopped onto his legs, burrowing her head into his lap.

Seyanna began to plead, "Don't give up, Jet. You can't die. I can't live without you."

"Renowned is like famous," whispered Jet. "What do we know is famous?"

"Uh…"

"A crusade is an adventure, but with meaning. What adventure has meaning?" Jet repeated both concepts a few different times. He finally said, "I need *The Sorcerer's Guide*."

Jet found that Iris's head lay on his ring as if she knew the answer. She poured in a bit of energy, and he pulled out the tome.

"What is it?" she asked.

"There's always been something weird about this fable. Some of the numbers are spelled out, and some of the numbers are actually numbers." Jet shouted, "Go to the dials, and I'll read out the numbers."

The creature, only mere feet away bellowed so loudly that Jet could smell its breath.

"Is this going to work?" Seyanna demanded.

He stammered. "The first number is ten."

Seyanna frantically rolled the first dial. "It only goes up to nine."

"Use a one and zero as the first two numbers."

Jet felt the air shift next to him as a claw struck less than six inches from his leg. He began reading, but it was almost impossible to concentrate.

"Done."

Iris began hissing at the Chupovana.

Jet said, "Five. Then four. Then four, two, and three."

"Done."

The creatures next swung sliced into Jet's arm. Peering back at the tome, he read the last few lines and shouted, "Two, six, and five."

"That's ten," Seyanna screamed.

From the corner of his vision, Jet could see that the Chupovana had won despite all their efforts. Its next swipe would kill him. Time slowed as the claw struck at him. Without warning the stone ground below the Chupovana broke away, and the supersized polar bear went sprawling into thin air and down into the crevice. The scarab stone door jerked upward as if on an ancient pulley system, inch by inch. Iris quickly ducked inside as Seyanna knelt next him.

She began crying in earnest. Finally, she said, "It's a complete miracle we're not dead." Her arms wrapped around his neck, and she dragged him inside.

CHAPTER 38

Seyanna held onto Jet for a long time. Her cheeks pressed against his, and she gripped onto him as if there was a risk that he would slip away into the darkness. He was not in a comfortable position, but he didn't want the moment to end, so he said nothing.

"Sorry," she whispered as she let go.

"You saved us," replied Jet.

"No. You did," she said as she stood. "What is this place?"

"Are we inside the mountain?" questioned Jet.

Taking a few steps, Seyanna said, "I think you might be right."

The most startling thing that Jet noticed next was the unexpected aroma of plants, fresh air, fertility, and even dirt. Somehow the entrance was bright, and it soon became clear that the walls were not made of stone but of ice. They reflected a light from an unknown source and cast a glow into this unique cavern.

Iris set off to sniff the walls and the floor as if trying to decide if they were on friendly ground.

After another few steps, Seyanna came to a sudden halt. "Look down."

"I can't on my own."

She tiptoed back to him and helped him into a position where he could look down. A sudden sense of vertigo rushed over him. "Is that what I think it is?"

"We were wrong. We aren't standing on a mountain. We're standing between them, directly over the ocean."

"How's this possible? Water shouldn't be this high up."

"These mountains must be underwater." Pointing below and behind where Jet lay, she added, "That mountain is acting like a dam. I've never seen anything so beautiful."

"What are the chances of the ice breaking?"

"None. That ice is almost five feet thick."

"How can you tell? It looks so clear."

"Check out the sidewall, where it meets in the corner."

Jet stared awestruck. That's when he noticed the thickness of the walls. It was just as Seyanna had said. "That is some scary blackness, the deeper it gets."

Seyanna let out a small scream. "I see an orca swimming. Incredible."

"A what?"

"A killer whale."

"Oh, right."

Iris darted around and slid across the ice floor like she was playing.

Seyanna stood and walked to the nearest wall, placing her hand on the ice. "How is it this warm here, but nothing is melting?"

"*Magic?*" replied Jet, and he struggled to store *The Sorcerer's Guide*. Once finished, he said, "It's way too hot in here. I need to take off some of this gear."

"Good thinking." Seyanna removed his outer layers and his mid layers. From her backpack, she took out a pair of jeans and a shirt. She placed his cloak off to the side. She kept on his thermal underwear and struggled to get him dressed. Taking out a wipe, she cleaned and wrapped his injured arm. The last thing she placed back on was his cloak.

"Can you store your winter clothes?" she asked.

"No problem."

Seyanna quickly removed her outer layers as well. She pulled on some jeans and a sweatshirt under her own cloak. Once they were finished, she stared at Jet, and muttered, "How are we going to move you?"

Acting as if she understood the question, Iris rushed to Jet, ducked her head, and nestled it near his hands. "What is it?" he asked. She nipped at the sleeve of his cloak and tried hauling him onto her back. She almost succeeded.

"She wants to give you a ride."

"How?"

"I have an idea." Reaching into her bag, she pulled out some rope, tying his hands together after maneuvering him onto Iris's back. His weight didn't affect Iris in the slightest. Once finished, Iris ambled forward slowly. Jet was efficiently dragged behind her.

The first part of the entrance was far longer than it was wide. The floor and walls were extremely smooth. Iris's golden coat continued to give off a light glow, but it wasn't needed to see. The brightness diminished only slightly the farther they went.

"Jet, are you seeing this?"

"Trying," he replied, but he was struggling to keep his eyes open. "My energy is gone." When he managed to open his eyes, he could see that they were in a substantial chamber, bigger than two dozen basketball courts. Close by, birds were chirping and flying around the enclosed area. Steam rose in several different places, and it was warm and humid.

Seyanna said, "Part of the floor is stone, and part is ice. I can still see the depths of the ocean, but there's a lot of dirt and soil in here. Ferns are growing here. I see other plants and trees. I count at least three small lakes with fish swimming in them. There must be dozens of animals in here." Turning to Jet, she exclaimed, "An oasis in the middle of a freaking frozen island. Who would've guessed?"

"It's incredible." Jet agreed, but his eyes had fallen shut. "Where to now?"

"I see a few different options. There are a bunch of rooms in here, but there's another tunnel with a scarab carved into the stone."

Weakly, Jet said, "That has to be the way."

Iris picked up the pace.

Seyanna continued the commentary. "I wonder how the animals get in and out of this place." A dozen steps later, she added, "Oh my gosh. What a breathtaking waterfall. It's huge, maybe thirty feet or more. I wish we could go swimming."

Jet's eyes fluttered open. To their right and down some stairs was a chamber twice as large as theirs. He could partially see the waterfall, and it looked stunning. There were rocks and a deep pond. Jet thought he saw a moose drinking from the edge and thought of Alces. A group of tuna swam on the other side of the ice wall at the farthest end. It was surreal. This entire area felt like an underwater aquarium or lab. If he were healthy, he could sit and explore this place for hours.

"We're here," Seyanna said.

Jet was limp, and he could barely lift his head. "Let's rock and roll."

Iris crept into the hallway, scampering on several stone blocks placed in the ice. The route was just large enough for one of them to enter at a time, and the light began to fade away.

A few minutes later, Seyanna said, "It looks to be opening up."

The next room was rectangular in shape and approximately the size of a typical classroom. The walls were longer on their left and right, and an aqua blue luminosity shone behind the walls.

Seyanna stepped next to him. "I can see your breath."

"Same."

"What is this place?" asked Seyanna.

"It's a tomb," replied Jet, as his head flopped to the side.

"There have to be at least twenty scarab carvings throughout the room," said Seyanna. Pointing to the opposite wall, she added, "The most intricate and largest is across the chamber."

Jet said, "Are those Egyptian gods carved into the walls?" He noticed six such gods on the right wall, and some were as high as the ceiling. "What's on the left side?" he asked, unable to see that far.

Stepping out of his view, she said, "I see a bunch of hieroglyphs and other symbols as if it's telling a story."

"Iris, turn," commanded Jet. This allowed him to get a better look at the wall behind them. "I've seen one of those weapons before."

"What do you mean?"

On the back wall were five bigger-than-life weapons that had been carved and painted. He said, "Kaya attacked me with the whip up on the far right."

"They didn't find it next to her body," said Seyanna. "I was there when the Brotherhood came and took the bodies of Alces and Kaya."

He couldn't remember the name Kaya had used, but Alces's voice entered his mind. He repeated her words. "One of the five missing Chalua."

Seyanna said, "I wonder where it went."

Jet's eyes wandered to an image below the whip, a long wooden stick, a staff, that split apart at one end with a deep green stone at the top.

Before he could get a good look at the other weapons, a powerful and enchanting voice boomed throughout the tomb. "Have you come to collect my soul?"

Iris rotated in circles. It was impossible to tell where the voice had come from. An ice altar rose from the middle of the room, with a majestical black cube perched on the top, like a display.

"Have you come to rob me of my power?" asked the voice.

Jet wasn't sure what to say.

"Will you conquer the world with my influence?"

Jet wavered.

The voice became shrill. "Are you strong enough to do what is right?"

Jet became fearful.

The entire ice structure around them began to shake. The voice cried, "Will you command me to be your slave?"

Seyanna was knocked to the ground. The knot on the rope holding his hands together disintegrated, and Jet was lifted into the air and made to stand while Iris was pushed forward next to him.

"What makes you worthy to stand here before me?"

Concentrating with as much effort as he'd ever exerted, he quieted his own mind, thoughts, and feelings. He pushed away the doubt, the self-loathing, the fear, and his own feelings of embarrassment, pulling out *The Sorcerer's Guide*.

The book opened of its own accord, and golden light splashed outward, filling the room. Jet called out,

"I command no one, but I am here to ask for your help. I control the Elements, but I am dying. Will you heal me?"

The voice went silent. An unseen force pushed Seyanna to the back wall.

The voice proclaimed, "You are not who you are."

Jet was unsure what this meant, but he replied, "I am who I choose to be. But I was given an elixir for safety that blinded me from magic. At times magic slips through my hands, uncatchable."

The being cackled. "Of course. Not only do you want me to heal you, but you also want me to fix you."

"It's the only way to make me whole."

"Who is with you?"

Jet tried turning to face Seyanna. He muttered, "My friend."

"No," the voice replied. "Who is within you?"

Alces's voice spoke. "My lifeforce granted Jet the strength to come here and face you. But chaos and the evils of the world are winning, and without Jet, the Mikado, their victory is guaranteed."

"You gave a magical breather your lifeforce?"

"It was the only way," replied Alces.

"Do you trust him this much?"

"I trust the Kings, Leotyton, Lady Gaea, and my mother, Aurora. All things have led to this boy."

"He doesn't appear strong enough."

"He isn't. Without you, he never will be."

"He might deceive you; he might deceive the both of us."

"Honestly, we can't control that." Alces's heart warmed again but stronger, and Jet felt her immense love for the land, the people, her family, and herself. She pronounced, "Ella Dastria, life is unfair, and we can only hold ourselves accountable for *our* choices, not what others do with our kindness, love, and especially our minds. End this exile and join the war against Arisol. If you do not help this boy, that will become your biggest regret, dwarfing what has already transpired."

"You know not what you speak of," Ella Dastria replied.

"Make a choice, Grandmother," Alces's words were fading. "Goodbye, Jet. My time is over. A part of me will stay with you forever. If you live, never forget the sacrifices of those that came before you. Farewell my friend."

He felt her lifeforce flame out and knew that this meant he was dead. He could no longer breathe, and the warmth drained from his body.

Seyanna screamed, "No, Jet. We didn't come all this way for this."

He couldn't speak, and the light faded from his eyes. Iris, still standing next to Jet, toppled over, unable to control herself. The last thing that entered his mind was the being's voice; it said, "Your parents, the man who gave you the tonic, and Alces have killed you in the end."

Jet's mind responded with telepathy. "You're wrong. We saved each other. I'm not perfect, but I die with no regrets. Can you say the same?" The question lingered for what seemed an eternity.

His body was lifted and placed on the ice altar. The black cube converted into a mist and blanketed his body, preparing him for burial. Iris's limp body was pulled next to the alter.

Seyanna screamed uncontrollably.

Time nearly stopped.

Then the cold air was sucked from the room, the mist becoming absorbed into every pore on Jet's body, and in an instant, his body, soul, and mind were made whole again.

The voice spoke without a hint of bitterness or hatred, full of the most overwhelming joy and relief. "I think that we will save each other in the end. I gift unto you, Jet Black, the Mikado of Elemental magic, my lifeforce, the Soul of Anesidora."

THE END

ABOUT THE AUTHOR

L. SCOTT CLARK is intrigued by the magical world surrounding each of us. He writes young adult novels influenced by the incredible beauty of nature, the vastness of our world, and the psychological complexities between each of us.

Born and raised in Colorado, L. Scott has a deep love of nature, mountains, oceans, and the sense of adventure that awaits us each time we step outside.

He is the author of **The Sorcerer's Guide** YA Fantasy series and hopes to expand his writing capabilities. He has written two books in the series – *Path of the Phoenix* and *Soul of Anesidora*. He plans on having seven books in the series. He has written stories in YA, mystery, Short Stories, and more.

His path to becoming an author started in high school with his love for reading and writing. Initially, he pursued a degree in Physician Assistant Studies and has worked for many years in the medical field, correctional medicine.

L. Scott Clark began writing shortly after graduation and it has been his own adventure to become a published author.

You can visit him online at www.LScottClark.com or on Twitter (@LScottClark) or Instagram (@lscottclarkauthor)

If you enjoyed reading this book, please leave a review on Amazon or Goodreads (or both). This is an incredible way to support authors and we appreciate each and every review. I read the reviews with an open mind and equally important, they help new readers discover my books.

Additionally, you can sign up for my Newsletter at my Author Website https://lscottclark.com/. This will give you the chance to stay up to date on the latest book news, promos, and other awesome opportunities that might come down the line. It will also give me the opportunity to get to know you better. I try to update my readers at least once a month.

THE SORCERER'S GUIDE
TO THE

GRAVITY
OF
DECEIT

CHAPTER I

A small amount of decency within a person can simmer, undergo growth, and blossom, or it can be cast out by the simplest of decisions in a moment of anger or wrath. This was a belief Queen Aurora had held onto, taught to her tribe, and passed on to her children. Compassion and principles such as this might lead to love, enlightenment, or even victory. But the opposite can induce wars, betrayal, hatred, and bring about the end of civilization. The margin between the moral and the ruthless might be nothing more than a breath of calm.

Kaya treasured the land around her and had spent years and even decades trying to catch the fae and other living beings tucked away throughout Illustina. Her sister, Alces, was far more interested in order, cleanliness, and the understanding of the hints of magic swirling around them.

One day, the Grey Panther, a gentle man, beckoned Queen Aurora to meet him at the Cascade Quarry. He was the leader of the Council and had devised a flawless plan to reunite the five magical groups under a single assembly. For years, the Elementals and Runics had waged war against each other. The kingdom had suffered death and despair, but with this new plan, hope had begun to spread across the lands. The Grey Panther wanted to combat wickedness and hatred with knowledge, tolerance, and sacrifice, despite magic being on the decline. The two books detailing magic were opening less and less, and the other three were lost completely.

The Grey Panther envisioned a world of advancement, harmony, and amity between the creatures of Goth Airtha. This included those gifted with magic, the many creatures and tribes in the land, and the Mayeians or the nonmagical. Queen Aurora was torn because she wanted to invite her close friend, Lady Gaea, to the occasion but believed the Grey Panther wanted to be careful about the details of his proposal.

The splendid waterfall overlooking the quarry was nearly as large as a mountain. Queen Aurora approached from the south, giving way to the sunrise on her left. Her animal form was a caribou, and she was regal and majestic. Her fur was thick, and she was muscular and proud. Peering down to the bottom of the falls, she found the striking and impeccable Grey Panther waiting for her. Peering up, he saw her, and waved energetically for her to come. The smile on his face could trick mold into believing it was beautiful.

The path was not difficult, but it was steep. Halfway down, an impressive green-and-golden boar, the size of an elephant strode out from behind a gigantic fern, blocking her descent. This creature was nothing like anything Queen Aurora had ever seen. Its hide was more like dazzling reptile scales instead of fur, and she was drawn to the three horns on top of its elongated head. Two of the horns were positioned upward, but not entirely, while the third horn, much smaller, curved forward. This creature roared angrily, moved swiftly, and attacked the Grey Panther.

Queen Aurora galloped after the beast, but by the time she arrived, it was too late. The Grey Panther had been gravely injured and lay on the ground with a deep cut through his abdomen. She did not know any magical words to heal the leader of the Council, and therefore she prayed to her goddess for the wisdom and strength to restore him with a portion of her soul. She had been taught the words to give of her lifeforce and intended to do so.

The Grey Panther, in a faint voice, whispered, "Aurora. Please. Don't give me of your soul. I'm not worth that. There must be another way."

The gash in his chest covered the entire width from his left shoulder to his right hip. She was sure that his insides were extensively damaged under all that blood. Aurora answered, "You must live. The magical world and our friendship must survive. I can't sit here and do nothing."

He smiled kindly. "You're more important than I am. You might find a way to bring about peace, where I have failed."

"I couldn't. You're far more influential."

He jerked suddenly, pain spreading across his face.

"No," she screamed. "I can't let you die."

"I believe fate has spoken."

"I refuse to stand here and do nothing." Her head bowed and she transformed into her human form. "Your ideas of changing the Wepet Sumuran are brilliant. You must be there to make those changes."

His laugh was hollow. "I don't think that it's written in the stars. I've lived a good life."

"My soul will give you the strength to heal from this attack."

He coughed noisily. When he recovered, he whispered, "There's not enough time, and I fear that I will leave you unprotected if I accept your soul."

Aurora mumbled, "Maybe there is another way."

In a tortured voice, full of pain, the Grey Panther hissed, "I know of no object that can heal me. This is how the gods wanted it to be."

"Wait." Queen Aurora straightened. "I have an idea." Closing her eyes, she pictured her eldest daughter, Alces. Through telepathy, she communicated with her and then cut the connection.

"What just happened?" asked the Grey Panther. "You were glowing."

"The cure is coming. I know what to do."

Alces arrived within minutes, delivering six black stones. A gigantic purple moose presented the stones to her mother and stepped back several paces.

The Grey Panther had fallen unconscious, and Aurora worked quickly. She built a fire and cast the stones into the depths of the flames. Several minutes later, the stones were removed and doused in the water of the quarry. Next, the stones were positioned evenly on the stomach of the Grey Panther. Aurora spoke three words: "Dexican, Fuliminus, Sensoitor."

"Mother?" asked Alces. "What are you doing?"

"Saving the leader of the Council. Bonding the nomads with the Council and ensuring that magic will be reborn."

"Those are hidden fae words and Father's stones."

"He will understand," responded Queen Aurora. "And the Incrementum clan have the other seven. This bond will bind us with the Grey Panther, and neither he nor anyone from the Council can attack us."

"Is it worth the cost?"

"What cost?"

"This man will possess these stones until he needs to use them again." Her eyes landed on the injured man. "What happened to him?"

"One of those creatures attacked the Grey Panther."

"What creatures?"

"Those who thirst to steal magic."

"Why?"

"They must've caught wind of the plan to bring back magic to where it can do the most good."

"Where's Father?" asked Alces. "Does he know that you're meeting with the leader of the Council?"

"He's with the Natu, and they're searching for the den of the enchantress Khalicaans."

"Why did we send our greatest warriors?"

"Father believes that they're aligning themselves with these magic stealers, the Chupovanas. They needed the greater strength."

The reddish-brown skin coloring of the Grey Panther started to improve.

Turning to her daughter, Aurora whispered, "I'll be back home soon. Praises for your swift action. You helped save this man and I must take him home to recover."

The Grey Panther stirred, his eyes fluttering.

Before Alces left her mother, she hissed, "I hope you know what you're doing."

"I do."

# # #

Standing before an ornate mirror the length of the entire room, a tall woman brushed back her unusually long brown hair as two servants helped her get dressed. The excitement of tonight was etched across her lovely face. Her skin was soft and smooth, a brownish gray, and she had six fingers on her left hand, which played with a portion of her hair. She wore a long, subdued, wine-red dress that fit perfectly with her triangular body with its close-set shoulders and broader hips. She knew that many believed her to be one of the most magnificent women in the land, but that was only because she was a goddess, or once was.

First, they attended to her hair, placing golden clamps every few inches. Since her hair nearly reached the back of her knees, this took some time. The arranged jewelry was not only pleasing to look at but also to smell. It was as if the rubies had been bathed in pine needles and lemon balm.

Chloe, the youngest servant, asked, "Where's Tigerus taking you tonight, milady?"

"Oh, haven't you heard?" remarked the older servant, Shanira. "The master is taking the princess to the Island of Demaro."

"Oh my," gushed Chloe. "The stories I've heard about that paradise. What I wouldn't give to cross an ocean with my true love."

Shanira retorted quickly, "This is Princess Dastria's first visit to the island. Master Tigerus has been there many times."

Ella Dastria spoke, her voice full of excitement. "Tigerus will show me things that I never thought imaginable. He told me that I would not likely forget this night for as long as we shall live. I will meet creatures from the underwater that no one has ever beheld. I will visit and see the heart of the island. Our love will burn forever after tonight."

Soon the servants were finished with their work, and her knight, Braverly, escorted a beautifully decorated princess. A heavily clad giant with a big sword taller than Ella waited outside her room, holding a resplendent black box.

Ella said, "Thank you for bringing Pandora."

"Yes. My lady."

He escorted her through her castle and down the cobblestone walkway to the harbor. They strolled past a dozen boats until the last open bay. Together they waited for the grandest ship of all to arrive. As the silence passed, Ella felt that Braverly was staring at Pandora. She asked, "Have you never been curious about what is inside this box?"

"No. My lady." He straightened slightly. "Curiosity is not within me to feel. I am determined to fulfill my oaths and commitments. As you say, the other things are just dust on top of a barn's dirt floor."

"I see that about you," Ella replied. "That's why I called upon you once the transformation was complete and after my marriage to Tigerus."

"Happy to protect and assist," Braverly replied with a slight nod.

"You have done everything as I have asked. I thank you for that."

Without answering directly, he nodded once again. Quickly he added, "Lord Tigerus's ship has arrived."

Princess Dastria gazed upon the water and felt a jolt of excitement as the colossal ship with three masts came into port. Tigerus, in splendid attire, stood near the foremast. His grin was so genuine and enormous that she could see his blazing teeth even from this distance. He treated her like she was the most important woman in the world. His love for her was beyond ordinary, and she thanked him every day.

"My Joyella. It's wonderful to see you again after these long two months. I'm sorry that my work took me away from you. I intend to take the next several days to make up for my absence. Will you ever forgive me?"

"Depends," replied Ella coyly. "What do you have to make up for my loneliness?"

A pair of deckhands brought over a basket full of oysters. They opened them quickly, and Ella beheld the largest pearls she had ever seen.

Tigerus responded, "We found these in the seas of Quartz, and I knew that they could only belong to you."

Ella realized her mistake a second too late. The excitement on her face revealed her true thoughts. She tried to muster a frown, but her facial expressions always showed a glimpse into her heart.

Tigerus laughed heartily. "This is not all, my princess."

A massive treasure chest was brought forth. Ella was slightly confused as the deckhands opened the lid, revealing gold and black jewelry.

Hastily, Tigerus said, "I know that you aren't impressed by riches, so I hid the true nature of this gift underneath."

The necklaces, diamonds, coins, and such were quickly removed to reveal two pieces of long-lost artwork. The lump in her throat caught her off guard—these two paintings had been fashioned thousands of years ago. The one on the left was of three sisters, Lady Gaea, Bio Vita, and Aqua Felis. She knew these women all too well. The other painting was of herself and her sister Atmos Geni.

"Where did you find these?"

Tigerus replied, "Hidden in a library on the island of Avalon."

Ella Dastria glanced up quickly. "That place doesn't exist."

"For you, my Joyella, it does. This is the gift I've been promising you. That is why I went away for so long. But I'm back now, and I'll do everything to make it up to you."

She ran to Tigerus, jumping into his broad shoulders as he lifted her, kissing her passionately.

For the next two weeks, as they traveled to the Island of Demaro, happiness and bliss followed in their wake. Fish of all sizes and shapes swam close to their ship. This trip quickly became one of Ella's most treasured experiences. She reflected on her time as a Matron with such fondness, she adored her time with Tigerus with equal affection. She missed her sisters but felt resolve and understanding at her choices.

Magic had never been stronger than in these last centuries, and that would continue for the foreseeable future. Rumors of a hidden evil were quashed quickly by Tigerus, Braverly, and her other commanders. Even her letters from her sisters reassured her that the stories were exaggerated.

She had a budding secret of her own. The life that she and Tigerus had known over these last twenty years was about to change. They were adding a third party to their pair.

"There she is," Tigerus announced.

A set of islands more spectacular than Ella had ever seen came into view. The epic cliffs, tall mountains, valleys, and millions of trees were breathtaking. But what she loved the most were the active volcanoes splashing lava into the sea. She had heard of the Island of Demaro before but had been too busy to look.

They anchored near a beach with black sand a few hours later, and four deckhands took Tigerus and Ella to shore. Braverly remained on deck as a sentry. She held her black box, and for the first time, she noticed that Tigerus held a long cedar box of his own. Once ashore, the four men from the ship stayed on the beach and started a fire.

Tigerus led the way through a cave, and they wandered for nearly an hour toward the island's heart.

"Joyella, we're almost there. This is one of the most spectacular and special places in the world. Have you ever heard of the Heart of Demaro?"

"Only vaguely."

He stopped and smiled so brightly that her heart melted. "It isn't every day that you can find a secret that a goddess doesn't know. What a blessed day."

The cavern they entered was as large as a small mountain, but it was mostly hollow this time. Gazing upward, Ella thought she could see an opening at the top.

"This is Demaro," Tigerus said, trembling with admiration. "I never imagined it would be this delightful."

"Is this a volcano?" asked Ella.

"One that has been asleep for hundreds of thousands of years. This is the mother of this island, and she only wakens when angry. She has not been angry for a long time."

"It is remarkable."

Tigerus asked, "Did you bring your gift?"

"I brought two."

"Really?" Tigerus replied, surprised. "Two gifts for me? You are the kindest woman to have ever lived."

Pointing around the entire cavern, she asked, "Why exactly are we here?"

"A celebration. This is where we'll exchange gifts that will forever be etched into the hearts of many. I discovered an ancient ritual that will provide balance and acceptance to all those on the earth. An exchange of gifts must happen in the heart of this mountain."

"I have brought mine."

"Wonderful," Tigerus said. "We must give these gifts of our own free will. Without hesitation."

"I'm willing," Ella said.

"Come to this altar," Tigerus said.

Ella hadn't seen the large stone altar in the exact middle of the cavern. It was positioned directly below the opening.

Tigerus said, "I will go first. Your gift and mine can never be used again. They will be driven into the altar and remain here forever. I have brought you a staff so powerful that darkness fears its existence. It holds an enchanted blade, a clout gem, and is made of magical wood from an ancient Koa tree." He removed a wooden staff from the cedar box and speared it into the altar. The ground shook slightly.

Ella watched as the altar accepted the gift with finality.

She put her box on the ground. It was far smaller than the cedar box. She whispered a few words, and the box opened. A midnight-black blade only six inches in length with a wide black handle sat on a black pillow. For the first time in centuries, Pandora's box was opened again. Whispers in the darkness spoke of its unique and hidden power. Reaching inside, she pulled out the knife.

A glimmer of desire shone on Tigerus's face. It made her happy to know that she was fulfilling his wishes. Walking to the altar, she repeated the action of her husband. Once again, the altar accepted the sacrifice, and the ground quaked.

Dozens of hands exploded from the ground below them, entrapping her, holding her in place. She screamed and watched in horror as the face of Tigerus changed. Soon he was leering at her, a darkness in his eyes.

"What have you done?" demanded Ella.

Tigerus said quickly, "It's selfish to think that magic should only be given to the goddesses. The rest of humanity has a right to hold magic in the palm of their hands and use it as it was meant to be."

"What are you saying?"

"The Matrons will be no more."

"That blade cannot be used to kill anyone."

"Oh, I know," seethed Tigerus. "But it can be used to remove the protective glow around your sisters. The time for a new world of temptation, lust, and progress will be ushered in by me."

"Let me go," demanded Ella.

"This is your new prison," replied Tigerus.

He sailed to the altar with glee, and his hand gripped the black blade. A silky and sinister voice spoke to Tigerus. "You can only remove one. Choose wisely. I showed you the direction to the Staff of Gravity so you could take the Dagger of Pandora."

"Yes, Master."

Ella screamed, "What are you going to do to my sisters?"

The sinister voice answered, "Hunt them."